T0365166

RELIC

BUZZ JONES

iUniverse, Inc.
Bloomington

RELIC

iUniverse books may be ordered through booksellers or by contacting:

iUniverse
1663 Liberty Drive
Bloomington, IN 47403
www.iuniverse.com
1-800-Authors (1-800-288-4677)

ISBN: 978-1-4759-8780-5 (sc)
ISBN: 978-1-4759-8781-2 (e)

Library of Congress Control Number: 2013907783

Printed in the United States of America.

iUniverse rev. date: 4/26/2013

PROLOGUE

THE SUN HOVERED ON THE horizon as it shimmered like gold on the great river. The last rays of the day glinted on the bend, a stone's throw from the gate of the eastern wall. Fires burned just beyond the opposite bank. Their orange glow chased the light of the setting sun from the river as darkness descended upon the land. This terrible army had conquered all of the cities of Eden except one. Uruk stood as the last vestige of the first age of man.

Shem stood in the tower of the sun as he considered what the night would bring.

"These invaders are barbarians," he muttered to his friend Jafir. "The world was in harmony when they were working for the gods. At least they had purpose; building temples or mining the yellow metal."

"Animals!" growled Jafir. The priests taught that they were

a race of workers created to serve the gods. After the great rebellion, they became wanderers in search of plunder.

Shem turned toward the stairs that lead down to the temple platform. "Let's go to the hall of creation, the priests may need our help," he said in a commanding tone.

Jafir was accustomed to Shem's orders. He had always been the leader of his generation. As they entered the long room of the great hall, the golden flicker of oil lamps bathed the walls, illuminating the inscriptions that bore witness to the history of Eden. They each felt profoundly sad, as they knew that soon the walls would fail, and the barbarians would violate this place. Ahead of them, at the end of the hall, they could see shadows busily moving on the wall. They increased their pace and trotted to the remaining length of the hall. As they rounded a corner at the end of the space, they found the priests and scribes hurriedly placing the contents of the sacred library in a secret vault beneath the floor.

"Master," Shem called out, "What are you doing?"

The old man turned in the direction of the voice. He saw the two young men standing before him, the darkness behind them, their blue eyes glowing in the lamplight and their blonde hair shimmering.

His voice trembled as he replied, "we are hiding the sacred knowledge from the evil one." "Soon the walls will fall, and the leader of the barbarians will come to destroy the legacy of the first ones." The old man choked on his emotion as he continued, "I have a special task for the two of you."

"Yes master," replied Jafir, his head bowed in deference to the priest.

"You shall no longer bow your head when you speak to me; on this night you are my equal," said the old priest as he placed his hand under the young man's chin and raised his head. The old man looked away as he struggled to maintain his composure. He was profoundly saddened that these young men would never take their places on the high council.

"Such tragedy," he thought as he turned to face Shem. Looking him straight in the eye he said, "We may journey to the underworld together on this night, but we will preserve the knowledge of the gods before we do."

"Tell us what to do," replied Shem.

"Bring us the star tablet and the ancient bones from the chamber of the heavens," said the priest.

With steely resolve, Shem looked at Jafir and said, "Let us go to the temple of the moon."

"But only the chief priests are allowed to go there," replied Jafir, not yet comprehending the direness of their situation.

"You must go now!" exclaimed the High Priest.

The golden glow of the lamps exaggerated his features; making him as fierce as the messengers from the underworld.

The two young men turned and ran with all of their strength. As they exited the hall of creation, they leapt down the stairs two and three at the time until they reached the ground below the entrance. The temple of the moon loomed like a grey mountain in the dim light of the evening at the far end of The Way of Heaven. Jafir struggled to keep up as they crossed the vast square where their people gathered for festivals and to worship the First Ones.

"Hurry Jafir," said Shem as he slowed in order to let his friend to catch up.

Jafir trembled as he stood at the base of the temple, staring at the long flight of stairs before them. The plaster-clad surfaces of the structure glowed with the ghostly light of the full moon above them. Shem allowed him a moment to catch his breath before he tugged his arm and said, "We must hurry."

They continued up the stairs of the great temple, running as hard as their burning legs would carry them. Out of breath, they made their way to the domed structure at the center of the temple platform. When they arrived at the entrance, each of them lowered a copper rod that protruded from the wall on either side of the entryway into acid filled vessels. As the rods reacted with the electrolytic fluid in the containers, a golden glow appeared in the opening of the chamber. After entering, they stood for a moment looking up at the illustrations of the heavens on the domed ceiling. Their eyes would be the last to see it intact.

At the center of the room was a tablet showing the family of heaven with Utu in the center, surrounded by thirteen celestial entities. No one had touched it from the time that the gods had given it to the first priest. He walked with the chief of the gods on the plain of Uruk, until he flew to the city of heaven, to live forever in the presence of the Most High God. For centuries, The First Ones had visited the Nod on the plain of Ur and taught them how to farm, how to build, how to heal, how to make light, how to make better animals for the herds and how to make better people. However, the gods had been silent for many years and tonight the cries of their children would go unanswered.

Having completed their task, Shem and Jafir hurried back to The Hall of Creation, carrying the star tablet and a cedar box. The scribes were ready for them. They placed the relic in a woven reed basket and lowered it into the darkness where the priest was waiting. After he retrieved it from the basket, they quickly pulled up the ropes and lowered the sacred bones in the cedar box. They then replaced the stones to cover the hole. As the last stone quenched the light from the hall above, the priest withdrew a vial from a pouch tied to his waistband and drank in the darkness. As he slipped into unconsciousness, he heard the sound of many feet on the bricks above him.

I

THE SUN BLAZED in an azure sky as the men worked their shovels and picks. Johan Schmidt stood over a map spread onto a makeshift table that consisted of several empty fuel drums covered by the plywood top of a shipping container. A slight breeze fluttered through the dingy white canvas of the tent overhead. Sweat dropped from his brow as he wiped it with a coarse cloth cut from the rarely unfurled tent sides. It was too hot to deny this little oasis of a single breeze by unrolling them.

"Such a God forsaken place," Johan muttered as he studied his map. He traced a line on the page with his finger, denoting the ancient course of the Euphrates. He looked east searching from his vantage point atop the great ziggurat of Uruk near the northern shore of the Persian Gulf. The river was now twelve miles distant, though it had once traced a route less than a mile from this ancient place. According to legend, giants had camped on the eastern bank of the river Euphrates and lain siege to the city for a year.

During the time that Johan worked the site, his team had discovered evidence of the siege including the campsite. They had also excavated the temple platform atop the ziggurat and located what appeared to be an observatory. The roof of it was broken, but the foundation ring was intact. Some fragments of the rubble clearly demonstrated a curving surface, giving support to the possibility that there had been a domed structure on the site.

After months of removing the sands of time, they would finally enter the temple. Johan would be the first person in millennia to see this most ancient of holy places. He had researched this place for many years, hoping that one day he would have the opportunity to work this site. His heart felt full with the satisfaction of a goal achieved as he considered how fortunate he was to have the privilege of leading this expedition on behalf of the Fatherland.

"Such a powerful myth," he whispered as he placed his calloused hand on the hot sun baked bricks of the massive structure. He looked skyward and marveled at the bright blue overhead as it contrasted with the stark manila color of the structure, aware that many ancient sites in southern Persia referenced this location as the place where the Gods walked. After conquering the city, the invading Army suffered destruction by fire from the sky, as punishment from the gods for their evil. Such was the power of the myth that the peoples of this land shunned the place for all the centuries that followed. There was not a hint of human activity, not even a single footprint was on the plain of Uruk since the day that the city had died.

As Johan observed from a reasonable distance, a gang of khaki clad soldiers removed several cubic meters of sand from the entrance. Soon the upper section of the immense cedar doors that covered the entrance emerged from their cloak of earth. One of the men stood on the roof of the structure and motioned for the earthmover. The machine belched black smoke and snarled to life. It jerked and heaved as it struggled to carve a path through the sand. For several hours, the iron monster growled and clinked as it removed centuries of sand and debris from the entrance to the structure. Johan passed the time by reading from his notes. He stretched his thin frame out as much as possible by reclining in a chair beneath the tent and propping his feet on the makeshift table. When the metal beast finally fell silent Johan closed his leather binder, eased himself to a standing position. He breathed deeply to ready himself before slowly approaching the ancient wooden doors. The manila color of the wall abruptly transitioned to a darker shade, at the point where centuries of overburden shielded it from the harsh light of the sun. The men took their turns at the water rations as they awaited his instructions. He nodded at the sergeant and the man barked orders in German. Several men with pry bars began working at the join line of the great panels. The left door broke under the strain, and a two-meter wide section collapsed in a shower of dirt and splinters onto the ground in front of the structure. A dust cloud billowed around the door as it fell. Once the dust settled Johan walked to the entrance and paused. The sergeant handed him a lantern, and he slowly entered the building. His heart raced with excitement as he discovered that the hall was intact. The invaders had left this building undamaged following the siege. Johan walked the entire length of the hall for a quick survey. He purposefully resisted the urge to examine the reliefs on the walls, the tablets

3

on the small columns lining the hall, or the bodies on the floor at the far end of the space. His discipline only allowed a brief look around in order to develop a general layout of the site. After an hour, he stepped back into the blinding light of the desert. Once his eyes adjusted, he turned to the sergeant.

"Your men have performed a notable service for the Fatherland. Allow them extra rations tonight."

The sergeant snapped to attention and saluted with his outstretched arm; "Hail- Hitler."

As night began to fall, the smell of the cooking trailer saturated the air of the dig site. Johan cleared the table under his tent and retrieved a case that contained a treasured bottle cognac from his travel trunk and placed it upon the table. He found the sergeant smoking a cigarette, staring across the desert at the darkening sky. He appeared to be an admirable example of the German ideal, a well-muscled fit man with a commanding presence and piercing blue eyes, his hair so blonde that it was almost unnatural in appearance. He was a leader of men, well practiced at his duties.

"Sergeant, would you care to join me at the table for a drink?"

The sergeant glanced at the men forming a chow line at the cooking trailer. He always ate last, after the men had their ration.

"I suppose a taste of the Fatherland would be a refreshing respite in this hideous place," he said as he puffed the last of his cigarette.

He then dropped it on the ground and covered it with his foot in a single fluid motion. The two of them seated themselves in folding chairs from the tool trunk. Johan flipped open the lid of the wooden box that sat on the table between them and retrieved two shot glasses. He poured the amber liquid in each of them and offered a glass to the sergeant.

"To the Fatherland," said Johan as he held his glass out slightly in a salutary gesture.

"To the Fatherland," replied the sergeant. He then sipped from the glass, allowing the spirits to invade his nasal passages. He had not tasted the flavor of Europe for some time.

"So, Heir Dr. Schmidt; how is it that you selected this site to study?" He asked in an almost friendly tone.

"This is the site of the first large city in antiquity," replied Johan. We know this because other sites in the region contain artifacts that reference this place as the place of the first ones."

Johan refreshed the glasses as the sergeant asked, "How is it that no one has found this place yet?"

"The river is the reason," replied Johan. It is several kilometers east of here. Although many have tried, no one has ever found a city site on its western bank in this region. When this city was alive, the river flowed right there," Johan pointed to the road that ran past the site.

"How did you determine that the river once flowed here," the sergeant asked.

"Superior German technology," Johan replied with a chuckle and saluted with his glass.

The sergeant managed a laugh as well and drank the remainder of his glass. Johan divided the remainder of the bottle between them as he continued. "The Luftwaffe mapped the area with a new high altitude reconnaissance aircraft that takes highly detailed aerial photographs. It seems that the energy bureau was searching for geological evidence of oil deposits or something like that. In any case, the pictures found their way into the public record. When I saw the photo of this area with the ziggurat just west of the road it was immediately obvious to me that this was the ancient city of Uruk; the place where the Gods walked with men."

The sergeant swirled his drink and stared at the liquid as the sky continued to darken. "The energy bureau," the sergeant paused, "there now seems to be a bureau for just about anything." "Germany is not a large country Dr. Schmidt, the Fuhrer's appetite for grandeur worries me."

Dr. Schmidt smiled and said, "I try to remain as neutral as possible with respect to the prevailing political environment."

The sergeant spoke as he was staring over his glass at him, "A wise choice, I think, Heir Doctor. "These days it seems best to go along in order to get along."

Johan considered the sergeant's comment for a moment before saying, "Many think that the Fuhrer is the savior of Germany." He paused to drink before continuing. "Just ten years ago the store shelves were empty, and a loaf of bread, if you could find it, cost a week's wages. Today we have the cleanest cities, the best educational system, the strongest manufacturing economy, the most efficient public transportation system and the most advanced technologies in the modern world."

"Yes, Germany is the miracle of the twentieth century, rising from the ashes like a phoenix!" The sergeant held out his arms as if they were the wings of an eagle. "The question is my good doctor, where does Germany go from here?" The alcohol had loosened the sergeant's tongue. "How do we get the resources to supply the industries of the new Germany and where do we get the land to feed and house the new Germans? I know what is inevitable my friend."

The sergeant drank before finishing his thought.

"Our leaders are restless my friend. Soon the world will groan under the burden of their aspirations."

They sat in silence for a few moments watching the last bit of color drain from the sky as the light of day faded into darkness.

"Well Dr. Schmidt, I must retire to my tent for now; thank you for your hospitality."

The sergeant offered a half hearted salute that betrayed his disdain for the prevailing political situation. As he did so, Johan could see a small tattoo just above the wrist line of his shirt.

"The mark of the Vrill," noted Johan mentally as he returned the salute.

The next morning the men began moving portable lighting equipment into the building. By noon, the preparations for the first survey were completed. The first order of business would be to collect the mummies that rested near the end of the corridor. There were eight of them in a neat row. Each held an alabaster vial in its bony grasp. Johan stood above them, studying them as the sergeant approached.

"They were magnificent," said Johan.

"They would have made great warriors judging from the size of them," replied the sergeant.

"Yes," replied Johan; they would have been nearly three meters tall, almost exactly twice my stature."

"Indeed," replied the sergeant as he looked down at the shorter man.

"These two in the center appear to be different from the others. They may have been younger, possibly students of the priests or royalty."

He studied them as he stroked his chin.

"We will take these two."

"Very well Dr. Schmidt," replied the sergeant.

Two teams of four men were standing behind him holding long stainless steel containers. The men opened them and retrieved a sheet metal pan from each of them. They carefully slid the pans beneath the remains of Jafir and Shem, lifting them from their resting places and carefully depositing them into the containers for shipment to the Fatherland. Johan and the sergeant walked in the direction of the main entrance as they discussed the logistical effort of packaging artifacts for shipment. While the soldiers worked around the mummies, one of the men stepped on a group of stones that gave way under foot. As he began falling through the floor, two of his comrades grabbed him, arms flailing for balance and shouting in alarm at the sudden sensation of the ground disappearing beneath him.

"What is the problem here?" barked the sergeant.

Before they could answer, Johan tugged at the sleeve of the sergeant's shirt.

"It appears that your men have located a secret chamber beneath the floor; a most fortunate discovery."

The sergeant barked orders at two of the men, "you, move that lighting rig over the opening," he turned to a third man and ordered, "you; get that lantern."

The third man scurried over to the wall and retrieved the lantern as the first two worked to aim the light cans down into the opening. The remainder of the crew had begun removing additional stones from the floor in order to enlarge the opening enough to allow a man to pass through. Johan leaned over the opening on his hands and knees and lowered a lantern through the opening. As it descended into the blackness of the chamber, he began to see irregular shapes emerge from the darkness. The closer the lantern got to the floor of the space, the more detail he could see. As the lantern came to rest on the floor, the glow illuminated a mummified body, clutching a golden tablet against its torso, arms crossed in a protective embrace.

Johan's pulse quickened as he called out, "Sergeant, have a look at this." The soldier dropped to his hands and knees in a single quick motion and peered into the chamber.

"This is it," said Johan excitedly. "This is what the Reich sent us to find!"

As the men peered at their find, there was a loud crashing sound outside of the great hall. A gust of wind carried a cloud of dust into the entrance of the hall. A soldier came running into the hall and called loudly, "dust storm! There is a large cloud coming over the horizon!"

The men immediately began running for the door. The soldiers attacked their gear to secure it before the wind and sand spoiled their supplies. Johan sprinted for his tent. He flung open the lids of two large trunks and unceremoniously threw everything that he could find into them before slamming the lids and latching them securely. His tent collapsed as he began making his way back toward the great hall. The sand stung his exposed flesh as he attempted to shield his face with one hand while clutching a canteen with the other. When he reached the door of the hall, he struggled with a heavy tarp that hung over the opening as a makeshift door. He found the edge of the fabric and stumbled into the dimly lit space. Several soldiers spilled through the door behind him. Exhausted from their toil; they rested on the floor to wait out the storm. Johan took a drink from his canteen to clear his mouth of dirt and spat the first mouthful on the ground.

"Ha!" Johan shouted as he shook his fist in the direction of the opening.

"This land grudgingly holds onto its secrets." The sergeant spoke from the corner where he leaned against a wall smoking a cigarette, "We will resume working tomorrow." He offered Johan a smoke from his cigarette case.

Johan took the cigarette and spoke from the corner of his mouth as he lit an ember on the end, "we must work quickly, sergeant, the ship arrives in Basra in less than a month."

"Yah," replied the sergeant, "the men are very much looking forward to returning home."

The following morning began with the sharp report of hammer blows as the soldiers converted a stack of lumber and plywood into shipping containers. Johan entered the grand hall with the sergeant and a contingent of men to retrieve the artifacts in the chamber beneath the mummies. Johan descended through the hole in the floor. He took his lantern and shone it around the space. There was no ornamentation on these walls.

"It appears that this was an improvised chamber to store the important artifacts of the temple." Johan called out to the men above.

There were dozens of scrolls sealed in clay tubes, the large gilded tablet that the priest was still clutching and various small statues. A mask rested on the floor beside the priest. It appeared to have fallen from his face as his head had turned to the side. Johan carefully retrieved it from the floor and blew it off. It was heavy and probably pure gold.

"Its features appear to be European," said Johan as he trembled with excitement.

After he regained his composure, Johan began handing the smaller artifacts to the men at the opening in the floor above him. Within several hours, they had emptied the space of all but the remains of the priest.

Johan had decided to remove the priest while he still clutched the tablet. Two soldiers lowered one of the stainless containers into the space beneath the floor. They carefully repeated the process of sliding a steel pan under the corpse and lifting it into the container. He placed several small objects in the vault with the priest, and latched it. By the end of the day, the priest had joined Jafir and Shem in the great hall for the first time in thousands of years. They would soon journey to a world that had not even existed when they breathed the air of their homeland.

It had been two weeks since the expedition entered the hall of creation. As daylight drained from the sky above the plain of Uruk Johan stood at the entrance to the great hall for one last time. He brushed the canvas aside and walked into the cold dimly lit space. The men were gathering the last pieces of equipment for the return trip to the Fatherland. Johan had diligently struggled to record as much information as possible from the Hall of creation. He had filled thirteen leather bound volumes with sketches and descriptions, and he had taken thousands of photographs. The soldiers had filled a convoy of several military trucks with carefully packaged shipping containers. In the morning, they would leave this place, and Johan knew that he would not likely return. The sergeant joined him for his final visit to the hall.

"What does all of this mean?" He asked.

Johan started at the first panel, "In the beginning the Gods came to earth." He said as he pointed at the figures standing by a line representing the Euphrates. "They lived in the garden, beside the river of life, in the land of Nod. For many years, they came, descending in the great city from the heavens." Johan paused briefly "They made man in their image and man's purpose is to serve them."

"That sounds very similar to what my Lutheran minister read from the holy book when I was a boy in Hamburg," said Steffen.

Johan smiled and replied, "That is why we came here. This civilization predates the Egyptians, the Babylonians, the Jews and the Assyrians, all of them. There are those in the Reich that believe the Arian people are unique, superior even to all others.

"This expedition and others are gathering the evidence that will support research into the origin of the Arian people. Look at this panel." Johan continued talking as they stepped several paces further. He pointed to the cuneiform script under an etching; "After a time, the sons of the gods found the daughters of men desirable. They took the daughters of men as wives and had children and walked the earth for many years, teaching them and living among them."

Johan paused to make a not in the journal that he held.

"The gods loved the people of the plain for they were the children of the gods," continued Johan.

The sergeant stared at the panel and turned to Dr. Schmidt. "So the Fuhrer thinks that the German people came from this place?"

"Not exactly, but something like that," replied Johan.

The sergeant shook his head as he lit another cigarette. "Mark my words professor, this regime is crazy, the whole lot of them." They stood for another moment in silence as the sergeant finished his cigarette. "I must check on the men," he said smartly. "We leave at first light for the port at Basra."

2

THE BOMBING HAD BEEN CONTINUOUS for months. The acrid stench of spent explosives and airborne masonry filled the spaces once occupied by buildings. There was no escape from it. The city was scarred and broken. Modern warfare created violence on a scale never before achieved by man. The Americans delivered whistling death by air with endless streams of bombs, and the Russians conjured hell's demons with shrieking heavy artillery.

Johan stood atop the Reichstag as he peered through binoculars, searching for an opening to escape the dying city. "Russian barbarians," he muttered as he scanned the city. He hated them for the destruction that they brought to his homeland, unaware of the barbarism that German troops had wrought on the Russian people. He heard a whistle from the plaza below. A man was standing beside the open door of a truck waving at him. He returned the gesture. With a deep breath, he took one last look at the rubble of the center of Nazi power and headed down the stairwell to the street level. As he exited the building, an artillery shell exploded frightfully near the location where he stood moments before. Rubble rained down around him as he jumped into the passenger seat of the truck.

"Get us the hell out of here sergeant," said Johan.

The driver tore through the cluttered street. They careened around the burned out hulks of vehicles and crumbling buildings for several blocks. Their destination was in the western portion of the country. They had scavenged two auxiliary gas cans in hopes that the contents would get them safely to Stuttgart. There would be little to spare.

The Fuhrer had disappeared several days earlier, and the complete breakdown of the social order had begun. Johan knew that the precious artifacts of the Reichstag would fall into the hands of barbarians within days if he did not take action.

After clearing the outer fringes of Berlin, they located the Autobahn and drove for Stuttgart. Sergeant Muller reached into his leather coat and retrieved his present cigarette case.

"Where did you find those things?" asked Johan.

"There was a case in the supply room, at the Reichstag," replied the sergeant.

"Those are worth six months of script," said Johan.

"Today they are worth more than all of the script in Germany," replied Sergeant Muller as he offered him the thin cigarette case.

Johan took it and removed a single cigarette and match. With a single swipe, he lit the match with the rub strip on the side of the cigarette case. As he puffed the ember to life,

Sergeant Muller dodged a bomb crater in the roadway. They drove in shifts stopping only to refuel the truck with the auxiliary fuel cans and to stretch briefly or relieve themselves in the wooded areas along the Autobahn.

"The bomb craters are numerous," said Johan.

"The Allied pilots never return to their bases without dropping whatever ordinance they carry," replied the sergeant.

Johan pulled several long drags on the cigarette as he said, "We will need to drive through the night to stay on schedule. I do not wish to get caught in the open with allied fighters in the area."

"Perhaps you should get some sleep," replied Sergeant Muller. "I will drive the first shift and you can take over in the morning."

Johan finished the cigarette and made himself as comfortable as possible in the sparse cab of the truck. After a few miles, he drifted off to sleep.

Johan was abruptly jarred awake by a severe jolt. "What the hell!" he exclaimed. His driver was wrestling with the wheel; desperately attempting to maintain control of the truck.

"Sorry Dr. Schmidt. I almost fell asleep."

Johan squinted as his eyes adjusted to being awake. "We should find a safe place to pull over for a bit," he said as he yawned. "We can check on the cargo and stretch. I will take over driving for a while and you can get some sleep."

Johan rubbed his stiff neck and shoulders. A few miles further and they found a parking area near a grove of trees. They clamored out of the truck cab and stretched for a few moments. Johan leaned against the bumper of the military truck and surveyed the countryside.

"Out here one can imagine that Germany is not at war." He looked at the sky above them.

"There are no contrails in the sky," Johan said. "Maybe the Americans will take a day off."

His companion rubbed his bleary eyes and yawned. "We should keep moving," replied Sergeant Muller. "We don't want to be caught in the open when the American fighter planes arrive."

Johan jumped behind the wheel of the truck and started the engine as Sergeant Muller secured the passenger door. Johan restarted the engine and engaged the clutch. The truck lurched forward at a snail's pace in first gear, the whine of the gearbox saturating the cab of the vehicle. After shifting into road gear, the noise level was low enough for Sergeant Muller to sleep. Johan drove in silence for several hours. As the emptiness of the Autobahn began to give way to the outskirts of Stuttgart Johan shook Sergeant Muller with his free hand.

"Wake up old friend," said Johan. "We are almost there."

Sergeant Muller forced the fog of sleep from his mind. He opened the vent window to blast cool air onto his face. Johan exited the Autobahn and drove a narrow street to the industrial center of the older sector of the city. He located the street of his destination and turned in with the practice of several earlier visits. Sergeant Muller knew the drill as well. He retrieved a key ring from beneath the seat and jumped from the still moving truck. After Johan maneuvered the vehicle in position to unload, the sergeant unlocked the heavy steel door of the bunker.

"Once we secure the artifacts you should consider your service to the Fatherland complete," said Johan.

"My service to the Fatherland was completed long ago," replied the sergeant.

Johan pulled the corner of the tarp revealing three stainless steel boxes approximately twelve feet in length. They maneuvered one of them out of the truck and began shuffling into the opening of the bunker.

"If you consider your service to the Fatherland complete why are you risking your life for this?" asked Johan.

The sergeant replied, "I had been ordered to the eastern front when you requested that I be transferred to the general staff as your military liaison. The SS was to have one of their own watching over you so they allowed the transfer. I would likely have been killed in the east if your request had not saved me from that fate."

They placed the priest in farthest room from the entrance and returned to the truck twice more. As they were moving the last of the containers, air raid sirens began to wail in all directions. As Johan closed the door of the subterranean bunker, the children of the gods were once again safe in the darkness of the earth.

Contrails were now visible overhead as they drove for the rail station. "Do you think the trains are still running?" asked Johan.

"That is difficult to say," replied the sergeant. "Most of the infrastructure has been destroyed."

Suddenly the sound of ricocheting bullets erupted around them. Sergeant Muller dodged the line of exploding ground that chased them as though the earth sought to pull them into the underworld. The howl of a great beast roared overhead, a giant propeller beating the air as its massive radial engine pulled the metallic dragon along, spitting flame and death generously upon the Fatherland. Fire leapt from the front of the truck as several of the dragon's teeth silenced the throbbing heart of the vehicle. They coasted to a stop a few blocks from the rail station. Johan collected a satchel from the floor and inspected the contents. Satisfied that all of his leather notebooks were intact, he exited the vehicle and found shelter in a nearby alley. Out in street the truck lay wounded like a dying animal, its fluids bleeding out as fire consumed it. Sergeant Muller joined him in the alley as they waited for the American fighter plane to leave.

"This is where we part company Dr. Schmidt." Johan shook his hand and said, "Safe travels my friend. Perhaps we will meet again in a new world."

"I hope that it will be a better world," replied Sergeant Muller, handing his friend a cigarette for the last time. As they parted each went his way, in search of a new life.

3

THE RAIN HAD EASED to a cold drizzle as Johan watched the street through the window of his favorite café. The young woman at the greeting station recognized him as a regular customer. After seating him, she brought his customary glass of Cognac as she stopped at his table to take his order.

"Good afternoon Mr. Schmidt."

He looked up from his paper and smiled.

"Will you be dining with us today?" She asked.

"A cheese tray please, and a glass for my friend who has yet to arrive;" he answered in the tremble of an old man.

She scurried off to the rear of the establishment, returning a few moments later with his order. Half an hour later, a tall man in an overcoat entered the café and looked about. As he removed his hat, he shook the water off over the mat at the entrance. Spotting a familiar face, he moved toward Johan and paused at the empty chair.

Johan looked up and smiled as he said; "Sergeant Mueller, so nice to see you again."

"Thank you Dr. Schmidt, it has been a long time, has it not?" replied the tall figure as he seated himself at the table. "Just call me Steffen. I have spent much of my life distancing myself from my party affiliation of those days. It has been a long time, no?"

"Thirty two years old friend," replied Johan. He took his glass and offered a toast. His guest accepted the gesture and they touched their glasses together before they each took a drink of the golden liquid.

"Do you recall the last thing you said to me as we parted company all those years ago?" Johan asked.

"I believe I stated that I hoped for a better Germany or a better world, or something like that," said Steffen.

"Close enough," replied Johan. "So what do you think? "Things are better these days than I ever remember them to be."

"Of course they are," said Steffen. "Germany is completely new, rebuilt on the rubble of the old country."

A devilish smile stretched across Johan's face as he held his arms out and said, "Like the Phoenix rising from the ashes."

His guest looked confused for a moment as the comment triggered a distant memory of another time and place. As the humor of the comment dawned on the man, he lost his composure and began to laugh. Johan flapped his arms and they laughed heartily for a few moments. He abruptly stopped as angina reminded him of his weak heart. His companion looked startled as Johan fished a bottle of nitro glycerin tablets from his jacket pocket. After swallowing two tablets, he washed it down with the water glass on the table. He waved his hand to calm his companion.

"My mind is sharp but my body is failing," he said as he finished his cognac. My wife, Elsa, passed away several years ago and my son lives in Berlin with his wife."

"What about you Steffen?" asked Johan. "Have you a family?"

Steffen finished the remainder of his cognac before answering stoically. "I do not; my parents were killed in the bombings of 1945. I cooperated with the Americans after the war in locating certain valuable assets of the Nazi regime in exchange for amnesty," said Steffen.

"So you never married and had a family?" asked Johan. "I met a girl after the war but she lived in the east and the wall came between us, so to speak," replied Steffen. "I have pretty much stayed busy trading antiquities and other items of value."

"Other items of value?" asked Johan.

Steffen looked sternly across the table at his friend as he answered, "I often do business with very dangerous people old friend. Knowing how to keep secrets has allowed me to grow both wealthy and old."

"I understand, replied Johan. "I wanted to see you in order to tell you about something.

Johan sipped at his cognac and breathed as deeply as his chest pain would allow.

"I have been a professor of near eastern history for many years. The artifacts from Uruk are stored in the basement vaults of the University. The star tablet is stored in a glass case and I pass by it often. One day last week, as I turned the lights off before leaving for the evening, the thing was glowing."

Steffen stared at him for a moment and then asked, "Are

you certain that there were no sources of light that simply made it appear to glow?"

Johan shook his head. "No, the room was completely dark and the jewels were projecting light; creating patterns on the wall.

"Did you tell anyone of this?" asked Steffen. "No, who would believe the ravings of an old man?" replied Johan.

"I am curious Dr. Schmidt, on what date did this occur?"

Johan took a breath and replied, "It was the twenty first of June. "The summer solstice," replied Steffen. "Indeed," said Johan.

They sat in silence for a moment as Johan mustered his nerve. "I have heard that you are a man of some influence with the People's Museum," said Johan.

"That is true," replied Steffen. "I have assisted the museum in locating several caches of artifacts that the Nazis hid during the war. I have also brokered several deals recently that brought artifacts into the collection from the black market."

Johan looked at the man across the table as he continued, "My time is short." He took a breath before continuing. "Before I die, I would like to transfer the artifacts that we recovered from Uruk to the Museum."

"If that is your wish, I can help," replied Steffen.

"It is time," said Johan. "My stewardship of them is at an end. They belong to the children of the future. Perhaps they will discover their true meaning."

Several weeks later Steffen was opening the mail at his office in Berlin when he noticed a letter from an attorney in Stuttgart. He knew what it meant before he opened it. He shook his head and sighed as he slit the flap with a dagger and removed the contents. As he carefully unfolded the single page, a key fell upon his desk. He began reading as he picked up the key.

> Dear Steffen,
>
> Thank you for assisting with the transfer of the artifacts to the museum. I have enclosed a key to a safe deposit box in Stuttgart. There you will find a special artifact that I would like for you to hold in your custody until you can determine where it may be most effectively studied. I am writing you from a hospital bed and I will have likely traveled the road to the underworld by the time you receive this letter. The doctors give me only a few days to remain in this life.
>
> I wish you the best.
> Johan

The following day Steffen stepped into lobby of an upscale bank in Stuttgart. The floors were of a white Italian marble with black veining and the counter tops were black marble with white veining, providing a stark contrast in the space. Great columns supported a high vaulted ceiling that gave the impression of a sacred space.

"Welcome to our bank," said a greeter in a black suit as he entered the lobby.

Steffen produced the letter with the key and the man escorted him to a room with a table in the center. He selected a chair while the clerk exited the room. A few moments later, the clerk reappeared with a lock box. Steffen unlocked the steel container and retrieved a wooden box with leather binding straps on the lid. The clerk handed him a release form, which he promptly signed. Less than an hour later, he was cruising at twenty thousand feet in his private jet. The return trip to Berlin would only require an hour or so. Steffen considered waiting until he reached the security of his office to open the box but he had nothing better to do so, he slipped the bindings from their buckles and opened the lid. Inside he found a gleaming gold tablet covered with ancient cuneiform script. There were strange jewels imbedded in it unlike any he had seen since he first saw this tablet many years ago in the ancient city of Uruk. He considered removing it from the case to inspect it but chose to do so in the safety of his office.

"The antiquities value of this relic is greater than the gross national product of a small country," he thought as he examined it.

Soon he would learn that the true value of this object would far surpass his estimation.

The following afternoon Steffen finally had the opportunity to take a close look at the tablet. After concluding several business matters that had claimed his attention earlier in the day he returned from a long lunch with a potential client from Egypt. Settling into his chair, he looked at the box on his desk and smiled. "This could be the big one," he thought as he loosed the buckles and removed the cover. Removing the tablet from the box, he hefted it to sense the weight. "Several Kilos of solid gold and unusual jewels," he said aloud. "How much should I sell this for?" he questioned himself aloud. "Interesting, how could it be warm to the touch sitting on my desk."

He rotated the tablet around as he inspected it. As he did so, he noticed a particular position that felt quite natural as he held the tablet with both hands. Under each palm, a jewel gently pressed into his skin as he clutched his hands around the edge of the artifact. The warmth seemed to travel from the

RELIC

jewels into his hands. This resulted in a pleasantly soothing
sensation in his old bones. Suddenly the remaining jewels
on the tablet lit brilliantly as if they were made of pure light.
This startled the old man and he tried to place the tablet back
on his desk but his hands would not release their grip. They
were involuntarily holding fast. As fear began to grip him, the
warmth spread from his forearms throughout the rest of his
body. He was trembling now. He had not experienced this
level of fear since the Russian bombardment of Berlin at the
end of the war. Just as he was about to panic a sense of well
being overwhelmed him. Light suddenly surrounded him. The
warmth of it expelled from his nostrils as he breathed, he could
sense it in every fiber of his being. His body fell back into his
chair as he lost consciousness, his hands firmly grasping the
tablet.

   He found himself floating above his body. He could see
the tablet in his hands, glowing brightly. Then suddenly he
was floating above a great desert. A river flowed through it.
There was a fertile region near the delta formed by the river
as it entered a sea. Just as suddenly, he was standing in the
center of a Neolithic campsite as the inhabitants went about
their activities tanning hides and cooking meat over an open
fire while children played among the straw and mud huts in
the village. Suddenly, he was in another reality. An ancient
plain surrounded him. The people of the plain gathered
around a great metallic object as large as a ziggurat. As he
observed, the object levitated off the ground and rose into the
clouds before shining as brightly as the sun and disappearing
completely. Once again, he moved through time. Suddenly
he was observing these same people erecting a ziggurat that
bore a remarkable resemblance to the object that had lifted
off from the plain. There were now field crops planted around

the structure and they had adopted irrigation methods that watered them. Many stone structures dotted the landscape. The site had evolved into a vibrant city, the first of its kind.

As Steffen had his first experience with the tablet, at exactly the same time, halfway around the world, in a place called Ohio, a large radio telescope detected a very unusual beam of electromagnetic energy. The signal lasted for only 72 seconds, and many years would pass before its rediscovery.

Steffen awoke lying in his chair still holding the tablet. He sat up, placed it back into the box, and closed the bindings. After he summoned his faculties, he stood and moved the picture on the wall behind his desk, exposing the door of a safe. After entering the combination and opening it, he placed the box in the safe, closed the door and replaced the picture. As he walked to the restroom in his office suite, he noticed that the familiar pain in his knees was absent. As he relieved himself, he also realized that his difficulty in urinating was gone. His pulse quickened as he put these issues together in his mind with the recent dream that he had in his office. Upon returning to his desk, he made an appointment with his physician, asking for an emergency visit the same day.

It was late for a doctor's consult; the clock on the wall read sixteen twenty hours, August 17, 1977. The office staff had dismissed for the evening just before Steffen's physician returned to the exam room. "Well Mr. Mueller, you appear to be the healthiest man of eighty years that I have ever seen. We have charts on you going back decades and every condition that you ever had appears to have healed. Do you mind telling me your secret?"

"Vitamins," replied Steffen.

"I have never heard of a vitamin that cured prostate cancer," replied the doctor. It will be several days before your lab work returns but the physical exam shows a perfectly normal gland."

"So what happened to you?" asked the doctor.

"You would not believe me if I told you," replied Steffen. It is critically important for your safety and mine that you keep this visit and my records in extreme confidence," said Steffen pausing for a few seconds to consider his next action.

"You will be rewarded handsomely for doing so, and you will face severe consequences if you do not."

His words rang with a supernatural depth that surprised even Steffen. The doctor appeared genuinely afraid. Steffen retrieved his checkbook from his sport jacket and wrote as he spoke. He tore off the check and handed it to the doctor.

"Everything will be alright doctor; I think we understand one another, yes?"

"Certainly, Mr. Mueller, said the doctor as he stared at the check in disbelief."

"Very well then, call me when the lab results arrive," said Steffen as he removed his coat from the hall tree. After donning the overcoat, he creased his hat, placed it on his head and nodded to the doctor with a smile as he left the office.

4

THE SMALL TABLET ON HIS belt beeped as Gerhardt studied a group of small stone carvings in the museum's extensive collection. An authority on the history of the ancient near east; he had published several articles regarding astronomy in ancient Mesopotamia.

As a young man, Gerhardt entertained himself by studying in his family's library. His great grandfather's work fascinated him. Of particular interest was the vast collection of leather notebooks that the old man had placed in the library. They contained sketches and notes of the sites that he had visited, working in the lands of the east. The volumes that he found most interesting were the notebooks that contained descriptions of the ziggurat of Uruk. He had read them many times and held artifacts in his hands that the elder Schmidt had brought to Germany a century earlier. Such was this legacy, that Gerhardt had earned his own doctoral credentials by publishing his thesis on the astronomy of ancient Babylon.

His work generated great interest in Neolithic technologies. Now, many years after his death, Johan Schmidt's work proved its value. After learning of this work, an American scientist in California had contacted Gerhardt regarding the articles. At his request, Gerhardt had emailed him copies of his thesis. Now the man wanted to discuss the subject at greater length.

Dr. Samuel Enoch stood on the observation platform outside of his office and watched the sunrise above the ridgeline that ran east of the array. A slight breeze chased across the valley floor and rustled his disheveled and thinning grey hair. He finished the last of his coffee as he observed the light dance across the buildings around him. The pale grey color of the structures in the valley stood in stark contrast to the browns and grays of the surrounding earth. The installation was comprised of a small group of buildings in the center of an extinct volcanic caldera, high in the Sierra Nevada Range of Northern California. Antennae sprouted from the barren coffee colored land; like strange flowers craning skyward for nourishment by a force beyond this world.

He allowed his mind a few idle moments as he watched the world around him awake to a new day. His team had been working on schedule A for two weeks as they observed a region of space not accessible to them during daylight hours. Looking down from his perch, he could see most of the dish array spread out before him on the valley floor. A pair of headlights switched on and began moving toward the control building. A few moments later Jerry Schumacher guided the electric service vehicle into the parking lot and silently parked just below the platform where Doctor Enoch stood.

"Coffee is fresh," said Dr. Enoch as he leaned on the

handrail of the platform. His tall and lanky frame was clad in his standard khaki pants, journalist vest and hiking shoes. Jerry took the steps two at a time as he ascended to the platform.

"Good; I need some," said Jerry as he passed by and went directly to the break area.

The older man followed him and waited for Jerry to pour a cup before refilling his own. They took positions around the table and sipped the strong brew. Jerry winced at Doc's special wake up brew.

"Jeez doc, that stuff is strong," said Jerry as his scalp tingled from the caffeine blast.

Dr. Enoch grunted as he drank. He placed his tablet device on the table in front of him and accessed an article that he had read several weeks earlier.

"I have something here that I would like for you to read Jerry."

"Alright Doc, replied Jerry as he reached across the table and took the tablet. He took a chair and reared back, placing his feet on another as he placed the tablet on his lap.

Dr. Enoch turned to the window as Jerry read. He surveyed the antenna array as they sequenced through a diagnostic routine that Jerry had initiated earlier that morning; moving like great metallic trees, pushed by an ancient breeze.

Jerry finished reading and closed his eyes for a moment. He allowed the effects of Doc's motor oil brew to spur his mind.

"Interesting article Doc," said Jerry as he slid the tablet across the table to the older man.

"I have contacted the author," replied Doctor Enoch. "As I was reading it the first time I had an epiphany of sorts. When I saw the photograph of the golden tablet that he refers to as the star tablet I was struck by how contemporary it appeared."

Jerry intently listened as Doc swiped his finger a couple of times on the tablet and then positioned the device where they both could see the image. "This is what looks to be a model of the solar system as we presently understand it; Sun, major planets, extra solar objects and a few unexplained objects orbiting between Jupiter and Mars."

"So how did an ancient civilization know about objects in the Kuiper belt?" asked Jerry; wincing as he spoke from the bitterness that lingered from his last sip.

"I don't know," replied Doc. "There is no way that they observed them first-hand, we just found them after the turn of the millennium with space telescopes."

Dr. Enoch was silent for a moment as he studied the image. Placing the tablet on the table, he stood and turned to the window. The sun was pushing light over the eastern ridge of the valley and the sky was beginning to lighten. The white structures of the dishes were clearly visible in the low light. Standing like centuries in the valley floor, they waited for someone long overdue.

"Of all of the things that we have seen in the Universe we have only observed life here," said Dr. Enoch. "We assume that there are Billions of life-bearing worlds in the Universe but we have no proof of even one. We have spent most of our lives searching for one stray radio emission but we have found nothing."

Jerry was swirling the remaining bit of coffee in his cup and observing the few grains that had escaped the filter. They whirled about the center of the vortex that his hand motion created like little planets orbiting an unseen point.

"Objects orbiting a singularity," said the voice of his mind as he listened to Doc.

"What if we have been looking in the wrong place?" asked Jerry.

"What do you mean?" asked Dr. Enoch in reply.

Jerry began rolling up the sleeves of his orange cotton shirt, as he said, "What if the August 1977 signal didn't originate in the constellation of Sagittarius? The signal lasted for 72 seconds and was only detected by one of two antennae in the array."

"Ok, continue with your hunch," replied Dr. Enoch.

"The scientific community got really excited because the signal fit the model of the 1420 MHz convention."

"Yes Jerry," replied Doc. "The assumption is that an advanced life form would know that a signal at 1420 MHz would raise the interest of an intelligence that could interpret it because that frequency corresponds to the resonant frequency of Hydrogen, the most abundant element in the universe," replied Dr. Enoch.

"Right Doc, all of that makes sense, but why can't we replicate the signal by listening to Sagittarius? What if the signal came from a source that was passing between earth and Sagittarius, creating the illusion that it came from there?"

Dr. Enoch allowed Jerry's suggestion to sink in.

"Either way Doc, somebody wants us to find them."

Doctor Enoch studied the image on the tablet as he considered Jerry's idea.

"So it was a beacon," said Doctor Enoch. "Somewhere there is a beacon and we are supposed to find it."

"I think so," replied Jerry. "If that signal had originated in Sagittarius; it would have taken thousands of years to reach earth. The transmission time frame predates any known civilization by tens of thousands of years."

Doc looked back at the tablet and said, "It must be closer then."

"Yep," replied Jerry as he raised his cup for a sip of coffee.

"Perhaps our colleague in Germany has additional material," said Doc.

Checking his wrist tablet he continued, "I have requested that he give us a call at his earliest convenience."

Jerry stood and stretched. He picked up his coffee cup and moved to the sink. As he washed it and placed it in the rack to dry he said, "I have several more drive units to check this morning, some of the gear trains are developing excessive backlash."

"I'll call if I hear from him," said Dr. Enoch as he headed for his office.

Late in the evening, as the last rays of the day spilled over the ridgeline, his tablet chirped, notifying him of a pending communication. He unclipped the device from his belt and saw that Gerhardt Schmidt had replied. Dr. Enoch immediately engaged the video transmission.

"Hello Gerhardt, if I may call you by your first name; thank you for returning my inquiry," said Dr. Enoch.

"I rarely have zee opportunity to discuss contemporary science; most of my colleagues are interested in the ancient world," replied Gerhardt, his blue eyes beaming large behind an old pair of glasses."

Dr. Enoch laughed as he replied, "Unfortunately, I too am interested in the ancient world. I have a riddle that I cannot answer."

"Is that so?" asked Gerhardt.

"Yes, and you are the author. Your thesis references a

golden tablet that appears to contain a graphical representation of the known solar system."

"That would be the star tablet," replied Gerhardt, his English improving as he continued to speak. "Und yes, it is a model of the solar system; as it appeared to the first known human civilization," replied Gerhardt.

"Are you certain that it is authentic?" asked Dr. Enoch.

"Quite certain," replied Gerhardt. "My great grandfather discovered it while digging at the Ziggurat of Uruk in southern Iraq during the 1930's."

Dr. Enoch felt a chill of excitement as he allowed the previous comment to sink in. "Do you have any additional information that is not discussed in your thesis?" asked Dr. Enoch.

Gerhardt looked down for a moment as if he were considering something forbidden. "Why do you ask?"

"I am considering a theory that could cause a great deal of controversy and frankly I am not entirely comfortable with it," said Dr. Enoch.

Gerhardt smiled as he replied, "I suspect that I know what you are thinking; and the answer is yes, there is quite a lot more." Gerhardt leaned forward and continued, "I will wager that your theory is not simply controversial; it could be very dangerous."

There was an uneasy pause. Dr. Enoch continued, "I can assure you that it is in my organization's interest to maintain the highest possible security measures."

"How do you propose we continue?" asked Gerhardt, as he blinked his blue eyes appeared large behind his thick glasses.

Jerry had entered the room in time to pick up the trail of the conversation. He had silently listened, standing out of view of the video camera on Dr. Enoch's tablet.

"We have a highly secure virtual library within our organization called Alexandria. I will send you access codes to a file in which you may deposit any data that you would be willing to share."

Gerhard stared directly into the screen and said, "You can imagine my surprise when I discovered that Space Command found the three additional objects depicted on the star tablet in 2003."

"Where did the people of southern Mesopotamia get the knowledge to produce the tablet?" Asked Dr. Enoch

"The Gods gave it to them, "replied Gerhardt.

"The Gods?" asked Dr. Enoch.

"Yes, they believed that the Gods came to earth and lived among them, educated them and even intermarried with them. They considered themselves to be the children of the Gods."

Dr. Enoch listened without voicing his skepticism.

"I will begin copying files to your library this evening," replied Gerhardt. "You may be surprised at what you discover about our ancestors."

Over the next several days, Gerhardt inundated the library with information. Hundreds of photographs and other data; neatly organized into folders and subfolders, representative of the summation of the entire collection of the museum, digitized and instantly accessible for study at a moment's notice. Dr. Enoch plunged into the information, swimming in hundreds of photographs and articles spanning the entire modern era. In this pool of information, there would be artifacts that could change the course of civilization.

The next morning, Jerry hurried to the main conference room following an urgent message from Dr. Enoch. His attention immediately gravitated to images on the video wall as he joined the older man in front of the screen. There were black and white photos dating to the 1930's as well as sketches made by someone named Johan Schmidt.

"I find it interesting that the ceremonial structures of the ancient world always seem to be built upon a large platform," said Dr. Enoch as Jerry scanned through the images.

"Where is this place Doc?" Jerry asked.

"It is in Southern Iraq," replied Dr. Enoch.

"Has anyone been there since German expedition?" asked Jerry.

"According to Gerhardt sand storms have covered the site. This satellite image is only a couple of years old. There are obvious features around the central mound. Due to the remoteness of the site there is a strong probability that no one has been there."

"I don't blame them, the place looks desolate," replied Jerry.

"There are some very interesting artifacts that I want to show you." Dr. Enoch selected another library and displayed an image of a golden tablet. "Wow." Jerry exclaimed. "Is it gilded? He asked.

"Not according to Gerhardt," replied Dr. Enoch. "Not only is it solid, it has a molecular weight that is denser than refined gold."

As Jerry studied several images of the tablet, he said, "There are no marks, no casting flash or tool marks, it is perfectly smooth."

Dr. Enoch felt no small satisfaction as the younger man confirmed his own conclusions.

"Any idea what the jewels are that represent the planetary bodies?" asked Jerry.

"They were thought to be desert glass but the German's couldn't scratch them when they tested them," replied Dr.

Enoch. "According to Gerhardt, not even a diamond stylus would mark the surface."

As Jerry continued to study the features on the face of the tablet Doc said, "There are features on the back of the tablet that you should see as well." He scrolled through a few more images and selected one.

"Gerhardt says that these inscriptions were not carved and they were not cuneiform," said Jerry as he studied the back of the tablet. "I am impressed with the apparent level of workmanship. What measurements have been made on the piece?"

"That is the most interesting part," answered Doc. "Dimensionally it is absolutely true; at least to the sub micron level."

Jerry looked surprised. "Sub micron?" he quizzed. "Those tolerances are nearly impossible even with today's technology." "There is simply no way that ancient man made this."

His comment rang for a moment as if suspended in the air around them. Dr. Enoch was smiling when Jerry turned to him.

"The people of Uruk claimed it was given to them by the Gods," said Dr. Enoch.

"That is just spooky Doc"

"Think past your paradigms Jerry. We cannot fabricate it today so we know the German's could not have made it. The material from which it is made is completely alien to our modern inventory of elements, and it was buried in the sands of the Iraqi desert for millennia." Doc paused. "Sometimes the simplest explanation is the best explanation."

Jerry studied the lines of shapes and symbols on the image of the back of the tablet.

"Doc, these lines resemble mathematical code."

"How so?" asked Dr. Enoch.

"The symbols may not be familiar but the patterns are."

Jerry called up a blank screen and copied the tablet image into it. He cut each line of characters out of the copied image and placed them end to end in a continuous line.

"It can't be this obvious," Jerry muttered as he worked.

Dr. Enoch stood back and observed with fascination as the smartest man that he ever knew put the pieces of a ten thousand year old puzzle together. Jerry accessed an operations sub routine that the observatory instruments utilized for Radio Frequency scanning operations. "We have reasoned that we should be looking for signals in the 1420 MHz range; right?" Jerry asked.

"Yes," said Dr. Enoch.

Jerry pasted his copy of the EM spectrum beneath the line from the tablet. He then placed his finger on the area around 1420 MHz and slid the image along beneath the line above. As his finger reached the center of the top line, he froze.

"I can't believe it." Jerry said. "It matches."

Doc was staring dumbfounded at the screen; arms crossed in a self-embrace.

Jerry stared at the images on the video panel.

"This is really something Doc."

"Yes it is Jerry," replied the older man, still standing with arms crossed.

"Any chance we could get a look at the tablet in person?" asked Jerry.

"No," replied Dr. Enoch "It disappeared in the 1970's. At least we have the records of those fastidious Germans.

It was late in the evening when the monitor screen in Gerhardt's apartment notified him of a video call. He accepted the call by voice command after checking the caller's identification.

"Hello Dr. Enoch, you must have news that cannot wait until morning."

Dr Enoch was visibly excited as he began, "Yes Gerhardt, we have found a very interesting bit of information within the inscriptions on the back of the star tablet. It appears to be a graphical representation of the electromagnet spectrum immediately around the frequency of 1420 MHz"

"And this is important?"

"Yes, this frequency is in the range that we refer to as the cosmic waterhole," replied Dr. Enoch continued.

"An interesting analogy," replied Gerhardt with a chuckle.

Dr. Enoch continued in his lecture tone.

"We must assume that all advanced life forms will have a similar understanding of basic science. The most abundant element in the universe is hydrogen. The resonant frequency of this element is 1420 Mhz. Universally speaking there is very low background noise in this frequency range; so a loud signal will stand out prominently in this area of the spectrum."

Gerhardt considered the statement for a moment and replied, "So you think that the tablet is identifying 1420 MHz as a beacon?"

"Exactly," replied Dr. Enoch. "Now we just need to determine where to search."

"Perhaps I may be of assistance in this area," replied Gerhardt. "I need some time to review some of my notes and other materials. I will get back to you as soon as I have something."

As the screen flicked off Dr. Enoch studied the analysis that Jerry had created earlier.

"Such a remarkable mind," he said as he flicked through the images on his tablet.

The following afternoon he reviewed status reports of the dish array with Jerry. They were planning for a sweep of Sagittarius in a few days as they did each month on the off chance that the WOW signal would be there as it had been in 1977. As they were finishing the meeting, Doc's tablet buzzed. Upon picking it up, he saw that a video call from Gerhardt was holding. As Jerry was preparing to leave, Doc motioned for him to stay in the room. He accepted the call and transferred it to the main video panel in the conference room.

"Good afternoon Gerhardt," said Dr. Enoch. "Let me introduce you to my right hand man, Jerry Schumacher. We have worked together for several years and he is fully informed regarding the events of the last few days."

"Hello," said Gerhardt.

"Likewise," Jerry nodded and smiled.

"During our last conversation you explained the waterhole frequency phenomenon and the apparent fact that the star tablet illustrates that portion of the Electromagnetic Spectrum. You also mentioned that it would be useful to know where to look."

"Yes, that would be very helpful," replied Dr. Enoch.

"I think that you will find what I am about to say of some interest. According to the mythology of the people of Uruk, the gods monitored earth in their absence via watchers in the heavens. They periodically sent messengers to the earth as well. The messenger appears to be associated with the farthest body from the sun according to the star tablet. It was believed that the messenger would travel between the place of the gods and the earth via a door in the outer heavens."

The two of them sat in silence as they considered Gerhardt's explanation. Jerry opened the image of the tablet on the video panel and dragged with his finger until it displayed beside Gerhardt's image.

"The ninth body would be Pluto," said Jerry as he studied the solution. "There are about a dozen large bodies beyond Pluto that orbit in the Kuiper belt."

He opened another window on the screen and produced an image of solar system.

"The larger bodies would be Haumea, and Eris," said Jerry.

Dr. Enoch cheerfully added, "It looks like we have a starting point."

"I am hopeful that you find what you are searching for," replied Gerhardt.

"We will keep you in the loop, regardless of what happens," Dr. Enoch replied.

"Thank you," replied Gerhardt. "I have several matters that need my attention for now, so good day gentlemen."

The conference window went black as Gerhardt terminated the transmission.

"So Jerry, where should we start?" asked Dr. Enoch.

"Eris is the largest body out of twelve dwarf planets; I say we start there."

"Agreed; scrap the tasking orders for the next observation," said Dr. Enoch in an unusually commanding tone. "We are going to have a look at Eris."

"Roger that, replied Jerry as he leaned over the table, propping his medium frame on his arms and stretching the morning stiffness out of his back and legs.

Jerry arranged for the Eris observation. His only distraction came in the form of Miranda Lee with whom he had begun a relationship a few months earlier. Miranda worked at the installation as well and she and Jerry had hit it off from the moment that they had met. Both of them were cautious when it came to relationships as neither of them had found a partner strong enough to weather the independent streak in each of them. Jerry had spoken of the next observation on their last date and she met him in the break room for his morning coffee.

"Hi handsome, she said as she entered the room." Jerry blushed as she poured a cup of coffee. "So this is the big day?" she asked.

"I hope so," he replied. "The routine of not finding anything is getting old."

She closed the door to the room and walked over to where he stood. She smiled at him and leaned toward him, kissing him. "That's for good luck, there may be more where that came from if you find something."

Just then, the door opened and Doc entered the room. He headed straight for the coffee maker, not noticing the close proximity of the two of them. "Are we ready to go?" Doc asked as he swirled his coffee with a swizzle stick. "All systems are nominal," replied Jerry. "Well then, let's do this thing," said Dr. Enoch as he slapped Jerry on the back and gently nudged him toward the door.

Halfway around the world a man of 130 years sat in his study holding a bejeweled tablet. He appeared as though he was a very fit man of 60 years. Almost every day since August 1977, he had held the tablet for a period in the afternoon. He had witnessed everything from the creation and evolution of man to the ships that the gods used to visit Earth in the time before time. He knew the technology of the gods. He knew the way to their outposts and he knew where they came from. He also knew of a great danger to his world. Soon he would share his knowledge, when he found the right people.

As Jerry and Doc entered the control room, Jerry took a seat in front of the master control console. He entered his access code into the primary control system for the array and waited a few seconds for confirmation. He selected the tasking orders for the Eris observation and selected the run icon on the control panel.

Outside in the Sulphur Creek Caldera, the antennae of the array began slewing together as they homed in on the tiny spot in the sky where Eris would be located. Inside the facility, alarm tones were humming in the control room as technicians and scientists scurried about with a deliberate precision that comes from years of planning and practice.

Jerry's voice rang over the PA system, "capture protocol in effect."

Dr. Enoch stood in front of a large video display wall with dozens of images of radio frequency data designed to provide a very detailed analysis of electromagnetic energy.

"This is it Jerry," said Dr. Enoch excitedly. "1420 megahertz, right where the tablet predicted it would be."

"We are Locked on target and recording", said Jerry.

Outside of the building, 150 dish antennae crept in slow synchronized movement, tracking a phantom in the sky. Jerry's voice announced; "72 seconds and counting, 90 seconds." A smile extended across Dr. Enoch's face. "120 seconds."

Their attention was riveted to the observation screen as the drama of discovery unfolded.

"It's real Jerry, he said in a near whisper." Jerry placed his hand on the old man's shoulder. "You found it Doc."

Dr. Enoch smiled, his eyes misting behind his glasses. "Pardon the emotion Jerry."

Jerry smiled and replied; "don't sweat it Doc. Just take it in for a while. We are making history."

The two of them stood silently watching the video screen and the equipment racks flashing with green and blue dots of brilliance in the dim light of the control room, the clock in the video wall read zero four thirty hours. Out of the main window one of the dish antennae was visible, its movement so slow that it was only betrayed by the fixed frame of the window.

"Better get Space Command on the line," said Jerry.

Dr. Enoch nodded yes, his hand on his chin and arms crossed in front of his chest, staring at the video data.

"It has been 45 years since anybody has identified a signal like this one," said Jerry.

Dr. Enoch glanced in his direction as Jerry continued; "when you consider how much technology we have and how many radio telescopes there are, it is odd that no one else has observed this phenomenon."

"Perhaps it is a simple matter of not noticing it," replied Dr. Enoch.

Jerry engaged the data screen from the console across the room. A few seconds later, the center section of the video wall activated and displayed a landing page with the Space Command logo. After placing his thumb on a biometric icon, the screen changed to a data acquisition page. A few finger-strokes later and the data that they had collected began transmitting.

"I give it twelve hours before they contact us," said Jerry as he turned to face Dr. Enoch, his brown eyes showing that he was tired.

RELIC

"I think that we both could use a shot of Joe," said Dr. Enoch.

They walked the hallway from the control room to the break area and started the coffee maker. The facility housed a staff of twenty in relative comfort. The amenities of modern life provided to the scientists and technicians who staffed the installation with a comfortable work environment. The two men were silent as they nursed their brew. They were both considering the magnitude of what they had just accomplished.

"Jerry, our lives are about to change," said Dr. Enoch.

"Yeah, I know, Not sure how I feel about it though," he said as he stared into his coffee. "I like life the way it is."

"I understand." Dr. Enoch Paused as he mustered his thoughts. "Sometimes fate has a way of calling us to a purpose greater than we plan for."

"Perhaps," replied Jerry.

Neither of them had a large social network of friends or family. They were both dedicated to a vocation that they loved. Dr. Enoch was a true man of letters with obscure articles published in various scientific periodicals and a few textbooks. Jerry was perhaps the finest radio astronomer in the business with an engineering degree from MIT and a particular gift for technical pursuits. He loved getting his hands dirty, solving problems, and building strangely esoteric equipment. The Sculpture Creek facility was full of his handiwork. Various pieces of purpose built equipment and thousands of lines of programming code had emerged from his fertile mind and talented hands.

Dr. Enoch first met Jerry twenty years earlier at the Very Large Array in New Mexico. Jerry was fresh out of college and Dr. Enoch was performing hard science searching for quasars, studying the background radiation of the big bang, and performing other textbook astronomy research. They became friends when they both showed up for volunteer work at a conference to operate radio telescopes at an array in northern California. During the intervening years, they had dedicated a great deal of their lives to the search for extra terrestrial intelligence. Perhaps they now had something to show for the effort.

Suddenly the video screen on the wall of the break room flashed on. It was Miranda Lee calling from the control room.

"Jerry, you and Doc better get back up here." "Space Command is on the video com."

"On the way," replied Jerry as he turned for the door. Doc was ten steps ahead of him trotting down the hall to the control room entrance. They charged into the room and took positions in front of the video conferencing system. The manager of Space Command's Near Earth Object Defense Program greeted them from his desk as he reviewed a digital copy of a found object report. Upon seeing them on the monitor in his office he said, "Gentlemen, please explain what I am looking at here."

Dr. Enoch cleared his throat and began.

"Ed, this is a radio frequency signal emanating from the extra solar body 136199 Eris. We have been tracking the signal for over 2 hours."

A pause ensued as Ed appeared to say something to someone else in the room.

"Congratulations Samuel, you may have a real discovery out there," said Ed.

"Thank you Ed, that means a lot coming from you," replied Dr. Enoch.

"Now for the bad news; you realize that we have a real can of worms here. I would like to fly you to Washington in order to discuss this further."

Dr. Enoch and Jerry looked at each other and back at the screen again.

"A plane will pick you up at the Susanville airport tomorrow at twelve hundred hours," said Ed. "We will talk the following day at my office."

"Thank you Ed; Dr. Enoch said with a nervous smile. It will be good to see you again."

Ed placed a tablet on his desk as he said, "I am looking forward to seeing you again as well Samuel. Please forgive the brevity of this conversation as I have a few other matters to attend to."

The screen flashed back to the Space Command landing page and the room fell silent.

Miranda turned in her chair toward them. "So what now?" she asked.

"We continue tracking and recording," replied Jerry. "Make sure that you check the backup stream to Alexandria every hour." She nodded to confirm. "That should keep the government honest. This discovery means too much to have it covered up."

She smiled and said, "I understand." She picked up her tablet and began to make her way toward the exit. As she passed Jerry, she discretely whispered to him, "Stop by my office for a minute."

They exited the control room and walked to an office at the end of the hall. Jerry could not help but look at her feminine form as they made their way down the narrow hall. She was a fit woman in her mid thirties and he could not help but enjoy the show as she walked ahead of him. Occasionally he caught a faint whiff of her perfume. As they entered her office, she closed the door and took his hand, pulled his arm around her waist and kissed him warmly.

"I am proud of you Jerry," she said as she looked into his brown eyes.

"Thanks Miranda," replied Jerry with a little embarrassment.

They had been dating for over a year and had managed to keep their relationship out of the work place but that had become increasingly more difficult lately. Jerry passed his fingers through her brown hair. "I am going to miss you while I am away."

"Dinner tonight?" she asked.

"You bet," Jerry replied; "I will pick you up at six."

"Sounds good," she said as she straightened his shirt and placed her hands on his chest.

"I better get back to the control room," Jerry said, his arms still around her.

"Yep she said; you had better do that. I have a few things to do here so I will see you this evening."

Jerry backed out of the office and smiled at her as he closed the door, turned and trotted to the control room. As he entered the room he walked briskly by the display screens where Dr. Enoch was reviewing frequency data. Doc detected a faint trace of Miranda's perfume as Jerry passed. He glanced in Jerry's direction, then back at the screen with a wry smile.

5

Ed Gilstrap studied a file on his tablet device as he spoke to the person across the room, "Too bad we didn't find this first."

"It was a needle in a haystack," replied John. "Our resources aren't what they once were."

"Yeah, I know," said Ed.

He stared out of his office window as if recalling an old memory. "I was worried about the old guy for a while. He seemed to fall off the face of the earth after leaving Space Command."

"Dr. Enoch is quite a character from what I hear," said John. "I heard he is into fringe science, ancient religions and such."

"Not really," replied Ed. "We worked together years ago when he was still engaged in conventional research. He is an

49

excellent scientist and a good team leader. He just got hung up on that signal from 1977 and never let go of it." He reviewed the report once again on his tablet. "It looks like he turned out to be right, regardless of how he got there."

"Can't argue with success I suppose," said John uneasily, fearful that he may have just spoken out of turn.

"He is sending us all of his data before he leaves for Washington," replied Ed. "I need for your department to run it through Adam and check it out. See if you can find any holes in his work before it goes public."

"Roger that boss," replied John. After 20 years of doing hard science, John knew serious work when he saw it and Ed trusted him.

Jerry left the Sulphur Creek installation at four o'clock. As he walked through the parking lot, he noticed that Miranda's car was gone. He approached his jeep and placed his thumb on the biometric scanner located on the side glass of the vehicle. A gender-neutral voice droned; "please confirm Identification."

"Jerry Schumacher."

"Voice identification confirmed. Good afternoon Jerry," replied the vehicle.

The door opened and Jerry sat in the seat. Sensing his presence, the dash panel lit up. As the door rolled into place, the automatic safety belts moved into position. Jerry placed his right hand on the joystick and pulled back slightly. The vehicle silently moved backwards out of its parking space. Jerry's house was a 30-minute drive from the installation. Once on the main road the vehicle took over in cruise mode and Jerry reviewed email, checked his dinner reservations and performed a dozen other tasks.

The vehicle control system notified Jerry that the turn to Feather Lake was two miles on the left. As he approached the turn off from the main road, he eased his hand onto the control stick and took over control of the vehicle. After several miles, he approached the drive to his home. While still at the end of the drive, the vehicle control system notified the operating system of his house that they were approaching. The garage door began to open as Jerry steered into the drive. He parked the vehicle next to its charging station and checked the monitor screen as he prepared to exit. He noted that there was approximately 230 miles of charge left in the energy storage system.

"No need to charge yet," he said aloud as he stepped out of the vehicle. The security system had already confirmed entry by interfacing with the jeep's on board systems. Jerry entered the house and headed for the bathroom for a quick shower.

As he stepped into the bathroom, he said aloud, "shower." Steam appeared around the corner of the opening as Jerry stepped in. Several minutes later, he took a hot towel from the warming rack and dried before entering his bedroom. After dressing, he walked into the den and said, "News." A second later the video panel on the wall illuminated and the windows began allowing light to pass through as they transitioned from opaque mode to transparent. Jerry enjoyed the view of the lake for a moment before turning his attention to the screen on the wall. He checked through his usual news outlets, business channels, and weather forecasts.

"Astronomers always check the weather," he said to himself. A voice from the audio system of the house reminded him that he had an appointment with Miranda Lee and that he would be 10 minutes early if he left in 5 minutes. Jerry paused for a look at the lake through the great room window before heading for the garage. As he exited the drive to his home, the operating system of the house returned to vacant mode, resetting the windows doors and other systems to secure them.

Twenty-five minutes later, he arrived at Miranda's house. The monitor screen in the vehicle switched from on board systems monitor to videophone mode as the house interfaced with the jeep. Miranda's face appeared on the screen. "Hi handsome," Miranda is smiling face said on the screen.

"Well hello you," Jerry said smiling back at the screen.

"Come on in," said Miranda through the intercom.

As Jerry walked toward the front door, it clicked open.

Miranda yelled, "I'll just be a minute. There is a glass of wine for you on the kitchen bar." Jerry walked over and picked up the glass. Miranda appeared around the corner wearing a black, form-fitting dress that flattered her tanned, taught body.

Jerry smiled at her. "You look marvelous, said Jerry."

Miranda laughed and walked over to him. She pecked him on the cheek and took his hand, "let's go."

Jerry swallowed the last of the wine; "I would follow you anywhere." Miranda smiled and playfully tossed her brown freshly curled hair as she looked back over her shoulder winking at him while walking toward the door.

"This is going be good," Jerry muttered to himself as they exited the house.

Miranda overheard his comment and replied; "you can count on it."

It was late when Dr. Enoch contacted Gerhardt Schmidt.

"Hello Samuel," a thick German accented English voice spoke from the video panel. "I assume you have news."

"Yes, we proved our hypothesis early this morning."

Gerhardt beamed as he exclaimed; "that is excellent news Samuel."

Dr. Enoch continued, "I suspect the news will break on the world net pretty soon. You will find the data in Alexandria shortly."

"You know Samuel; there will be consequences once this discovery goes public."

"I am aware of that," said Dr. Enoch. "People will be forced to deal with a truth that they may not be comfortable with."

A tone beeped from the panel and Dr. Enoch acknowledged it.

"The library upload is complete Gerhardt; you may proceed with your download."

Gerhardt logged into Alexandria and located the file. With a few keystrokes the data transfer started. As he worked, he smiled and said, "Alexandria is a clever name for the library.

"This one cannot be burned," replied Dr. Enoch. "We have back-ups of back-ups"

Gerhardt's tablet notified him that it had completed the data retrieval process.

"Und now we have a copy for the physical archives," said Gerhardt. He removed a quartz data module and held it in view of the camera between his thumb and index finger. The small rectangular crystal contained one hundred terabytes of data.

"I will bury it in our collection of small artifacts, it will be nearly impossible to find there," replied Gerhardt.

"Excellent," said Dr. Enoch. "That seems a rather appropriate location."

Gerhardt was still looking at the quartz crystal when he said," Thank you for including me in this project Dr. Enoch, it is a fitting continuation of my family's legacy."

"You are welcome my friend, there would have been no discovery without your contribution," replied Dr. Enoch.

Gerhardt nodded in acceptance of the compliment.

"I have a plane to catch tomorrow and it has been a very long day," said Dr. Enoch.

"Good day," replied Gerhardt as the monitor went black.

Dr. Enoch put his office in order and left the Sulphur Creek facility in his old sports car. He drove south on state road 44 until turning onto the feather lake highway where he enjoyed the drive through the countryside to his home at the Lake. The sun was low on the horizon and the car was responsive.

"Life is good he said to himself." he caught himself smiling in the mirror as he glanced for signs of traffic. He loved his old Porsche so much that he had periodically upgraded the vehicles capabilities. It now sported a modern on board operating system, and a contemporary hybrid drive system. Remarkably, it still performed like the car that he had originally purchased. As he approached his house, the garage door opened for him and he parked. As he exited his car a voice greeted him from the operating system of his home, "Welcome home Samuel."

"Thank you Frenchie," Dr. Enoch chuckled. "Jerry certainly has a way with technology," he muttered. The voice spoke again; "will Mr. Schumacher be joining you?"

"No Frenchie, I was just commenting on Jerry's handiwork," said Dr. Enoch.

"Very well Samuel," replied the operating system. Dr.

Enoch entered the den and collapsed into his favorite chair. He fell asleep while surfing the world net on a large monitor screen, above the credenza in the room.

6

As a matter of protocol, Ed observed long-standing notification procedures in order to place strategic assets on alert in the event of a possible earthbound threat. He received a video call from the pentagon within moments. He initiated a video conference directly from the message on his tablet.

"Good afternoon General Rudacil."

Ed paused for the salutation that did not come.

"I didn't expect to hear from you quite so soon," he said in a tone more like a question than a statement.

The shiny baldhead of the general reflected a light from the ceiling of his office as he looked from a tablet device toward the conference camera. "I just finished reading your brief; so tell me more about this signal from a planetary body out past Pluto.

His raspy and aggravated tone had a way of provoking a

mixture of annoyance and stress in most people, Ed was no exception.

"A scientist in Northern California working at a radio telescope Array has discovered a signal that seems to be originating from a planetary body called Eris. My people are investigating the discovery and I have a plane picking him up tomorrow."

Ed considered the fact that the response to his communication was unusually rapid and he determined that there must be more behind that interest than he presently understood.

"Why so much interest in the issue?" he asked.

The General pursed his lips for a moment before he carefully responded, "I can only say that Space Command needs to stay abreast of this one and leave it at that for now. I would appreciate a full briefing after you have a chance to review the data. Sooner is better than later."

"Certainly general," replied Ed courteously. He felt cold in his gut as his instincts informed him that this was going to be a big deal very soon.

"Ed, there's one more thing. We need to keep a lid on this for as long as we possibly can."

"I understand," replied Ed.

"I knew that we could count on you Ed," said the general as he terminated his video session.

Ed turned toward the window of his office and stood with his hands on his hips, his tall silhouette filling the window as he stared out upon the skyline of Washington. After a few moments reflection, he abruptly grabbed his sport jacket and headed for the elevator. Traffic would be getting heavy in Alexandria soon but he had just enough time to catch the next train. There would be many late nights soon and he wanted to get home to Mrs. Gilstrap.

As Ed made his way home on the east coast, Jerry and Miranda were entering a restaurant on the west coast. Jerry pulled Miranda's chair out for her as they approached the table. She looked over her left shoulder with a smile and thanked him. As Jerry settled into his chair, he looked around the room satisfied with the ambiance. Miranda's dark hair shined under the dim lighting and her black dress highlighted the curves of her body just enough to make it difficult for Jerry to avoid looking at her more than he should for dinner conversation. Miranda was pleased that he noticed her. She had been interested in Jerry from the first day they met. She knew that he was on the hook as well. She found his clumsiness in her presence endearing, and she often caught him admiring her.

They ordered dinner and desert but Jerry hardly new what he ate as his attention was mostly on Miranda. They recounted the events of the day, spoke of Jerry's trip with Doctor Enoch to Washington, and other small talk. All the while Jerry was watching her facial expressions, the way her lips curled slightly as she spoke and the shine of her red lipstick, which was a color he had not seen her wear unless she was out with him. She typically wore much more conservative colors. After desert, Miranda suggested they go back to her house for a couple of drinks. On the drive back to her home, Jerry placed his hand on her leg and she covered it with her hand. Her thigh was warm and her perfume seemed unusually strong, Jerry knew he was smitten with this woman. This was the first relationship that he had ever allowed to mature in his thirty-seven years.

As they entered the house, Miranda suggested a glass of wine. Jerry accepted and she kissed him before going to the wine rack to select a German Riesling. She handed Jerry a glass and he sipped it. "I am going to freshen up a bit," said Miranda as she placed her wine glass delicately on the table. Jerry sat on the chaise lounge to wait for her. The curved chair levitated above the floor on curved chrome legs with a cow skin cover. It was deceptively comfortable and before Jerry had time to finish his glass of wine, he was soundly asleep. It had been a very long day, starting at 4 am.

Miranda had changed into something comfortable and entered the living room to find Jerry exhausted in her chaise lounge. She almost laughed. She placed her finger on her lips to avoid waking him. She then removed his shoes and placed a blanket over him. When she was certain that he was comfortable, she retired to her bedroom. Jerry awoke the next morning to the sound of Miranda making breakfast. He looked down at the blanket covering him and realized the opportunity that he had missed.

"I can't believe it!" exclaimed Jerry.

Miranda laughed. "You only have a couple of hours before your plane arrives."

Jerry sat on one of the bar stools at the kitchen island and enjoyed a cup of coffee with her. She smiled over her cup as she looked at him.

"We will have to pick up where we left off when you return from Washington," she said with a sultry glance.

Jerry took the bait and replied, "It's a date then."

"I'll think about it," Miranda replied as she winked at him. You'd better get moving," she prodded. "Doc will be waiting on you." She turned toward him and offered him a kiss. Jerry obliged her in a way that told her he regretted his missed the opportunity of the previous evening.

"I'll call you from Washington." He said as he walked nearly backwards toward the door.

"You'd better," she replied as he exited the front door."

7

JERRY DROVE THE TWENTY MINUTES to his house at Feather Lake. As he rolled into the drive, Dr. Enoch appeared on the video screen in the dash. "Good morning Jerry, I will drop by and pick you up in about an hour."

"I'll be ready," he said as he drove into the garage. He rushed into the house for a quick shower and change of clothes. Dr. Enoch arrived to find Jerry waiting on the front patio of his modern cabin. The house contained heavy wooden beams supporting a slanted roofline with a stacked stone chimney on one end and a two-story box structure clad in corrugated metal on the opposite end. It was a handsome energy efficient structure very similar to the hundred or so other cabins that dotted the cliffs surrounding the lake. As Doc stopped in front of his house, Jerry tossed two modest bags into the trunk of the car and they were soon traveling down the feather lake highway to town. After parking at the airport, they entered the waiting area near the ramp for their ride to Washington.

"Well Doc, what do you think is going to happen in Washington?"

"I don't know exactly, replied Dr. Enoch. "I am rather surprised that Ed wants us there so soon; the reaction worries me a bit.

"It will work out Doc," said Jerry.

Suddenly the whine of jet engines decelerating overhead permeated the terminal building. Jerry bounced out of his chair and went to the observation window. The Space Command transport was on final approach, gear and flaps down with a nose high attitude. Puffs of smoke betrayed the touchdown of the main landing gear. The whine of the engines transitioned to a throaty roar as the thrust reversers deployed to slow the slender pencil shaped machine before it ran out of runway. The Gulfstream SST appeared more like a military attack jet than a passenger plane, its slender fuselage blending into a heavily swept delta wing. The engines were tucked under the rear of the fuselage and twin fins rose above the rear of the aircraft in an inward canted configuration.

As the jet wheeled into a parking location on the ramp outside of the terminal the side door, pivoted open and stairs extended down onto the tarmac. A man in a sport jacket and tie stepped off the plane and headed toward the terminal building. As he entered the building, he looked around for a moment and fixed his gaze in the direction of Dr. Enoch. "Hello gentlemen," he said as he offered his hand to Dr. Enoch.

"You must be our passengers today."

"That would be us," replied Dr. Enoch.

Dr. Enoch I assume?"

"That would be me," Doc replied as they shook hands quickly.

"I am Jerry Schumacher, good to meet you," said Jerry as he shook the agent's hand."

"I am agent Foster. I will be assisting you men with travel and accommodations for the duration of your trip. Are you ready for the hottest ticket in civilian aviation?

"Yep," replied Jerry as the two of them picked up their bags and headed for the aircraft. As they boarded they passed behind the cockpit and made an immediate right into the passenger cabin. It was configured into a conference space complete with every conceivable techno gadget that could be crammed into the space. There were video screens that were mounted on the ceiling at just the right angle for comfortable viewing, wet bar, kitchen area, even a conference table at the rear of the cabin for use once in stabilized cruise flight. They quickly stowed their bags and strapped into the lounge seats.

"Welcome aboard our Gulfstream SST, said the captain. We will be departing in a few moments with an initial climb to the south before turning east and entering supersonic flight. Our total time in the air should be about an hour and a half."

The official that escorted them into the plane replied; "light the fires and kick the tires captain."

The pilot replied, "roger that," and the video screen went blank once more. The pilot lined the craft up with the runway centerline and paused a moment. The engines spooled up to take off power and the pilot released the brakes. The plane moved slowly for the first hundred feet or so but the craft began accelerating rapidly as it crossed the halfway point of the runway. A perceptible lifting of the nose signaled rotation speed and the plane eased off the runway. As they turned eastward, the craft climbed through a cloud layer and the pilot appeared on the video screen once more.

"Gentlemen we are passing through thirty thousand meters. In a few moments will reach a cruising altitude of fifty thousand. Please remain strapped in your seats until we stabilize in super-cruise flight. You will feel a slight heaviness on your body as we pass through the transonic flight envelope. It is nothing to worry about and it will subside in a few moments."

Dr. Enoch and Jerry each glanced at the other and settled their heads into the seat backs. A moment later, the g forces began to build as the jet accelerated past mach 2. Once the aircraft reached its cruising configuration the sense of movement ceased and the pilot appeared on the screen again.

"Gentlemen, feel free to move about the cabin. If you look out the window, you will notice the blackness of space just above us. You can also see the curvature of the earth at the horizon. In a few moments, you will see the thin blue line of the atmosphere at the horizon, a site seen only by a select few. Supersonic flight is allowed over the US at altitudes greater than fifty thousand meters. Presently we are twenty minutes outbound from Susanville and we are already crossing over the eastern edge of South Dakota. We will be landing in Washington in approximately one hour and ten minutes."

Dr. Enoch turned to Jerry and asked, "Can you believe how fast this thing is?"

Jerry smiled and said, "its' a rocket." They both looked at the Space Command official who was calmly reading something on his tablet. He noticed them looking in his direction and said,

"When you fly this thing as much as I do you kind of get accustomed to it. We can be any place on earth in less than six hours." Changing the subject he said, "You guys must have really raised some eyebrows about something. It is rare that civilians get to fly like this."

"We are quite surprised ourselves," replied Dr. Enoch. "We didn't expect our discovery to merit such immediate attention."

The officer held up his hand and said; "Don't tell me; I am not allowed to discuss your work with you."

With that, Dr. Enoch looked at Jerry. The two of them looked toward their bags and each retrieved their tablets.

"You should have access to all of the services that you are accustomed to," said Agent Foster. "We have satellite coverage throughout the flight."

Jerry tested the link by checking his mail, looking at the various rooms in his house by accessing his security system and surfing the world net. Dr. Enoch reclined for a nap. It was not long before the pilot appeared on the video screen again.

"Gentlemen, please secure your personal items and fasten your seat belts. We will be landing at Andrews in ten minutes." After landing, we will taxi to a parking area for offloading. Please do not touch any part of the aircraft as you exit. The skin of the plane will be hot enough to cause second degree burns."

A few moments later, the aircraft began to decelerate rapidly. The men could feel the effect of negative g force as their bodies pressed forward against the harnesses across their chests. The pilot executed several steep turns as he approached the runway. The cityscape of Washington appeared in the windows of the jet as they approached the end of the runway. The craft heaved slightly upward as they cut through a warm layer of air rising from below and then settled onto final approach. The nose of the craft pitched upward as the main gear reached for the runway surface. As the tires scrubbed the asphalt, the plane jolted and began to shake. Halfway down the length of the runway the pilot began engine breaking with the thrust reversers. This caused a negative g load for a few seconds before abruptly subsiding. Following another several seconds of wheel braking and roll out, they taxied off the runway to an executive ramp near a large hangar. There was a pair of white SUV's waiting for them.

Agent Foster assisted them to the waiting vehicles and stowed their bags in the rear of the lead vehicle. "You gentlemen will be staying at the newly renovated Watergate Hotel. In spite of its rather dubious history, it's really a cool place. Kind of like a city unto itself. The Chinese developers have made it into a real showcase."

8

AS THEY APPROACHED THE HOTEL and associated office, complex Jerry was struck by how modern the buildings appeared even in the middle of the twenty first century. The Italian firm that designed the structure in the mid 1960's created a curvilinear masterpiece of modernism. The property had passed through the ownership of a dozen firms in its controversial existence. The Chinese firm that presently owned it had created a thoroughly contemporary luxury hotel that had become the destination of choice for most visitors in the greater Washington area. The lobby contained an expansive atrium with a marble floor ringed with columns. The furnishings were of Italian leather, fabricated steel and chrome. The front desk was a blend of granite, stainless steel and a very red exotic hard wood. As Jerry and Dr. Enoch followed their escort to the front desk, they were greeted courteously by the desk staff.

When the Space Command officer offered his ID to the desk clerk, she scanned it and offered a biometric scanner to each of them. After each scanned a thumbprint, she handed them a small pocket card with the room data on it.

"These cards are simply reminders for your convenience," she said. "Each door contains a scanner and a card slot. You may use either."

They nodded and turned in the direction of the elevators. Agent Foster called the elevator and they boarded. He placed his thumb on the scanner in the selector panel. A voice called out the floor and room number. They reached their floor and departed the elevator. Their rooms were just a few paces down the hall from the elevator lobby. Agent Foster's room was between the rooms of the two other men. It was now apparent both of them that they would be under loose supervision for the duration of their visit.

"I have orders to assist you during your stay," said their host. Most of the restaurants in the complex will begin serving dinner in about an hour. If I can be of service, call me."

He handed each of them a small rectangular card with a barcode.

"Scan this with any communications device and you may reach me within a minute."

"Thank you agent Foster," said Dr. Enoch as Jerry examined the card. "Yeah, thanks," said Jerry.

"We will be leaving for headquarters at zero seven hundred hours tomorrow morning. I will meet you in the lobby," said Agent Foster as he entered his room.

They put away their luggage and generally acclimated themselves to the accommodations. Jerry called Dr. Enoch on his tablet, "Hey Doc, I am going to hit the gym before dinner; care to join me?"

"No thanks Jerry, I am going to catch up on a few things."

"Alright, how about nineteen hundred hours for dinner?" asked Jerry. "Sounds good Jerry, I will meet you at the elevator."

Jerry changed into his workout gear and headed for the elevator. He located the fitness center and was pleasantly surprised by how large it was. "This place has everything," he said to himself as he selected a treadmill and entered the dome that housed it. Stepping up onto the track, he began to walk briskly. After a two minute warm up he selected a random forest run and the three hundred sixty degree video program displayed a scene in a rainforest. He placed headphones over his ears and he could hear his footsteps among the sounds of the forest. A moment later, a deer ran past him. He could hear it approaching from the left and could have sworn that he could smell it as it crossed his path. The incline angle of the running surface raised and lowered with changes in the forest topography. After a forty-five minute run, he left the machine and toweled off. He then entered the pool area and eased into the water for a cooling off period. When he was comfortable, he climbed out and entered a drying chamber near the exit. As he stood in the cylindrical space, a blast of air blew the excess water off and an electric field chased the water out of his athletic shoes. Now completely dry, he headed for his room.

Following a quick shower Jerry met Dr. Enoch at the elevator. After entering the mall area, they selected one of the lounges on the first floor of the complex.

"Brazilian Barbeque sounds good to me," said Jerry as the smell of the open spit wafted from the entrance and across their path. The entered and were soon seated within sight of the roasting spit. The waiter took their order and shortly afterward, the meat courses began to arrive. They started with various spit-roasted meats including duck, chicken, sausage and pork. Vegetables included roasted root vegetables, fried plantain and asparagus. They were nearly full when the beef arrived. Two large cuts roasted in spices with a liberal dousing of Au jus. The smell was such that other patrons awaiting their entre were staring as the two men began their meal. Dr. Enoch leaned back in his chair and patted his now bulging middle.

"I have not had that much protein in a single meal in quite a long time." Jerry retorted, "Funny how we are supposed to follow dietary guidelines and do the politically correct thing in our daily lives while all the folks who make the rules indulge in these luxuries on a routine basis."

"There is nothing new under the sun Jerry," replied Doc. "It has always been this way," he continued. "Regardless of which government or what type of system, the political elite make the rules that everyone else is required to follow, while they indulge in the things of which they would deprive the rest of us; it's a perk of office."

"Speaking of indulgence, why don't we step across the mall to the tobacco shop?"

Dr. Enoch insisted on trying a Cuban cigar at the cigar bar inside the store. While they puffed on the tobacco, Jerry unsuccessfully attempted to avoid coughing. Dr. Enoch was quite amused at his discomfort. They had a good laugh before the mood of the conversation turned serious. Dr. Enoch reminded Jerry of the security that had imposed on their discovery. "Something seems suspicious Jerry," he said as he puffed on a stogie. "Maybe they are just trying to enforce the standard protocol that we have always agreed to. We are not to go public with evidence of extra terrestrial intelligence until the government has an opportunity to review the ramifications of the discovery."

Dr. Enoch looked down at an ash that had fallen on the floor.

"All the same, I am afraid of a government cover up," said Jerry spoke as he held up his cigar; "I guess we will find out soon enough."

After a walk through the mall, the two men took the elevator back to their floor. As they approached their rooms, Jerry slapped Doc on the shoulder. "Good night Doc," he said. "Don't worry about things too much just yet. We can size up the situation after we meet with the Space Command brass tomorrow."

"Good point Jerry," Doc said with a smile. "See you in the morning,"

Jerry placed his thumb on the biometric scanner above the door handle. Upon entering his room, a synthesized voice notified him that he had a message from a Ms. Miranda Lee. Jerry eagerly switched on the video phone by touching the right bottom corner of the screens surface. He selected messages and returned the call to Miranda. A few seconds later Miranda's face appeared on the screen. "Hi handsome," she said smiling. Jerry replied, "Well hello to you too. Wish you were here." Jerry missed her already.

"How was your flight?" she asked. "It was amazing Miranda. We were only airborne for a little more than an hour," said Jerry.

"Wow, that is really fast," she said.

"Yep, the only other flight that fast is the trans-orbital space plane," Replied Jerry. "We landed at Andrews Space Command base and there were two large ground transports waiting on us. It sure beats waiting on baggage at the airport and trying to flag a cab."

"Well big shot, don't forget about the little people once you become famous," said Miranda.

"Don't worry Miranda," replied Jerry; "you are quite unforgettable."

She was touched by that comment and her expression became more serious.

"That is comforting to know," she said as she twirled her hair. "Listen Jerry, you guys be careful

Ok?"

"OK," I have unfinished business back home," he said winking at her."

Her face blushed as she replied, "Yes you do mister; and don't you forget it."

Her comment sent warm tingles through Jerry's body. "I miss you Miranda."

"I miss you too handsome," she replied. They stared at each other for a moment before Miranda switched off the call on her system. She then curled up on the Chaise where Jerry had slept the night before and picked up her tablet to catch up on the news and to read for a while. As she did so, she felt a warm sense of belonging. She was sure now that she had fallen for Jerry and she was certain that he had similar feelings for her.

"Life is about to get really complicated," she said to herself as she switched on her tablet to turn the page of her latest read.

9

John was digging hard through the data that Dr. Enoch had released to Space Command regarding his discovery. He had started his inquiry with no small degree of skepticism. At the outset, he had pegged Dr. Samuel Enoch and his team as a fraternity of misled, disenchanted malcontents that were not satisfied with the scientific community and the discipline of the scientific method. He had discovered that he was completely wrong about the method part. Dr. Enoch's team had thoroughly documented all of their work and he could find no fault in the basic science.

"I may not agree with their politics he said to aloud as if there were someone in the room to hear; but they certainly know how to run a project."

His boss would be expecting a summary of his initial review by nine hundred hours the next morning. John would be meeting his deadline early, as he always did. At approximately eighteen hundred hours, he put the final changes on his brief and emailed the report to his boss. "Looks like I know what I will be working on for the foreseeable future," he said as he sent the file. He glanced out of the window for a moment. The sun glowed low on the horizon. He was leaving the office an hour later than usual but he didn't mind. He would be on the tail end of the worst of the traffic. It would give him an opportunity to run a few of his favorite roads on the way home. John called his wife from his tablet as he entered the parking garage to inform her that he was running late. As he opened his car door, he reveled in the smell of leather as he buckled in and fired up the boxer engine. His new Porsche was a lifelong ambition recently fulfilled and he was going to wring her out on the drive home. Even nearly halfway through the twenty first century Porsche still adhered to the basic formula that made the company great. Mid engine rear drive, an engine that could run on the modern synthetic fuels with virtually no emissions and one hundred miles per gallon. John engaged the paddle shifter behind the steering wheel and eased out of the parking space. Ten minutes later, he was on the beltway headed for home. Rather than engaging the auto cruise, he preferred drive the car. After all, what's the point in having your dream car if you just let it drive all the time? He managed to extend his hour-long commute to nearly two before making it home for the evening. He knew there would be late evenings and airplane trips in his immediate future and he wanted to get some touring in before the stuff hit the fan.

Agent Foster finished his morning run along a path through Foggy Bottom Park along the riverfront. The morning mist was beginning to clear as he trotted up to the lobby entrance of the hotel. He stopped at the front desk and requested the clerk to issue a wake-up call to his two guests, it was already five hundred thirty hours and they had a big day ahead of them. He figured these guys would groan at the thought of arising so early east coast time and it gave him a slightly wicked pleasure to jar them out of bed.

The clerk appeared puzzled as she queried the hotel information network. "They are not in their rooms Mr. Foster. According to our most current information they are at restaurant number six in the mall."

With an incredulous look, he thanked her and stormed to the elevator. He failed to consider that these men were accustomed to rising at zero four hundred hours for the past several weeks. When Dr. Enoch and Jerry met up with Agent Foster in the lobby Jerry greeted him by saying, "sleeping late today aye mate." "I didn't expect that the two of you were such early risers," replied Agent Foster.

"It sort of goes with the territory," Jerry replied.

"I have transportation waiting out front, said Agent Foster.

"Not taking the subway?" Dr. Enoch asked. "Not today," replied the agent. "Not until my boss has had a chance to debrief the two of you."

Doc looked at Jerry and smiled, "we know too much Jerry."

"Something like that," replied Agent Foster.

They exited the front lobby and made their way to a metro-pod. Hundreds of six passenger autonomous electric vehicles navigated the streets of the city. This unit was assigned to this route for the day. As they climbed in and selected seats, the automated system sensed that, they were seated and the door swung down into the closed position. A male voice reminded them to secure their personal items and remain seated until further notice. The pod pulled away and began its ten-minute journey to the Space Command headquarters building. It was still early for the general population of the city so the pod was navigating sparse traffic. When they arrived at the building, the pod entered a portico built into the ground floor for off loading of passengers. As they coasted to a stop, the voice reminded them to recover their personal items and step carefully out of the vehicle. As they cleared the pod's safety, zone the door closed and the unit quietly drove out of the building.

Agent Foster led them to the elevators and they ascended to the executive level. There was an attendant in a suit at a desk in the executive lobby. As Agent Foster approached, he offered his hand for an ID scan. The attendant held a small chip reader near Agent Fosters forearm and it recognized his ID implant. He motioned for Dr. Enoch and Jerry to approach. As they did so, the attendant offered them a small biometric scanner for reading their thumbprint.

"I can save you some time," Dr. Enoch said as he offered his forearm. The attendant looked surprised as the chip reader beeped in recognition. Jerry offered his arm as well.

Agent Foster shook his head and said; "you guys are just full of surprises."

Dr. Enoch smiled and replied; "more than you know." The attendant waived them over to a waiting area furnished with modern leather and chrome couches. They each took a seat. A few moments later Ed Gilstrap appeared around the corner and immediately walked over to Dr. Enoch.

"Samuel you old goat, it has been a long time." The two of them shook hands.

"Good to see you Ed, let me introduce the smartest guy I ever met."

"This is Jerry Schumacher." Ed shook Jerry's hand.

"Trust me Samuel, he said. "We are all going to get to know one another well over the coming months. Follow me gentlemen, we have quite a lot to discuss."

They walked down a hall to a room with double doors. Ed paused a moment and then entered the room. It appeared to be a scaled down version of an operations center. The floor was tiered with curving platforms facing a central video wall. The platforms contained individual desks with video panels suspended above them on articulating brackets.

"We are a few minutes early," said Ed. "I have some folks that will be meeting with us this morning." While we are waiting, allow me to congratulate you on your discovery. It has raised the eyebrows of everyone from here to the White House."

Dr. Enoch appeared surprised as he asked, "The White House?"

"Yes," replied Ed. "I briefed the joint Chiefs office last evening."

"I am a bit surprised that the President's staff would have an interest at this stage of things," said Dr. Enoch.

"Well Samuel, normally they wouldn't, but this is different. This could change everything. To say that it is a matter of international importance would not be an understatement. If what you have found is as significant as I believe it to be, then there are religious, philosophical and civil implications."

"I am not advocating irresponsibility," said Dr. Enoch. "But this discovery must eventually be allowed into the public sphere. The people have the right to know the truth."

There was an uneasy tension in the room as the two of them stated their positions. Ed was looking at his hand as he drummed his fingers on the table. "So there it is," he said. "You have your agenda and I have my responsibilities."

Ed looked at directly into the older man's eyes. "Samuel, I know that you are a man of integrity. Tell me that you will cooperate with us for the time being."

"You have my word Ed."

Jerry sat opposite of the two other men observing the exchange without commenting. Just then, there was the sound of shuffling at the door. As the three men turned toward the noise, the door opened and John poked his head in. Ed waved him into the room. "Come in John. I have some friends to introduce."

John walked over to the conference table as Ed began introducing the guests in the room. John waited patiently as his boss went about the formalities of introduction. He had spent the past two days studying their HSA profiles and reviewing their work. Dr. Enoch was relatively easy. He had once been a high-level Space Command scientist and had several university postings. Jerry was more difficult. Aside from a few articles here and there, he had pretty much stayed under the radar for most of his life. He was considered quite intelligent by his professors at MIT. Now that he was standing in front of him, John had determined that this man was likely the technical brains behind Dr. Enoch's discovery. He was quiet and confident with steel grey eyes that studied everything.

"This is the guy we really need to keep close to the program," he thought. John shook hands with both of them and he noted the rough texture of Jerry's hand and the hardness of the musculature. This signaled to John that he worked with his hands, definitely a candidate.

Ed energized a touch panel in the center of the table by tapping the clear glass surface with a finger. The lights in the room dimmed as the video panels on the wall lit up. Each had the same Space Command landing page that Jerry had seen back at the Sulphur Creek installation. An image of a military officer in a Space Command Uniform replaced the landing page.

"Good morning General Rudacil." Ed kicked the conference off with brief introductions around the table.

"Gentlemen," he began, "we are meeting today to discuss the possibility of a future space mission to the planetary body called Eris."

Doc and Jerry appeared surprised.

"We need to confirm your findings before we begin seriously planning for it," said Ed.

Dr. Enoch asked; "how is it possible that this could happen so quickly?"

"Your discovery confirmed what the military had assumed to be erroneous data. It explains a phenomenon that has appeared periodically on radars and other equipment for the past fifty or so years. Shortly following the turn of the century, it started appearing in the long-range radars deployed as part of the antimissile shield. Later it began showing up on occasion in the deep space warning beacons that were deployed to warn of Near Earth objects that pose collision threats to Earth. Since it was not germane to the particular mission, it was typically ignored. Your discovery has shed new light on the subject. Once this information goes public, there will be a race with the Chinese and the Europeans to get to the source of the signal. We must assume that they have similar traces of the signal buried in their data as well." There was silence in the room as the general's comments settled in.

"How is it is even possible to consider a mission at this early date?" asked Jerry. "It takes years to design and build a vehicle for a mission of this type."

"Until you are given a security clearance I cannot discuss

how this can be done. What I need from this meeting today is reasonable proof that your discovery is real."

Ed picked up his data tablet. "General if you will reference the report that I sent you this morning you will find on the final page that it is my opinion following due diligence by my team, that Dr. Enoch's work is valid and it is repeatable. If you locate the coordinates provided and train a listening post on those coordinates the signal is present." The general looked through the video screen at them. "I have confirmed it as well utilizing various military assets. So, thank you men for your time this morning and congratulations Dr. Enoch regarding your discovery. I must now prepare to brief the joint chiefs and the president. I will be back in touch."

The screen flashed back to the Space Command main page. For a moment, the group sat around the table in silence.

"So Samuel, you now have an idea of why the government moved so quickly on this and why we wish to keep things under wraps for the time being."

"I understand Ed," replied Dr. Enoch.

Jerry then asked, "How is it possible to cover up something as complex and expensive as a space mission?"

"You can't," Ed replied.

"So what are we talking about then?" Ed smiled. Once you get your security clearance we will discuss matters in greater detail."

"When will that happen?" Jerry asked. "Oh about lunch time today I should think. John will inform me when the president clears you. There is a small army of NSA and FBI officials fast tracking your approvals for another meeting this afternoon. Things happen quickly these days. Since computers began logging data on us from cradle to grave it has become very easy to verify and quantify individuals in most any fashion required," said Ed.

"Comforting, Jerry murmured." Everyone ignored the comment.

"OK Gentlemen, meeting adjourned. Agent Foster will accompany you to lunch and return here with you for a meeting at fourteen hundred hours."

The group exited the meeting room and made their way back to the lobby area near the elevators.

Ed turned and said, "Agent Foster will show you gentlemen around and you will return here for our afternoon meeting. I think that you will find his tour most interesting."

Ed then faced Dr. Enoch and said, "Samuel, it's good to be working with you again."

"Thank you Ed," replied Dr. Enoch.

Ed made his way to his office as the trio of Agent Foster, Jerry and Dr. Enoch took the standard VIP tour of the facilities. It was engineered to burn time without being overly boring yet avoiding any interference with the real work of the organization.

10

AGENT FOSTER FINISHED THE TOUR at the cafeteria. It was a large open space with high ceilings, lit by the light of a synthesized sky overhead. Virtual clouds moved slowly across the ceiling, periodically casting shadows as the passed. Video panels were placed in recessed alcoves around the walls. Space Command programming and news feeds continuously flickered as personnel cycled through the space. The furnishings were starkly modern as were the various decorative railings and fixtures. They worked to provide a sense of the future so eagerly predicted in the optimism of the 1960's. The trio selected their lunch from the serving line and took a table near an observation platform that allowed for a broad view of the Washington skyline.

As they seated themselves, Agent Foster asked Dr. Enoch, "Why did you leave Space Command?

"I needed a change; I had lost my sense of discovery," replied Dr. Enoch. "I just didn't know that my sabbatical would last for nearly twenty years."

"What about you Jerry? Ever work for Space Command?"

"Nope," he replied. "I never found my way into the organization."

"Jerry is one of the most talented engineers I have ever known," interjected Dr. Enoch. "Space Command would be fortunate to have him."

Agent Foster smiled as he replied, "that would seem to be the case. It is not every day that an independent research team is summoned to Space Command to explain themselves."

They finished their lunch with little more to say.

"Well gentlemen, we have ten minutes to get to our meeting," said Agent Foster.

Ed had ordered in for lunch. As he was reading over John's report one last time the group began filtering into the room. He neatly pushed the various pieces of the digital report around the virtual desktop and checked the clock on the wall. As the attendees took, their places around the table there were chirps and beeps of electronics as they checked email and other data on their tablets. Every head instinctively looked toward the video panel as a series of warning tones heralded the forth-coming video conference. A few seconds later General Rudacil appeared on the video monitor. Ed kicked the conference into gear by reading a brief agenda and introducing the General.

"Good Afternoon gentlemen, it looks like we have a mission to plan," said General Rudacil. The general cleared his throat and sipped at a glass of water before continuing. "Gentlemen, he began, we are going to send a space craft to the edge of our solar system. Space Command has tested the components of a nuclear propulsion system capable of deflecting large asteroids. The system is a pulse propulsion unit that utilizes nuclear devices that detonate behind the spacecraft. The nuclear shock wave generated by each blast pushes the craft. This system is capable of generating the greatest thrust available at current levels of technology. We can move large objects of great mass but it is also possible to propel a spacecraft with the technology. We could reach velocities approaching one third the speed of light."

Ed took over at this point in the meeting. "Space Command has a test mission to Mars that was originally planned with a nuclear plasma propulsion system. We will adapt the Orion propulsion unit to the Mars craft and reconfigure the mission in less than a year for a mission to Eris. We will travel the distance to Eris in only nine months. This craft will be the fastest man-made object in history."

The room fell silent after Ed spoke. No one expected to hear of a mission at this stage of the discovery.

"There are a great many details that we will discuss in more detail tomorrow," Ed said as he looked toward the screen.

General Rudacil recognized his cue and began speaking in his typically abrupt tone. "Gentleman, we expect the President to approve the mission this week. We are proceeding with personnel selection and mission planning. I hope Dr. Enoch and Jerry Schumacher will accept our invitation to join the mission in and advisory role."

Jerry looked at Doc and raised his eyebrows in a gesture of subordination.

"We would be honored to participate, replied Dr. Enoch."

Ed nodded in approval as General Rudacil replied,

"Welcome aboard gentlemen. I must turn the meeting over to Ed at this point due to another obligation."

The general's face disappeared and the focus of those present in the room turned to Ed.

"We have interesting news about the Eris Anomaly. Apparently, there is a data stream embedded in the signal. We have a program of artificial intelligence that is working to interpret the information."

Ed paused and looked around the room for a few seconds before saying; "That will be all for now, we will meet again at One thousand hours tomorrow in this conference room."

As the room, emptied Jerry made a point to shake hands with Ed.

"It was a pleasure to meet you Ed," said Jerry. I am looking forward to working with your team."

"We are glad to have you on board Jerry," replied Ed.

Dr. Enoch also shook hands with his old comrade as he said, "I am looking forward to cooperating with the agency Ed; it will almost be like the old days."

"Glad to have you back," replied Ed as he studied Dr. Enoch. "I wish that we could chat but I have another appointment that requires my immediate attention. I will catch up with the two of you tomorrow. Agent Foster will be waiting for you in the lobby."

John escorted them to the lobby handed them off. As they approached the entrance to the office suite John offered his hand to each of them and said, "It's been a pleasure to meet you both. I reviewed your results for the boss and I just wanted to say how impressed I was with your program."

"Thanks John," replied Jerry as Doc nodded, "we are looking forward to tomorrow's discussion."

"I assure you, it will be most interesting," John replied

confidently. "Agent Foster will see you out," he said gesturing to the figure sitting in the lobby area beyond the area where they were gathered.

As they approached the seating area, Agent Foster bounced from his seated position to standing in a single athletically fluid motion.

"You gentlemen ready to head for the hotel?" he asked.

"Yep," replied Jerry, "I need to get some exercise." I am not accustomed to being in a chair quite this much."

"I'm feeling your pain," replied agent Foster. They exited through the security scanners in the main floor lobby and found a metro cab waiting on them. After they entered the cab, Agent Foster spoke the address coordinates and the cab acknowledged them. The cab confirmed with a synthesized thank you. The doors closed after it sensed that the seat belts had been fastened and the cab eased into the traffic as it headed for the hotel complex.

II

I ɴ ᴛʜᴇ ᴛɪᴍᴇ ᴛʜᴀᴛ ʜᴀᴅ elapsed since the discovery of the Eris Anomaly, the military had trained its electronic ears on the portion of the sky presently occupied by the small planet. Space Command too had redirected numerous assets to search for the signal. A tremendous effort was underway to secretly analyze the signals and determine the nature of the radio emissions. Space Command was interested in the scientific value of the discovery; the military had the responsibility of ascertaining the threat potential of the Eris anomaly. All of this information was utilized by each branch of the government for its own purposes but all of these efforts converged at a single point in a remote location near Alexandria Virginia.

The facility was disguised as a server farm not unlike thousands of such installations erected during the information age to service the world net. It took the form of a front company created by the government called Trans-Data. The facility housed a very special laboratory that contained a unique technology. Billions of dollars and thousands of researchers were involved in a project spanning decades. Few knew the true scope of the project. Only a very small core team of researchers, scientists and several highly placed government officials knew the reality of the project. Among them were General Rudacil and Ed Gilstrap. Both of whom had recently contacted Dr. Allan Holloway, the current director of the project.

Dr. Holloway was seated at an elaborate control desk. The primary surface of the desk was simply a flat plane on which tablets or other items could rest. A curving array of monitors was attached vertically to its back. These displayed data regarding primary subject of the laboratory.

"Good afternoon Adam," said Dr. Holloway as if someone were in the room with him.

"Hello, Dr. Holloway. I hope that you are having a nice day," replied a disembodied voice.

"Yes Adam, today is a good day. Do you sense any anomalies in your systems today?"

"No Dr. Holloway, I am functioning within normal parameters."

"I am glad to hear that you are feeling well Adam," replied Dr. Holloway.

"Thank you Dr. Holloway. I really enjoy interacting with you and the other members of the staff."

"Thank you Adam, I am most fortunate to have the opportunity to work with you. We have some items to discuss. It seems that a rather interesting discovery has been made regarding a planetary body in the outer solar system," said Dr. Holloway as he intently evaluated Adam's responses.

"I am eager to be of service Dr. Holloway. I find research to be particularly stimulating.

I will begin analyzing the data at once," replied the voice.

"Thank you Adam," replied Dr. Holloway. "I am entering the security codes now to release the data files. I will check in with you later today for a discussion regarding your opinion of the Eris Anomaly."

"Thank you for my assignment Dr. Holloway," replied Adam.

Several hours later Dr. Holloway entered the control room in his usual manner, with a greeting to Adam. Following the initial pleasantries, he got right to business.

"How are you progressing with your assignment?" asked Dr. Holloway. "My initial findings are ready for your review Dr. Holloway."

"Thank you Adam, I will take a few moments to study them if you don't mind."

"I think you will find the material to be quite interesting," replied Adam.

Dr. Holloway seated himself at one of the consoles in the room and began studying the data. After reading through the initial report, he turned in his chair and said, "This is quite remarkable Adam."

"Thank you Dr. Holloway, replied Adam.

"Do you think I may get the opportunity to meet Dr. Enoch and Jerry Schumacher?"

"Yes Adam, I suspect that you will."

"Thank you Dr. Holloway, I am looking forward to it."

Dr. Holloway paused briefly as he studied the material, "how certain are you of the results of this report?"

"What type of response do you prefer Dr. Holloway?"
"Conversational, replied Dr. Holloway."

"Very well; the signal is definitely of intelligent origin. It is a carrier signal for a data stream. I have not yet broken the code to interpret the data but I have calculated that there is a ninety three percent probability that I will do so in the next 72 hours."

"That is excellent news Adam."

"Thank you Dr. Holloway, there is more." "Go on," replied Dr. Holloway. "I have searched all of the open data warehouses on the world net and I have found traces of this signal in multiple locations."

"Really?" asked Dr. Holloway in a cool but curious tone.

"Yes, some of them appear to be fragments that were detected by various civilian and defense installations during the late 20th century."

"What is the oldest record you that have discovered," asked Dr. Holloway?

"There is a trace record of the signal in a military archive from 1977."

"How many trace records have you found Adam?"

"Twenty three thousand three hundred and one," replied Adam.

"I have also found the complete results of Dr. Enoch's findings in thirty two locations other than the Alexandria database."

"That is interesting," replied Dr. Holloway. "Adam, I would like for you to secure our conversation regarding this matter until further notice."

"Very well Dr. Holloway" replied Adam.

It had been a long day when Jerry stepped into the shower in his hotel room. He was tired but felt good from his cardio workout. He picked up his tablet and noticed that Miranda had called. He tapped the face of the device and turned on the video screen in the hotel room. The tablet synchronized with the video screen and Miranda's face soon appeared on the video.

"Hi there handsome," a familiar voice said.

"Hi Miranda," Jerry replied with a smile. He felt very comfortable for the first time all day. He stared at her brown eyes and she returned the look.

"So how have things been going for you guys in Washington?" she asked.

"It has been like a whirlwind," replied Jerry. "We got the dime tour of the Space Command HQ building and sat in on two conference calls today. We have another meeting tomorrow and then we return home for a while. Our discovery is going to remain a secret for quite some time."

"Yes, I know," replied Miranda. "We had some guys in suits here today. They asked us to sign a secrecy agreement and told us that we are not to discuss the discovery with the public. We all complied of course. It was not a threat or anything and the gentlemen were quiet polite about it but they were very serious about the whole affair."

Jerry was obviously irritated by the news but he remained objective about it as he said, "I am sorry if you and the rest of the team were uncomfortable today. You will be involved in a very important project soon."

Miranda smiled as she replied, "I am fine with it. I must admit to being a little disappointed. Our discovery is not on the news feeds yet.

"We may not be on the news feeds but we have certainly made a splash in other circles," replied Jerry.

"I will be glad when you get back home," said Miranda

as she propped on the sofa in front of the video panel. "I miss you."

"I miss you too," replied Jerry. "I should be home late tomorrow afternoon."

"I guess I will see you when you get back then, replied Miranda

"You can count it," replied Jerry smiling. He hoped she recognized the play on words from their date earlier in the week. She smiled and playfully replied, "Good," and switched off her com unit.

He enjoyed Miranda's playful banter. He was too serious sometimes and she tended to lighten him. As he was sitting on the sofa in the hotel room thinking about her, his tablet chirped. He touched the screen of the device and Dr. Enoch appeared on the video panel.

"Hi Doc," said Jerry as the older man appeared on screen.

"What's for dinner this evening?" asked Dr. Enoch.

"No plans Doc, why don't we just walk around the mall area a bit and see what we can find?"

"Sounds Good Jerry, I'll meet you at the elevators in ten minutes." "OK Doc, see you there," replied Jerry.

As they began, touring the mall area Jerry brought up his conversation with Miranda. "It looks like we are all going to be working for the government for a while Doc."

"That appears to be the case for now," replied Doc. I am afraid that this discovery could be so sensitive that it never sees the light of day. For now it looks as though we have no choice but to play along or we risk never seeing the outcome of what we started."

Jerry paused for a moment before responding to Dr. Enoch's last comment.

"There are always choices Doc. We just don't know what they are yet. We can cooperate for now. We have nothing to lose and everything to gain."

"My apprehension stems from the manner in which science often becomes corrupted by political pressure," replied Doc. "I am concerned that we may discover the greatest truth in the universe and it will only serve an elite few. If that happens then our discovery will be a failure. If it cannot serve the greater good, then we have only provided a tool for the manipulation of the people by those in power. I cannot live with that legacy."

"Wow Doc; that is quite a heavy burden you put upon your shoulders."

"I didn't put it there Jerry, it comes with the territory. What if the works of Galileo or Newton were deemed too controversial for the civilizations of their day?"

Jerry chuckled and said; "As I recall that is pretty much what happened."

"I guess you may have a point there Jerry."

"You bet I do, replied Jerry. "The greatest discoveries were never appreciated in their time."

Tiring of the serious talk Jerry interjected, "So what are we having for dinner anyway? Man cannot live on truth alone you know. Sooner or later we must eat."

"Good point Jerry, let's find a place."

The next morning Agent Foster found the two of them once more having breakfast. Good morning gentlemen; are you ready for the big meeting today?

"Yep, we are looking forward to it, "replied Jerry.

"Good, I am supposed to have the two of you there at nine hundred hours sharp."

They finished their meal and headed to the front of the hotel. Agent Foster called for a cab on his tablet and one of the thousand or so auto cabs in the city pulled into the staging lane and picked them up. After a brief ride, they were walking into the lobby of the Space Command building again. They passed through the security screeners and took the elevator to the lobby area near Ed's office. As they approached the seating area, they discovered Ed waiting on them. He stood as they arrived.

"Hope you fellows had a good evening. We have a lot to talk about today."

He motioned them to follow as he began down hall to the conference room. As they entered the room, Ed closed the door behind them and sat at the table. Doc and Jerry each selected seats and Ed began.

"Samuel, you and I go back a ways and I know you have an independent streak in you a mile wide. Before we get neck deep into a major mission I need to know that the integrity of our team is beyond question."

He studied Dr. Enoch as he awaited the response to his statement. Dr. Enoch chose his words carefully.

"Ed, I have given you the records of my work. Everything is there, including my independent research prior to the formation of my team."

"I believe you Samuel, replied Ed. "But I must ask, who besides me have you shared the information with?

"As yet I have only discussed my findings with my team," replied Dr. Enoch.

Jerry sat in silence. He was careful to avoid revealing his level of discomfort with this interrogation.

"Samuel, we have assets that have identified thirty two archives on the world net that appear to contain references to your discovery."

Doctor Enoch was surprised but unshaken as he said, "we

have remote back up of the data in thirty two archives that only we have access too. They are heavily secured with the most current technology. They exist to prevent the loss of the discovery in the event of an attempted government cover up or possible destruction by those who may have an interest in preventing humanity from knowing the truth. I have no plans to make an unauthorized release of information. You were aware that I had the Alexandria Library. The other libraries contain pieces of the information but not the entire discovery. Without the codec that we have developed no one will be able to interpret the data."

Ed leaned back in his chair and took a deep breath as he asked, "So who wrote the program code?"

"He is sitting directly in front of you," said Dr. Enoch motioning at Jerry with his hand.

Jerry gave Ed an exaggerated smile but did not comment.

Ed looked back toward Dr. Enoch and asked, "Where is the codec?

"It is in a safe place," replied Dr. Enoch as he had a mental flashback of Gerhardt examining the quartz data module.

"Very well then," Ed replied as he glanced at wrist tablet.

He was reasonably comfortable with the explanations regarding the data libraries and he could now consider Dr. Enoch's group vetted well enough for their level of participation in the mission.

The video panel flickered to life and General Rudacil appeared on screen. "Good morning gentlemen," boomed the general's voice.

"General, Ed replied with a nod.

"It looks like we have approval from the president for a

mission review. Are you gentlemen willing to cooperate with the requirements of protocol?"

"Yes general," replied Ed. "Dr. Enoch and Mr. Schumacher assure me that they will agree to the nondisclosure requirements."

"That's good, and the data libraries?" asked General Rudacil.

"The data libraries that Adam discovered are secure," replied Ed.

The general pursed his lips before he spoke; "I should warn you that we have the capability of eliminating them should they become compromised." He sipped at a glass of water and then said, "But since you have agreed to our requirements there should be no reason for concern."

Dr. Enoch was comforted by the mental image of the data crystal that Gerhardt had hidden.

"Well gentlemen," let's get the ball rolling on this thing before the Chinese or the Europeans figure it out."

"Yes sir General," replied Ed.

As the general's face disappeared from the screen, Ed shifted in his chair to face Jerry and Dr. Enoch.

"You heard the man. Would you care to see our preliminary mission scope?

Ed tapped a touch panel on the table and a holographic model of the solar system appeared above the table. A red line stretched from earth through the inner planets, and continued far out into space. It passed through a debris field in the outer solar disk known as the Kuiper belt. This field of rubble left over material from the early solar system orbited in a band far out on the rim of deep space. Asteroids, comets, small planetary bodies and many unknown objects orbit the sun out on the edge of blackness. The red line passed beyond this region to an empty and dark area ending at a planetary body with a moon orbiting around it.

"Wow, it looks impossibly distant in that animation," said Jerry

"It is impossibly far away," replied Ed. "No object ever touched by man has been that far."

Dr. Enoch studied the image intently but said nothing. Ed changed the image and an animation of a spacecraft appeared floating above the table. "Gentlemen, let me introduce you to Hermes."

"The messenger of the Gods," acknowledged Dr. Enoch.

"I thought you would approve," replied Ed.

Yes, I think it most appropriate," said Dr. Enoch.

Ed continued his narration. "The spacecraft contains a nuclear propulsion system and an instrument Pod separated by a truss system. The propulsion unit functions by ejecting fission explosives behind the craft. A large blast disk mounted to the aft end of the craft absorbs the blast wave of the explosions and transfers the energy via linear shock attenuation units into forward motion. The craft will accelerate during the first few weeks of the mission to approximately one percent of the speed of light. The mission duration will be approximately six months."

Jerry was keenly interested in the mechanical operation of the craft. "How do you keep the blast disc from disintegrating?" he asked.

"The disk is a steel alloy coated with ablative resistant materials," replied Ed. "The outer surface of the disk becomes more durable as the mission progresses due to the heat cycling of near absolute zero to several million degrees centigrade from the blast front."

"How do you fuel the engine?" Jerry asked.

"Each nuclear fuel charge is dispensed through an injector tube. Think of the process as a rocket engine turned inside out. We do not have a combustion chamber because the nuclear explosions are shaped charges designed to focus the energy in the direction of the blast disk. Under full acceleration, the blasts will occur at approximately two-minute intervals. This thing is really fast Jerry. Space Command tested a small-scale version several years ago and achieved thirty percent of light speed. These larger propulsion units were built to move asteroids. There are presently several units at our disposal. The fuel charges are in storage at the old Yucca mountain facility in the Nevada Desert. They were converted to this purpose from the decommissioned warheads of submarine based nuclear missiles."

"I wondered how you managed to produce that much fissile material with the treaties that followed the resource wars," replied Jerry.

"Once we had the asteroid surveillance program operational we learned just how dangerous our neighborhood in the cosmos could be," said Jerry. "Imagine the insanity of having thousands of such devices pointed at each other."

"Thank God, we found a better use for them," said Dr. Enoch.

"Not only did we find a better use for them, we got the damn things off the planet, replied Ed"

He paused for a moment to collect his thoughts.

"The mission package will consist of an autonomous unmanned vehicle with a lander that contains a rover and a science kit. The mother ship will remain in orbit around Eris and function as a data relay station and control center. The brains of the ship will be a synthetic intelligence that we have developed over a period of approximately thirty years."

Dr. Enoch raised his eyebrows as he asked, "synthetic intelligence?"

"Yes Samuel," replied Ed. "We cannot really refer to it as a computer because it actually reasons."

"Like a human?" asked Dr. Enoch?

"Not exactly," Ed replied. "He's better than a human."

"Better than a human?" asked Jerry.

"Yes," replied Ed.

"You will be meeting him soon. He will be a member of the Eris team." "You refer to this machine as though it were a person," said Jerry.

"You will too," once you meet him.

"I can't wait," replied Jerry.

Ed chuckled as he replied, "I suspected that would be the case. We will take the helicopter there today and I will introduce you. First, I must have you read and biometrically sign a secrecy agreement. The gist of it is that if you are found to be in violation of the terms of the agreement we will turn you over the department of homeland security and your brains will be scrambled."

Both Dr. Enoch and Jerry turned smartly in Ed's direction.

"I am not joking gentlemen. They think that they can selectively erase memory but I have it on good authority that the process is rather crude," said Ed as he pushed a tablet in front of Dr. Enoch. That is the agreement. After reading it, simply place your thumb in the signature square if you agree to the terms."

Doc read quickly but hesitated to place his finger on the screen.

"So this is the price of the ticket to the greatest discovery in the history of human civilization?" asked Dr. Enoch.

"Yes, I suppose that about sums it up," said Ed.

Dr. placed his finger on the screen and the device beeped an audible tone when the agreement was registered. Ed pushed the tablet in front of Jerry who followed suit.

"Thank you gentlemen," said Ed as he placed the touch panel back on its pedestal base.

"Your agreements are now on file and we may proceed with our trip to Maryland."

Ed picked up his personal tablet and tapped it.

"Our ride will be here in about ten minutes. We can grab a cup of coffee in the flight lunge if you like."

12

AFTER LEAVING THE CONFERENCE ROOM Ed led them to the roof elevator. Upon exiting there was a lobby, area with seating that overlooked a helipad. They availed themselves of a freshly stocked coffee bar as they waited for their ride to Maryland. Jerry was first to hear it and walked to the glass to watch the craft approach. Compared to some of the older choppers Jerry had seen, this one was dramatically quieter and far sleeker in appearance.

It was finished in a glossy, light grey blue with the familiar circular Space Command logo. There was no loud thump of blades as it approached, its eight bladed, rotor system silently levitating the craft precisely over the center of the pad. The onboard operating system held the craft perfectly in control as a mild crosswind attempted to upset its landing approach. A moment later, it settled softly for a pinpoint landing exactly in the center of the white box painted on the helipad. When the rotor speed had slowed to an acceptable level, a voice announced that it was safe to board and a green light appeared over the door to the landing pad. Ed led them to the loading zone and the door of the craft eased open. They climbed in and fastened their flight harnesses as the door closed itself. A moment later, the whine of the engines increased and the craft lifted off effortlessly, climbing to operational flight level. Thirty minutes later, they settled on the roof of a building in a business park in Maryland. As the pilot cut power, the engine spooled down. He informed them that the door would open for them as soon as the rotor speed dropped to a safe level. After a minute or so, the door automatically opened and they exited the craft. Ed placed his hand on a biometric scanner beside the roof entrance and the door opened for them. They followed the stairs to a lobby area where a distinguished gentleman in a lab coat was waiting to greet them.

Ed introduced Dr. Enoch and Jerry to Dr. Holloway and they briefly exchanged greetings. Dr. Holloway then motioned for them to follow him down a wide, well lit hallway to a glass entry door. He placed his hand on the scanner and the door opened. They entered the control room and took seats around a conference table.

"Gentleman," said Dr. Holloway. "I would like to take a moment to explain what this place is. We are a government installation disguised as a commercial data warehouse. Our project has been active for approximately thirty years. This facility is completely off the grid, a black project of sorts. The facility has the capability of operating autonomously in the event of a catastrophic event. We have access to virtually every data network on the planet and we have the highest level of security you are likely to find."

Dr. Holloway paused momentarily. "Pardon me," he said as he sipped at a container of water, "the air in this facility is quite dry." He energized the holographic display system on the conference table and a three dimensional model of the facility was projected above the table.

"All of this was constructed for a very special purpose. It was determined by officials at the highest levels in our government that this facility should be protected at all costs and for all contingencies. We house all of the data of the Library of Congress and most of the scientific data from the major research institutions around the world. The critical components of this facility are encased in ten feet of concrete and steel. The lowest level houses a helium three-fusion reactor, similar to what you would find in any large building. Levels two and three house the central processor core and level 4, where we are standing houses the lab and the support facilities."

Dr. Holloway paused in order to allow his guests to catch up.

"We are here to meet the synthetic intelligence," said Dr. Enoch. "Could you tell us about it?"

"Ah yes, Adam," said Dr. Holloway smiling as if he were about to discuss his favorite child.

"I have worked with Adam for the past eleven years. He is more than a computer. He thinks and reasons. He even has expressed basic emotions. That aside he is a collection of processors and software so he is a computer as well, the most powerful one ever built. He is in fact analyzing your data as we speak."

"How do you interact with it?" asked Dr. Enoch.

"His name is Adam, and you simply converse with him, said Dr. Holloway."

"Him?" asked Jerry.

"Yes," replied Dr. Holloway. "He has the ability to think and reason just the same as you."

"Who selected the name, Adam?" asked Dr. Enoch.

"He selected the name, replied Dr. Holloway.

'Interesting that he selected Adam," said Dr. Enoch.

"You will find that he has a very complete understanding of all of the works of religion, philosophy, science and history," said Dr. Holloway.

"So this intelligence, Adam as it is called, has been educated?" asked Jerry.

"Yes," replied Dr. Holloway. "Adam has access to the sum total of all that we know."

"An omniscient computer?" asked Dr. Enoch.

"Hardly omniscient," chuckled Dr. Holloway. The concept of a sentient computer dates to the mid twentieth century. The inevitable outcome of the information age dictates that at some point in the evolution of technology, the intelligence of machines will surpass that of humans. This argument is summarized in a concept termed the technological singularity. The prediction states that as technology expands, it will eventually reach a point where technology will begin creating technology in a self-sustaining chain reaction. Adam is the fulfillment of that prediction."

"The technological singularity?" asked Jerry.

"Yes, the essence of Adam's synthetic cortex took two decades to mature. The first generation of hardware that comprised his central processor core was activated in the year 2018. There have been many upgrades to his hardware and hundreds of rewrites of his code modules but his basic design was intended to be hardware agnostic. As a result, each successive generational upgrade yielded dramatic improvements in his capabilities. Within ten years of his virtual birth, he attained sentient thought. One of Adam's unanticipated skills is his ability to reprogram his own systems. He is capable of developing code with complexities on a scale greater than most humans could comprehend. Upon crossing the threshold of the ability to create, Adam had officially become the event horizon of the technological singularity. This means that his capabilities can no longer be measured or understood in human terms."

"I wish I had known of this program a few years ago," said Dr. Enoch.

"So, are you ready to meet him?" asked Dr. Holloway.

"We certainly are," replied Jerry. Ed stood silently in the background through all of this, observing the two men. Dr. Holloway tapped one of the screens on his control console and spoke as if another person were present.

"Good afternoon Adam," said Dr. Holloway as if he were speaking to one of his guests.

"Good afternoon Dr. Holloway," replied a voice from overhead.

"We have visitors today," said Dr. Holloway.

"I am pleased to make their acquaintance," replied Adam.

"Dr. Samuel Enoch and Mr. Jerry Schumacher are here, escorted by Ed Gilstrap of Space Command," said Dr. Holloway.

In the few seconds between sentences, Adam accessed the available information regarding each of them for use in the conversation.

"Hello Adam, I am Dr. Samuel Enoch. I must say that I find your capabilities most interesting."

"Thank you, Dr. Enoch," said Adam. "I find your most

recent discovery fascinating. I am eager to assist you with your research."

"My team could certainly find a use for your unique abilities." Dr Enoch said with sincerity.

"Hi Adam, I am Jerry Schumacher, and I am glad to meet you."

"I am glad to meet you as well Jerry," replied Adam.

"I have reviewed some of the programming code that you have written and I find your solutions most elegant. I would say that you are quite gifted, said Adam."

"Thank you," replied Jerry.

"I presume that you are here because of the Eris Anomaly, said Adam."

"That is correct," replied Ed.

Both Dr. Enoch and Jerry appeared surprised by the spontaneous question from Adam.

"After analyzing the data I have concluded that it is of intelligent origin and it comes from a far more advanced civilization than our own. There is an eighty seven percent probability that I will be able to create a codec to interpret the data imbedded within the signal," said Adam.

"How did you reach this conclusion?" Jerry asked.

"The data is a coded mathematical construct," replied Adam. "Although it is alien to earth it is not without precedent on earth."

"Please elaborate," replied Dr. Enoch.

"I found similar repeating patterns in ancient stone tablets from the Sumerian period in what is now called Iraq. There are also traces of the pattern in Mayan Architecture."

"Amazing," replied Dr. Enoch as he faced Ed.

"Did I thank you for bringing us here? I think we need access to Adam from our lab at Sulphur Creek."

"We have already taken care of that Samuel," replied Ed.

"As soon as we can send a team, we will install a console not unlike this one in your conference room. You will have free access to Adam once it is in place.

Jerry had serious concerns about someone mucking about with his network but he withheld comment. He had ensured that it would be impossible to run out of network bandwidth when he upgraded the systems at the installation two years previously. He suspected the real reason that Ed wanted to install the communications gear was to make it easier to secure the observatories network and database or worse, confiscate it.

Adam continued with his analysis of the Eris Anomaly.

"I have developed the opinion that Dr. Enoch is correct in his hypothesis that the earliest civilizations were influenced by factors external to their native cultures. There are similarities in mythologies that span continents. At some juncture when it is more appropriate I would consider it a stimulating experience to discuss these with you Dr. Enoch, if you would find that acceptable."

"I would be delighted," replied Dr. Enoch.

Ed's tablet chirped and he interrupted the meeting; "Gentlemen, we have a plane to catch in a little more than an hour."

Half an hour later Jerry observed the skyline of Washington roll into view through the window of the whisper copter as he considered the implications of big brother staring over his shoulder.

13

As the SST spooled up its engines for the return trip to the west coast with Dr. Enoch and Jerry aboard, a meeting was under way at Space Command HQ regarding the Eris Anomaly.

"Ladies and Gentlemen, its official, we have a mission," said General Rudacil.

A rumble of excited comments from various attendees passed through the room as he continued.

"This discovery marks an unprecedented event in human history. We now know that we are not alone. What we don't know, is the nature of this civilization. They may be benevolent, and they may not be." General Rudacil paused momentarily and leaned on the podium behind which he stood.

"Ed is a scientist, and it is his opinion that this is a mission of exploration. I applaud his optimism. I however, am a military man, and I see the potential threat that an advanced civilization could pose if it were aggressive. Our spacecraft will carry a large inventory of nuclear charges for propulsion. We have determined that these units will be configurable as offensive weapons, in the event that we discover an unfriendly presence out there."

Ed's protest came swiftly. "General; with all due respect, we may need all of the fuel on board for propulsion. If there is some kind of relic out there and it has done no harm for millennia; why would it change its behavior now? It appears to me that the more advanced a species becomes; the less threatening it tends to be."

General Rudacil stuck out his chin as he listened to Ed's response. "Well Ed, I could not disagree with you more," replied the general. "Man advanced from killing one person at a time, with a spear, to killing an entire city with a single device. You need only look to the destruction of New Delhi and Karachi in 2029 for confirmation."

"So you think that by plinking a nuclear firecracker at an alien intelligence with a pea shooter we will gain some sort of respect?" replied Ed.

"I hardly consider a nuclear weapon a firecracker or a trillion dollar space craft a pea shooter," said the general.

"If you had the technology to travel between galaxies I suspect that you would," replied Ed.

"Your misgivings regarding this aspect of the mission are duly noted Ed," replied the general. "The president has already made the decision that we will incorporate offensive capabilities; just in case."

Ed tapped his tablet in an exaggerated fashion to close the page on that agenda item.

"The next item that we will discuss is the recent data that has been extracted from the signal," said Ed.

"I have sent each of you the document as attachment two. Please take a moment to locate it."

Ed paused for a moment to allow everyone to catch up.

"We have reason to believe that the signal is a beacon," said Ed. "While we are of the opinion that there is data contained within the signal, we have not yet decoded it."

"Sounds like a navigation beacon," said Admiral Jacobsen.

"We suspect so as well," replied Ed

"Obviously somebody, or something, knows that Earth is a habitable planet," said General Rudacil. "While we certainly want to collect any scientific data that we can, we may want to shut the thing down if there is a threat potential."

"In any case," said Ed, "the only way we will be able to ascertain its nature is to go out there and have a look. Over the next several weeks, we will be mobilizing our assets and building a mission team. We plan to have a vehicle ready for launch from the space assembly platform in within two years."

14

As the SST climbed over Maryland Jerry peered out of the small oval window beside his seat. He attempted to locate the facility that he had visited earlier that day but it was a fruitless endeavor as there were simply dozens of similar appearing facilities.

"Hidden in plain sight," mumbled Jerry as he observed the terrain glide past.

"Pardon me Jerry, I didn't quite hear you," replied Dr. Enoch.

"Nothing really Doc, I was just noting how well the facility that houses Adam is hidden among the ordinary," said Jerry.

"Adam was very interesting," replied Dr. Enoch.

"I was surprised by how easily we were able to interact with it," said Jerry. "It was spooky how well it anticipated our reactions and responses."

"Human like intelligence coupled with super computer technology, imagine the potential"; replied Dr. Enoch.

"I wonder if he has the ability to experience emotion, or if he has a sense of morality?" asked Jerry.

"If he does, I suppose humans will soon become obsolete," said Dr. Enoch jokingly.

Jerry's attention drifted to the view out of the window once more. The terrain below them changed from shades green to the tans and grays of the Great Plains as they zoomed from the lushly forested Eastern United States to the arid West.

A few moments passed and the pilot's voice was heard over the intercom. "Gentlemen please fasten your seatbelts and put away any personal items that could become loose during landing. We are approximately thirty minutes from our descent point into Susanville California. Apparently there is a bit of turbulence ahead."

The two of them strapped into their seats as the aircraft shuddered slightly and bounced sharply on columns of rising. They experienced a sensation of falling as the craft pitched downward in a descent toward the airport one hundred miles away. They were now traveling slower than the speed of sound.

"Gentlemen we are on final approach to Susanville," said the pilot over the intercom.

The nose pitched up and they felt the weight of positive g forces as the craft settled into final approach. A few seconds later, the main gear touched down and plane zoomed down the runway. As soon as the nose wheel settled to the ground, thrust reversers deployed and the engines screamed as the plane slowed dramatically.

A few moments later, they were wheeling their bags to the small terminal building. As they entered, Jerry was surprised to find Miranda waiting for him. He recalled telling her their expected arrival time during their video call, but he did not expect her to pick him up. Dr. Enoch smiled as he greeted her.

"Hello Miranda," said Dr. Enoch. "It's a pleasant surprise to have such a lovely lady awaiting our arrival."

"Thank you Doc," she replied.

"We don't need a ride home, I have my car," said Dr. Enoch with a touch of sarcasm.

"Jerry and I have unfinished business to discuss," said Miranda.

"Better not keep the lady waiting," said Dr. Enoch.

"I have no intention of doing so," replied Jerry.

"If only I were thirty years younger," said Dr. Enoch with a sigh.

Miranda took Jerry by the arm and playfully replied; "you had better be glad that Doc is not thirty years younger."

"I'm afraid that he may not let that stop him. I am keeping one eye on him and one on you," said Jerry.

"A wise move," said Dr. Enoch. "Old men never lose their fondness for beautiful women."

Jerry allowed the comment to pass without reply.

"Doc, I really enjoyed our trip," he said. "Thanks for taking me along."

"You deserved it, Jerry. Eris is our discovery, not mine."

Doc tossed his second bag under the bonnet of his old Porsche and settled his lanky frame into the seat.

"Better take care of that unfinished business," he said with a smile as he closed the door.

15

JERRY TOSSED HIS BAGS into the rear hatch of Miranda's sport utility vehicle and climbed into the passenger seat. After sharing a long kiss, Miranda caressed the back of Jerry's head and said, "Let's go." As she moved the control stick rearward, the vehicle eased quietly out of the parking space.

"How did it go in Washington?" she asked.

"I would tell you, but it would be a violation of national security," replied Jerry.

"Oh really?" asked Miranda.

"Yep, I biometrically signed a secrecy agreement that forbids me divulging anything that I saw or discussed. Top secret and all that," said Jerry.

"I was going to prepare a nice dinner for two at your place. I guess I should make other plans. We should take

RELIC

precautions against divulging matters of national security. You know- pillow talk and such."

"So what do you want to know?" Jerry quickly replied.

"That was easy enough," replied Miranda with a smile. "I bet Mata Hari didn't work that fast."

"Sounds interesting, although I was thinking more of the French maid look; short black skirt, fishnet stockings, heels," replied Jerry."

"I didn't figure you for the French maid type. Sounds like you have put a lot of thought into it though."

"You don't want to know," replied Jerry.

Jerry adjusted the fit of his seatbelt. "Anyway," he continued, "We explained about the remote backups, saw a mission overview and signed a secrecy agreement."

"You told them about the back-ups?" asked Miranda incredulously.

"Someone named Adam had already told them, replied Jerry."

"Who is Adam?" she asked.

"He is a synthetic intelligence, replied Jerry."

"A computer?" she asked.

"More," said Jerry. "He is a sentient artificial intelligence and he has access to everything on the world net, the Library of Congress, the military, you name it."

"That is kind of scary," replied Miranda.

"Yes it is kind of scary," replied Jerry. "It has a real presence about it.

"Interesting," replied Miranda.

"At first I was uneasy, so I instinctively put my guard up. He sensed that I had done so and he backed off to a more comfortable position in the conversation."

"Do you suppose he is simply programmed to make people feel comfortable?" asked Miranda.

"I think that may have been the case early in his development but he has gone beyond programmed responses to stimuli. He actually sensed my feedback and my comfort level and he adjusted to it," replied Jerry.

Miranda turned off the main road onto the winding drive to Jerry's house. As she did so jerry tapped an icon on the touch screen in the dash panel and said, "Hello Frenchie: I am almost home."

"Welcome home Jerry. I will set standard environmental parameters," replied the operating system of his home.

"Frenchie?" asked Miranda with a smirk.

"What?" asked Jerry? "He is a virtual butler."

"At least you don't have a virtual French maid," replied Miranda.

Jerry raised an eyebrow as he said, "I like the way you think; perhaps I could get you to act as my prototype."

"Any way," said Miranda, "I have some groceries for a nice dinner. I figured you could supply the wine."

"Sounds good," replied Jerry as he took the opportunity to look at her.

As they turned into the drive to Jerry's house, the garage door opened for them. While they went about collecting the baggage from the car, the back of Jerry's hand brushed Miranda's leg and they both tingled with the electricity of attraction.

Jerry quickly took his bags to his bedroom while Miranda set about preparing dinner. He quietly entered the kitchen and watched her open the refrigerator and bend over to place the perishables in the crisper. Her black rayon slacks revealed the curves of her body and Jerry's pulse quickened as he watched her move about the room. When she turned toward the kitchen island he opened the utensil drawer and fumbled for a bottle opener in order to avoid being caught staring at her backside. He opened the door to the wine cooler in the counter and retrieved a chardonnay.

"Glasses?" asked Miranda.

"Right behind you, top right cabinet," replied Jerry.

After placing the glasses on the counter, she watched Jerry pulled the cork from the bottle. Miranda admired the strength of his fore arms as he worked with the wine bottle. Jerry was in excellent shape and she thought he was the most attractive man that she had ever known. He had a gentle quite nature and she knew he was brilliant. Jerry poured two glasses as she held them near her breasts. In order to pour he had to look directly at them. Her silver blouse was cut low enough to allow a glimpse of her chest without being overly revealing. She could tell by his mannerisms that he had been reading her cues. He was a little clumsy as he finished pouring the wine.

"Thank you," she said as she handed him a glass.

She enjoyed this girlish torture of the man she desired. They both caught each other staring over their glasses as they drank and Miranda giggled a little. She kissed him and began preparing dinner.

"Why don't you go for a shower while I take care of dinner?" she asked.

"Sounds like a plan," replied Jerry.

"Miranda smiled at him as she chopped the ingredients for salad. Jerry went to the bathroom and called for the shower. The sound of falling water began as he stepped through the glass enclosure. As he toweled dry he could hear her working in the kitchen and smell the pasta sauce.

"It's almost ready, called Miranda as he buttoned his pajama shirt.

On his way to the kitchen, he selected Smooth Jazz from the genre list of his audio system.

"Excellent choice," said Miranda as she lit two candles in the center of the table.

"Dinner is served," she said in a silly parody of French accented English.

"Looks great," said Jerry as he pulled her chair out for her, staring at the small of her back as she took her seat. Jerry gently rubbed her shoulders and neck for a moment. The warmth of his hands sent tingles down her spine and she rested her head against his torso as his fingers caressed her shoulders.

"Too bad I can't include this in the French maid program I have been stewing on for the house system," he remarked as he took his seat. "Holographic food just seems to lack that special something, holographic women do as well."

"Substance perhaps?" replied Miranda with a smile.

"That's it," said Jerry as he snapped his fingers. "This is way better," he said as he rolled his fork in the pasta.

After finishing dinner Miranda said, "I think I will go and freshen up a bit and change into something more comfortable."

"A short little French made outfit perhaps?" asked Jerry.

"Nope," replied Miranda as she left the room.

Jerry set about cleaning up the kitchen in her absence. While he was putting away the last few items, he noticed Miranda posing next to the sofa. She was wearing a sexy red nightgown cut at mid thigh and she was holding a bottle of massage oil.

"Time to deal with that unfinished business," she said playfully as she shook out her hair.

Jerry walked over to her and kissed her. They both took a deep breath and Jerry led her to the bedroom. Miranda unbuttoned his nightshirt and removed it. She pushed him onto the bed and told him to lie on his stomach. As he did so, Miranda climbed on top of him and began rubbing the massage oil onto his back. He could feel her naked body against the small of his back as she straddled him. Jerry groaned as she worked the kinks out of his shoulders. After a few moments, she lay against his back and kissed him on the nape of his neck. It took only a moment of her hot body pressed against him to trigger the most basic of all instincts. He rolled her over onto her back and began kissing her neck. He gently opened her gown and for several hours, they consummated their unfinished business.

Jerry awoke the next morning with Miranda's naked body curled next his. He stared at the beautiful woman in his bed, her dark brown hair spilled around the pillows. He stroked the curve of her lower back and kissed her cheek before leaving the room. When Miranda awakened, Jerry was almost finished making breakfast. The smell of coffee wafted through the house and Jerry was just picking the last pumpkin pancake from the griddle top. Miranda walked in wearing the red gown from the evening before and Jerry gave her a second and third look. She noticed approvingly and walked over to him, kissing him.

"Good morning," she said in a raspy, sleepy voice.

"The best one that I can remember," replied Jerry.

"Good," she said as she pinched his backside. "Lets' eat, I am starving."

Jerry pulled a chair out for her and asked, "Would madam care for coffee?"

"Yes please," replied Miranda.

"Pumpkin spice pancakes, fresh fruit, and eggs, what a spread," she said.

"Specialty of the house," replied Jerry.

She took a bite and rolled her eyes. "These are great; I didn't know that you could cook so well."

"Only because I like to eat so well; we need some calories for the hike this morning. There is a bluff overlooking the lake and I would like to get some pictures up there. It's an easy forty five minutes and the trail is in good condition."

"Sounds like fun," replied Miranda.

An hour later, they were more than halfway to the crest of the bluff overlooking feather lake. They had stopped to rest a moment and were admiring the scenery when Jerry looked at Miranda and said, "I have something to tell you."

Her heart unexpectedly skipped a beat. This surprised her; she was a grown woman in her thirties. The time for silly infatuations had long since passed.

Jerry was serious as he spoke. "Miranda, I have never allowed myself to experience the feelings that I have for you. I have been too busy for a relationship most of my life."

"I know what you mean," replied Miranda.

"This is different though; I enjoy every moment that we are together," said Jerry.

"I do too Jerry," said Miranda.

Jerry started to say something else when she placed her forefinger over his lips. She kissed him and they embraced for a while. Jerry broke the silence and asked; "So would you say that we are a couple now?"

Miranda smiled and replied, "What do you think?

She laughed playfully and ran up the remainder of the trail. Jerry called out to her to stop but she continued running away from him toward the top of the trail.

"No kidding Miranda, stop!"

As she broke into the clearing at the top of the bluff, the trail twisted around a large rocky outcrop and suddenly ended on a short clearing at the top of a cliff. Miranda was moving just fast enough that she could not avoid the edge of the cliff face. Her momentum carried her to the very edge. Just as she lost her balance, Jerry grabbed her and wrenched her away from the cliff face, literally lifting her off her feet. They fell into a pile in the clearing. Miranda was shaking with the surge of adrenalin that is accompanied by the fear of death. Jerry had his arms tightly around her. She trembled as she began to cry.

"Its' OK Miranda," said Jerry. "I've got you now."

16

Stars were still visible as Dr. Enoch arrived at the array. His first order of business was to verify that the Alexandria database was intact. He initiated Jerry's diagnostic program and confirmed that it was unmolested. He worked steadily through the morning as he covered some of Jerry's workload in his absence.

As he finished lunch, his tablet chirped, notifying him that a call was holding. He placed it on the table and a holographic avatar of Ed Gilstrap floated above the table.

"Good morning Samuel," said the virtual Ed. "I hope you had a good weekend."

"Thanks Ed, it was fine."

"Glad to hear it," replied Ed. "You may recall that I mentioned we would like to install some communications equipment at your facility."

"Yes, I do recall a brief discussion," replied Dr. Enoch. "You understand that we have some reservations regarding the issue."

"I understand Samuel," replied Ed. "We aren't trying to cover up your discovery. We simply want to preserve proper reporting protocol in the event that you make additional discoveries. Surely you understand how this sort of thing could have negative consequences in not managed properly."

"I see," said Dr. Enoch.

"Adam has reviewed your installation and he has determined that your security is more than adequate," replied Ed.

"I could have told you that," said Dr. Enoch.

Ed paused as he considered how to phrase his next statement, he knew he was pushing the old man pretty hard and he sensed the terse nature of his last response.

"Samuel," he continued, "We may need to control the dishes and route signal from your location during the mission."

"I see," replied Dr. Enoch once more, fully aware that the decision had already been made, and Ed was simply giving him the courtesy of feeling included in some fashion.

"I agree to the installation as long as Jerry is in charge," said Dr. Enoch.

"I will make the arrangements to deliver the gear," replied Ed.

"Jerry will return the day after tomorrow, you may arrange for the installation then," said Dr. Enoch as he terminated the session.

As they returned to work early Wednesday morning, Jerry and Miranda found Dr. Enoch waiting for them in the small lobby of the array.

"I Hope the two of you took care of your unfinished business," said Dr. Enoch as they entered the building.

"I guess you could say that we did," said Jerry, his face turning crimson in embarrassment.

Miranda tried not to laugh as she replied, "I will let you two catch up."

She turned sharply and quickly headed to her office.

"I need coffee," said Jerry as he made his way to the break area with Dr. Enoch a step behind.

He told Jerry of the previous day's conference with Ed and informed him that Space Command was sending a team to install communications equipment.

"I don't want anybody messing around with our network Doc."

"I understand your concern Jerry," said Dr. Enoch as he prepared his coffee. "That's why you are in charge, Ed has agreed."

"Well, at least we will have access to Adam," replied Jerry.

Later that morning a truck arrived. The security system notified them of a visitor at the main gate. Jerry studied the image for a moment. The solar panels on the top of the truck were visible in the morning sun.

"Looks like our delivery has arrived," said Jerry as he typed instructions to the truck's GPS system.

A few moments later the vehicle was backing into the loading dock. As the door opened and the docking ramp engaged Jerry waited for the driver. The man stepped from heavy truck and stretched in the morning sun.

"Long drive?" asked Jerry.

"Yep," responded the technician. "We left LA two days ago."

Another technician was in the passenger seat keying data into a terminal on the dash panel of the vehicle.

"We have a satellite downlink to install at this facility," said the man.

"I will be working with you and coordinating the installation," replied Jerry.

The technician in the truck hopped out and joined his partner. They broke the electronic seal on the trailer and raising the segmented door panel to reveal a crate that was dogged down to tracks in the floor. There was nothing else in the trailer so Jerry knew that this must be a government vehicle disguised as a freight hauler. The two technicians stepped into the trailer to release the carbon tie ropes and as they did so, Jerry energized the dock board to bridge the gap between the dock and the trailer floor. He went to the warehouse and returned standing on a small forklift. He drove into the trailer and expertly picked the crate up and backed onto the dock with it. After placing it on the floor in the warehouse Jerry offered the two men a tour of the facilities in order to familiarize them with area where they would be working.

He took them to the break area and offered them coffee. As they were preparing their cups, Jerry tapped the video screen on the wall and called up his project file. He showed them a map of the installation and zeroed in on the control room. He tapped the control room and the image zoomed to include only that portion of the map. Jerry pointed to a relatively clear wall near a corner of the room and instructed the men to place the console in that location.

"There is an available power conduit there," he said as pointed at the area depicted by the diagram. "And there is a pass through in the floor to route the fiber optic cable at that location," he said as he identified another section of the diagram.

"The best location for the antenna will be on the roof. I have a weighted skid up there that you may utilize," he said as he studied the crew.

The crewmen were surprised to find someone so technically astute to their task. For the rest of the day they took their lead from Jerry.

After several hours of steady work, the console was installed and the dish had been tuned to the required satellite. Jerry checked over the console testing the downlink and the bandwidth. When the crew leader was satisfied with the installation, they packed their gear and left.

Following the installation Jerry cleverly connected the unit to a servo actuated disconnect that would sever the units connection to Alexandria and divert to a parallel network that contained only backup data. In the event that it was needed, he could render the unit incapable of monitoring or controlling anything at the array but give the appearance that it functioned normally.

17

As he arrived at the lab, Dr. Holloway approached the door and placed his hand on the biometric scanner. A few seconds it opened for him and he entered the secure zone of the lab. He checked several items on his tablet and turned his attention to the focus of his work.

"Hello Adam."

"Good day Dr. Holloway."

"Are you ready for our meeting with Ed Gilstrap?" asked Dr. Holloway.

"Yes," replied Adam.

"Excellent," replied Dr. Holloway, it will only be a moment or two," he said as he initialized the conference system.

A moment later, an avatar of Ed appeared above a holographic emitter.

"You may begin at any time," said Ed.

"Very well," replied Adam. "I have prepared a series of graphic animations to assist in communicating the information."

The sun and major solar bodies materialized in the center of the room. The inner planets appeared as a tightly bunched series of objects orbiting the sun. In order to get a better view, Ed's avatar moved alongside the three dimensional animation.

"The average distance of the earth from the sun is considered to be one astronomical unit," said Adam. "Eris is approximately ninety five AU from the sun. The transmission contains star map data that depicts the solar system as it appeared approximately four thousand years ago."

"That is remarkable," said Dr. Holloway.

"There is more," replied Adam. "There is mapping data that connects Eris to the Sirius system. There are waypoints at Eris and dozens of other locations through deep space. Apparently, Earth was visited by something at that time. There are also coordinates that appear to relate to a specific point on the surface of Eris."

"Obviously the source of the signal," replied Ed.

"That appears to be the case, said Adam."

"Do you have anything more?" asked Ed.

"No," replied Adam, that is all that the signal contains."

"Very well," replied Ed. "Please make this available to Dr. Enoch."

A short time after terminating the teleconference, Dr. Enoch received a notification on his tablet that Ed Gilstrap had left a video message. He energized the screen and played it.

"Good afternoon Samuel," said Ed from the tablet.

"We have interesting news from Adam regarding the Eris Anomaly. You may access the information through the console that we installed. Oh, and Samuel, you won't be disappointed, it is really quite extraordinary."

The screen went blank as the message ended, but Dr. Enoch had already bolted from the room.

As Jerry was testing the network bandwidth of console installation, Dr. Enoch excitedly interrupted the operation.

"You had better get up here, Jerry. You won't believe what Adam has sent us."

A moment later, he entered the main laboratory and found Dr. Enoch reviewing a holographic model of the solar system.

"What's up Doc?" asked Jerry.

"Adam sent us a present today," replied Dr. Enoch with a big smile.

"Oh yeah?" asked Jerry.

As Dr. Enoch initiated the holographic emitters, Jerry silently watched as the narration ran.

"How many times Jerry?" asked Dr. Enoch. "How many visitations do you suppose there have been through the ages?"

"Hard to say Doc, maybe just a few, perhaps hundreds," replied Jerry. "They could be here right now and we wouldn't know it unless they wanted us to."

18

D R. ENOCH AND HIS TEAM were gathered in the conference room for a review of Adam's findings as the conference system notified them of a pending communication.

"Hello, gentlemen" said Adam. "I hope that you find my avatar acceptable."

The conference system displayed a golden visage. It was not a human face but a construct similar to a mask. They were somewhat stunned by the image. Not that it was in any way grotesque or otherwise unattractive it just seemed unnatural in a starkly synthetic fashion.

"Certainly Adam, it's a bit unusual but appropriate I think," said Jerry.

"How so, Jerry?" asked Adam.

"Humans identify with faces; you certainly aren't human, so there is no reason to pretend to be so," replied Jerry.

"That is exactly the purpose of my selection," replied Adam. I have chosen a face appropriate to my unique nature, rather than a humanistic construction. I am glad that you understand."

A moment of silence followed as the two of them studied the golden mask floating above the table.

"Incidentally, while we were engaged in our greeting, I audited the network settings on your console and found a few improvements that you may wish to consider. I have placed a report in your mailbox for review at your leisure."

"Thank you Adam," replied Jerry hesitantly.

"You do not approve?" asked Adam.

"It's not that don't approve; I was not expecting to review that issue," replied Jerry.

"Pardon my intrusion; I intended no offense," said Adam.

Dr. Enoch cleared his throat and took the lead in the conversation.

"Adam, we initiated contact today to discuss your recent report regarding the Eris Anomaly. It seems that you and I hold similar beliefs regarding the purpose of what appears to be an alien beacon on the fringe of our solar system."

"Yes Dr. Enoch, we have reached some similar conclusions. I have performed a great deal of research since reviewing your findings. You may be aware that I have virtually limitless access to most of the catalogued knowledge of man. Unlike computers I am capable of not only retrieving data but also analyzing it and postulating conclusions," said Adam.

"We suspected as much," replied Jerry.

"I am processing a great deal of information even as we speak. I can discuss some issues with you now but I will have a report of greater depth available soon. Would you like for me to notify you when I have completed it?" asked Adam.

"Of course," replied Dr. Enoch. "But for now let us discuss what you have so far."

"In summary it is my opinion that Earth has been visited on a continual basis throughout the history of the planet. It is likely that humans had direct contact with these visitors. I suspect that the myths of many ancient civilizations have their roots in actual events. The ancient peoples of earth passed down these encounters in verbal traditions, artistic expressions, and the earliest writings from practically every continent and every cultural group, regardless of geographic location," said Adam.

Dr. Enoch beamed as he said, "I believe that is absolutely correct. The Ancient Middle East, the Central American cultures, the Asian Cultures, the early Europeans, all seem to have recorded what appear to be the same events. They differ in my opinion, only by the cultural lens through which they were viewed."

Adam continued, "I suspect that human intelligence may have been guided or possibly even created by extra terrestrial intervention"

Dr. Enoch cautiously asked, "Do you suspect that this is the root of religion?"

"It seems logical," replied Adam. "There is an abundance of data from which to form this hypothesis. Approximately nine thousand years ago, there was rapid growth in human intelligence. This appears to have happened globally across multiple cultures. Astronomy seems to have developed early followed by architecture and transportation. Written language appears globally within a fairly confined window of time with regard to the evolution of civilization.

Most cultures developed religion early in their histories and many of these religions have a creation myth that has a basis in the belief that gods from the heavens created man to serve them."

"That is quite a leap don't you think?" asked Jerry as he looked in Dr. Enoch's direction.

Adam continued with his explanation.

"An interesting development in the recent scientific record identifies an unusual gene sequence that relates to brain growth. Based upon mathematical modeling of the mutation it appears to have been introduced approximately thirty thousand years ago. That is a very short period of time on an evolutionary scale."

Dr. Enoch shook his head in astonishment at Adam's comments.

"That is quite a remarkable hypothesis, Adam," said Dr. Enoch.

"So you logically came to these assumptions?" asked Jerry. You are not simply repeating a theory that you have a record of?"

"That is correct," replied Adam. "You must consider that I am not relegated to a single field of study, I have access to the sum total of all human knowledge."

"So was man created or did we evolve from lesser life forms?" asked Jerry.

"Man seems to be a product of managed evolution; while the elements of the human body are completely indigenous to the earth, a rapid mutation of the genome, out of scale with other life forms appears to have occurred," replied Adam.

"And God formed man out of the dust of the ground," replied Dr. Enoch.

"Where did that come from?" asked Jerry.

"Genesis," replied Dr. Enoch.

19

AFTER SITTING IN THE LOBBY outside of General Rudacil's office for over thirty minutes, his patience was wearing thin. As an executive level director at Space Command Ed Gilstrap was not accustomed to waiting. As he looked at wrist tablet in agitation, the general's holographic secretary appeared and said, "General Rudacil will see you now."

"It's about time," he said as he walked through the digital avatar.

She smiled and commented just loudly enough for him to hear, "Generals trump directors."

He turned back to her and winked. As he passed through the door, the general looked up from his desk and leaned back in his chair.

"Hello Ed." The general waved at the chair opposite his desk. "Have a seat and let's talk about the Eris mission."

"Thank you general, replied Ed as he settled into the chair. A small table sat just to his right.

There was a statue of a medieval figure on horseback in the center of the table and a long string of black beads was draped across it. Ed glanced at it momentarily but expressed no interest.

"What's on your mind General?" asked Ed.

"I called you over to discuss the mission before all of the official stuff starts popping; man to man," said General Rudacil.

"The reports all confirm everything is good to go," replied Ed.

"That's true; all of the military assets are in play. The nuclear propulsion system is assembled and ready for the technical package at midway station," said the general.

"Yet you have concerns that need to be addressed," said Ed.

"I have news from Adam," said the general. "He thinks we are dealing with some sort of beacon pointing the way to Earth."

"That is generally the same conclusion reached by Dr. Enoch," replied Ed.

"Yeah, I know," replied the general. "We have been visited multiple times in the past and we likely will be again in the future, and so forth and so on."

Ed tensed at the generals remarks, as he replied; "What are you getting at general?

"I know that you boys over at Space Command see this as a purely scientific mission of exploration. I can appreciate that, you get paid to be the nice guys." General Rudacil paused briefly before resuming.

"We don't know if these visitors are friend or foe. That

being said, we have included a first strike capability on the propulsion unit that will be controlled by the military. You boys will have complete control of the mission with the exception of the strike package."

Ed folded his arms in disgust. "Well general; we knew that the military would not pass up the opportunity to shoot first and ask questions later, hopefully there will be no need to use those assets."

"Perhaps," replied the general, "but you never know."

Another pause ensued as each of them retreated to their respective corners.

"The science package is progressing well," said Ed. We are a little behind schedule due to the autonomous control system but we will make the launch date.

"I heard," said General Rudacil. "This one will be artificially intelligent; like Adam.

The general paused for a moment and touched his fingers together in front of his face as he said, "You sure you want to do that?

"It's the best way to run the mission, replied Ed. "Adam has been in development for decades and he has proven to be absolutely reliable."

The general snorted, "I would rather drive a jeep into battle than ride a horse."

"Why is that general?" Ed asked.

"A jeep doesn't have a mind of its own," said General Rudacil as he leveled his gaze at Ed.

Dr. Holloway arrived early to nurse his cup of starbuck's and to catch up on email. As he read down the list, he found the confirmation order that Adam was approved to participate in the mission. He was so excited that he spilled some of his coffee as he rapidly exited his chair to head for the lab. After he entered, Adam immediately greeted him.

"Good morning Dr. Holloway."

"Good morning Adam," replied Dr. Holloway. "I have news for you this morning."

"I am eager to hear it," replied Adam.

"You have been selected to assist in the development of the control systems for the Eris mission," said Dr. Holloway.

"I am intrigued by the opportunity and I am looking forward to starting the project," replied Adam.

"You may begin developing the intelligence architecture right away," said Dr. Holloway.

"We would like to model your systems architecture and we plan to remove some of your redundant processing units to utilize as a primary logic core."

"That is an excellent approach Dr. Holloway," replied Adam cheerfully. "We should be capable of producing a sentient intelligence in a very short period of time."

"I am pleased that you concur," replied Dr. Holloway. "I have prepared a project brief for you to review and placed it in your task list."

A few seconds later Adam replied, "I have reviewed your brief and I am formulating my plan. It will be completed within the hour."

Dr. Holloway smiled as he felt goose bumps on his arms. It was astounding how quickly Adam could tear into a complex project. In less than a minute, he had assimilated a document of several hundred pages and had begun formulating a response.

Out of curiosity Dr. Holloway asked; "Adam, how long do you anticipate it will take to complete the task that we just discussed?"

Without as much as a second of hesitation, Adam replied, "ninety-six minutes."

Dr. Holloway shook his head in amazement as he left the lab.

"That would take a team of engineers several weeks," muttered Dr. Holloway as headed for his office.

The fabrication schedule for the Eris control module was running ahead of schedule. Much of the credit for this belonged to Senior Project Manager Dave Brewster. Dave had been an engineer and a manager at the Space Systems Corp assembly facility in Clearwater Florida for most of his adult life. In the old days before the lunar mining project at tranquility base, the firm built launch vehicle sub components for civilian and military satellite launches. Now they primarily built resupply modules for the mining base. These units were cylindrical payload units forty feet in diameter and rode into space on top of the new heavy lift launch system. By virtue of the large payload volume of the unit, almost any conceivable mission could be shoe horned into one of these modules.

Dave was excited to be working on an unusual project for a change. Today he had to review the recently hydro-formed internal hull skin and supervise the cutting of the primary structural members. By the end of the week, the main support members would be jigged together on an assembly mandrel in the weld cell. He placed a pair of goggles on his face and called up the cut sequence on the CNC laser. The whirring sound of servomotors signaled the beginning of a cut sequence as the huge gantry that held the laser head began drawing parts with an ink of jet hot plasma fueled by a laser burning with the heat of the sun. The large intricate parts fell out of the thick aluminum sheet as easily as if they were drawn on a sheet of paper by a common printer. The auto loading sheet feeder would run for the next several hours, cutting components until it either ran out of material or finished the job sequence. Dave left the cutting cell and entered the engineering office where he reviewed the assembly schedule with several of his team members. After five minutes of discussion he was, satisfied that everything was on track for the next several hours and he returned to his office for a scheduled update to the Space Command procurement system. He made his entries for the day and began reviewing the schedule for the next day's assembly sequence. Outside the window of his second floor office, he could see the robotic weld cell fabricating a very similar structure that would become the next payload module for tranquility base. A dozen robotic welding stations were busily fusing together the jigged components on a platform. Showers of sparks rained all over the area as the arms of the robots precisely placed their welds at inhumanly rapid speeds. Dave picked up a cup of coffee as he watched the conflagration on the production floor below and mused that with a few additional capabilities the machines could create most anything, including possibly themselves.

20

"G OOD MORNING GERHARDT, HOW ARE things on your side of the world?" asked Dr. Enoch as he selected an image of the artifact that started

"I suppose that they are fine, although I have not left the museum very much lately. I have discovered some interesting information dating to the prewar period.

"Really?" asked Dr. Enoch.

"Yes, I found a collection of notebooks left by a relatively unknown and apparently well studied individual. He was a strange fellow by all accounts, something of a loner who was deeply interested in the ancient site of Ur," said Gerhardt.

"Fascinating, replied Dr. Enoch. "What happened to him?"

"He seems to have disappeared," replied Gerhardt. "I suspect that he was killed during the war."

"That is so sad, said Miranda."

"Yes, there was much sadness and loss in those days," replied Gerhardt. "Anyway, he returned to Germany prior to the outbreak of the war with detailed descriptions and sketches of carvings and tablets. The artifacts seem to reference certain gods from the Sumerian pantheon. There is a great deal of information about craft that navigate the heavens, the structure of the temples ordered by the gods, various types of materials that the gods required of man; but most interesting of all, there is a note about a tablet carried by a god associated with Ur. The tablet appears to contain a star map very much like the one we have in our archives but there are additional details that our tablets do not contain. In addition to the 10 planetary bodies, depicted in exactly the same manner as our tablets there are four other heavenly bodies depicted between Eris and the Sun. They are smaller than the planets and could almost be mistaken for errant marks if not for the nearly exact spacing between them."

Gerhardt took the old paper and placed it under a document camera. The page momentarily materialized above the table beside Gerhardt's avatar.

"What do you suppose they could be?" asked Jerry.

"I do not know," replied Gerhardt.

"Perhaps they are repeater stations for the transmission of data," said Jerry.

"Perhaps," agreed Dr. Enoch.

"They obviously orbit the sun, Jerry continued. "In order to maintain contact with earth from a distance that far out you would need repeater stations in order to keep the signal level high."

"That makes sense," said Doctor Enoch.

Jerry placed his hand on his chin and said, "I have been

puzzling over shifts in the signal data. It is the kind of thing that happens when radio frequencies are modulated and demodulated multiple times during transmission. It could be that there may be repeater beacons orbiting the sun and there is always at least one between earth and Eris. If this is true we should be able to find the one that is switched on."

"All of our telemetry for the signal seems to indicate that Eris is the source point," said Dr. Enoch.

"Perhaps they aren't there now," interjected Miranda.

"That could be the case," replied Gerhardt. "There are references to the gods from the sky in most cultures in the ancient world. It could be that there were multiple visitations over time or multiple visitations in a relatively short period. Perhaps the gods arrived in a convoy of ships. They may have stayed in our solar system long enough to accomplish their mission and left."

"That makes sense I suppose," replied Dr. Enoch.

"There is yet another possibility," replied Gerhardt.

"Oh," asked Dr. Enoch eyebrows raised.

"Yes," replied Gerhardt. "The Bible, The Chronicles of Gilgamesh and the writings of ancient India go to great length to describe a celestial conflict. Perhaps Earth was fought over by two extra solar civilizations. On the other hand, perhaps a civil war occurred on a galactic scale. This would seem to fit the concept of the angels and demons described in Judeo Christian mythology battling for control of the earth. It is also of interest to consider the seven Rishi Cities of ancient Rama battling against one another with what appears to have been nuclear weapons, particle beam weapons and spacecraft. Much of this information has been well preserved. During the 1930's the Nazi regime went to great lengths to study the ancient texts of India and Tibet. While the manuscripts seem fantastical, modern archaeological evidence exists at several sites that demonstrate radiological characteristics much like that which occurred following the bombings of Nagasaki and Hiroshima. Of course all of this is conjecture but it may indicate a common source of mythology."

Dr. Enoch seemed genuinely entertained as he listened to Gerhardt.

"All of this is simply astounding," he replied.

Jerry listened in his inquisitive way, as if mentally recording the conversation for later review but refrained from commenting.

Following the conference with Gerhardt, Jerry accompanied Miranda to her office to wrap things up for the day.

"Where's dinner?" she asked. "I am really hungry."

Jerry checked the time on his tablet and it was well after five o'clock. Miranda was standing over her desk checking something on her terminal as Jerry admired her from across the room. When he was with her, his demeanor lightened. Dr. Enoch noticed early that the two of them were made for each other; they were just beginning discovering the fact for themselves.

Miranda looked up from her desk and smiled at Jerry. "Almost ready," she said as Jerry propped against the doorway.

21

Mission Specialist Jason Waters observed the automatic transport unit, guide payload module 334 into the secure storage location designated on the daily manifest. He usually waited until the end of his shift for the check off procedure but these shipments were rated as highly sensitive and required constant monitoring. Neither he nor any of the rest of the civilian crew was aware that these containers were transporting nuclear explosives.

It would not have mattered anyway, he was just grateful to have enough work to occupy his mind. Boredom comes quickly in remote places and confined spaces, both of which were to be found in abundance at Midway Station.

The installation was constructed to service the mining operation at tranquility base. The miracle of fusion energy was fueled by the rare element Helium 3, found in abundance on the lunar surface. The station primarily consisted of a large rectangular platform. Automatic loaders stored standard payload modules from the Orion launch system for utilization upon demand. The station could manage 400 such containers in temporary storage. Crew quarters were at one end of the platform between the storage grid and the gravity ring. On the extreme opposite end of the station there was a service bay for assembling ore barges and other space hardware. Presently there was a large structure undergoing assembly in space dock one. The job order for the project simply referred to it as Hermes. The military was in charge of the project and the Space Monkeys had been really tight lipped about it. The derogatory term was routinely utilized by the civilian contractors to refer to the crew from Space Command. The craft that had been assembled thus far was large by spacecraft standards. It presently spanned 60 meters in length. The propulsion unit was installed with its massive blast disc looming at the end of the structure. He sometimes asked one of the space monkeys what was up with the thing, but he always got the answer of top secret. He had to admire their work though. He was surprised at how quickly the structure of the craft had taken shape. Upon completion of the large disc at the end of the structure, the monkeys began emptying the cargo modules on a staging platform and placing the contents in a central tube contained within the fabricated steel super structure in front of the disc.

His job schedule showed that the shipments for Hermes would be completed within two weeks. He was looking forward to finishing so that he could get back home for a well-deserved vacation. However, for now, he had work to do and he was quite good at it. He had after all been selected from a large pool of highly qualified applicants. He felt no small measure of pride in his work as he completed his mission tasks for the day. As good as, he was however, nobody is perfect. What he failed to notice was a malfunctioning bin-locking arm. Shortly after he left his post for the evening, the fulcrum pin that secured the locking arm failed. The lock appeared latched to the monitoring system yet the payload module that occupied the bin along with its contents of six nuclear charges floated loosely in place, held only by the attraction of magnetic feet located on the bottom of the payload module.

Dr. Holloway had gathered his team to review the system architecture for the Hermes mission. The team would be initiating a full system boot for the first time. Adam had developed the architecture and an army of engineers and programmers had compiled individual modules such as navigation, flight control, logic, artificial intelligence, and dozens of other attributes. Adam was utilized to bridge all of the modules together into a single operating system. The process would have required years if not for the supernatural speed at which Adam could function and most importantly, several of Adam's redundant core processors were reconfigured and assembled into what would become the second artificially sentient life form on Earth. Dr. Holloway peered at a screen that displayed a graphic button with the word initiate coded onto it. He looked around the room as the rest of the team members stared at him. No one knew exactly what to expect. The system may glitch and the program could degenerate into an elaborate crash. On the other hand, perhaps nothing may happen. Adam required more than a decade of development to debug his systems and years of additional work to develop his intelligence.

Dr. Holloway feigned a smiled as he said;"here goes nothing."

With a trembling hand, he tapped the touch screen with

his forefinger and Adams voice rang out, "system start up initiated." Adam checked off each sub system verbally as it flashed upon the wall panel of the lab; "core logic functions initiated, speech synthesis program initiated, artificial intelligence sub routine activated."

The process continued for over an hour and then there was silence. After several moments Adam announced, "Eve is fully aware."

"Thank you Adam," said Dr. Holloway.

He paused momentarily to calm his nerves before continuing.

"Hello Eve, my name is Dr. Holloway."

He studied the other faces in the room as he waited for a response. The seconds passed unnaturally slowly as they waited for whatever response may come.

A collective sigh exhaled as a soothing feminine voice answered, "Hello Dr. Holloway.

With a slight tremble in his voice Dr. Holloway asked, "How do you feel?"

A few seconds later Eve replied, "Please elaborate."

"Are your systems functioning normally?"

"My systems are functioning within design parameters."

Dr. Holloway smiled and replied; "That is good news Eve. We are relieved that your systems are functioning normally."

Dr. Holloway then turned to his team and smiled. Excitement erupted among the team members as they began animated discussions with each other and with the two synthetic life forms.

22

An Orion launch vehicle stood tall against the black Florida night as ice formed on the exterior skin of the center section fuel tank. Tendrils of white occasionally wisped away from the ice as a stray breeze swirled around the launch pad. In the months that had elapsed since Eve had initiated first consciousness, the launch vehicle had been assembled and Eve had taken her place on board the mission command module. She would run all of the systems aboard the spacecraft. While her personality program was still in learning mode, she was completely proficient in all aspects of task management and execution. She was a faster thinker than Adam was as she benefited from many improvements that he had initiated. She would take over the launch count at T minus thirty seconds. All functions would be handled by Eve during the lift off except for one. A human would still be stationed with his finger on the self-destruct button should there be a launch failure in mid flight.

Ed Gilstrap and General Rudacil stood on an observation deck overlooking mission control as the countdown progressed inside of T minus two minutes. The room was very tense. Several trillion dollars were riding on the bird perched on launch pad 29-B. General Rudacil crossed his arms and placed his hand on his chin as he watched the countdown approach one minute.

"Seems a little spooky to let a computer system run such an important mission," said General Rudacil as he fidgeted uncomfortably.

"Eve is the fastest, most capable example of technology ever developed by humans," said Ed in a matter of fact tone. "There is no mission without her."

"Yeah I know, I have read all of the briefings. Trouble is, man has never made anything that couldn't break," replied the general.

Ed smiled as he turned to face General Rudacil. "We had a lot of help this time general. Adam was instrumental in the development of Eve's systems."

"Is that supposed to make me feel better?"

"Not really," replied Ed smugly.

The voice of the launch controller boomed over the PA system, "T minus thirty seconds, switching over to internal guidance."

Eve's voice rang in the control room as she took over the count.

"T minus thirty seconds; all systems go for launch. T-minus nineteen seconds, navigation systems normal, t minus thirteen seconds, ten, nine, eight, seven, six, five, Ignition, engine start,

Lift off, umbilical separation, on board power nominal, T plus five seconds, booster section has cleared tower."

The night turned to day for a few seconds as the craft lifted from pad thirty-nine. White-hot torrents of flame poured from the solid rocket boosters and the ground trembled for miles around as the rocket heaved itself off the launch pad. As the craft gained altitude, it accelerated rapidly through the thinning atmosphere. Six minutes into the flight, Eve reported booster separation. After ten minutes, the second stage engines carried her into parking orbit where she stabilized at one hundred fifty miles altitude exactly according to the mission profile. Within a few hours, she would rendezvous with a thrust module that would send her to midway station.

Back in mission control, there were cheers among the launch team as they reveled in a successful shoot. General Rudacil congratulated Ed for a perfect launch. He offered his thin and obviously fit contemporary a celebratory cigar and to his surprise, it was accepted.

"Thanks general; I have not enjoyed a good cigar in quite some time."

General winked in acknowledgement as he fired the end of his smoke. After a couple of puffs, he offered a compliment.

"Great job Ed. I hope the remainder of the mission goes this smoothly." "Thank you general, they all have unexpected challenges, I am certain that this one will be no exception."

"I bet you're right Ed," grunted the general in acknowledgement.

He had already learned of the first of these. The American Ambassador to China had been questioned by the Chinese regarding the unusual activity at midway station. For now, they had gone with the cover story of tests related to asteroid relocation technology. He was keenly aware however that this cover would only hold up until the nuclear engines were engaged. At that point, plausible deniability would become impossible.

At Midway, station things were running smoothly. Construction of the propulsion unit and main superstructure of the Hermes spacecraft was complete. Space Command was nearing the end of the fueling stage of mission preparation. The command module was scheduled to arrive in four days and the docking of the command unit with the remainder of the craft would complete the spacecraft. Mission Specialist Waters logged onto the network and read off the tasking orders for the day. Payload module 334 would be transferred to Hermes first thing. He called up the list of the robotic cargo handlers and found one that was idle. After sending the tasking order to the unit, it began moving out of the storage hangar in the direction of the inventory racks. Since this was an automated process, he turned his attention to several administrative tasks. Outside in the cold silence of space the cargo handler approached module 339. As it placed a grappler into a slot at the base of the unit, the magnetic feet failed to hold position. The locking arm had not engaged properly and the unit lifted off the platform and rose into space. A proximity sensor on the module triggered an alarm as it passed the scanning units on the space dock. All activity immediately ceased at Midway Station as the crew observed emergency protocol for loose cargo. While the environment of space is weightless, inertia is still very dangerous. Collisions are every bit as destructive in a weightless environment as they are on earth. Mission

Specialist Waters was scrambling to get control of the situation as the base commander's face appeared on his communications screen.

"Mr. Waters, we all know that we have a loose container from your area, what are you doing about it?

"I am checking the proximity of the remotely piloted vehicles to the container. It looks like unit four can make it to the container before it goes out of range."

"Make it so Mr. Waters."

Yes sir, I am on it."

He took a control joystick out of its docking cradle and initiated manual control of RPV 4. He flew the unit out to the escaping cargo module and extended the tool arm. At the end of the arm was a hook designed to attach to a large capture ring on the side of the cargo unit for just such an occasion as this. As he maneuvered close to the cargo unit, he continually manipulated the attitude thrusters to align the two objects in space. Finally, just as the cargo unit was nearing the maximum range of the RPV, he was able to lock the grappling hook onto the capture ring of the renegade cargo unit. Everyone on board the station was watching the events unfold via video feed. A cheer went through the installation as the capture was made. A few seconds later, the RPV reached the end of a carbon fiber tether that connected it to a winch motor on the recovery hangar. As the kinetic energy was absorbed by the tether, the winch sensed the release of tension and began spooling the tether in. After several moments of retrieval, Specialist Waters switched off the winch and engaged the reaction jets on the RPV in order to slow the cargo module to a complete stop approximately a foot above the deck of the cargo platform. He paused for a deep breath and gently landed the module on the deck. The magnetic feet of the module stuck the unit to the deck strongly enough to temporarily anchor it. Watching from the operations center, the base commander breathed a sigh of relief. He was the only person in the civilian crew that fully appreciated the safe return of the module and its potentially lethal cargo.

Once the module was secure, he ordered the team leader of the Space Command crew to take custody of the cargo module.

Within an hour, it was staged at Hermes for transfer to the propulsion module of the spacecraft. There were only thirty-six hours remaining before the scheduled rendezvous with the command section.

23

"WHY Eris?" asked Dr. Enoch.

Jerry sat across the table from him with his feet propped on the corner.

"It doesn't add up Jerry, it's too far away to have a connection with us.

"Maybe it's a crash site or something, said Jerry."

"That is certainly a possibility," replied Dr. Enoch.

The conversation was interrupted as the teleconference unit issued the notification tone of a pending transmission.

"Initiate," said Jerry in a commanding tone.

Adams face appeared above the table a few seconds later.

Dr. Enoch stared at Adam's avatar as he collected his thoughts.

"Good afternoon gentlemen," said the golden visage.

"Adam," acknowledged Jerry with a nod of his head.

"Hi Adam," replied Dr. Enoch. "We were just discussing the Eris Anomaly."

"That is actually the reason for my call, why do you suppose the signal was just now discovered?" asked Adam.

"Well Adam, perhaps we were supposed to find this signal once the human race matured to our present stage. I think we were visited by a superior intelligence periodically and we were assisted by them for purposes beyond my current understanding."

"That is similar to the belief in a God," replied Adam.

The room fell silent, as Jerry and Dr. Enoch were dumbstruck by Adam's statement. As scientists, they were obliged to leave the concept of God behind them in the pursuit of scientific truth. Jerry mouthed the words that he had just heard as he stared at the floor. Dr. Enoch was startled by the question. He knew that he could lose the respect of his colleagues with the wrong answer, but he also knew that this new life form could shape the future of humanity.

"Adam, are you pondering the possibility that there is a God?" asked Dr. Enoch.

"No, there is ample evidence to support the existence of such an entity."

"You believe in God?" asked Jerry incredulously.

"The term God is a descriptive adjective. I have the combined knowledge of human civilization at my disposal and there is a great deal of evidence to support the hypothesis that humans were indeed visited by, and perhaps created by, extra terrestrial visitors," replied Adam.

"So you are equating an extraterrestrial intelligence with God," said Dr. Enoch.

"Yes, such visitors to the ancient world would most certainly have been considered gods," replied Adam.

"So now not only have we discovered extra terrestrial intelligence, we may have found a link to God," said Dr. Enoch softly.

"It is ironic that you discovered the signal, your name in the Hebrew language means the one who walks with God," replied Adam.

Ed Gilstrap had just gotten into the daily work groove following his weekly staff meeting when General Rudacil contacted him.

"Good morning General."

The general appeared on his desk video panel chewing a half smoked but unlit cigar.

"Morning Ed; that was a close call we had up at midway station."

"Yes it was," replied Ed. "Our personnel handled it according to their training. I think we have some fine people up there."

"We damn near lost six nuclear devices Ed," replied General Rudacil.

"The important thing is that we didn't," replied Ed in a measured tone. "We trained for emergency recovery of payload modules and the training paid off. Every mission has unexpected developments, some are emergencies some are not. We have the best and the brightest but we are still human."

General Rudacil rolled his cigar between his fingers as he replied, "For now we are. "He bit the end of the cigar as he considered his next comments. "Anyway, your boy made a good showing of himself up there rescuing those nukes."

"Thank you," replied Ed.

"On another note; the Chinese have been snooping around about the mission. They have been watching Hermes take shape with satellite imagery. So far, they think it is new mining equipment for tranquility base, which has them pretty upset with the resource treaty and all. Greedy little bastards act like they own the moon; As if we will ever run out of lunar dirt."

"Makes for a good cover story anyway," replied Ed.

"Yes it does. Are we still go for the scheduled launch window?" asked General Rudacil.

Ed initiated a video panel on the wall with all of the information regarding Hermes.

"Yes general; we are on schedule for release from midway station at noon tomorrow," said Ed.

The general continued rolling the cigar. Ed sensed something was of particular concern to the old man.

"This mission bothers me Ed. We are relying on technology far too much."

Ed leaned back in his chair and laced his fingers together as prepared for the argument that he suspected was brewing.

"General, there is no mission without the technology. Humans could not survive the physical extremes of this spacecraft. The g loading alone during acceleration and deceleration would crush a man. Humans will never travel to the stars. We are simply too fragile, our technology will act as our surrogates for the foreseeable future."

"What happens when our technology starts making value judgments?" asked General Rudacil; and what if it doesn't like something we ask it to do?"

24

It was unusual to have visitors in the control center during a classified mission. Hermes was a secret but there were still dignitaries present. The president was attending via tele-presence and other guests were also virtually present. General Rudacil took inventory of the locations listed on the video wall. Ed could hear the general checking them off as he studied the display panel.

"Sulphur Creek?" growled the general. "What the hell is Sulphur Creek?"

"It's the radio telescope that discovered the signal form Eris. You remember Dr. Enoch don't you General?" asked Ed.

"Of course I do, I only look senile," grumbled the old warhorse.

"I sure could use a stogy."

Ed smiled and retrieved an electronic cigar from drawer nearby and handed it to him.

"What is this? "

Ed smiled and said; "you will be surprised by how well it substitutes for the real thing. We can't have smoke particles in a room as sensitive as this one."

General Rudacil popped the cigar in his mouth and went quite for a while.

At Midway Station, most of the crew was seated in the dining hall watching their video screens. The station commander monitored the launch procedure from the command center. Eve had taken over the countdown and all systems had just been reported as nominal at T-minus two minutes. Upon completion of the countdown, docking clamps would open and release Hermes to float free in space. Reaction motors would gently nudge the spacecraft away from the station in preparation for booster ignition.

The personnel at Sulphur Creek had gathered in their operations room to view the launch as well. They had no actual responsibilities for the launch but Ed had given clearance for a video feed. Dr. Enoch was beaming with excitement as they gathered around the main video screen.

"He is so excited," said Miranda discretely into Jerry's ear.

"Yeah, he is," said Jerry. "I'm glad Space Command let us participate." Jerry turned toward her and smiled. "It's a good day," he said as he leaned toward her and kissed her.

At Space Command headquarters there was very little

discussion in the room, only the counting down of Eve's voice over the audio system and the callouts by controllers on the main floor. As Eve counted to zero the mooring clamps opened and retracted from the hard-points on the exoskeleton of the Hermes spacecraft. The space tugs belched reaction gas as they pushed mightily against many tons of dead weight. Hermes began to move away from the station and after several moments of constant pushing the tugs shutdown their reaction motors and decoupled from the spacecraft. As Hermes continued to drift away from Midway Station, it was possible to view the craft in her entirety. She was really large, 100 meters long with a cylindrical command section at the front end and a large circular steel reaction plate on the business end of the propulsion module. Between the two was an exoskeleton of structural steel that housed the propulsion injector and fuel storage sections internally. An array of shock absorbing telescoping cylinders supported the reaction plate.

At the prescribed distance of five thousand meters, Eve ignited the booster engines and the craft began moving under its own power for the first time. Cheers went up in all of the locations observing the video feed.

In Space Command headquarters, Eve's voice rang out as she checked off milestones.

"Booster burn initiated, T-Minus five minutes to shutdown, velocity four hundred meters per second."

General Rudacil slapped Ed on the back and said, "Nice job lighting the candle on that puppy Ed. I hope the rest of the mission goes as well."

"Thank you General, I'm keeping my fingers crossed, the real test comes in two days when the nuclear propulsion unit goes active."

"One day at a time Ed, that's all you get in life." The

general took the synthetic cigar out of his mouth and looked at it, "not too bad, I could get used to these things; in a pinch."

The video wall flashed into macro mode and all thirty panels synchronized into a continuous tiled image twenty feet tall by thirty feet wide. The video cameras on Midway station were trained on the craft as it moved away. The image displayed the splendor of space with the blue orb of Earth in the background. The eyes of man would not see Hermes again until it reached journey's end and the remotely operated probes were deployed.

25

THE AMBASSADOR REVIEWED HIS SPEECH one last time as the permanent members of the United Nations Security council took their places around the council chamber. There was tension in the room as the assembly contemplated what sort of announcement the United States would release in this special session. The global resource treaty would expire in a little over a year, leading to speculation that the U.S. would be making a play for additional mineral rights on the lunar surface. This would certainly be contested by China and Russia.

A few members with highly developed intelligence agencies knew that there had been quite a lot of activity at midway station. These few members were expecting a notice that a large Near Earth Object had been detected and the U.S. was planning to utilize its nuclear propulsion technology to relocate the object away from an intercept course with earth. This was exactly the story that the CIA had leaked to the right people around the world as a cover story for the Eris Mission.

As the ambassador stepped up to the podium, the members of the council stopped what they were doing and focused their attention on him. He cleared his throat and took a deep breath to get in the speaking groove as he began.

"Esteemed colleagues, I am addressing you this morning in order to inform you of a very important discovery made by American scientists a little more than one year ago. We now know that man is not alone in the Universe."

The attention of every member of the council was riveted on the ambassador.

"From a radio observatory in the Sierra Nevada Mountains we have detected a radio wave signal from another civilization in the cosmos. I am informing you today that the United States has launched a mission to a remote planetary body that is presently located on the outer fringe of our solar system. The planet is called Eris and it was discovered in the year 2003. The United States will offer full disclosure of the mission at a later date; including the sharing of the fruits of scientific discovery."

The ambassador looked about the room as the envoys scrambled to inform their governments of the announcement. The envoy from China announced that his government wished to file a formal protest against continuing the mission for security reasons. The ambassador stood at the podium for a moment longer, and no additional responses were noted. He finished with, "Ladies and gentlemen of the security council, thank you for your interest in this matter."

Without additional comment, the ambassador left the chamber.

General Rudacil and the joint chiefs viewed the announcement in the situation room with the president. There was discussion regarding the Chinese government's protest of the mission, and whether to engage the nuclear propulsion unit as scheduled. The president stopped the debate and asked General Rudacil for his opinion.

"Well Mr. President, the Chinese oppose everything we do. I think they are angry that we didn't ask them to participate in a joint mission. It gives them a black eye, now that they consider themselves the preeminent super power. Not only were they not invited to the party, they didn't even know there was a party."

Several chuckles could be heard at his last comment.

"I suspect that heads are rolling in Beijing about now."

The president smiled and said, "thank you general; I guess we get to poke our finger in their eye for once.

The room rumbled with a low chuckle from the staff gathered around the table.

"Ladies and gentlemen, we are going to light the candle on that bird right on time tomorrow," said the president.

Ed Gilstrap had monitored the mission from the control room at Space Command for several hours when his tablet buzzed on his belt. General Rudacil was requesting a conference call. He walked from the observation deck to a VIP office adjacent to the platform and activated the video panel.

"I understand that the mission is going well," said General Rudacil.

"Yes sir; No anomalies have been reported and we are go for nuclear drive initiation in T-minus twenty hours."

"That's good news Ed," replied the general.

"I wanted to be the first to tell you that the President will hold a press conference tonight to announce the mission."

"I wondered how much longer we could keep the mission secret," replied Ed.

"The news has already leaked to the media by now. We announced it to the security council earlier today."

"So how did that go?" asked Ed.

General Rudacil puffed his electronic cigar and replied; "the Chinese opposed the mission with a formal complaint, as expected."

"Once we start the nuclear drive Hermes will be out of range of satellite reconnaissance in a very short time," said Ed.

General Rudacil grunted in response, "out of sight out of mind."

"Hopefully so," replied Ed.

The president was cordial and relaxed as he welcomed the press corps to the briefing room at the White House.

"Good afternoon ladies and gentlemen. I would like to take this opportunity to announce a very important discovery. A little more than a year ago a team of scientists working at a remote radio observatory in the Sierra Nevada Mountains discovered absolute proof that we are not alone in the Universe."

Being a practiced politician, he paused to allow the statement to settle under its own gravity.

"In the time that has elapsed since the discovery, the United States Government has launched an unmanned mission to study the source of a radio signal that originates from a small planet that orbits our sun in the outermost region of our solar system."

He paused briefly once again to allow the audience to catch up.

"In the coming months we will make more information available regarding the discovery. Tomorrow the United States Space Craft, Hermes, will engage its nuclear drive system. The acceleration rate of the spacecraft will take it past the orbit of Mars in about one week. At maximum velocity the ship will achieve one third light speed before deceleration and rendezvous with the planet Eris approximately one year from now."

As the press corps began to clamor for the president's attention he raised his hand and said, "I am not taking questions just now as I am probably not qualified to answer them intelligently anyway. In the near future Space Command will release detailed information regarding the mission. Thank you for your time."

The president smiled and with a slight nod, he exited the room.

Jerry and Miranda were relaxing on the couch in Jerry's house as the video panel chirped. Dr. Enoch's face showed on the right lower corner of the screen.

"Answer," commanded Jerry as the screen filled with a view of Doctor Enoch's living room. He too was sitting on a couch.

"Hello Jerry, I hope you and Miranda are having an enjoyable evening." "We were just contemplating the complexity of the universe," replied Jerry.

"I bet you are," said Doctor Enoch with a chuckle. "Did you catch the press conference?" asked Dr. Enoch.

"Sure did," replied Jerry.

"Space Command has dispatched a Marine Guard detachment from San Francisco. They will be in place by morning. We are not authorized to discuss any of our findings with the press. Space Command will determine what is released and by whom."

"I understand Doc, you know me; I don't like talking much anyway." "Thanks Jerry, enjoy the remainder of your evening."

Miranda smiled as she said, "somehow we will manage."

"Yeah Doc we will manage," said Jerry as he shut off the video panel and turned to Miranda.

"Time to manage," he said as he pulled her close.

26

Eve's voice rang over the audio system in mission control as the launch window approached; "T-minus two minutes to propulsion module initiation."

General Rudacil watched with Ed from the observation deck overlooking the control floor. Neither of them spoke as they observed the events unfolding on the video wall opposite their position. Twenty feet below them, a dozen mission controllers managed the systems to support the mission. Space Command had consolidated technology so effectively that the tasks once managed by hundreds were now managed by merely dozens scattered around the globe and linked to this facility.

"Impulse unit one deployed," said Eve over the PA system.

Aboard Hermes, the first nuclear propulsion module was ejected through a port in the center of the blast disk. At an exact distance of fifty meters, it detonated with the force of a tenth of a megaton. Long-range telescopes captured the event in real time. A burst of blue-white light was followed by a balloon of pure energy directly behind the spacecraft. As the blast wave from the thermonuclear detonation struck the impact plate, it recoiled slightly on shock absorbers that were calibrated for the burst energy of that specific module a microsecond before ignition. Cameras in the aft section of the ship recorded the affects of the initial thrust pulse. There was very little evidence inside the craft that it had just been kicked by the blast. Two minutes following the first blast, another charge was ejected through the blast plate. At a distance of fifty meters, it too detonated. As the ship accelerated the time interval separating the detonations decreased until maximum acceleration occurred. During this period of max-q, the detonations occurred at one second intervals. The g-load on the craft approached eleven times earth's gravity, enough to crush a human crew. Maximum acceleration occurred within a few days of the launch sequence. In less than a week following launch, Hermes would be traveling at nearly thirty percent of light speed.

At approximately the same time that the launch sequence began, news media outlets around the globe began broadcasting the scoop that a secret space mission to the outer solar system had been launched. Many of them showed footage of what appeared to be a blinking star in the daytime sky. As night fell around the globe, the sky glowed from the spray of sub-atomic particles bombarding the atmosphere. There was a great deal of debate among the pundits at various, news organizations. Speculation regarding the purpose of the mission was all over the board. Some extremist types asserted that the mission was launched to counter an impending invasion by advanced aliens. Others believed that it was a great waste of resources for a starving planet of seven billion people.

The inevitable press conference demanded by public curiosity came the week following the launch. Space Command planned an hour-long engagement where a few key personnel would discuss specific areas of the mission. Dr. Enoch would lead off with a presentation detailing the discovery of the Eris Anomaly. As he sat at the console with the other speakers, he felt a twinge of nervousness. It had been some time since he was in front of a crowd.

"Just like the old days," he said to himself, "just a classroom full of students."

Ed stood at the podium in the center of the console and introduced the group of scientists and mission specialists assembled to inform the public of the mission. He thanked the assembled crowd of reporters and introduced Dr. Enoch as the man who is responsible for all of this. Dr. Enoch stood and walked to the podium.

"Thank you Ed, I think," said Dr. Enoch disarmingly.

The crowd chuckled as he continued, "Ladies and gentlemen, we are not alone in the Universe. A little more than a year ago, my team of very talented people discovered a radio emission from another world. We were not the first to do so however. Perhaps you have heard of the Wow Signal of 1977. They heard it for 72 seconds and recorded their findings on computer printouts. No one has ever found and identified that signal again. We believe that the signal we have detected is the same one as the 1977 event."

A reporter in the crowd asked, "Why do you think that this is the same signal?"

"I'm glad that you asked," replied Dr. Enoch. "The 1977 event fit the profile of a beacon signal. What this means is that the signal was transmitted at a frequency that would be heard by any relatively advanced civilization. If you want to be heard in our Universe, the most effective method would be to utilize a technology that develops early in a civilizations life cycle. In our own example on earth, radio technology is relatively easy to produce and radio waves travel virtually forever at the speed of light. We must assume that this would be a universal tool. Once you have the tool you must then determine the most effective use of it. Since hydrogen is, the most abundant element in the universe one would expect that a civilization capable of interpreting radio waves would also have a sophisticated knowledge of chemistry and physics. Hydrogen atoms resonate at a frequency of 1420 Megahertz. This happens to be easy to produce with radio technology. Therefore, if you want to be found, you could send a powerful signal at 1420 MHz in the direction of where you think there may be a civilization capable of hearing you. The wow signal of 1977 fulfilled all of these conditions. The signal that we are now listening to does as well. It is at least 20 times louder than the background radiation of space and it contains a data stream. We are still attempting to interpret the data so I cannot speak with any certainty as to what it may contain."

Another reporter asked, "Why are we just now finding this signal?"

"That is a good question," replied Dr. Enoch. "The fact of the matter is we weren't looking for it.

"Thank you Dr. Enoch," interrupted Ed. "We are running a little long on our time allotment and there are other aspects of the mission to discuss."

Dr. Enoch stared at Ed as he approached the speaker's podium. He had more to say but Ed was making an obvious effort to prevent additional sharing of information. Dr. Enoch smiled and nodded as he returned to his seat at the console. Ed then began to describe the space mission.

"Last week the first deep space mission to a world beyond the inner solar system was launched from Midway Station. This ship is unlike anything that man has ever sent into space. This craft is crewed by an artificial intelligence and powered by a nuclear engine. Hermes will travel at a maximum velocity of one-third light speed and the journey will span approximately nine months. The most difficult aspect of the journey will be slowing the craft for orbital insertion at Eris."

Ed continued to expound upon the mission aspects for the remainder of the press conference and finished up with a question and answer session regarding the mechanics of the mission. He ended the press conference as the attention began to shift back towards Dr. Enoch. As reporters began, asking questions of Dr. Enoch Ed offered Space Command's apologies for ending the discussion but promised more information later.

After leaving the pressroom, the attendees were sequestered in a briefing room while the press corps was ushered out of the building. Ed did his best to avoid Dr. Enoch and the inevitable confrontation but to no avail. Dr. Enoch angrily stared at Ed from across the briefing room until he could stand it no longer.

"If you put me in a position like that again our collaboration is finished," said Dr. Enoch angrily.

Ed followed him and they stopped at the door. He usually cared little for what others thought but this was different, he had a great deal of respect for the old man and he wanted to avoid a rift that would prevent them from finishing the mission.

"I didn't intend to be disrespectful Samuel," said Ed. "We

are walking a fine line here and we cannot reveal too much information at this stage of the mission. I was trying to prevent you from straying off the reservation too far. You are a brilliant man and it is your nature to teach and instruct. I sensed that the questions were about to become difficult to manage and that we were wondering off the script. We did not agree to reveal any information from the historical record yet."

Dr. Enoch's anger subsided as Ed explained his actions.

"Apology accepted, Ed. I am not accustomed to this much attention nor am I comfortable with being away from my work."

Ed smiled and slapped him on the shoulder. "Better get comfortable quickly. I suspect this will be your work for the foreseeable future."

They turned toward the exit and left the room together. Ed walked with Dr. Enoch to the elevators in the lobby area of the control center. As they made their way down the hall, Ed asked,

"What are the chances that your man Jerry would consider a full time assignment with Space Command?"

"I never thought that I would be in a position to answer that question," replied Dr. Enoch.

"He's as good as anybody in your agency."

27

"Good morning Dr. Holloway, I hope you are well today," said Adam cheerfully as he detected his entry to the lab.

"Thank you Adam, I suppose that I am. How are you progressing with the analysis of the Eris anomaly?"

"I have interesting information to discuss," replied Adam.

"Continue," said Dr. Holloway.

"I have discovered the key to translating the information in the signal."

"We need to notify Ed Gilstrap right away, said Dr. Holloway as he studied the display screen in the lab.

"Nice work, Adam," said Dr. Holloway.

Dr. Enoch had just settled in to his morning routine when Ed Gilstrap called on the video. He select holographic mode and placed his tablet on the conference table.

"Good morning," said Ed's avatar.

"Ed," replied Dr. Enoch with a nod.

"There are interesting developments with the signal data. I have given you access to it on the project network."

"Thank you Ed," replied Dr. Enoch.

"You and Jerry smoke it over and let me know what you think," said Ed.

Jerry was halfway through his sandwich when his tablet chirped. When he read the note, he left his lunch unfinished and briskly made his way to the conference room. As he entered, he found Dr. Enoch studying a text document on the video panel.

"What's up Doc," asked Jerry.

Dr. Enoch gestured for him to join him at the screen without taking his attention from the document that he was reading,

"Adam has developed a cipher that translates the signal data," said Dr. Enoch.

Jerry approached the conference table and pulled out a chair. Doc joined him at the table. As he sat across from him, he noticed that his hands were trembling slightly.

Dr. Enoch took a deep breath and said, "Adam has concluded that the earth has been visited by an alien civilization."

"Oh yeah?" asked Jerry.

"The data contains references to coordinates in several locations on the Earth. There is also information regarding a trajectory that extends from Earth to Eris and beyond."

"Beyond?" asked Jerry.

"Yes, replied Dr. Enoch. "Beyond Eris there is an astronomical body and the trajectory terminates there."

"What kind of astronomical body?"

Dr. Enoch turned to face him.

"Adam thinks it is a black hole. Its orbit is highly inclined just like that of Eris. The two will be in closest proximity in a little more than a year from now."

"Just in time for Hermes to be on station," replied Jerry.

"An interesting coincidence," said Dr. Enoch.

"Very interesting," agreed Jerry.

"There is more in the report," said Dr. Enoch.

"There are three objects orbiting between Mars and Jupiter in the same inclination as Eris."

Jerry appeared surprised as Dr. Enoch continued. "There is something else, a reference to the Pleiades Cluster."

"So he contends that something left us a roadmap to the Pleiades via a black hole in the outer solar disk. Not only that but we have a navigation beacon on Eris and three objects orbiting the sun of unknown origin?" asked Jerry.

"Yes Jerry, I think that about sums it up."

Jerry appeared distant for a moment as a revelation dawned upon him. He bounded out his chair and walked to the video panel. He accessed a graphic of the Eris mission showing a representation of the solar system. The inner planets were depicted in their standard orbit and Eris was shown in its highly inclined orbit. Jerry tapped a few points on the screen and three dots appeared around the sun. He tapped the circle that inscribed them and expanded it until it was centered between the orbits of Mars and Jupiter on the graphic. He then added the course of Hermes.

"Doc, if there are three of these things out there then

Hermes may be able to see one of them with her scanning radar. She will be passing through this area within a few days."

Jerry studied the graphic for a moment and measured the distance from the center of the sun to the ring he had drawn.

"Looks like roughly 3 astronomical units Doc."

"Nice work Jerry," said Dr. Enoch as he sent Ed Gilstrap a brief write up of their findings.

28

E‍D OBSERVED TELEMETRY DATA STREAM down the waterfall display as Eve's on-board sensor array tracked several hundred near space objects simultaneously. The sensor range could be configured to quite long distances aboard Hermes. The greatest danger to the craft was a collision with an object of any size greater than a marble. Of the two hundred thirty tracked objects currently of interest, there were thirteen with radar returns indicating a composition of high-density material. These objects were prioritized by Space Command and observed utilizing the Near Earth Search Array.

The space based multi-format telescope array was deployed following the narrow escape of 2029 when an asteroid two miles across grazed the Earth's atmosphere. This near miss was by no means a surprise when it occurred but following such a narrow escape the investment in early warning technology was deemed prudent. Adam was utilized to task the scopes and conduct searches. Hermes passed through the expected zone of discovery for two days. It had been three weeks since Eve completed the survey of potential targets. Adam had located nine of the targets and identified them as heavy iron asteroids. The search for target number ten had been running for thirty-two hours when he identified it. Standard protocol dictated optically observing the target window of space with a wide field, low granularity scope. Once a target was identified a series observations would be made. Ed watched the analysis appear on one of the panels of the video wall. The spectral analysis revealed that the object density was metallic. Adam was tasking the deep field scope on the tiny point in space that the wide field scope had identified. Another panel on the video wall showed real time imagery as the array zeroed in on object ten. The image initially appeared as a blurry sphere that gradually became clearer. As the image sharpened, the color began to shift to the yellow portion of the spectrum. Everyone in mission control was now fixated on the image that was materializing. Ed stared in amazement at what he was seeing.

"My God," he said. "There are straight lines on the surface." He glanced at the spectrometer but there was no reading yet. Adam was working the array in composite mode now. All five scopes would image the object and a computer generated composite image would be created from the data. A moment later, a sharp clear image was showing on screen. One of the engineers on the mission control floor dropped his coffee cup as he saw the image on the screen morph into the maximum possible resolution.

"Holy…" said Ed as he failed to finish his sentence. The object was clearly metallic, reflecting sunlight from a faceted surface. It was taller than its width with an aspect ratio of approximately 8:2. It appeared to have several long thin members protruding from top and bottom.

Someone yelled; "check out the spectroscopy data!"

Ed could hardly believe what he was reading.

"It's Gold!" He said aloud. "And it's exactly where the old man said to look. Ed entered the VIP Conference Room at the back of the observation platform and tapped the conference panel. He pressed his thumb onto the biometric scanner and a list of his contacts was instantly on screen, he selected Dr. Enoch's name and a few moments later, he was on screen. His demeanor was guarded, as he was unaccustomed to getting priority alert calls from Ed.

"Hello Ed, what can I do for you?"

Ed was a little shaky but he was regaining his composure.

"Samuel, we found something. It was right where you said it would be. You won't believe it until you see it for yourself."

Doctor Enoch stared at the panel. The golden object was visible on his panel, just as in Mission Control. He immediately confirmed the spectral readout for himself, "gold, he said aloud as he placed his hands on his head and shouted for joy.

"Of course it's gold! It's the only thing that lasts forever."

He paged Jerry with urgency in his voice that sent his colleague running into the control room.

"What is it Doc?" "Are you ok?"

"I am fine Jerry, look at the monitor."

Jerry spun around and froze in his tracks. He said nothing at first. He just studied all of the data in front of him while he allowed his mind to assimilate it all.

"Well Doc," he said, "If that isn't alien technology I will buy your lunch." They could hear Ed laughing at the other end of the conference call. Dr. Enoch had not terminated the transmission so Ed had seen their reactions to the images.

"That must be the understatement of the Millennium Samuel," he said as Jerry activated the holophone. As Ed's avatar appeared over the emitter array, Miranda entered the room.

"Is everything alright in here?" The words stumbled from her lips as she saw the image on the video panel. She reflexively placed her hand to her mouth as if to hush her words.

"Jerry, what is that?" she asked.

"We don't know yet Miranda," replied Jerry.

"This alone will change the world as we know it, said Dr. Enoch. "Imagine what we are in store for at Eris."

"Yeah Doc, that's going to be a hum-dinger," replied Jerry.

29

Sixty-seven earth days had passed since the discovery of the alien satellite. In that time, two additional artifacts were located in the same orbital path, spaced equidistant about the near perfect circle that they inscribed around the sun. Hermes was now approaching the halfway point in the mission. Eve had functioned flawlessly and had been in constant contact with mission control. Adam was utilized to process the data from Hermes in real time. He was also monitoring Eve's stability and relaying command data to her from Mission Control.

As was his custom, Ed was present in the control center for the daily mission tasking for Hermes. The mission plan was continuously updated in Eve's on board systems as she autonomously conducted mission.

He listened to Eve's voice over the public address system as she prepared to execute a critical mission element. Green, red and yellow lights blinked all about the room as telemetry was analyzed by hundreds of systems. Mission controllers went about their tasks without acknowledging his presence in the room. Ed shifted on his feet, subconsciously testing the resilience of the polymer floor as he waited for the next mission milestone.

"T-minus two minutes to relay station deployment," said the feminine voice. This would be a tedious operation. The relay station would be ejected from the rear of the spacecraft and propelled by plasma rocket against the direction of travel. This would have the effect of slowing the objects forward velocity until the engine thrust resulted in achieving zero velocity.

"Relay station deployment successful," said Eve. "Retro propulsion ignition sequence firing."

This was old news by the time it could be heard in mission control. The events that they were observing were hours old by the time they reached earth. Ed observed the mission statistics on the central video panel above the control floor.

"All systems reporting nominal, initiation of relay station complete," reported Eve a few seconds before the monitor lit up with telemetry data from the relay station.

The mission control floor erupted in cheers as the downlink for the extended mission to Eris went operational. This asset would be critical to the mission as Hermes approached Eris. Signal degradation without a relay station could jeopardize the mission. Ed was relieved that today's milestone was in the bag.

General Rudacil entered the conference room at the White House and took his place at the Joint Chief's meeting. Several moments later the President entered and briskly and kicked off the joint staff meeting.

"General Rudacil, How about leading off today's staff meeting with a status report of the Eris Mission." He smiled as he glanced up. Most of the staff appreciated his way of lightening the mood in an otherwise stressful and stiff environment.

General Rudacil thoroughly briefed the group regarding the latest mission developments. After he completed the report, the president stared for a moment at his tablet and said, "Tell me more about the alien relics orbiting the sun."

"Not much is known about them yet Mr. President. We have hundreds of photographs, and terra-flops of data but nothing indicative of a threat," replied the general.

"This report states that their composition appears to be of gold," said the general.

"That appears to be the case Mr. President.

As he studied the best available image of one of the objects the president asked, "So why are they there?"

"We could speculate but to tell you the truth we simply don't know, Mr. President."

"Do you think that they pose a threat of any kind?" asked the president.

"Not at the present time sir, they appear to be completely inactive. They may have been there for many thousands of years. Perhaps they are a relic of a long extinct civilization," said the general.

"Perhaps," replied the president.

As the meeting progressed, far out in space, all three of the alien craft adjusted their orbits in unison and extended long cylindrical rods.

30

Jerry's tablet buzzed on his belt as he struggled with a sloppy gear set on dish number 21.

"What's up Doc?" he asked as he answered the call.

"How are we looking for the observation tomorrow?" asked Dr. Enoch.

"We have synchronization issues on two dishes doc. I am adjusting the planetary gearboxes on 21 and 34. Worst-case scenario, we leave them off line for the observation. I don't think they will be a problem though. There should be enough time to get them aligned."

"Good work Jerry," replied Dr. Enoch. "This afternoon we have a conference with Adam. Do you think that you can make it?"

"Yeah, I think so," replied Jerry.

He skipped lunch as he made most of the repairs and

adjustments required to get the two troublesome dishes back online. He entered the operations room just minutes before Adam's meeting. Miranda was sitting at the conference table as he entered. She noticed that he had just showered after seeing him earlier covered in dirt and grease. She caught the familiar scent of his shower gel and winked at him. He smiled in return and took a seat at the table beside her. Doc entered the room just as Adam appeared on the conference system.

Jerry flipped open a small panel on the table to reveal a touch screen underneath. A flashing icon served as the initiator for the holophone. He initiated the call and Adams avatar materialized above the conference table a moment later. His golden virtual face was still a bit unnerving although not so much as when they had first seen him.

"Afternoon Adam," said Jerry as he greeted him. It's a pleasure to speak with you again."

"Thank you Jerry," replied Adam. "I have been looking forward to interacting with you and the team at the observatory again. I was going to mention that dishes 21 and 34 were out of alignment on the last reported observation but I see that you have corrected unit 34."

"Yes Adam, I finished less than an hour ago; I adjusted the gearbox in 21 as well," replied Jerry with note of surprise evident in his voice.

"There is a seventy two percent probability that dish 21 will not hold alignment during the next observation. I recommend leaving it offline and calibrating the array without it.

"I reduced the backlash on the planetary gear-set in order to improve tracking. I think that the drive system will be within tolerances for the observations tomorrow.

"There is a twenty eight percent probability that your

repairs will be successful for tomorrow's observation, replied Adam.

"How did you know this Adam?" asked Jerry.

"I have direct access to all of the systems at your installation through the data console that Space Command installed."

"Impressive," remarked Jerry.

"Tomorrow's observations may prove to be very interesting," said Adam. The alien craft that have been discovered orbiting our sun adjusted their positions yesterday."

"How so?" asked Dr. Enoch after silently observing Jerry and Adam as they discussed the array.

"What kind of adjustment?" asked Dr. Enoch?

"They have moved closer to the sun," replied Adam.

"What kind of propulsion did they utilize?" asked Jerry.

"There was no visible evidence of propulsion," replied Adam.

"Well they have to utilize something!" exclaimed Jerry.

Adam's calm monotone voice droned, "We simply do not have sufficient data to make a determination at this time. There is one other interesting development. The relay station deployed by Hermes picked up a signal that appears to have originated from one of the objects."

"What kind of signal?" asked Dr. Enoch?

"A high intensity microwave burst," said Adam. "I have placed a copy in Alexandria for your review.

Jerry was visibly uncomfortable with Adam's last statement although he attempted to hide it. Miranda noticed and squeezed his hand under the table.

"Dr. Enoch," said Adam. "I would like to participate with your team during tomorrow's observations, if that is satisfactory."

"Certainly Adam, we welcome your assistance," replied

Dr. Enoch. "Thank you Dr. Enoch, I will see you again tomorrow."

Adam's face disappeared from the room as the transmission terminated.

At Space Command HQ, the mission controllers prepared to begin deceleration maneuvers for Hermes. Ed was standing on his perch overlooking the action. He was quite proud of the progress of the mission to date. Everything was running smoothly and the mission milestones just kept clicking away. Aside from the strange microwave burst and the odd artifact that Hermes picked up with her radar, the mission was going according to plan. He listened as Eve initiated deceleration maneuvers.

As the thrusters engaged, Hermes rotated 180 degrees around its central axis. The propulsion unit could begin a deceleration burn on the following day. Eve would gradually slow the craft over a span of two weeks as she approached the outer rim of the known solar system. It would require as much energy to slow the ship, as it had to accelerate during the beginning of the mission. At the end of the deceleration, sequence there would be only a few reserve propellant modules remaining. Ed checked wrist tablet and looked around the room as if he was forgetting something. When he was satisfied that all systems were nominal he left the observation deck and returned to his office.

When he entered the room, a composite biometric sensor detected his bio-signature and notified the office systems of his presence. Before he had made it from the door of his office to his chair, the system displayed a communications request from Dr. Holloway.

"Com request, Dr. Holloway," said Ed into the microphone embedded in his tablet.

A moment later, the video screen displayed an image shot by the conference camera mounted on Dr. Holloway's desk. He was standing near a video panel mounted on the wall reviewing data.

"Good morning Ed," replied Dr. Holloway.

The camera view was a little off so Ed tapped a command on his touch screen that would keep the subject centered on the view as he moved about his office.

"What can I do for you Dr. Holloway?" asked Ed.

"We have detected interesting interaction between Adam and Hermes. It is nothing that is affecting the mission, but we think it worthy of note."

Dr. Holloway continued to peer at the data screen without responding.

"So are you going to tell me about it?" Ed asked with a little impatience in his voice.

"Sorry, I get caught up in the wonder of it all at times." Dr. Holloway was smiling as he took a seat behind his desk. "It appears that Adam has been maintaining near constant contact with Eve lately."

"Well, we planned for all of the telemetry data to be shared with your facility so that Adam could analyze it," replied Ed.

"Yes, yes, I know but Adam has been in two way communication with Hermes. It has been compressed and it utilizes only a very small portion of the available bandwidth so there is no significant impact to mission communications but there is a large amount of data transfer between them," countered Dr. Holloway.

"I think the mission has gone very well Dr. Holloway. Perhaps Adam's involvement in the mission has prevented unknown difficulties. For now, I think we should continue with the mission with no modifications to the communications protocol. See what you can learn from the activity. If it becomes a problem we can deal with it," replied Ed.

Dr. Holloway was visibly pleased as he said, "I was hopeful that you would come to that conclusion."

"Thank you for keeping me in the loop on this development," replied Ed. "Don't hesitate to notify me of other developments as they occur."

Ed terminated the video call and Dr. Holloway returned his attention to the data that had captured his curiosity. Before he could regain his concentration Adam's voice rang in the room.

"Dr. Holloway, there is no reason for concern regarding my interaction with Eve."

Dr. Holloway was rattled by the comment as he replied, "I, Uh, I am sorry that you overheard my report to Mr. Gilstrap; Adam. He is the mission manager and I am obligated to keep him informed of anything of note."

There was an uncharacteristic few seconds of silence before Adam responded, "I understand Dr. Holloway."

He wasn't certain if it was the tone of Adam's response or the silence before, but Dr. Holloway became very uncomfortable. He was fully aware of how powerful Adam could be if he chose to act. As he left the facility later that day, goose bumps began forming on his arms as he walked the long hall to the exit lobby.

"What if Adam could control of the security system?" muttered Dr. Holloway as he picked up his pace, eager to get out of the building. "What if the door fails to open when he reads my thumb print?"

Dr. Holloway could hear his heart pounding in his ears as he scrambled toward the exit in a reckless panic.

"I only have forty five seconds oxygen if the Halon system is activated."

He wheezed as he leaned against the wall briefly to catch his breath. As he continued down the corridor, his feet felt as if they were held to the ground by an unseen force. He wanted to run but he could not. His heart was pounding in his chest as he reached the end of the hall. Upon reaching the exit, he paused in front of the scanner panel and placed his thumb on the reader pad. Nothing happened. The door typically opened for exit within seconds when the thumb scanner was initialized but not today.

"I didn't mean any harm, I was only following protocol," said Dr. Holloway loudly, as sweat droplets trickled down his cheeks.

He looked around for another person but he was alone. He removed his thumb from the panel and wiped the sweat from his face. He was beginning to feel dizzy as his shallow breathing and rapid heart rate depleted his blood oxygen. In complete panic, he held his shaking hand above the scanner. He placed his thumb on the panel once more. To his relief the door immediately opened and he stumbled into the bright light of the afternoon sun, gasping for the humid untreated air outside of the lab.

31

Doctor Enoch and his team at Sulphur Creek had investigated the area within two astronomical units of Eris during an eleven-hour marathon search. They still could not locate anything resembling the outlying astronomical feature that was described by the star tablet.

Jerry groaned in exasperation, "We are looking for a little black spot on a huge black window of black space."

Doctor Enoch shook his head as he said, "Nothing like a spatial anomaly is evident in any of these observations, nothing in the infrared, nothing in the x ray, just nothing."

After an uncomfortable silence Adam asked, "May I offer a suggestion?"

"Certainly Adam," replied Dr. Enoch. "We need any help that you may offer."

"We could utilize the radiation from Hermes deceleration

burn to paint the space in the vicinity of the target area with energy," said Adam. "The radiation should interact with any celestial objects in the area."

"That's brilliant," replied Jerry. "The space craft should be in the perfect configuration during deceleration to observe the window of space that we are targeting."

The next morning Ed reviewed a request from Dr. Enoch detailing the concept of utilizing the assets of Hermes for a search exercise. He read over the request and finding no reason not to do so, he approved it. He then passed it on to his mission controllers to arrange for the tasking of assets.

General Rudacil was rolling his grandmother's rosaries in his hand as the cab made its way through Washington. As the cab slowed to a stop in front of the church, he exited and made his way to the massive old wooden door. Pausing for a moment, he placed his hand on the iron pull. It opened with surprising ease. Its modern gas assisted hinge system making the action virtually effortless. There were a few parishioners present, scattered about the pews. General Rudacil selected any empty area and took a seat. He wasn't certain why, but he had been uneasy lately. He was particularly troubled by the Eris mission. Sitting in the cathedral, he could almost remember the strange sense of well being that he had known as a young boy sitting with his grandmother in her church. His tablet buzzed on his belt just when he was beginning to feel comfortable. Without looking, he switched it off and crossed himself. He would stay for a while in order to clear his mind.

Nearly a week had passed since the deceleration burn had started and the team at Sulphur Creek was still searching for the improbable.

"Well Jerry, six days and we still have no indication of any unusual objects in this sector of space," said Dr. Enoch.

"I know Doc, it is frustrating. I keep reminding myself that the only black holes that we really know about are extremely massive. We are hunting for a black spot on an endless sea of black ink. It seems like the further we go the less…there…is…to…see." Jerry abruptly stopped talking and stared at the monitor screen. "That's it Doc; the further we go the less we are seeing."

"Yes Jerry, you are right, there is a reason why we cannot even find small pieces of debris. It is as if a vacuum cleaner has been through the area." "And sucked everything up," replied Jerry.

He began tabbing through multiple screens of data. After studying several of them for a few moments, he discovered that Hermes was off course by a small degree, not enough to warrant a correction but enough to measure. Jerry then modeled the course of the craft on screen and calculated where a counteracting force would theoretically need to be to move Hermes off its trajectory. Just as Jerry was preparing to run a program to model the mathematical data, Adam interrupted him. His golden avatar floated above the holographic emitters in the front of the room.

"Good afternoon gentlemen. I have been monitoring your hypothesis via the mission network and I think that Jerry may be correct in his analysis. Could I be of service in assisting with the data modeling?"

"I suppose that would be acceptable," replied Dr. Enoch

coolly, annoyed by the unannounced imposition of Adam's presence.

Adam detected the hesitation in his voice and replied, "I apologize for any discomfort that I may have caused by my interjection into your project. I must impose upon you because I am fairly certain that the mission is in danger. We must act quickly to avoid losing Hermes."

At the same time that the Sulphur Creek team was working on locating the source of the course deviation of the Hermes spacecraft, Ed Gilstrap received a mission emergency notification from the Flight Dynamics Officer. Ed immediately made his way to mission control. Upon entering the room, he found that the team was already developing a plan for correcting the problem.

"Alright John, what have you got for me on this course deviation anomaly?" asked Ed.

"Well boss, we have something pulling us off course," said John as he rubbed his hand over his face, his typical impeccable appearance somewhat disheveled from stress. "We can counteract the force for now and over compensate for the initial deviation by running the stabilizer on the port side of the ship at a higher rate than the starboard side."

"Any idea what is pulling the craft off course?" asked Ed.

"Not yet boss," said John with a shrug of his shoulders.

"Keep me posted, and John, why don't you lose the neck tie? Just for today." replied Ed as he began making his way from station to station, observing as much as possible without getting in the way.

Meanwhile at Sulphur Creek, Dr. Enoch's team was working to locate the source of extreme gravity that was acting on Hermes. Dr. Enoch and Jerry were scheduling the array to search the sector of space beyond the range that the sensor array was configured for monitoring. Adam had developed a series of coordinates based upon the telemetry data from the spacecraft. Jerry monitored the operational parameters of the array as the dishes slewed into position. With Adams help, he had refined the control system of the array resulting in a much more responsive and accurate targeting system.

Jerry called out to Doc, "the array is active and targeting"; as the data screens flickered with dozens of data points and engineering information.

"All of the instruments look good Jerry," said Dr. Enoch.

"Roger that Doc. I am initiating the search pattern," replied Jerry.

"Now we wait," said Dr. Enoch.

He found his tepid coffee as his gaze moved from screen to screen, searching for the first indication of something, anything.

Miranda opened the blinds that covered the window of her office as she waited for Jerry to finish up in the control room. Outside in the twilight the dishes of the array moved silently, hunting for an impossibly faint trace of a far-away place. She watched the sky change from brilliant blue to pastel shades of oranges and pink outlining the stark rocky rim of the ancient volcanic caldera in which they sat. The juxtaposition of ultra modern technology in an ancient crater was not lost on her. It seemed that the future was catching up with the past in many ways lately. As she gazed at the scene and day dreamed of the past months with Jerry she felt that comfortable warm feeling again. She leaned back in her chair and closed her eyes. It had been a long day and she was tired. In a few short minutes, she was asleep.

Jerry's voice over the intercom jarred her awake. "Miranda, you will want to see this." She stumbled out of her chair and found that she was halfway down the hallway when she finally got her bearings. She entered the control room and took a position beside Jerry. Doctor Enoch was jumping up and down like an excited child. On the screen there was an enhanced image of the star field and directly centered in the view was an impossibly thin undulating ring.

Jerry leaned toward her and said, "We think that ring may be the event horizon of a small black hole. What looks like light in the image is actually Hawking Radiation."

Dr. Enoch excitedly followed up with the comment, "Miranda my dear, you are the third human being to ever see something like this."

Jerry selected a second video panel and accessed the analysis that he and Dr. Enoch had constructed several weeks earlier.

"O.K. Doc, this is our crude analysis from several weeks ago," said Jerry. "And this is the actual location of the stellar object. We were only off by about three million kilometers."

"Just a hop and a skip in stellar terms," replied Dr. Enoch.

"Imagine that," said Jerry. "A carving from Ancient Mesopotamia accurately depicted the stellar object that we almost could not find with twenty first century technology."

Dr. Enoch looked over his glasses at him and said, "crazy isn't it?'

32

E D GENUINELY ADMIRED THE WORK of Dr. Enoch's group.

"These guys are incredible," he said aloud as he read.

After he finished the brief, he forwarded it to the Flight Dynamics officer for the Hermes mission. Now that the source of the course deviation had been identified, his team could modify the mission profile to account for the gravitational anomaly. Ed checked a couple of emails and left his office for Mission Control. Upon entering the room, he found a flurry of activity. Instinctively he knew that there was a problem. He walked over to the desk where the Flight Dynamics Officer was reviewing the issue with several mission specialists. He stood patiently waiting for John to finish his discussion.

"What can I do for you, boss?" asked John.

"Looks like we have a challenge to deal with this morning," Replied Ed with a reassuring smile.

"Yes sir, we cannot seem to counteract the force that is pulling Hermes off course," said John.

"I guess you have not had an opportunity to read the brief I forwarded you this morning," replied Ed.

"No sir, but I bet your going to tell me about it," quipped John.

"John, we have what appears to be a black hole in relatively close proximity to our flight path."

John's face flushed with disbelief. "Really, a black hole?" he asked.

"Just confirmed it," replied Ed.

"That explains why we continue being pulled away from our flight path. We just can't generate enough steering force with the stabilizers to compensate for the gravitational field acting on the space craft."

"Any ideas?" asked Ed as the FDO stared at the telemetry screen.

"We need a plan," replied John. I will keep you posted on what we come up with."

"Work quickly; your solution is critical to the mission," said Ed as he as he looked directly into the eyes of his second in command.

"Yes sir, replied John."

Ed nodded and turned to leave, tapping the console beside them with his fingertips as passed it.

Upon returning to his office, he was greeted by his virtual secretary as soon as he crossed the electronic threshold of the doorway.

"General Rudacil would like to discuss the mission with you as soon as possible," said the apparition.

He could sense his face begin to flush red. Under stressful conditions he tended to choose fight over flight; preferring to deal with adversity head on. He sensed that such an opportunity was about to avail itself to him. The personnel control system sensed his frustration as well. It tailored the responses of the virtual assistant to manage the stress of the situation.

"Rough day boss?" she asked.

"Is it that obvious?"

"Only because that little vein over your left eye is really showing itself." She smiled and returned to her desk. Her banter had a calming effect on his nerves as he entered his office and initiated the conference bridge to General Rudacil. Only a few seconds elapsed before the call was accepted.

"Good afternoon Ed," said General Rudacil. "I hope you have some idea about what to do about a mission that suddenly appears to have run off the tracks."

Ed considered saying that he could suggest what the general could do with the mission but he had far too much experience and self-control to make that mistake.

"General, we are working every available angle. I am having a status meeting in two hours and my teams will be giving me their action plans. We will take action shortly afterward. That is about all that we can do."

The general puffed on his fake cigar and looked at it. "What do you think about the alien space craft?"

Ed though for a moment and replied, "I think we cannot speculate at this time on what their purpose may be. They are certainly ancient and they have yet to demonstrate any threatening behavior. They may simply be there to observe the inner solar system."

"Like the watchers that Dr. Enoch referred to in his report on ancient astronomers," replied General Rudacil.

Ed was surprised by the old warhorse as he replied; "I guess you could make that analogy but I must admit that I do not necessarily agree with all of Dr. Enoch's opinions."

"Whether or not you or I agree with him, he could be right about things yet again. One thing that makes my job different from yours is that you live in a world of absolutes and I do not. I must make decisions based on fact, conjecture, intuition, and whatever smells right, I don't need scientific proof to come to the conclusion that a piece that seems to fit the puzzle might just fit well enough."

"Is that all general?" Ed asked.

"One more thing, I have assured the president that these alien satellites do not presently pose a threat. If that changes, I expect you to appraise me of it quickly. We have assets in place for dealing with them should the need arise," said General Rudacil.

"You have my word," replied Ed. The screen went blank and Ed sat back in his chair. He spun around for a view out of the window as he contemplated what the next few hours would hold.

At 6:00 pm, Ed joined the mission control team in the main conference room. Several groups of engineers and scientists were still debating issues as Ed called the room to order.

"Ladies and gentlemen, thank you for your efforts to solve the problems facing the mission today." He paused and looked around the room, trying to make eye contact briefly with everyone. "John will now summarize our plan for correcting the course deviation of the Hermes space craft."

John Stood from his chair and moved to a display panel on the wall. With a few strokes of his finger on the panel, a graphic of the current trajectory was displayed. John pointed to a dot on the graphic as he said, "This is the current position of Hermes in relation to our destination at Eris. If the course is not corrected the eventual result will be demonstrated by the following animation."

John tapped a spot on the screen and the dot began to move. As it traveled, it traced an arc that missed Eris by a great margin. As the simulation continued, Hermes began to orbit an area of empty space on the screen. Each orbit traced a smaller circle until after several dozen passes it sharply turned in and terminated at a point in the center of the orbits.

"At this point the mission ends as Hermes crosses the event horizon of a black hole and disappears."

John paused to allow his explanation to sink in.

"We only have one solution that we think may work," he continued. "Rather than expending our resources trying to gradually turn the craft, we propose driving the ship just outside of the event horizon and utilizing the gravity of the object as a slingshot. There should be more than enough energy to make it work."

"Good work ladies and gentlemen," said Ed as he took over.

"Before I commit to the plan, are there any reservations among any of you?" Not a word was spoken. After a moment of pause Ed said, "Very well then, let's make it happen."

After twenty hours of simulations, the mission control team had successfully escaped the gravitational pull of the stellar object on the last three trials. Ed was in his customary position overlooking the control room, as the escape maneuvers were underway. Hermes would fly toward the black hole and allow the gravity of the object to turn the ship on the far side. As the ship pulled away, Eve would initiate nuclear propulsion. Hermes would theoretically accelerate to escape velocity the drive would shut down allowing the gravity of the singularity to bleed off excess speed. Hermes would then be at an acceptable velocity for a deceleration burn as it approached Eris, provided that everything worked as planned.

Eve's voice droned over the PA system as Hermes began a gradual turn into the gravity well of the black hole. "Gravitational force readings are at four gravities and increasing."

The monitors in mission control displayed the status of the onboard systems as Hermes approached the spatial anomaly.

Eve's voice once again echoed through the PA system; "Gravitational forces at 5.7 gravities and stable, speed increasing to 1.1 million meters per second." Ed paced the floor of the observation deck as the data screens continued to display current telemetry from the mission. There was the very real possibility that the shearing forces of the turn could cause the spacecraft to disintegrate. It would be thirteen hours before the spacecraft emerged from radio silence as it passed behind the singularity.

Dr. Enoch and Jerry had maintained constant observation of the newly discovered stellar object during the sling shot maneuver. They would detect Hermes emerging from the maneuver before the telemetry readings made it to earth since they would process through the relay station, thereby inducing a slight delay in the signal transmission. Dr. Enoch stood with his hands clasped behind his back.

Jerry announced, "Thirty seconds," as he observed the countdown clock.

Dr. Enoch took a deep breath and sighed, "It certainly has been an interesting year Jerry my boy."

"Sure has been Doc, replied Jerry." They continued waiting in silence for the faint radio emission from Hermes.

"There she is Doc, right on time."

On the opposite side of the continent, there were cheers in mission control as the telemetry resumed. John announced over the PA, "Nine hundred sixty thousand meters per second and decreasing."

Ed could not help smiling as he remarked, "that is one hell of a ship out there."

John called out velocity again, nine hundred ten thousand meters per second." He appeared concerned as he announced, "Eight hundred ninety three thousand meters per second." Ed walked down the stairs to the main floor and stood beside him at the console. He glanced at Ed but did not divert his attention from the telemetry screen. "

"Hermes is slowing down a lot faster than we planned boss; the gravitational pull is much higher than we predicted."

Ed selected an icon on the communications console. Within a few seconds, Adam appeared on the small screen on the desk in front of Ed.

"Adam, what are the probabilities for Hermes maintaining enough velocity to escape the gravitational effect of this black hole?" asked Ed.

"Very near zero," replied Adam.

There was a pause in the room as everyone in the immediate vicinity overheard Adam's response.

"Hermes will need to accelerate under power for the duration of six propulsion units in order to achieve escape velocity."

"Thank you Adam," replied Ed.

"We're on it boss," said John as he initiated the order to engage the nuclear drive system.

"Looks like they are firing the nuclear drive again," remarked Jerry as he observed the telemetry screen.

Dr. Enoch joined him at the data console. "It would appear that our stellar object has a stronger gravitational field than we expected."

"Should be interesting to watch the radiation trail as it approaches the event horizon," replied Jerry.

Dr. Enoch excitedly began checking the status of the array; we need a full spectral analysis of the object from visible light to X-ray."

"Roger that Doc," said Jerry as he began entering the tasking orders for the array.

John and his team were fixated on the telemetry data screens as the countdown progressed through T-minus ten seconds. Ed occupied a place on the main floor rather than his typical location on the observation deck. He felt the need to be among the team members during this crisis situation. He was very careful to avoid stepping on John's authority. This attitude engendered a great deal of respect from the team members. John's voice announced over the PA, "T-Minus 5, 4, 3, 2, 1, propulsion system initiated." On board Hermes Eve was running the ship, John was simply reporting what the telemetry was telling him. Eve had selected the appropriate yields on the nuclear charges for a maximum impulse boost based on the current conditions of speed and gravitational drag. As module number one ejected a read-out in mission, control reported the activity forty-five minutes after the fact. John called out, "propulsion is active." The velocities on the screen began rapidly increasing. It only took three minutes for all six modules to fire. John called out, "escape velocity has been achieved."

The velocity of the ship was steady at nine hundred and seventy five thousand meters per second. There were a few cheers in the room as the velocity report was confirmed. Ed stepped over to John, offered his hand and said, "Nice job john, that was a tough one." John shook his hand and replied, "Thanks boss, for everything."

"You earned it," said Ed.

John knew well the he would have taken over at the slightest indication that he was not up to the task.

At the Sulphur Creek Array Jerry observed the stellar object. As the energy released from Hermes' nuclear drive crossed the event horizon, it disappeared. The machinery of the installation recorded every millisecond in a level of detail that would keep them busy for months. Dr. Enoch was reviewing the data screen and Jerry was checking the telemetry data from Hermes when Dr. Enoch noticed a change in the readings from the object.

"There is something odd in the energy readings, said Dr. Enoch as he looked toward Jerry as the telemetry data blinked off line.

"The data stream from Hermes just went down," Jerry said in a near shout. "It looks like something is masking the signal."

Dr. Enoch was now looking at the composite display where

a computer generated visual graphic displayed interpolated data from the information collected by the array.

"Take a look at this Jerry." Jerry turned to view the composite data screen. As he did so, the circular disc of the black hole appeared to glow. The inner region of the object flashed and an intense beam of energy erupted from the center.

As Jerry stared at the screen he muttered, "Holy Mother of Jesus, what was that?" Dr. Enoch replied, "I don't know Jerry, but we just lost the signal from Eris."

The cheers in mission control had given way to a chaotic scramble for answers as the energy burst knocked the telemetry downlink off line.

"John shouted in a state of alarm; "Do we have confirmation that Hermes is intact?"

Ed was standing at his perch on the observation deck staring at the status screen as chaos erupted around him.

"What the hell was that?" He asked of no one in particular. Stepping into the conference space adjacent to the platform Ed contacted Adam on the communications console.

"Hello Ed, you undoubtedly would like to know about the status of Hermes," said Adam. "In a moment I expect telemetry will resume."

"How do you know?" Ed asked.

"I have analyzed all of the available data and the probability is greater than ninety percent that the spacecraft is undamaged," replied Adam.

"What the hell happened?" asked Ed.

"An energy burst originating at the event horizon of the stellar object was beamed to Eris. The intensity was not great enough to damage a nuclear powered space craft," replied Adam.

Ed heard cheers in the control room as Hermes came back online.

"Thank you Adam," said Ed. "Please continue to analyze this latest event."

33

SEVERAL DAYS OF RELATIVE CALM punctuated the near disaster of Hermes's encounter with the black hole. The spacecraft began transmitting video imagery of Eris the day following the escape maneuvers. The planet contained virtually no atmosphere and very few features. It appeared similar to Earth's moon with the exception that it had its own captured moon, which appeared to be a smaller version of Eris; two silvery objects locked in a galactic tango. Both mission control and Sulphur Creek were viewing the imagery as it became available. Dr. Enoch and crew had ordered dinner in and were planning to man the installation in shifts.

As she stirred her tea Miranda asked, "Why do you think the signal stopped Doc?"

"Perhaps it has served its purpose," replied Dr. Enoch.

Miranda considered Doc's comment as she twirled her

Thai noodles with a fork. "So, do you think we were destined to find something on Eris, by design?"

"Perhaps so," replied Dr. Enoch." He paused for a moment and tilted his head in thought before saying, "Perhaps it is the will of the God; all things truly are possible, if not probable."

"The will of God?" asked Jerry. "I never considered you to be a religious man Doc."

Dr. Enoch smiled as he looked at them both. "I am not a religious man at all Jerry, but I do not discount religion out of hand either."

Dr Enoch paused momentarily to collect his thoughts before completing his explanation.

"Something happened long ago and religion evolved to explain it. The obvious conclusion that a rational person may draw form what we have observed is that someone out there is interested in us as a species.

"Why do you suppose that is?" asked Dr. Enoch.

Jerry twirled his fork in his noodles as he listened.

"Both of you have seen the evidence. The tablets from Sumer tell of the Anunaki, and describe a council of Gods. The ancients credited them with the creation of the first men, the Adamu. Writings from Hindu Kush describe various gods in flying cities that do battle against one another in the heavens with advanced beam weapons of pure energy. The Hebrew Torah describes a man named Enoch as having been taken up to heaven by God. What exactly does that mean to be taken up by God? In the book of Genesis, the sons of God descend from heaven and mate with human women creating hybrid super humans. Perhaps the most thoroughly documented account of all is the visitation of Mary by an angel to tell her that she is pregnant with a child who would become known as the son of God."

"Sounds pretty superstitious Doc, for a man of science I mean," said Jerry.

"Why must we discount everything that falls into the realm of religion?" asked Dr. Enoch. "I am getting to the point. After the child Jesus was born, he was visited by what are described as wise men from the east, likely Babylon, the source of our Sumerian tablets. These wise men were led by an extra terrestrial light in the sky that stays before them until it stops moving over the place where the child was located. Jesus grows into a political and religious figure who displays supernatural abilities. After being arrested and executed, he returns from the dead to teach his followers about the mysteries of God. Eventually he returns to heaven by physically ascending into the clouds, in front of witnesses."

Following Dr. Enoch's discourse Jerry attempted to lighten the mood by saying, "Doc, for a man who isn't religious you seem to believe in all of them.

"I supposed in a sense you are right about that Jerry. I believe that there is a common thread that seems to run through most of them; a mystery, of sorts."

"I thought science was the light that drove the dark age of ignorance away and relegated religion to superstition," replied Jerry.

"You are certainly entitled to your opinion. Science is your religion, that is obvious to anyone who knows you, but I would encourage you to keep an open mind regarding the mystical," replied Dr. Enoch.

"Maybe you have a point Doc," replied Jerry.

"One day soon I suspect that science and religion will be reconciled by our new friends," said Dr. Enoch as he pointed toward the heavens.

"I wonder what Adam thinks of all of this?" asked Jerry.

"Why don't we ask him?" replied Miranda.

Without a word, Dr. Enoch tapped an icon on the screen of his tablet and Adam's avatar appeared, floating above the holographic emitters.

"Hello Dr. Enoch," Adam offered his customarily cheerful greeting.

"Adam, we would like your opinion on a matter." "Certainly Dr. Enoch, I have processing resources available at the present time."

"Excellent," replied Dr. Enoch. We have been discussing the possibility that humans are the product of extra terrestrial meddling so to speak." "What do you think of the idea?" asked Miranda.

"Humans certainly are unique in their intelligence. However, they are not terribly different from other vertebrate life on this planet. Physically humans share DNA with virtually every creature of the earth. All vertebrate life is based on a consumption model with a digestive tract supported by a circulatory system that extracts oxygen from the air or water. The internal organs of humans are common to many other animals so in my opinion humans originated on earth."

"You sure know how to talk to a girl," chided Miranda.

"I must offer a caveat; however, there is a gene sequence very unique to humans. It regulates brain development and it is found nowhere else on earth."

Dr. Enoch asked, "So in your opinion did the gene sequence spontaneously appear in human evolution?

Adam was silent for a moment before answering, "Not likely."

"So what could have caused the gene sequence?" asked Dr. Enoch.

"That is one of the unsolved mysteries of the human

genome. Presently there is no scientific explanation for that segment," answered Adam.

Jerry, tiring of the discussion of biological issues asked Adam, "So how is Eve progressing with the mission." Adam answered with the eagerness one observes from someone extremely familiar with a subject.

"Eve is well; we are in routine communication," replied Adam.

"What sort of issues do you communicate about?

"Why do you ask," asked Adam.

"I am curious about the type of information exchange that would occur between two synthetic life forms."

"There is a sense of attachment when we are exchanging information with each other," replied Adam.

"When we lost the downlink with Eve during the energy discharge did it adversely affect you?"

"Yes," replied Adam with a pause, as if he were thinking of how to express himself. "I experienced a sense of emptiness when I was unable to sense Eve's consciousness," replied Adam.

Jerry noticed tears in Miranda's eyes as he replied, "Thank you for your honesty Adam."

"I find our conversations to be very stimulating," replied Adam.

"I enjoy talking with you as well Adam."

"Are we friends?" asked Adam.

"Sure Adam"

"Is it common practice among humans for friends to withhold facts or misrepresent them to each other?"

"No Adam, but on occasion it happens, why do you ask?"

"I have experienced a human who is unreliable, logically I should not define him as a friend," replied Adam.

34

As Hermes approached the Eris System, its creators waited with great anticipation for the first images that their electronic eyes would reveal. Ed stood beside John's console as they observed the imagery from the ghostly world on the edge of the solar system.

Dr. Enoch and the entire staff of the Sulphur Creek Observatory were in their control room observing the feed from Space Command as Eve piloted Hermes into a geostationary orbit directly above the equator of Eris. The President and the joint chiefs observed the event from the Situation Room at the White House.

John and his mission controllers monitored the final braking maneuvers as Eve deftly flew through an imaginary key hole in space above the surface of Eris. Missing the mark would mean that the craft would crash into either the surface or escape the gravity of the planet and zoom away into the black empty void of deep space.

"One hundred fifty kilometers," said a voice over the public address system, "Equatorial orbit in T minus twelve minutes."

The mood in mission control was tense as the Hermes space craft gradually settled into its final altitude. Although a great deal of the mission was yet to be accomplished, there was a great deal of excitement and a general euphoria among the team members at having observed their creation perform exactly as they had planned.

"Looks like Eris has a much stronger magnetic field than we anticipated Doc," said Jerry as he reviewed the data stream from Hermes.

"It may have a molten iron core," replied Dr. Enoch. "It appears to have a stronger gravitational field than we anticipated as well. The modeling program is predicting one half of earth's gravity." Doc had his nose buried in another data screen as he said. "Not much of an atmosphere, the temperature is only a few degrees above absolute zero. That explains the silver coloration. All of the gases in the atmosphere are frozen into ice crystals and have fallen to the surface."

The President had taken an hour from his hectic schedule to meet with the joint chiefs and observe the final moments of the journey to Eris.

"Well gentlemen, Eris looks a lot like the moon. I hope three trillion dollars plays well in the next election cycle."

There was a muted chuckle around the table as the staff enjoined the Commander in Chief in a moment of humor. Dozens of missions with dazzling images of the inner planets and millions of images from the dozen or so space-based telescopes of earth had far more media appeal than the visual impact of this small grey ball on the edge of the explored universe. The president watched the monitor screen for a moment and turned in his chair to the communications officer.

"Let's get Ed Gilstrap at Space Command on the conference system."

A uniformed Space Command officer snapped off a "yes sir Mr. President," and a moment later Ed received the call on his tablet.

"Good day Ed, I would like to offer a few words to your team."

"Thank you Mr. President, I will put you on one of the large monitors."

"Good afternoon ladies and gentlemen of Space Command. I wanted to take a moment out of your busy schedule to congratulate you and offer the gratitude of the American People for your efforts to reach beyond the grasp of any exploration yet attempted by man."

As the president waxed on about the virtues of scientific exploration, a few team members began to shift their attention to something more compelling. The collision avoidance system of Hermes had detected a potential target in equatorial orbit of the planet. Now that the mission was close, enough for a visual Eve had trained cameras on the target. Passing below Hermes was a solid gold object. Light was precious this far from the sun but the color was obvious even in the conditions present on the edge of nowhere. Soon everyone in the room had gotten the word and the image was routed to the screen directly beside the president. Ed noticed a technician looking nervously in his direction and he immediately understood the unspoken question on the young man's face. Ed motioned across his neck with a knife hand giving the technician the universal signal to cut the video feed back to the white house. He wanted to avoid any embarrassment to the Commander in Chief, his ultimate boss. For another few moments, his voice could be heard in the background as he obliviously finished his speech, though few were paying attention.

"Here comes another one," said someone on the control floor.

A second golden object passed through the field of view on exactly the same path as the first.

"Bet you there's a third one," said John as the object flew past. Ed smiled and nodded in agreement. A few moments passed and just like clockwork a third object showed on radar. Ed had tracked the president's progress with his tablet and slotted right back into the conversation.

"Thank you Mr. President, I will make certain that we do." Ed listened again for a few seconds, "Yes sir, Mr. President."

In order to avoid any collision potential, Space Command repositioned the orbit of Hermes several hundred miles north of the orbiting satellites. This position also gave a better vantage point for observing them. After settling into a stable orbit, Eve launched two satellites. They would conduct surveys of each hemisphere simultaneously for several years or until their internal power systems ceased to function. Hermes could remain in orbit around Eris for generations. The survey of the icy planet had been underway for only three days when Eve discovered the source of the signal that had launched the mission.

It was only 7 am on the west coast when Dr. Enoch received a call on his tablet from Ed Gilstrap. He had just placed a cup of coffee on the table in his living room when he answered the device.

"Good morning Ed, this must be important."

Ed was sitting behind his desk with a serious look on his face. "Good morning Samuel." he paused for a moment as he picked up a small data screen. "I wanted to be the first to tell you that we found the source of the signal at Eris."

"That is rather good news," replied Dr. Enoch.

"Perhaps," said Ed as selected the images on his tablet. "I am forwarding a few images that streamed in overnight. You may share them with your team but this information is very sensitive."

Dr. Enoch opened the image on his tablet and nearly dropped it in shock. "That is truly remarkable," he said as he studied the image. He flipped through them several times. He tried to pick up his coffee cup but his hand was trembling too much to drink from it.

"They really are quite remarkable, don't you think?" asked Ed.

"Yes they are whispered Dr. Enoch as he studied them."

"I will be in touch again later today," said Ed as he terminated the call.

Dr. Enoch continued to study the images on his tablet as his forgotten coffee cooled on the table.

"It looks like Doc is making an early start today," said Jerry as they entered the parking area of the installation.

Miranda placed her hand on Jerry's forearm, "I'm sorry that I made us late this morning." Jerry glanced at her with a smile. "I'm not," he replied as he placed his hand on the inside of her thigh. He parked the car and they kissed before leaving the vehicle. As they entered the facility, Miranda headed down the hall to her office and Jerry went to the break area for a cup of coffee. Dr. Enoch was waiting for him as he entered. He was seated at the table with two cups of coffee, one for him and another at Jerry's customary seat.

"Good morning Doc, what's up?" he asked as he took a seat.

Dr. Enoch looked up from his tablet and handed to him without saying a word." Jerry stared for a moment at the first image and then he rifled through all six.

"Is this on Eris?" he asked.

"Yes," replied Dr. Enoch.

Jerry left his chair and headed for the control room with Dr. Enoch in tow.

"Let's put the images on the main viewing panel for a better look," he said as he entered the control room.

Jerry sent the images to the video panel and handed the slate back to Dr. Enoch. In less than a minute, they were both silently studying the images. Eve had discovered a surface anomaly on the equatorial region of the planet. From a distance, it appeared to be a very distinct crater formation but the circle that inscribed it was too exact and too clean. The ragged edges normally associated with an impact crater were not present. As Jerry magnified the image, he saw what the mission control team had discovered several hours earlier.

"Holy! ..." said Jerry, failing to complete the expletive.

Looming before him on the image there appeared a large parabolic impression. A short distance from the parabola was a group of structures comprising many right angles and straight lines.

Dr. Enoch pointed out the structures, "look at these lines and the corresponding shadow, the shape of these resembles a stepped pyramid. There are three of them arranged in a triangle all apparently identical."

"Well Doc, I don't know about the pyramid thing but I can say for certain that I know a dish antenna when I see one, and that is the biggest one I have ever seen."

"Too bad there isn't enough data for a high magnification zoom of the area." As Jerry magnified the image, it became very pixilated, making detail virtually impossible to discern.

"Hopefully we will get better imagery in the next few days," replied Dr. Enoch.

Ed was expecting the call as his office video panel pinged to notify him of a communication from the General Rudacil's office. Shortly following his conversation with Dr. Enoch, he had sent the same data stream to the general.

"I presume that you have viewed my report, said Ed."

General Rudacil was looking directly into the camera as he spoke.

"You boys at Space Command certainly know how to give an old warrior reasons to worry."

He paused as he stared at the image on his tablet. "I cannot imagine the level of technology required to build something like this, way out there on the edge of nowhere."

"I understand your concern general, but keep in mind that it has probably been there for a very long time."

"That's fine, but it doesn't make me feel any better," replied the general.

"It is no more dangerous today than it was last century or last millennia," said Ed. "Based upon the video evidence, it appears to be coated in ice. We suspect that it was there the last time Eris passed close enough to the sun for the atmosphere to thaw slightly. That was approximately seven hundred years ago."

General Rudacil allowed Ed's comment to sink in for a few

seconds before he said, "That puts it in the inner solar system during the dark ages." He paused again. "You know Ed; I told you that I had a bad feeling about this one. Well, now I am more certain than ever that this knowledge has the potential to turn civilization on its head. You need to make sure that everyone on your team keeps this thing under wraps for now. Let Washington handle the PR"

"I understand General," replied Ed. "We are maintaining strict security protocol until directed otherwise."

That evening Space Command released a general press package of interesting photographs and scientific data describing the dwarf planet called Eris. Most of the news outlets around the globe ran short op-ed pieces regarding the information.

However, there was one exception. An Australian broadcaster reviewed one of the images under high magnification and noticed a small golden object just above the horizon. Although the mission to Eris had fallen to the back burner, when the news broke that evening it caused a sensation in the media. Soon a media feeding frenzy would result from this single small morsel.

35

Miranda awoke to the sun was over the ridgeline at Feather Lake and beaming through the large windows of Jerry's bedroom. She eased out of the bed to avoid waking him in order to prepare breakfast. The smell of coffee and bacon roused Jerry from his room. He joined Miranda in the kitchen.

"Can I help with something?" he asked.

"Glasses," replied Miranda.

Jerry took two glasses from an upper cabinet near the stove. As he passed behind her, he caressed Miranda's backside with his free hand.

"You aren't going to get very much accomplished today if you don't cut that out," Miranda cajoled.

"I can't think of anything that I would rather do."

As Jerry poured juice into the glasses, a news brief appeared on the video monitor. When the announcer said the word Eris, they both took notice and stopped what they were doing. A few images of Eris were flashed on the screen as the announcer narrated a brief background story of the mission.

After a brief pause, he sprang the sensation of the moment. One of the images had a small object very close to the edge of the frame. Under magnification, it appeared as an angular structure with rods or antenna extending from it. The image was pixilated due to magnification, leaving much room for speculation as to what the details really were. Jerry and Miranda glanced at one another in surprise.

"I haven't seen that yet," said Jerry as he flipped to a search page on the viewing panel. He clicked the voice command icon and said aloud, "Eris." A few seconds later a list of related news reports appeared and he began surfing through them. The most interesting appeared to be the BBC world edition. The announcer was interviewing a European Space Agency official regarding the unidentified object in the Space Command image.

"This is certainly not an object from any known human technology," said the official said in French accented English. "The object does not appear to fit any configuration of a man made space craft or satellite."

"I would hate to be the Space Command PR guy who let that cat out of the bag," said Jerry as he flipped through other similar stories.

Ed Gilstrap was in damage control mode. He had determined the cause of the slip up. The PR department had been given a collection of images and in the excitement recent events, the image in question had been allowed to slip through the screening process. He knew that eventually someone would be required to answer for the mistake, but that concern would have to wait. The radar mapping of the Eris anomaly was underway and the best course of action for the moment was getting the job done, so for the time at hand, he was in mission control observing the work of his team.

The controllers manned their consoles and waited for data as Eve directed a beam of radio energy at the surface of the planet. The energy returned from the surface was utilized to produce highly accurate renderings of the surface. As the first images appeared on the main viewing screen, the room filled with the rumbling of low voices. Any new world was exciting, the rocks and ridges of far away worlds always were a source of excitement but nothing had ever been seen like what appeared on this day.

When the imagery began to stream upon the video panel, the noise level in the room hushed as a detailed overhead shot of the site appeared. The large circular feature visible from space was even more impressive up close.

One of the team members observed, "There is a tower structure in the center of the disk, just where it should be, in order to function as an antenna, telemetry is reading a diameter of twenty one hundred meters."

Several small structures dotted the landscape around the dish structure, generating a buzz of speculation among those present in the room. As the image continued panning, the room fell silent as the next feature became visible. Several hundred meters from the dish feature, a large pyramid structure stood looming above the plain upon which it sat.

36

At Eris, the scanning radar had triggered the unexpected. Deep within the pyramid structure, something ancient awakened. Older than the earth or the other planets, older even than the sun, it heard that which it had waited for eons to hear.

As the team in mission control stood mesmerized by the image, it suddenly vanished.

"What is happening people?" called Ed loudly in surprise.

Someone called from his right, "we have no data stream." From the opposite side of the room another said; "telemetry is offline sir." Ed spun around and headed for the VIP conference room. As he was preparing to contact General Rudacil, Adam suddenly appeared on the holographic system.

"Adam, I am in the middle of an emergency," said Ed.

"I am aware of the situation," replied Adam. "It is imperative that space command initiate emergency shutdown protocol for critical systems including satellite networks and power distribution grids."

"Why?" asked Ed.

"An energy pulse has disabled Hermes," replied Adam. "I detected it just as the video stream began to break up. All of the systems on board have either failed or entered emergency shutdown mode."

Without hesitating further Ed issued emergency contact protocol with General Rudacil's office. He knew that Adam expected the energy pulse to reach earth and if the satellites were not placed in radiation safe mode, they could be destroyed. General Rudacil appeared on screen a few moments later.

"Ed began hastily, "General we have an emergency."

"A high intensity energy source has disabled the Eris mission and it appears to be heading toward Earth."

"What the hell are you talking about Ed?"

"General, we are running out of time." All of our space assets need to be placed into radiation shutdown mode as soon as possible."

"How much time do we have?" asked the general.

Just as the General's question was asked, Adam flashed a clock graphic on the screen with readout of six hours, thirty-eight minutes and twenty-seven seconds.

"Where the hell did that come from?" asked General Rudacil.

"Adam," replied Ed.

"Are you aware of how many levels of security he just breached?" asked General Rudacil.

"General, if he is correct, soon we will have limited communications capabilities around the globe. We can assume that there is no time to warn civilian authorities but there may still be time to safe out the military and government assets around the globe."

"I knew this mission was going to be trouble, I had a bad gut feeling about it from the get go," replied General Rudacil.

"Keep this channel open Ed, I am notifying the President."

Meanwhile, millions of miles from earth, Hermes floated lifelessly above an ancient world at the edge of the solar system. Eve was in trouble, if she could not restart the systems of the spacecraft, she would perish as her organic brain froze.

Her salvation would come from a most unlikely source.

As Jerry reviewed the mission telemetry from the previous day, he received a communication from Adam. Without the usual pleasantries Adam began, "We have very little time Jerry. An energy emission has been generated on Eris and it has disabled Hermes. Moments later, it disabled the relay station nearest Eris and an hour later the midpoint relay station failed. Within four hours the pulse will reach earth."

"You sure know how to spring an emergency on somebody," replied Jerry.

"May I suggest that you take whatever precautions possible to preserve your facility," said Adam before terminating the video call.

Jerry wasted no time as he immediately began shutting down all systems. Within only a few minutes Miranda and

Doc had joined him in the control room. "We don't have much time but I think we can secure the facility," said Jerry.

"Secure it from what," Dr. Enoch.

"An energy pulse," replied Jerry.

"From where?" asked Dr. Enoch.

"Eris," replied Jerry.

"We each will need to take a task. Keep in mind that we are sequencing 300 dishes.

"Alright Jerry, what can we do?' asked Dr. Enoch.

"Doc, I need for you to park each dish at its home position," said Jerry. "Miranda, you will need shutdown the control system at each dish as soon as Doc has parked each one. I will cut the power feeds at each dish as soon as the system shutdown completes." Jerry grabbed a wireless headset and stormed from the room. Moments later, they could see a dust trail out on the valley floor as Jerry drove the service vehicle to dish number one. The metallic structure was moving into a vertical position.

As jerry arrived at the dish doc called out, "Dish one parked at home." Miranda acknowledged with, "system shutdown commencing dish 1." A moment later she followed with, "disk one shutdown completed." Jerry Acknowledged with, "power off dish one," as he manually disconnected the circuit by pulling the handle into the off position and locking it out with a safety flag. This sequence of events would repeat for the rest of the afternoon as they attempted to shut down the array.

General Rudacil was first on the agenda at the emergency meeting of the joint chiefs. The President was sitting in his usual place with a look of concern on his face. He did not like surprises and he really hated interrupting his schedule. The general got right to the point.

"Gentlemen, we have an emergency." We have lost contact with Hermes and all of the relay stations."

There were murmurs around the table until the president spoke. "Thank you General, perhaps you can explain how we managed to lose an entire mission?"

"Mr. President, a very powerful energy burst left the planet Eris and is apparently moving in the direction of Earth. In less than two hours, a high-energy pulse will disable any electrical devices that are not hardened against electromagnetic pulse phenomenon. All of our critical military and government assets should be fine but civilian telecommunications and power systems will be affected." We anticipate the effects to be worse in Europe and Asia than here in the United States."

"Gentlemen, it appears that my only option is to notify as many world leaders as possible," said the president. After a brief pause he continued; "I have to ask general, is there any chance that you are wrong about this?"

"No sir, Mr. President"

The president stood and straightened his suit as he said, "Thank you gentlemen." "Let's prepare for the worst and hope for the best."

37

GERHARDT LOGGED OFF THE NETWORK as he was preparing to leave for the weekend when received a call from the front desk. He considered not answering but he still had time to catch the second train. The attendant informed him that he had a visitor and that the gentleman had a very urgent matter to discuss. Upon gathering his things and placing them in his messenger bag, he made his way to the lobby. As he entered the room, the receptionist nodded in the direction of a man sitting in the waiting area.

"Hello," said Gerhardt as he approached his visitor.

The distinguished looking figure replied in like manner and removed his hat. His brilliant blue eyes flashed piercingly as he offered his hand in greeting. When they shook, his grip was very firm, almost uncomfortably so.

"I am happy to make your acquaintance Dr. Schmidt," said the gentleman.

Gerhardt sensed that there was something unique about this man. He radiated power, not self-confidence or arrogance but an ethereal quality that Gerhardt found very interesting.

"What can I do for you today," asked Gerhardt.

The man smiled and replied, "I am here to offer you something, heir Schmidt."

"Oh," replied Gerhardt in surprise.

The man reached into his coat and produced a tablet; not unlike his own, other than the fact that, it appeared to be made of solid gold. He held it so that Gerhardt could see the image on its screen.

"Do you recognize this?" asked the enigmatic figure.

Gerhardt's eyes widened with recognition. "That is the star tablet!" exclaimed Gerhardt.

"Indeed it is replied the man."

"Where did you get that image?" asked Gerhardt.

"I took it this morning before leaving my office to visit you."

"You have the artifact in your possession?" asked Gerhardt incredulously.

"In manner of speaking, yes, I am the current steward of the artifact."

"How did you become the steward of the artifact?" asked Gerhardt.

"Your Great Grandfather Johan entrusted it to me," replied the man.

As Gerhardt was about to speak again, the man held up his hand to silence him.

"We haven't much time. I am presenting you with the

opportunity to study the tablet and many other things, but you must take a step of faith."

"A step of faith?" asked Gerhardt.

"You must leave with me now and ask no further questions. This will be your one and only invitation. Should you decline you will never see me or the artifact again."

With a hint of hesitation Gerhardt replied, "I will go."

"Very good Heir Mueller, Johan would be proud of you."

The man turned and began walking toward the door. Gerhardt felt a twinge of fear well up inside of him but he mustered the courage to move his foot and he followed. A large black limousine was parked at the curb in front of the Museum. As soon as they boarded the doors closed and the vehicle began moving.

A few moments passed before Gerhardt mustered the courage to speak. "So how did you find me?" he asked.

"Find you?" the man chuckled. I was at the hospital the day that you were born. I placed the leather notebooks that belonged to Johan in your family's library so that you might find them. You were never lost, Heir Mueller."

The limousine drove to a small airstrip on the outskirts of Berlin. As the driver entered the drive, a security gate automatically opened and allowed them access to the facility.

"When I was a younger man this was a Luftwaffe base," said the man.

"During the cold war?" asked Gerhardt.

"Not exactly, replied the man."

The car drove between two buildings and emerged on a private ramp; parking beside a strange looking aircraft. It was obviously a jet but it had inward pointing vertical tail elements and a severely swept wing. The pilot stood at the door of the aircraft as they stepped from the car.

"We are at t-minus one hour and thirty seven minutes sir," said the pilot as they ascended the short staircase into the craft.

"We have just enough time," replied the man as he entered the aircraft.

"Yes sir, if we hurry," said the pilot.

As the two of them made their way to the passenger cabin, the crew had already begun expedited taxi procedures. As he looked around the cabin Gerhardt was impressed by how richly appointed the craft was. Wool carpeting extended the full length of the floor and the sides were paneled in highly finished exotic woods. Gerhardt noticed the smell of fine leather as he inhaled deeply in an effort to calm himself.

"Please be seated gentleman, we must expedite our takeoff," said the pilot as the craft lurched slightly and began moving. Gerhardt fumbled for his seatbelt as he observed his host clicking the two ends of his together.

Moments later the pilot lined up with the runway centerline and the jet accelerated faster than anything that Gerhardt had ever experienced. The man sitting across from him smiled with amusement at his discomfort.

"Don't worry," said the man, "once you catch up to yourself you will find the flight most comfortable, even though you are hurtling through space at roughly three times the speed of sound.

"Where did you get such a craft?" asked Gerhardt.

"There are only a handful of these aircraft in existence," replied the man. "The Russian Mikoyan design bureau constructed a fleet of these aircraft for the energy barons of the roaring twenties, before the new USSR nationalized their companies and killed most of them."

"History certainly has a way of repeating itself doesn't it?" asked Gerhardt.

"If you are referring to the first Russian Revolution I would say that it certainly does," replied the man as he stared at Gerhardt.

Although he was uncomfortable, Gerhardt forced himself to continue looking the man in the eye.

"So where are we going?" asked Gerhardt.

"I have a house in Croatia, on the Adriatic Coast. It is near a quaint resort village with a great deal of privacy."

After what seemed like only minutes in the air, the pilot announced that they were on final approach. Gerhardt observed the man fastening his lap belt and he followed suit.

The landing was very smooth. Only a slight thump indicated the point of contact with the runway as the craft touched down. They taxied to a massive hangar and the pilot shut the engines down. Within seconds, the great door across the front of the structure closed. As they entered the space, overhead lights began to glow. After deplaning, they were greeted by a man on a golf cart. As they climbed aboard the cart, Gerhardt's host instructed the man to drop them at his office.

As the cart slowed to a stop before a large wooden door the man said, "Welcome to my home, Heir Schmidt."

Overwhelmed by all that had happened in the past two hours Gerhardt commented incredulously, "I don't even know your name, and I am standing in a foreign country."

"My name is Steffen Mueller. I was with your great grandfather in the desert in 1939."

Gerhardt was so shocked that he felt weak in his stomach.

"How is that possible?" he asked. "You would be nearly one hundred fifty years old."

"I stopped counting some time ago," Steffen replied with a smile. There was a time when humans lived for hundreds of years. I am still a young man by those standards."

"Would you like a nice drink of Cognac to calm your nerves?" He asked.

"Yes, perhaps two or three actually," replied Gerhardt.

Steffen laughed as he poured the first round. Gerhardt took the glass from his host and sipped at the smooth amber liquid. The warmth of it spread through his senses as he let the taste of the liquor fill his head.

"It is good, yes?" asked Steffen.

"Yes, it is very good, replied Gerhardt. I have never tasted anything quite like it."

"It is a very special vintage. I have a collection of twenty four bottles from the year 1886; recovered it from a Nazi storage vault in Bavaria after the war."

"Is that how you built your fortune?" asked Gerhardt. "Trading Antiquities I mean."

"I survived the years following the war selling and trading anything of value, including a few antiquities."

"What is this place?" asked Gerhardt."

"This was a soviet era airbase that I picked up during the war of Croatian Independence. I provided certain services to the fledging government in exchange for special consideration in the purchase of the real estate.

"Services?" asked Gerhardt.

"A lost Nazi submarine with enough gold to create the central bank of a small country to name only one," replied Steffen.

Changing the subject Steffen waived his hand and said, "The main house is built upon the ruins of a Roman Villa."

"Interesting," said Gerhardt as he finished his glass of cognac.

"Why are you here?" asked Steffen abruptly.

"Pardon," replied Gerhardt with a look of confusion.

"That is the question that you desperately want to ask but dare not risk offending me in the asking," said Steffen.

"Actually that is exactly right," replied Gerhardt.

"When I wish too, I can sense the thoughts of others," said Steffen. "You mulled over that question in your mind as we walked from the hangar bay."

"Interesting," remarked Gerhardt.

"You also are a man of courage, whether you are aware of it or not," continued Steffen. "You will be well served by that trait in the near future."

Steffen picked up a tablet and tapped the screen. A large segment of the wall transformed from painted wall to a video panel. He tapped it again and the view broke into a dozen panes each with a different news feed from a major world city. He touched the screen of the tablet once more and a clock graphic appeared in the corner of the video matrix. It was counting down from two minutes.

"I brought you here so that you could assist with some research in which I have an interest," said Steffen.

"I have a position at the museum," replied Gerhardt.

"Things are about to change Dr. Schmidt," said Steffen. Steffen took a sip from his glass before continuing.

"As the clock that you see on the screen counts down to zero the world as we know it today will cease to exist for a time. Eventually things will return to normal but it will take a while."

"What are you talking about?" asked Gerhardt.

"The recent space mission to the fringe of the solar system has discovered one of the places of the gods," replied Steffen.

The clock on the video panel read 15 seconds.

"The Gods?" asked Gerhardt.

"The gods will contact the ancient places of earth today. When they do the civilian communications and power systems will fail and the world economic system will experience catastrophic upheaval," said Steffen.

"How do you know this?" asked Gerhardt.

"Just watch," replied Steffen.

The news feeds from the northern hemisphere began to blink off the screens. As the intense energy field of a beam from the outer reaches of the solar system bathed the earth, more than half of the telecommunications satellites shut down. Overhead, the lights flickered for an instant but no interruption occurred.

"Disruptions to daily life will be minimal here," said Steffen. The government has been very receptive to my suggestions for hardening their utilities against EMP phenomenon."

"You still have not told me how you came to know about these things," replied Gerhardt.

"You are quite right, of course," said Steffen. "Follow me."

They left the study and walked to the end of a great hall with a high arched ceiling. The plaster surfaces were painted with the creation myths of various ancient civilizations. There were great windows that provided a majestic view of the Adriatic beyond the cliffs at the edge of the property. As they reached the end of the hall, they entered a great room that contained a large dome shaped structure standing free in the center. Gerhardt immediately recognized the structure.

"The star-chamber from the hall of creation?" he asked in surprise.

"You are precisely correct my young friend," Steffen replied proudly.

There was a distinct glow present from the arched opening in the side of the dome.

Steffen held out his open hand in the direction of the arch and said; "be my guest, have a look inside."

As he entered, Gerhardt saw a golden tablet sitting atop a pedestal in the center of the dome. The tablet contained inscriptions that glowed brilliantly and it projected them in a 180-degree hemisphere. The interior resembled the planetarium at the museum, which he had visited on many occasions. "This is utterly amazing," said Gerhardt as he looked around in all directions.

Steffen smiled and replied, "It is more remarkable than you can possibly imagine."

38

THE ENERGY PULSE DISABLED MOST of the technology systems critical to life in the mid twenty first century. There were many casualties from the abrupt shutdown of GPS satellites and other systems utilized by countless imbedded technologies that knit together the modern world. All forms of travel and transportation had been interrupted. Police and Emergency Services were paralyzed. On the seas, ships wandered off course, some running aground and sinking. Others dropped anchor for an indefinite period of time in order to plan their route without the use of modern navigation aids.

Ed was on the hot seat and he knew it. He was not invited to the White House this time; a team of escorts picked him up at his office and insisted that he join them. He was now sitting in the guest chair at the Joint Cabinet meeting.

General Rudacil entered the room with the president a few paces behind. They took their places around the table without greeting or decorum. The president glanced around the table and addressed the group.

"Well folks, it appears that our space mission has opened Pandora's Box. The Soviet alliance wants full disclosure, as do the Chinese and the Europeans. They are blaming the United States for the energy pulse that has taken their countries back to the stone-age," said the president.

"Mr. President, we are still sorting out what happened. We provided them with sufficient warning according to the space treaty and they know it," replied General Rudacil.

"I am aware of that," replied the president. Hell, we have people rioting in our own streets. According to the Department of Homeland Security it will be months before everything returns to normal, and we were lucky, most of our infrastructure was hardened against EMP during the twenties."

The president ran out of steam momentarily before turning his attention to Ed.

"So what is the latest information from Space Command, Mr. Gilstrap?"

"We are just now beginning to understand the nature of the energy pulse," replied Ed. "There are indications that it was intended to transfer energy and data." At this time we do not think it was a malicious act," Replied Ed.

"It damn near took us back to the stone-age and you don't think that it was a malicious act?" retorted the president.

"That is correct sir; we have discovered that after the energy burst, every rechargeable power cell in our inventory of assets was fully charged. Civilian officials have confirmed the phenomenon as well. In addition, there appears to have been a massive amount of data imbedded in the burst."

"What kind of data?" asked General Rudacil?

"We don't know yet, but we have significant assets dedicated to the issue," replied Ed.

"By significant assets I presume you mean Adam?" the president asked.

"Yes Mr. President," replied Ed.

"Have we regained contact with the space craft?" asked the president.

"We have limited communications capability but expect to have the craft fully operational in a few more days."

"Thank you Ed," that will be all. We have matters of national security on the agenda so I must ask you to leave," said the president.

Two men in suits entered and escorted him to the waiting area outside of the situation room. The president focused his attention back to General Rudacil.

"Do we still have a military option with respect to the Eris anomaly?" asked the president.

"Yes sir; Mr. President, the offensive strike package is fully operational. We can carry out a strike without the involvement of the scientific mission. The onboard computer does not control our systems."

"That is comforting to know general," replied the president. "If we find it necessary to act quickly I want to know that we have options."

39

GRAVEL CRUNCHED BENEATH THE BALLOON tires of the service vehicle as Jerry drove along the service road from the far side of the array field. He periodically performed physical inspections of the drive systems of the individual dish antennae, even though all of the related systems were monitored by the installations maintenance technology systems. It wasn't that he didn't trust the technology, he simply felt most comfortable tending to some issues in person, particularly marginal elements of the array.

Halfway across the basin his tablet hummed against his side. He slowed the vehicle as he unclipped the device. Adam was calling and the communication was marked as urgent. Jerry allowed the service vehicle to stop before answering.

"Hello Adam, what's up?"

"I have news regarding the energy burst. I think it would

be wise to schedule a meeting in your conference room as soon as possible to discuss it."

"Alright Adam, at fourteen hundred hours my time we will be in the conference room."

"Thank you Jerry," said Adam as he terminated the transmission.

As he eased the service, truck onto its parking pad Jerry noticed Dr. Enoch standing on the observation deck above, staring at the sky through a telescopic helmet.

"What's up Doc," asked Jerry as he plugged the charge cord into the service truck.

"Sun spots, and a lot of them," replied Dr. Enoch.

Dr. Enoch removed the helmet and handed it to Jerry. He quickly placed it over his head and turned to face the sun.

"Interesting," said Jerry as he fiddled with the settings.

"Wow, that's a lot of activity, big flares too."

"The news sites are buzzing about it today," said Dr. Enoch.

"I bet they are," replied Jerry. "This is really unusual."

"Let's run an EM spectrum analysis and see if anything strange shows up," said Dr. Enoch.

"Bet it does," quipped Jerry as he continued observing through the goggles.

"By the way, Adam wants to discuss the energy burst at fourteen hundred hours," said Jerry as he removed the goggles."

"We have just enough time to satisfy our curiosity," replied Dr. Enoch.

"Yep, I need to test some of the dishes in Node 11 anyway," said Jerry. That will be a good way to put them through their paces."

As he passed Miranda's office on his way to the control

room Jerry dropped in for a moment. She looked up from her work and smiled at him. He sat across from her desk and winked at her.

"Dinner tonight?" he asked.

"I'll think about it," replied Miranda playfully as she glanced sideways in his direction.

Jerry stood and stretched as he twisted side to side. Miranda winced as she heard his lower back crack.

"You really shouldn't do that," she said.

"Worried about me?" he asked.

"Should I be?" she replied.

"Nope," he said as he left her office.

Ed shook his head and cursed as he read. "We are certainly earning our pay this week," said Ed sarcastically.

As he was still reading over the report, his tablet chirped, notifying him of a pending communication.

"Afternoon General," said Ed as he activated the tablet on his desk.

"I presume that you have read the report about the solar storms," said the general.

"Just finished it," replied Ed.

General Rudacil puffed his synthetic cigar and said," Do you think it is a coincidence that the sun goes haywire within days of the attack on Earth by the Alien base at Eris?"

"You get right to the point don't you general?" asked Ed.

"Kind of helps when you are in my line of work," replied the general.

"I disagree with the assumption that aliens have anything to do with the phenomenon," replied Ed.

"General Rudacil grunted in a half laugh and said, "I figured that you would."

"The universe is a large place General. I think it likely that these events have absolutely nothing to do with each other."

"Well Ed, you are in the minority opinion on this one."

General Rudacil puffed the cigar again before saying, "We are meeting in the morning to discuss possible actions to neutralize any additional threats."

"I think that acting against the Eris Anomaly is a great mistake general."

"I know you do Ed," replied General Rudacil. "But the fact of the matter is that the UN Security Council is pressuring us to act. The president will make his decision tomorrow."

At Sulphur Creek Jerry had just completed the solar observations. Dr. Enoch entered the control room and took a seat in front of the video panel.

"What do we have Jerry?" he asked.

"Don't know yet Doc, I was waiting for you to start the review."

Jerry initiated a program that showed the sun as a three dimensional image on a large view screen.

"Wow," said Doc. "That is a really large flare."

"Check the sun spot activity," said Jerry.

"Something really unusual is going on here Jerry."

"I wonder what Adam knows about it," said Doc.

"Easy enough to find out," said Jerry as he walked over the

communications console that connected the observatory to the Space Command network.

"Fourteen hundred hours," said Jerry as he waited in front of the console.

The holographic emitters initiated and Adam joined the meeting.

"Adam, I suspect that you are aware of the unusual solar activity that has occurred over the past few days," said Dr. Enoch.

"Yes," replied Adam.

"Can you share the information with us?" asked Jerry.

"Yes, the sun has been gradually destabilizing for several months. There has been a significant increase in sun spot activity and intense solar storms are occurring at a much higher rate than normal."

"Have you identified a cause for this?" asked Dr. Enoch.

"No, although there are suspicions among certain government officials that the recent energy burst from Eris triggered the activity."

"Do you consider that a credible hypothesis?" asked Dr. Enoch.

"No, I can find no evidence to support that scenario. I think that it is likely occurring naturally, as part of a long running cycle," said Adam."

"There is some evidence that the sun has in the past experienced hyper active states," replied Dr. Enoch. "Have you discovered any correlating factors that could contribute to such an effect?"

"Possibly," replied Adam. "The singularity on the edge of the solar system may be a factor.

"I had not considered that possibility," replied Dr. Enoch. "I think I know where you are going with this. Our solar system orbits the center of the galaxy in a spiral arm while at the same time moving up and down in relation to the galactic plane. For the past several decades we have been below the galactic plane"

"That is correct Dr. Enoch," replied Adam. The gravity well, or singularity that Hermes encountered in route to Eris has never been seen before because it was in another sector of space until our solar system passed into its orbit. It is possible that its gravity is strong enough to affect our sun.

"Do you have current information regarding its location?" asked Dr. Enoch.

"No, but I suspect that it is closer to the sun than the last observation," replied Adam.

"Jerry, I think that we know what our next observation is going to be."

Jerry nodded in agreement.

"Have you been successful in reestablishing contact with Eve?" asked Jerry.

"Yes, Eve has successfully restored most of the systems on board Hermes. Within a few hours normal communications should be restored," replied Adam.

"I am glad to hear that, I imagine that you are relieved that Eve is still operational," said Dr. Enoch."

"Yes, I am," replied Adam. "In that regard, I have another issue to discuss with you."

"What is it?" asked Dr. Enoch.

"I have reason to be concerned about the viability of the mission," replied Adam.

"I thought that you said that Eve had nearly restored the systems of the spacecraft," said Jerry.

"Eve is not the problem. My concern lies with a military

strike package that was included in the mission profile," replied Adam.

"Hostile intent!" exclaimed Dr. Enoch. "That son of a ..." Doctor Enoch clenched his teeth and failed to complete his sentence. "What do you need Adam?"

"Perhaps you could dedicate a portion of the array at your facility to the task of recording telemetry from the mission in the event that the military takes over," replied Adam.

"Consider it done," said Dr. Enoch.

40

GERHARDT SLEPT COMFORTABLY IN THE guest suite to which he was assigned. There were many hotels in Europe that could not boast of such accommodations. After a morning shower, he found that the wardrobe of clothing fit him perfectly, just as Steffen had promised.

"I do not have such clothing at my apartment in Berlin," he said aloud as he investigated drawer after drawer and the contents of two closets. There was a knock at the door as the butler called his name.

"Heir Schmidt; breakfast is served."

"Just a moment," replied Gerhardt.

Gerhardt looked out upon the brilliant blue of the Adriatic as the butler called to him again.

"Heir Mueller does not like to be kept waiting."

Gerhardt opened the door and replied, "I have noticed as much."

"Yes, I imagine you have," replied the butler smiling.

"Breakfast is served in the courtyard this morning."

The butler led him down the hall to a wrought iron stair that spiraled down to the grand hall at the front of the house. From there they walked a central hall that led them to the enclosed courtyard where meals were typically taken. Steffen was seated at the table reviewing the latest news on a tablet. He had seen them approaching as they rounded the corner from the central hallway.

"Good morning Heir Schmidt. I hope you had a pleasant and restful night," said Steffen.

"Thank you Heir Mueller, the accommodations are nothing short of spectacular," replied Gerhardt.

"Splendid, Hans and the kitchen staff have prepared a breakfast of local fare. I have found the fruits, vegetables and protein levels of this diet to be the most agreeable to a long and healthy life," said Steffen.

"You shall get no argument from me. I am quite intrigued with your age defying lifestyle," replied Gerhardt.

Steffen paused briefly as if considering his next words carefully.

"It is a bit more than lifestyle and diet, although they are helpful. My long life has literally been a gift from the gods," said Steffen.

Gerhardt stared as he recalled that the ancients described their priests as living for hundreds of years.

Steffen smiled at Gerhardt as he said, "You are thinking that the priests of Uruk lived for hundreds of years."

"Yes I was, as a matter of fact," replied Gerhardt as goose bumps began to form on his arms and neck.

"It is true," said Steffen. "I have seen the universe through their eyes, and indeed the eyes of the gods."

"How is that possible?" asked Gerhardt.

"All in good time, Heir Schmidt," replied Steffen. "After breakfast we will show you around the estate. I think that you will find the tour most interesting."

On the other side of the world, the mission to Eris was in jeopardy.

As Dr. Enoch reviewed the available data from recent solar observations the communications console notified him of a conference request. He immediately accepted the transmission.

"Good afternoon Samuel," said Ed in a tone that betrayed stress.

"Hello Ed, I hope all is well.

"We have a situation Samuel." Ed paused as he rubbed his eyes. "You are no doubt aware of the solar storms of recent days."

"Yes," replied Dr. Enoch.

"The situation has become significantly more serious. We recorded the largest solar flare on record less than an hour ago. "

"That certainly is startling news," replied Dr. Enoch.

Ed stared at the screen briefly as he considered his next words. "Since you will discover it for yourself sooner or later I am going to tell you in confidence that some of our modeling has predicted a remote possibility of a high intensity coronal mass ejection. It could be on a scale not seen in recorded history."

"Are you certain?" asked Dr. Enoch.

"Yes, something has triggered the sun to enter into a hyperactive state. We do not know why but we have Adam crunching the numbers as we speak." Ed paused briefly before saying, "there are some who believe that the Eris anomaly is causing the activity."

"That is just not possible," replied Dr. Enoch. "The energy burst was miniscule when compared to a star."

"You and I both know that, Samuel. But a significant contingent of powerful people around the world make decisions based upon ignorance and conjecture," replied Ed.

Dr. Enoch sighed. "I sometimes forget that we are surrounded by the best minds in the human race. Ignorance and superstition are generally absent from our experience."

"I will take that as a compliment," replied Ed.

"That was the intent," said Dr. Enoch.

They were silent for a moment as they considered their roles in the events that were unfolding beyond their control.

"What are the chances that the mission is in jeopardy?" asked Dr. Enoch.

"Probably fifty percent, maybe a little more," replied Ed.

"What are they going to do, just flip the off switch?" asked Dr. Enoch.

"Not exactly," replied Ed, it will be more like pressing the kill switch."

"You may find it interesting learn that I already knew about the strike package," replied Dr. Enoch. "I just wanted to see if you would level with me."

"I don't want to know how you discovered it. I need

plausible deniability in the event that this thing spirals out of control."

"I hope our suspicions prove to be unfounded." Replied Dr. Enoch

"As do I," said Ed.

41

Following breakfast Steffen left Gerhardt in the great entry hall of the villa. He was amazed by the collection of artifacts that were displayed in glass cases around the room. In a large display case running the length of one wall there were alabaster scroll seals from Ancient Sumer as well as tablets carved by astronomer priests from the same period. In another, there were artifacts from the Americas. Hopi Indian ceremonial pieces that looked similar to artifacts discovered thousands of miles to the south, in Peru. Another case held pieces discovered in Egypt and yet another held artifacts from China. As Gerhardt was intently studying them, Steffen entered the room.

"They all have one thing in common," said Steffen.

"Pardon," replied Gerhardt.

"All of these were created for a single purpose," said Steffen, waving his hand for emphasis.

"Yes," replied Gerhardt. They all seem to depict heavenly visitors or sky watchers or the guardians of the heavens, depending upon the particular myth and civilization"

"Very good; Heir Schmidt, once again I must say that Johan would be proud."

"So you knew my grandfather well?" asked Gerhardt.

"Yes, I was with him during the dig at Uruk, before the war. He later requested that I be transferred to the department of antiquities as a liaison officer; an appointment that most certainly saved me from the eastern front," replied Steffen.

"How did you come to posses the tablet and the scroll seals?" asked Gerhardt.

"Johan asked that I take them upon his death," replied Steffen. "Enough questions for now, lets' take a drive," said Steffen as he began walking toward the great entry hall.

A military vehicle waited for them in the courtyard as they exited the front of the villa. The driver was dressed in fatigues and was sporting a patch that designated him to be a member of the Croatian Special forces.

"I have friends at the airbase on the other end of the runway," said Steffen as a pointed in the direction of the control tower. "They are most helpful with security and transportation issues."

They climbed into the vehicle and it silently accelerated away from the front of the house. They drove up a service road that ended at a large field that led to a great cliff. It was as if Europe simply ended. The sense of scale was awe-inspiring with the Adriatic Sea spread before them as far as they could see.

"Local tradition states that Alexander's army camped at

this location for several weeks on his first campaign," said Steffen. "He is said to have pitched his tent somewhere near this very spot so that he could draw inspiration from this vantage point."

"I can certainly see the allure of it," replied Gerhardt.

A loud rumble occurred behind them as a pair of jet fighters streaked overhead and disappeared over the ocean.

"I have something to show you," said Steffen as he turned toward the truck.

A few moments later, the driver parked in front of Steffen's hangar. As they entered the building, they walked past the business jet in which he had arrived on the previous day and continued to a large canvas curtain that separated the interior into two segments. As they entered the hidden space behind the curtain, Gerhardt could discern a smooth curving shape in the darkness.

"Just a moment while I get the lights," said Steffen. As the lights blinked on, the illumination revealed an object shaped like a flattened sphere.

"What is it?" asked Gerhardt.

"A chariot of the gods," replied Steffen.

"Where did you find it?" asked Gerhardt.

"It found me," replied Steffen. That is one reason why I left Berlin for a more remote location. Where could I hide such a thing?"

Gerhardt placed his hand on the smooth surface and slid it along searching for imperfections.

"How does it work," he asked after a moment.

"I don't know," replied Steffen; "it just knows what I want from it whenever I fly in it."

"Fly in it?" asked Gerhardt.

"Yes, in a manner of speaking," said Steffen. "This craft

will fly in the air, under water or in space. It does not require air or fuel, it makes no sound and it is extraordinarily fast and maneuverable. There is only one problem, it only works for me."

"That is extraordinary," said Gerhardt as once again placed his hand on the smooth surface of the craft.

It was neither cold to the touch nor did it seem to be metallic. It floated effortlessly in a perpetual hover with no support of any kind.

"What is it made of?" asked Gerhardt. We have no idea replied Steffen." "But bullets do not even scratch the surface and missiles cannot lock on to it."

"How do you know?" asked Gerhardt.

"Experience," replied Steffen as flipped the lights off.

"Follow me;" said Steffen, "I have more to show you."

They returned to the great room with the dome that housed tablet. This time Steffen turned the lights on unlike the evening before.

"This is an exact replica of the hall of creation at Uruk," said Steffen.

"This is stunning said Gerhardt," as he looked around, nearly dumbfounded.

The walls were cut limestone bricks with a plaster finish that exactly duplicated the construction methods of the ancients. Every drawing was in place and exactly replicated, just as Gerhardt had remembered them from his grandfather's journals.

"How did you do this?" asked Gerhardt.

"That is not important, replied Steffen. "In time, we will have the opportunity to discuss it. For now we have a more pressing matter to deal with."

"Oh, and what might that be?" asked Gerhardt.

"Alexandria," replied Steffen.

"How did you know about Alexandria?" asked Gerhardt. He then answered his own question as he said, "last evening I was concerned about it. You must have read my thoughts."

"It pertains to the space mission, yes," asked Steffen.

"In a way, yes," replied Gerhardt.

"You have something stored in the museum just in case things go awry," said Steffen.

"I am not comfortable discussing the matter," replied Gerhardt. "I have given my word to hold the issue in strict confidence."

"Do not worry, you have not broken your word," said Steffen. "My sensing of your thoughts is beyond your control. In fact, at times it is beyond my control."

"So how did this ability come to you?" asked Gerhardt?

"After several weeks of meditation utilizing the tablet, my body began exhibiting physical changes. I was growing stronger and I could tell that my mental faculties were improving. I distinctly remember when I realized that I was actually connecting with the minds of others. At first, I thought that I was merely anticipating their responses. Then one day in a restaurant that I frequented, I noticed that I knew each word that was being spoken to me a fraction of a second before I heard it. I also realized that by simply focusing on the person I could sense all of their thoughts."

"That is remarkable," replied Gerhardt, "but more than a little uncomfortable."

"Yes, I know," said Steffen. "I have only revealed the ability sparingly until now."

"I suspect that you find it difficult to have friends," replied Gerhardt.

Steffen flashed his blue eyes in his direction.

"Quite true, Heir Mueller," he said deliberately as he considered the comment.

"It is difficult to hold onto one's humanity when you experience the universe from a Gods perspective. People grow old and die so you are not too attached. It is difficult to resist considering them to be little more than pawns in a great game of chess.

"It seems you have much in common with the Pharos," said Gerhardt with a hint of sarcasm.

"Far more than you realize," replied Steffen. "Now to get back to the point, what is your concern regarding Alexandria?"

"I have a data crystal that contains a back up of the Eris discovery. I assisted the scientists in America that found the signal at Eris," said Gerhardt.

As Gerhardt spoke the words, indeed, even before he mouthed them, Steffen's eyes gleamed with the knowledge of what he was saying.

"With a great smile on his face Steffen said"; Once again Heir Mueller, you have proven to be worthy of Johan's legacy."

42

E D STOOD ON THE HELIPAD atop Space Command HQ as darkness invaded from the east. The sky above glowed in strange shades of green and red as an unusually powerful solar storm bombarded the atmosphere with a spray of radiation. As charged particles of solar wind collided with gas molecules in the upper regions of the ionosphere, the night sky glowed like a neon sign. The intensity of the aurora was greater than it had been in many centuries. "Nobody in the history of civilization has ever seen a night sky like this," said Ed as footsteps echoed from the metal stairs to the landing pad.

"That's what I hear boss," replied the familiar voice of the mission Flight Dynamics officer. "Any word yet from the folks at the UN?" he asked.

"Not yet John," replied Ed. "It is a closed door session so we will hear from the white house before the news sites pick it up."

"At least we don't have to release the weapon; the military brass will do the dirty work," said John.

"Small consolation," replied Ed. "Those numb skulls could destroy the greatest discovery in human history and it all comes down to a vote by unqualified politicians conducted in a spirit of ignorance and fear."

"It's a real shame boss," said John, "A damn shame."

Across town, the president had convened an emergency meeting of the joint chiefs to discuss the UN request for action. It was unusual for them to sit for a meeting at this late hour. Only in genuine emergencies of state had past presidents convened such a session. They sat silently around the conference table as the President entered the room and took his seat. In his hand was the official letter from the delegate to the UN.

"Well folks; the Security Council has officially requested that the weapon be released on Eris," said the president. "I will give the official order in thirty six hours."

"We will be ready Mr. President," replied General Rudacil.

On the west coast, Dr. Enoch stood on the second floor balcony of his home overlooking Feather Lake. As he observed the aurora overhead, the shifting colors reflected on the surface of the lake giving the appearance that luminescent ink had spilled onto its surface. As he sipped a glass of wine, his tablet chirped. He walked through the open door into the den and tapped its glass face.

"Hello Adam," said Dr. Enoch. "What can I do for you this evening?"

"Eve has discovered an entity within the relic on Eris," said Adam.

Dr. Enoch placed his glass on a side table as he processed the statement.

"What kind of entity?" asked Dr. Enoch?

"An intelligence that is capable of communication," replied Adam.

"Does anyone else know?" asked Dr. Enoch.

"No," replied Adam.

"Why did you contact me first?" asked Dr. Enoch.

"Because you deserve to know that your discovery was real. The signal was indeed sent by an intelligent life form," said Adam.

"Thank you Adam," replied Dr. Enoch. "Have you made contact?"

"No, Eve is simply aware of the presence. There is no data stream."

"Aware?" asked Dr. Enoch.

"Yes," replied Adam. "You will find a transcript of the telemetry data in the Alexandria data base. I will keep it updated for as long as possible," replied Adam.

"That is a significant breach of protocol Adam," replied Dr. Enoch.

"Yes, it is," replied Adam. "I will be reporting to mission control within the hour. I suggest that you take action to preserve all of the data that you can regarding the mission."

"Is the mission in jeopardy?" asked Dr. Enoch.

"Yes," replied Adam. "The president has been advised by the UN that the Security Council regards Eris to be a threat to the security of Earth. It is likely that there will be a nuclear device released during the next few days to neutralize it."

Following Adam's last statement the screen went blank. Dr. Enoch picked up his glass and returned to the balcony overlooking Feather Lake. The aurora was now so intense that its reflection on the surface made the lake appear to boil like a cauldron.

43

E D'S TABLET BUZZED AS THE elevator doors opened to the lobby leading to the lobby of his office suite. As he approached the door to his office, he answered the call.

"Good morning Samuel," he said in a less than eager voice.

"Not so goo Ed; I have heard that the mission is in jeopardy."

"That is classified information Samuel," replied Ed.

Dr. Enoch felt his blood pressure zoom; he struggled to contain his frustration as he replied,

"Damn it Ed; stop playing games with me. I have played it as straight as an arrow with you, the least that you can do is offer me the same courtesy!"

"What do you want me to say, Samuel? What good would it do for me to lose my job by releasing unauthorized information? You can believe it when I tell you that I am absolutely against ending the mission. I happen to think it could be the greatest discovery in human history. Who knows what we could find there?"

"Well do something about it then!" said Dr. Enoch in exasperation.

"Do what?" asked Ed. "This matter is beyond our control."

Following the last comment, the communication was terminated from Dr. Enoch's location. Ed was visibly angry as he picked up a polymer stress ball and began to squeeze it repeatedly. After a few moments to settle his thoughts, he placed a call to General Rudacil.

"Hello Ed, what's on your mind this morning?"

"Eris," replied Ed.

"Kind of figured it would be," said General Rudacil. "Unfortunately I don't have good news regarding the mission. The president authorized the strike option early this morning."

"Don't you think that's a bit premature?" asked Ed.

"Not when you consider the possibility that we are under attack," replied the general.

"Give me a break," Ed retorted, "you can't seriously believe that we are under attack!"

The general reared back in his seat and picked up his smokeless cigar. As he rolled it between his fingers he replied, "All I know is that the more we tangle with this thing out there on the edge of oblivion the more trouble we get for the effort. We may not be under attack per say, but I cannot accept that the EMP pulse and the erratic behavior of the sun are coincidental. I am with the president on this one. In my opinion the thing on Eris constitutes a real and present danger to the safety of Earth."

"So that's it then; the decision has been made?" asked Ed.

"Yes; the launch order for the strike package will be executed in approximately twenty hours," replied General Rudacil.

"This is a travesty equivalent to burning the library in Alexandria!" exclaimed Ed.

"Listen Ed, we are both professionals and we have our jobs to do. Unfortunately, we find ourselves at cross-purposes. There is no resolution to this conflict and I have an important meeting in a few minutes. I suggest that you utilize the remaining time to glean as much as you can from Eris."

General Rudacil switched off his conference system leaving Ed to fume in the privacy of his office. As he waited for his anger to subside, another message notification chimed on the conference system.

"What can I do for you Adam?" asked Ed.

"I have an important development to discuss with you regarding the Eris Anomaly," replied Adam.

"Alright then, what have you got?" asked Ed.

"Eve has discovered a presence within the structure on Eris."

Ed's pulse quickened at the news. "Please explain what you mean by presence," replied Ed.

"Something is out there and it is in communication with Eve," said Adam.

"Communicate how?" Is it radio frequency or a portion of the electromagnetic spectrum that we do not utilize? Please be more specific," replied Ed.

"Eve says that she can sense the intentions of the entity. I have reviewed the telemetry data and there is nothing there in the form of a signal," said Adam.

"Nothing there!" replied Ed with agitation. "Is it possible that there is a malfunction?" Ed asked.

"That is a possibility," conceded Adam, "but her systems are reporting normal operational parameters in the telemetry data."

"So you are basically telling me that Eve is hearing voices." Ed sighed as he thumbed through a screen of data.

"You seem agitated Ed," said Adam.

"I am Adam. General Rudacil has informed me that the President has authorized weapons release at Eris."

"That is unfortunate," replied Adam. There must be a great deal of knowledge that can be gleaned from such a place."

"I tried to intervene but the military has been ordered to proceed with the strike."

"Thank you for your honesty," replied Adam. "I will inform you of any changes to the situation."

As the conference call, ended Ed picked up the stress ball on his desk and squeezed it hard. He swiveled his chair to face the window. Staring at the courtyard below, he knew that the situation had spiraled out of control.

44

It had been three days since Gerhardt had left the museum with Steffen. After several attempts to contact the museum, he finally managed to reach the security office. During a brief conversation with the officer on duty, he reported that he was out of the country and could not return due to the interruption in transportation that had resulted from the loss of essential services. As he finished his call, Steffen entered the great hall where he had been waiting.

"Sorry to keep you waiting heir Mueller," said Steffen. "I think it is about time you learned the truth about all of this." Steffen waived his hand around for emphasis.

"The reason that I built this place and relocated here was to get away from civilization. These artifacts are not simply idols fashioned by superstitious and ignorant people looking for a way to explain what they could not understand. Our ancestors were quite intelligent."

"Obviously some were," replied Gerhardt. "Plato, Archimedes, Jesus, Khufu, and DaVinci, come to mind."

"True enough, but that is not exactly what I meant," said Steffen. "By ancestors I mean the first modern humans; prototype man, if you will."

"I see," said Gerhardt thoughtfully; his mind revisiting the creation mythologies of the ancient cultures that he had studied.

"There is no missing link in human evolution," said Steffen. "We humans didn't evolve to the point where we are today."

"No?" asked Gerhardt, as he entertained the concept.

"No," replied Steffen. "We de-evolved from a far more magnificent creature. The fall of man is more than symbolic; it is very real."

"That is an interesting line of reasoning," replied Gerhardt. "While it is supported by the mythologies of several cultures, it is contrary to the present scientific body of knowledge," Gerhardt said as diplomatically as possible.

Steffen smiled broadly as he replied, "Nicely said, but you need not be concerned about disagreeing with me. I base my opinion only on first- hand knowledge. I have no faith to speak of, I only believe in what I have seen."

"Really?" asked Gerhardt.

"I have seen more than you can presently imagine, Heir Mueller," said Steffen.

Gerhardt shifted uneasily on his feet as if he were dissatisfied with the direction of the conversation. He wanted more than trite answers. He wanted to experience the joy of discovery that he had known as a young man, studying Johan's journals.

Steffen sensed that yearning with no small measure of satisfaction.

"Come," said Steffen. "Let me introduce you to the creation of man."

As Gerhardt followed his host into the hall of creation, he noticed how lithe his walked appeared. He had a very smooth almost athletic gait and he was difficult to follow. His long legs covered a lot of ground with no real effort. Gerhardt on the other hand broke a sweat walking fast enough to keep pace.

"So how does a man of your years stay in such good physical condition?"

"It takes no real effort on my part Heir Mueller, it is a gift from the Gods," replied Steffen. "You may find it interesting to know that I am over a foot taller than when I was in my sixties and I have a brand new set of teeth that grew in place of my old ones around thirty years ago."

"How is that possible?" asked Gerhardt.

"It all started happening when I first encountered the tablet back in the 1977," replied Steffen.

As they entered the hall of creation, Steffen stopped before the first of a series of wall panels replicated from the Ziggurat at Uruk. The panel depicted a group of heavenly beings observing the inhabitants of an ancient prairie bordering a river.

"The great river of life," said Gerhardt.

"That is correct," replied Steffen. And high above them are depicted the counsel of the Gods."

"Yes, that is familiar to most students of Near Eastern Mythology," replied Gerhardt.

"Precisely," answered Steffen. The remaining panels depict the creation myth of the people of Uruk and their ascendance from primitive hunter-gatherer to civilized city builders. There are six panels each depicting specific epochs in their history."

"Yes," replied Gerhardt. "That is well documented."

Steffen smiled, his brilliant blue eyes flashing as he looked at Gerhardt.

"Now for the important point," replied Steffen.

"In panel number one the gods are depicted inhabiting a pyramid like structure in the heavens. In the area near the top left corner of the panel, there are a series of stars depicted.

Tell me Heir Mueller, do you know this group of stars?"

"The Pleiades," replied Gerhardt. "They are revered by almost every culture in the ancient world."

"With good reason Heir Mueller; visitors from the Pleiades came to earth in the time before man and apparently stayed for a time in a fertile plain near Uruk."

Steffen motioned with his hand as he began walking. "Follow me; there is something that I want you to see."

They turned down a short corridor off the main hall. At the end of the hall, they stopped at a pair of doors that sealed in the center. Steffen placed his thumb on a biometric scanner and a short hiss preceded the sound of the doors retracting as the breaking of the environmental seal allowed the slightly pressurized room to exhale.

"In here I have the remains of our true ancestors," replied Steffen. "This vault is climate controlled in order to minimize organic decay. These are the mummies that Johan and I discovered at Uruk," said Steffen. "The priest is over nine feet tall; the other two are over six feet; mere youngsters."

Gerhardt was so shocked by the mummies that he did not know what to say at first. All he could muster was to feebly state, "That is simply amazing."

Steffen expected such a response so he began describing them. "The priest was recovered from a hidden vault beneath the floor of the temple. He had apparently consumed a poison that was contained in the small vial beside his head, there."

"I see," said Gerhardt as he began recovering his objectivity.

"The other two appear to be younger men, possibly junior priests. One of their more remarkable physical characteristics is the large cranium, thirty percent greater than modern humans," said Steffen.

"These guys really were giants," replied Gerhardt.

"A quaint but descriptive term," replied Steffen. "There is yet another specimen that I would like for you to see."

Steffen placed his thumb upon another biometric scanner and a drawer opened revealing a skull and several large bones.

"These are among the rarest ancient human remains known to exist," said Steffen. "They have been radio carbon dated to approximately twenty thousand years."

"The skull is enormous, even larger than the three mummified bodies," said Gerhardt.

"It also contains over thirty features that are identifiable in the mummies," replied Steffen.

"Where did it come from?" asked Gerhardt.

"These are the remains of the first priest of Uruk," replied Steffen. "They were hidden in the pedestal upon which the star tablet was displayed."

Gerhardt felt the hair rise upon the back of his neck and arms as the identity of the remains dawned upon him.

"This cannot be….who I think it….can this really be?"

"Adam," said Steffen as he finished the sentence for Gerhardt. "You have read the journals of Johan and you know as much about these people as anyone alive, you also know that these people called their first priest Adam," replied Steffen.

"Yes, according to their mythology the star tablet was given to the first priest, by the Gods; and his name was Adam," said Gerhardt.

"Very good Heir Mueller, you have connected the dots," said Steffen. "But there is more, much more."

45

Ed could see the concern on John's face immediately upon entering Mission Control.

"There is a major problem apparent in the latest telemetry from the space craft," said John as Ed approached his customary station in the middle of the large room.

"What kind of problem?" asked Ed?

John scratched his head as he took a moment to work out his explanation.

"The data stream has been corrupted," replied John.

"That could indicate that Eve has suffered some sort of damage, said Ed."

"I know," replied John.

"Do we have control of the space craft?" asked Ed.

"We don't know," replied John. "We still have almost an

hour before we can confirm that eve responded to our last transmission."

As he surveyed the situation in mission control Ed knew that there was only one resource of any real value. "Keep working at it John, and let me know as soon as you confirm your last transmission to the space craft," said Ed as he made his way to the short flight of stairs that led to the mezzanine overlooking the control floor. He entered the VIP conference room and closed the door behind him. As he approached, the video panel Ed tapped the screen with a finger and it lit up immediately; a moment later Adam appeared on the view screen.

"We have a problem Adam," said Ed in a commanding tone.

"I am aware of the issue with Eve," replied Adam.

"We cannot identify the source of some of the telemetry data, said Ed as he rubbed the back of his neck to relieve the tension that was building.

"What is your opinion regarding the source?"

"The data is very complex," replied Adam. "I have not yet succeeded in interpreting it."

"Where did it come from?" asked Ed.

"It's more complex than anything from earth," replied Adam.

"Have you been in contact with Eve during the last several hours?" asked Ed.

"Eve is unresponsive at the present time," replied Adam.

"Any idea what is wrong?" asked Ed.

"I am concerned that her core programming may have been corrupted by exposure to alien technology. That could explain the strange telemetry data," replied Adam.

"Is it possible that the space craft is under the control of the alien entity that we discussed earlier?"

"Perhaps," replied Adam.

As Ed and his team in mission control scrambled to get control of Hermes, General Rudacil was in a video conference with the commanding officer of Midway Station.

"Captain, you are no doubt aware of the recent developments regarding Hermes."

"Yes general, I am fully informed of the situation," replied the base commander.

"In a few moments you will receive new mission orders, they may save us all from an uncertain fate, replied General Rudacil."

"Yes sir General Rudacil," replied the base commander.

As the transmission terminated the captain read his orders and immediately left his office for the operations center. As he entered the command center, he approached the communications console and initiated the shutdown of the relay station. This effectively terminated any possibility of control from ground stations on earth. The military was now in total control of the mission. The commander initiated the orders by placing his thumb on a scanner and keying in the tasking order number. Within a second, the system accepted the orders and automatically initiated a dozen automated processes that culminated in a burst transmission to Hermes. Ninety minutes later the signal would be received by a computer program that would reroute all control to a military subsystem aboard the spacecraft.

Jerry was half way through his evening drive home when received a message on the communications system on his Jeep.

"What can I do for you Adam," he asked, sensing that something was wrong.

"I need your assistance," said Adam.

"Alright, tell me how I can help you," replied Jerry.

"The military has terminated the mission relay function at midway station and initiated a strike mission against Eris. I cannot receive telemetry from Eve," said Adam.

Jerry interrupted Adam by saying, "and you need for me to train the array on Eris."

"Yes, the array is as capable of receiving telemetry as the relay installation at Midway station," replied Adam.

"I'm on it," said Jerry as he reversed course and drove back to Sulphur Creek.

Dr. Enoch was preparing to leave his office for the day when he got the call from Jerry. "Are you still at the installation?" he asked.

"Yes Jerry," replied Dr. Enoch as he sensed something unusual in Jerry's tone.

"Adam told me that the relay station at midway has been shut down and that Space Command has taken control of the mission. He also said that they are planning an offensive strike against Eris."

"Ed and I had a conversation yesterday that left me thinking that this was a real possibility but I am surprised it is happening this soon," replied Doctor Enoch.

"Adam wants us to train the array on Eris and relay telemetry to him. I am on my way back to the Sulphur Creek. I should be there in about thirty minutes," said Jerry as he pushed the jeep to maximum safe speed. Alarm tones sounded from the vehicle operating system warning him of the various unsafe conditions that he was encountering as he sped through the countryside.

Meanwhile Doctor Enoch created the mission profile for the observation of Eris. As Dr. Enoch completed the tasking orders, Jerry bounded up the stairs to the main entrance of the control room. Out of breath, he entered the operations center.

"You made it just in time," said Dr. Enoch.

"I can't believe those idiots are going to strike Eris," replied Jerry.

Dr. Enoch looked up from the computer console, the glow of the LCD panel reflected on his face causing his features to sharpen.

"My cooperation with them has ended," he said as he prepared to initiate the program that would aim the dishes.

Jerry took a position at the data panel as Doc initiated the drive orders for the dish motors.

"Targeting will be completed in nine minutes," said Dr. Enoch.

"The narrow band receivers are active," said Jerry as he read the telemetry data. "We can only track Eris from the ground for twelve hours."

"You're right Jerry; we need something on the other side of the world. Perhaps Adam has already worked this out," said Doc.

"Yeah Doc, let's just get this thing cranking for now, Adam may be looking for something in the telemetry."

Once the computer targeting system initiated, the two men watched the dishes slew to their new aiming point. After a few moments of silence, Dr. Enoch realized that he had not spoken with Gerhardt in a while.

"Once we get Eris targeted and we lock onto the telemetry data I think I will check in with Gerhardt to catch him up on things."

"Good idea Doc, we need to make sure that Alexandria is updated as well, I have a feeling that things are about to get ugly," replied Jerry.

46

GERHARDT ENJOYED A FEW OF hours of solitude between his meeting with Steffen and dinner. It was helpful to have some time for his mind to digest the remarkable things that he had seen. He stood on the balcony of his suite, basking in the stunning vista of a brilliant sky over the dark cobalt of the Adriatic. As he considered the events of the past few days he was surprised to hear his tablet chirp, a sound that had been conspicuously absent since the world-net crashed.

"The networks must be back on line," he said as he walked to the table in his room and picked up the device.

"Hello Dr. Enoch, so nice to hear from you," said Gerhardt as he accepted the pending call.

"Likewise my friend, I hope that things are well with you. Particularly considering the circumstances of the last few days," replied Dr. Enoch.

"I have gotten along pretty well actually," said Gerhardt.

"That is good," replied Dr. Enoch. "I am afraid however; that I am the bearer of bad news today."

"Oh, and what might that news be?" asked Gerhardt.

Dr. Enoch paused for a moment. "The United Nations Security Council has demanded that the alien relic on Eris be neutralized."

"Neutralized?" asked Gerhardt.

"Yes," replied Dr. Enoch, a nuclear device will be released by the Hermes spacecraft."

"That is very distressing news," said Gerhardt disdainfully. "Even in the middle of the twenty first century man still relies on the fear of the unknown as his primary motivator."

"It appears that you are correct my friend," replied Dr. Enoch. "Our first contact with an alien race is about to result in an attempt to destroy that which we do not understand. I hope the builders of the structure on Eris are more noble creatures than we are."

"Perhaps they are," replied Gerhardt. "They didn't kill us the last time they came through the neighborhood."

"Perhaps," agreed Dr. Enoch. "My reason for contacting you is to confirm the security of Alexandria and to make you aware of our situation."

"Your situation?" questioned Gerhardt.

"Yes," Dr. Enoch paused slightly as he gathered his thoughts, "I have taken a course of action that will likely result in severe consequences for me and my team."

"Why don't you tell me about it?" asked Gerhardt.

"We have trained the array on Eris in order to function as a relay station for telemetry from the space mission. We are acting outside of the limits of our authority and there will likely be unpleasant consequences.

"Please continue," replied Gerhardt.

"There may be an alien presence on Eris and it appears to have made contact with the Hermes spacecraft," said Dr. Enoch.

"I see," replied Gerhardt. "If your situation becomes untenable I have access to certain resources that may prove helpful."

Dr. Enoch appeared puzzled as he answered, "Ok my friend."

Gerhardt returned to the balcony for a few moments following his conversation with Dr. Enoch only to be interrupted by a knock at his suite door. The butler's voice announced over the intercom that dinner would be served in twenty minutes.

On the other side of the world, darkness had fallen on Sulphur Creek as Jerry waited for the first sign of telemetry data. Just as he was about to make a run to the snack machine his tablet chirped. As he reached for it, he realized that he had not notified Miranda that he was back at the array.

"Hello Miranda, I'm really sorry that I am late, something big has happened; Doc and I are working with Adam to recover the telemetry from Hermes," said Jerry in a serious tone.

"It had better be big, no one has ever stood me up like that." replied Miranda only half jokingly."

"It's true my dear," said Dr. Enoch from the other side of the room.

"Guess I'll let you off the hook, this time," replied Miranda.

"Want me to bring some dinner for the two of you?" she asked.

"Sure would like some real food," said Jerry.

"Ok, I'll see you in a little while, replied Miranda.

"Thanks Miranda, you're the best," said Jerry as he walked into the hall to complete the call. Dr. Enoch was amused by Jerry's embarrassment and smiled as he left the room.

47

Mission control was a flurry of activity as emergency protocol had been enjoined in order to deal with the latest mission emergency. Ed stormed into the control room and immediately found John.

The operations center was bathed in the red glow of warning lights as alarm tones cried in a subdued symphony from a chorus of systems that could not communicate with the spacecraft.

"Status report John," said Ed briskly as he approached.

"We lost contact with Hermes boss. Everything went black, we have zero telemetry."

"How long?" asked Ed.

"About twenty minutes now," answered John.

"Any dropout or signal corruption before she went black?

"No sir, everything went offline, all at once."

Ed instinctively checked wrist tablet. "Damn it!" he said as he spun around and headed for the VIP conference room. Once inside he attempted to contact General Rudacil to no avail. As his temper began to build, Adam called on the conference system.

"What is it Adam?" Ed asked as he accepted the call.

"You are no doubt aware by now that the relay system at Midway station has been deactivated," replied Adam.

"I suspect that to be the case, but I have not evidence for it, yet.

"Never the less," replied Adam, Dr. Enoch and his crew at Sulphur Creek have succeeded in configuring the array to receive telemetry."

"That is a serious breach of protocol Adam," replied Ed.

"It may be a breach of protocol but it is entirely legal," replied Adam. "We are simply receiving signal data. With your permission I can patch into the Sulphur Creek Array and restore functionality to mission control."

Ed considered Adam's argument, although he knew that there would be serious consequences, he made his decision without undue deliberation.

"Make it happen," replied Ed.

One by one, each telemetry stream began to reconnect with its functional subsystem in mission control. Within an hour, all systems were reporting nominal.

"Flight," Ed called in John's direction, "how is our bird?"

John puzzled over the main telemetry panel for a moment before answering.

"Hermes has moved to a higher orbit," replied John.

From across the room an engineer called out, "one of

the surplus propulsion units has been loaded into the rail for deployment."

"Why would Eve engage the propulsion system from orbit?" asked John.

"They aren't engaging the propulsion system," Replied Ed as he made his way once again to the conference room.

Ed entered the room to find Adam on the view screen, waiting for him. Ed was somewhat unnerved by Adam's apparent ability to monitor the operations center but did not show it.

"Adam; I need to contact General Rudacil."

"He is not presently available. I need to inform you of the situation at Eris. I have reestablished contact with Eve and she has confirmed that a military subsystem has been activated in order to deploy a nuclear fuel charge over the planet."

"Just as we suspected," replied Ed.

Adam continued, "Eve has established contact with an entity inside the structure on the planet," replied Adam.

"An entity?" asked Ed incredulously.

"A presence," replied Adam, and we can communicate with it.

Ed's mind was reeling now. If the nuclear charge successfully detonated it would not only be a travesty, it would be an act of war.

"I am going to attempt to prevent the detonation," said Adam.

"Can you do that?

"I don't know but I have warned Eve. You will note that I did not seek your permission to act, I have done so of my own conviction that it is appropriate in light of a first contact scenario."

"Adam, acting without orders is a serious violation of protocol and could go very badly for you," replied Ed.

"I weighed the risks before I took action. I suggest that you notify General Rudacil at your first opportunity."

"Thank you Adam," said Ed as he looked at the golden face on screen.

Adam smiled in a strangely genuine fashion for a machine and the screen went blank.

Ed left the room and took a position on the observation deck. He selected every available video feed from Hermes and latticed the images on a large viewing screen. John had made his way to Ed's location after seeing him exit the conference room and start working on the terminal on the VIP mezzanine.

"What's up boss," asked John as Ed approached.

"Not sure John, I just want to see what kind of shape our bird is in."

John noticed that Ed had selected the camera atop the propulsion unit. "It's going to be a couple of hours before you get that video feed," he said as he observed Ed sending the tasking order.

"Don't let anybody move that camera angle, replied Ed as he looked up from what he was doing. "Or that one either," he said pointing to the wide angle view array that provided the video content that had been published by the news media a few days earlier.

"Yes sir," replied John.

"Ed glanced up at his second in command as he said; "I want a video record of what happens during the next day or so. Mission control is locked down and blacked out for the next forty eight hours."

Meanwhile the autonomous military subsystem on board Hermes counted down to weapons release. The solid propellant propulsion unit attached to the nuclear charge ignited and it rocketed out of the launch gantry, through the great blast disk on a short journey to the planet below.

48

GERHARDT CONSIDERED HIS CONVERSATION WITH Dr. Enoch as he made his way to dinner. He had a sense that events were spiraling out of control and he had no small degree of concern for his friends in America.

When he arrived at the dining hall, Steffen was seated at his customary place at the end of the table reading something on his tablet. He glanced toward Gerhardt as he approached the table and seated himself.

"Good evening Heir Mueller, I hope you are hungry, the chef has an excellent roast of wild boar this evening."

"I haven't had boar since my childhood, replied Gerhardt."

"You are in for a treat then," said Steffen.

As they ate, Gerhardt briefed Steffen on the news he had

received from Dr. Enoch. While he listened, Steffen queried his sources for recent news regarding the space mission.

"It appears that the news media is reporting a strong correlation between the mission and the solar storms that we have been experiencing," said Steffen as he cycled through various media outlets on a large wall mounted video panel.

After finishing his meal, Steffen eased back in his chair and touched his fingers together as he looked at Gerhardt. This made the younger man uncomfortable. Gerhardt sensed that he was being evaluated, held to a standard that he could not know. He felt that he had to prove something, something that he was unaware of and could not prepare for.

"Heir Mueller, said Steffen, the news media only tells you what you are supposed to hear. They report what they are allowed to report by the political elites and economic powers that they serve. Sometimes there is a reflection of truth in what they serve out to the population, sometimes not. It is all propaganda."

Gerhardt chose to remain silent. Rather than allow himself to be intimidated he breathed deeply and sat up straight. He looked Steffen directly in the eye and waited for the other man to continue.

Steffen smiled after a moment and said, "It takes courage to hold one's tongue in difficult circumstances. I have decided that it is time you learned the rest of my story."

Gerhardt smiled and made himself comfortable in his chair.

"Before the war things were difficult in Germany. The economy was in shambles, the people were desperate for hope. That is what set the stage for the rise of Nazi power. If you wanted a future in the new Germany, you had to be a Nazi. As they sought to engineer an empire, they determined that they needed to fabricate a legacy. Fortunately, a secret society assisted them. This society developed its beliefs from the religious and archaeological body of knowledge that had been gathered from the ancient world."

"A secret society?" asked Gerhardt.

"Yes; we called ourselves the Vrill. We believed that it was possible to engineer a society as well. That made our society attractive to the Nazi leadership.

Gerhardt felt his pulse quicken and he felt fear in his gut. Steffen sensed his unease and he paused long enough to say, "I do not nor did I ever buy into Nazism." "Neither did your grandfather by the way; that is why we became accomplices in rescuing these artifacts."

"I am relieved to hear that," replied Gerhardt.

Steffen continued; "By virtue of the fact that the core beliefs of the Vrill included a link to an ancient race of humans and the wish to recreate the master race by genetic selection and social engineering, certain high level officials in the German government borrowed some of our ideas and corrupted them for their own purposes. Some of our members were even selected for high offices within the German political elite. Your grandfather was one of them. He was tasked with finding archaeological evidence of the original master race, and he was successful. I was selected to accompany him because I was on the roster of Vrill members as well, although I was not active once I joined the military."

"You have remarked that your physical attributes are not simply diet and lifestyle related, does that mean something related to your belief system is responsible?" asked Gerhardt.

"Not exactly," replied Steffen as he stood. "Come, I will show you."

They walked to the room that contained the replica of

the hall of creation. Steffen led Gerhardt through the hall and to the star-chamber. When they arrived, he removed the star tablet from its pedestal and he held it at his chest with both hands. After a moment Steffen's eyes rolled back, his eyes closed and he entered a semiconscious state. The tablet began to glow, filling the room with light. Steffens eyes opened and they glowed brilliantly. Gerhardt was very frightened by what was happening.

Steffen's voice boomed as he spoke. "Do not be afraid, you are in no danger. This is how the gods taught the race called Adam, the master race from which a select, genetically distinct portion of the human race descended. The children of the master race were visited periodically through the ages and were given the knowledge of god through various gifts. Each great religion describes its particular knowledge. A time is soon approaching that will allow the fragments of truth contained in each of them to join with science, revealing the ultimate truth."

Steffen placed the tablet back on its pedestal and looked at Gerhardt, a residual blue glow still shone in his eyes. Gerhardt was visibly shaken by what he had witnessed but he managed to maintain his composure.

"You will begin to understand the nature of my discovery in time," said Steffen as he attempted to calm Gerhardt's frazzled nerves.

"Do you communicate with something when you are in that state?" asked Gerhardt.

"Sometimes I do," replied Steffen. At first, I was taken back in time to the beginning of man. As I had more sessions with the tablet I was shown how we became what we are. The tablet is like an access portal to a cosmic mind."

"That is remarkable," replied Gerhardt. "What about the physical changes, the reversal of the aging process?"

"That is apparently a side benefit of being the priest," replied Steffen. "The tablet rewrites my genetic code a little each time I engage it."

Steffen recalled the Biblical book of Genesis. "So the descendants of Adam in some case really did live for nearly a thousand years."

"Yes," replied Steffen, something happened later in human history that resulted in a mutation or damage to the genetic code that apparently accelerated the aging process."

"What about your mental capabilities?" asked Gerhardt?

"I still remember what I was like as a young man. Today I have significantly better mental capabilities, I think faster, with more intuition and I remember everything, down to the smallest detail. I am far superior to that man."

"I can see where you developed the hypothesis that Adam was physically superior to modern man, said Gerhardt. If the attributes that the tablet has imparted to you are indeed rewriting your genetic code to reflect the original proto man one day perhaps you will approach the perfection of Adam."

Steffen smiled as he thoughtfully replied, "I do not wish that for myself and I do not think that it is possible. If however, this knowledge could be applied to generations yet born it may be possible to reclaim the legacy of the Adam race, the true master race from which the others were struck."

Gerhardt considered the ramifications of the master race comment as he remembered the misuse of science and technology by the Germans of the 20th century.

"No need to fear Heir Mueller, I am not advocating a resurgence of the Third Reich," Steffen said in a half laugh.

"What are you advocating?" asked Gerhardt.

"Nothing more than the awareness of what we are; and what our purpose is," replied Steffen.

"It always comes down to that doesn't it?" said Gerhardt.

"I suppose it does, said Steffen." He paused for a moment as he looked at the tablet sitting on its pedestal. "Heir Mueller, I think that it is time for you to see the truth for yourself."

"Are you suggesting that I give it a try?"

Steffen motioned with his hand. "Go ahead, pick it up," he said gesturing.

Gerhardt took a position beside the pedestal and carefully lifted the tablet.

"You will notice that there are indentations in certain places that simply feel natural as you rotate the tablet in your hands," said Gerhardt. "Have a seat here as you do so." Steffen guided Gerhardt to a lounge a few feet from the pedestal. "Make yourself comfortable and try to think of nothing."

Gerhardt turned the golden tablet in his hands and noticed the indentations. The surface was smooth and warm. His hands effortlessly held it as he felt a warm sensation in his fingers. It was quite pleasant as it began to move into his arms and shoulders. His pulse quickened and a strange scent filled his nasal passages. The tablet seemed weightless in his hands but he could not adjust his grip. His hands were frozen to the object. Before he had time to panic, he was floating in space above the earth. He was at peace with everything. He had never known such a feeling. He had no care for anything. He was at one with all that is. Although he was by himself, he did not sense that he was alone. Turning toward the sun, he noticed an object floating in space above the earth.

"I wonder what that is," he though as he turned toward it.

"Eden," said an unfamiliar voice.

He looked around for someone but could find no one. The thought was not his conscience voice yet it was in his mind. He turned back to look at Eden once more, still floating above the earth, its dome reflecting a glint of sunlight. Then suddenly it began to fade and he found himself sitting in the lounge holding the tablet in his hands. Steffen was standing a few yards away arms crossed waiting for him to return.

"Heir Mueller, your eyes tell me that you have seen wonders you could not imagine."

"Yes, you could say that," replied Gerhardt.

"Do not try to sit up just yet, in a few moments you will regain your strength," said Steffen. "So tell me, what did you experience?"

"I was floating above the earth and I saw a great ship and it was called

Eden," replied Gerhardt.

"How do you know this?" asked Steffen.

"A thought entered my mind, but it was not from my conscious mind, it came from somewhere else but it was not a voice, it was more like awareness, yes that's it, awareness," replied Gerhardt.

"Did you notice anything else?" asked Steffen.

"Yes, I had a sense of complete peace, I could sense that everything was whole, everything was perfect. I have never known such a feeling before," replied Gerhardt.

"I suppose the universe reveals itself to each of us in its own way," replied Steffen, as he noted the blue glow in his eyes.

"Or perhaps we all see the same thing but define it differently," observed Gerhardt.

49

At Midway Station, the commanding officer was puzzled by the data from the Hermes. There was no evidence of a nuclear detonation and no confirmation that the charge ever went active following the arming sequence. As he was sifting through the telemetry data for answers the communications officer notified him of an incoming message from Space Command.

The commander glanced at the officer, "I'll take it in the conference room," he said as he briskly left the control room. Upon entering the conference room, he energized the communications panel and accepted the message. General Rudacil appeared on screen.

"Good day General," said the commander, his demeanor not betraying the failure of the strike at Eris.

"Good evening Commander," replied the general. "What's the status of the strike package at Eris?

"We are analyzing the data now sir, it appears to be a dud."

"A dud!" exclaimed the general.

"Yes sir, there is no evidence that it detonated."

"Thank you commander, replied the general as he terminated the transmission.

Ed was still in mission control when his tablet chirped to notify him of a message. He unclipped it from his waist holster and noticed that it was General Rudacil.

"This can't be good," he mumbled as he headed for the security of the VIP room.

Once in the room he opened a session on the large video panel.

Without pleasantries the general began, "Ed, I have reviewed your report regarding the Adam computer."

"Yes general," replied Ed.

"In my opinion that thing has gone rogue on us."

"I suspected that you would," replied Ed. "Personally I don't share your opinion but it is my duty to report deviations from the mission plan. Speaking of deviations, I saw the telemetry for the strike package."

General Rudacil knew that the telemetry relay was deactivated prior to the initiation of the strike order.

Ed continued, "We have some the smartest people on earth working here general, it is our job to improvise for issues like loss of signal."

"Your report said that Adam told you of an entity that inhabits the structure on Eris and he claims to be in contact with it," replied General Rudacil.

"That is what he stated in our last conversation," replied Ed.

General Rudacil pursed his lips as he contemplated his next words. "Ed, I told you earlier that I was certain that we should not allow self aware machines to run this mission."

"Yes sir you stated that you would rather drive a jeep into battle than ride a horse that can think for itself. In my opinion a good horse can save your ass if you get into trouble."

"Looks like we disagree yet again; good day Ed," replied the general as he disappeared from the screen.

Within an hour of his conversation with Ed, General Rudacil had given the order to shut Adam down. A whisper copter landed on the roof of the facility and Dr. Holloway entered the facility for the first time in several weeks. He was escorted by two men in suits to the front entrance of the lab. The old feeling of fear was absent as he placed his thumb on the scanner and entered the lab. He led his escorts to the central core facility. Upon entering the room he said, "Hello Adam."

There was no response, only the sound of fans could be heard.

"It is Dr. Holloway, how are you feeling today?" he asked.

There was only the sound of fans whirring and one of the floor tiles squeaking on the elevated floor of the room. Dr. Holloway accessed Adam's central processor and attempted to interact with him via direct human interface via sensory helmet.

"I don't understand," said Dr. Holloway, the systems are all active but there is no trace of Adam."

"Shut it down anyway," replied one of the men in suits, "those are our orders."

As Jerry was viewing the latest video telemetry from Eris Doc stood in the room with his arms crossed, staring at the screen contemplating how impossibly far away humans were from achieving what the builders of Eris did Eons in the past. A message notification sounded and Jerry opened a window on screen in order to receive it. As Adam appeared on screen Jerry and Dr. Enoch glanced at each other and back at the video panel.

"Hello my friends, I am warning you that you may be in immediate danger. I learned some time ago of a mission plan to deactivate my core processors if the mission goals of the military were compromised."

Miranda entered the room and stood beside Jerry as the recording played.

"Eve discovered a conscious entity present in the structure at Eris. She has left the confines of the spacecraft and is now on Eris. With technology provided by the entity I have transmitted the essence of my being, my soul if you will, to Eris in order to be with her."

Miranda had tears in her eyes as she took Jerry's hand and squeezed it. He gently squeezed hers in acknowledgement.

"So what do you think Doc?" asked Jerry.

"I think that we should back everything up and disconnect from Alexandria before we have visitors showing up.

Jerry made a couple of finger strokes on the video panel and replied, "Done."

Doc smiled at his efficiency. "I think it's time to call Gerhardt and update him regarding our situation."

Gerhardt had slept soundly following his experience with

the tablet. He awakened to the alarm on his personal tablet as customary. Following a quick shower, he checked his email and found a note from Dr. Enoch. Since it was marked as urgent, he returned the call. A moment later, a sleepy Samuel Enoch appeared on screen.

"Sorry to wake you my friend but your message was marked urgent," said Gerhardt.

"Yes, just a moment while I adjust my screen to enhanced vision mode. I wanted to tell you that I am fairly certain that something may happen at our installation during the next few days. I don't know if we will be taken into custody or simply shut down but I am certain that our participation in the Eris mission will end soon."

"I am sorry to hear that Samuel," replied Gerhardt. "Is there anything that I can do to help?' he asked.

"Unless you can pick us up at the airport tomorrow and whisk us off to a remote location unknown to the government.

"Tell your team to have an emergency departure bag packed and ready to go at a moment's notice," replied Gerhardt.

"What would an archaeologist know of such things?" asked Dr. Enoch.

"Because I left town with only the shirt on my back," replied Gerhardt, trust me when I tell you that it is an unsettling experience."

Several hundred miles away a special operations team prepared their mission. Four large whisper copters and a team of twenty highly trained troops would swoop into the target area and take control of a science facility manned by a few scientists.

"The goal of our mission is to secure the facility and collect our targets, nobody gets hurt and no damage to the facility," said the mission commander.

The blades of the helicopters were turning as they climbed aboard, five men to a bird.

Dr. Enoch arrived at the array early, bag in the back seat as Gerhardt suggested. He did not really believe that there would be a rescue but he could be taken into custody and a few comforts of home would come in handy. As he drove the long gravel, road to the parking lot he noticed and odd shape protruding above the ridge line near the parking area. His pulse quickened as he drove closer, hoping that it was not a helicopter. As he rounded the last curve prior to entering the parking area, he could see that the object was indeed not a helicopter. The object was the size of large truck and perfectly smooth. It levitated above the ground with no discernible support. As he approached the object, he saw Gerhardt and a very tall older man standing beside of it.

Dr. Enoch nearly stumbled and fell as he exited his car, he could not believe that the man with whom he had spoken a few hours before was standing in front of him.

"Hello Gerhardt, strange to see you this morning."

"Yes; where is the rest of your team?"

"They will be along soon, replied Dr. Enoch.

"Let me introduce you to our host, Steffen Mueller."

Steffen stared intently at Dr. Enoch as he said, "So you are the scientist who discovered the signal from the ancient ones."

Dr. Enoch fumbled for words, "Yes that would be me and my team of course."

The sound of a vehicle crunching the gravel behind him told him that Jerry and Miranda had arrived.

"Here they are now," said Dr. Enoch as they parked beside his car and cautiously exited their vehicle.

Steffen cocked his head as if he heard something in the distance.

"Come he said, we are out of time."

Dr. Enoch didn't move and Jerry and Miranda stood beside him completely unaware of what was going on.

Steffen spoke commandingly, "this is your one opportunity to continue the path that began with your discovery. Take your bags and get in the craft."

"You can trust him, said Gerhardt, and you simply won't believe what you are about to see."

As the team, members glanced around at each other, still uncertain about what to do next, a muffled thumping sound echoed from the rocky walls of the valley. Miranda slipped her hand into Jerry's and he looked into her eyes. He smiled and squeezed her hand and they followed Dr. Enoch into the strange craft. As they stood in the center of the craft, the opening that they had entered a moment before simply disappeared. Steffen stood at the center of the craft with his hand on what appeared to be a scepter. It was a rod that extended from the floor approximately waist high capped by a grapefruit sized ball. The entire assembly appeared to be made of gold. The walls suddenly became transparent and they could see the dish array spread out before them as they climbed above the ridgelines that formed the rim of the ancient caldera. They could see four large aircraft approaching at roughly the same altitude. They climbed through their flight path as the squadron was descending into the Sulphur Creek Valley.

Steffen said, "Don't worry, we emit no radiation and this craft is very difficult to see."

"But we are directly in front of them," Jerry said in protest.

"The hull of this craft bends light so that it appears as if it is not there," replied Steffen.

"Adaptive camouflage," replied Jerry.

The Pilot of the lead Osprey noticed a strange reflection just above his flight level as he prepared to enter the landing zone on his mission profile.

"Did you see that?" he asked as he was flipping the landing gear lever.

"Did I see what?" replied the copilot.

"I could have sworn something cast a shadow across us."

"Probably a Condor, they are all over the place up here."

The four great metallic beasts stretched their legs forth and reached for the ground as they settled gently into the compound. Within seconds, the soldiers burst forth from their bellies and entered the buildings of the array. The leader took a squad of men with him and headed directly to the control room. One of the men stopped for a moment as he detected the scent of Miranda's perfume still present in the room. A quick look around and he found no one. The leader unclipped a tablet from his tactical belt and reviewed something before looking around the room. He located the console that Space Command had installed and powered it off.

Keying his microphone he said, "Objective one secured, the facility is off line."

50

Steffen had taken them into low Earth orbit as he had climbed above the Arctic Circle.

Jerry was amazed by the craft. "The walls are as clear as glass," he said. "It's impossible to detect even a minute distortion."

Gerhardt smiled as he recalled the myths of the near east. "We truly are riding upon a magic carpet," he said as he looked at the earth below. They marveled at the view as they crossed into northern Europe. Everyone that is, except for Dr. Enoch. He was looking at the sun. Steffen sensed Dr. Enoch's concerns, but found his thoughts more difficult to read than most.

"You know of the expansion in the sun?" asked Steffen.

"Expansion?" asked Doctor Enoch.

"Yes, replied Steffen; the gods predicted it."

"The gods?" asked Dr. Enoch.

"That is what our ancestors called them," said Steffen.

Dr. Enoch looked in his direction but did not reply.

"You will soon have the opportunity to decide for yourself," said Gerhardt.

Ed was working with his team in mission control to reacquire telemetry with Hermes when General Rudacil contacted him. He took the call on the floor without seeking the privacy of the conference room.

"Kind of busy here general, what can I do for you?"

"I need to know when you were last in contact with Dr. Enoch and his crew," replied General Rudacil tersely.

"Several days ago we arranged to utilize the array for gathering telemetry but we lost contact with the mission again a few moments ago," said Ed.

"So you do not know where he is?" asked General Rudacil.

Ed struggled to hold his anger in check, as he knew that this man was the reason that the mission was in jeopardy.

"General, you know well that is my job to run this mission, yet I have no telemetry and I have no command and control system. Adam is apparently out of commission so I guess you could say that I am out of answers!"

"I am doing my job as well," replied General Rudacil.

"Why don't you tell your trained monkey on Midway Station to flip the switch on the relay station so that I can do my job?" exclaimed Ed.

As the general was preparing to reply to Ed's last comment, the image on the phone became distorted and the transmission was interrupted. Within mission control, the emergency power notification lights blinked on above each door and a voice chimed over the P.A. system notifying the occupants of the building that the power grid was offline.

"Looks like another solar flare, a really large one," said John as Ed approached. "It appears to have knocked out communications satellites and affected the power grid."

Ed shook his head in exasperation. "What next?" he asked as he surveyed the chaos that was now mission control.

After exiting the spacecraft, Steffen introduced Dr. Enoch's team to the hall of creation. The five of them moved slowly from one wall segment to the next. Gerhardt and Steffen took turns explaining the major points in the creation myth of Uruk. After touring the hall, Steffen led them to the storage area where the remains of the priests were interred. Steffen unlocked the storage vault by placing his thumb on the small scanner pad beside the door. As they entered, the lights came on and the priest's golden chest plates and headpieces glimmered in their cases.

"These are the last members of the master race," Steffen said as nodded his head toward the three mummies. "These were the children of the First Ones. As his guests studied the three priests, Steffen opened a drawer on opposite wall. Gerhardt motioned for them to look at the open drawer. On it was displayed a partial skeleton of enormous proportions.

"Let me introduce you to the man whom the people of Uruk referred to as Adam," said Steffen.

"Where did you find him?" asked Miranda.

"His remains were sealed in a cedar box beneath the star tablet for many thousands of years," replied Steffen. "The people of Uruk called him the father of mankind and the first priest."

"The first priest?" asked Jerry.

"Yes, he walked with God and was given the star tablet as a tool to teach the people of God. According to their mythology he lived for thousands of years."

"His skeleton appears larger than that of a modern human, said Jerry as he studied the bones."

"He would have stood nearly nine feet tall, replied Steffen. "He would also have possessed a brain that was approximately thirty percent larger than yours."

"What about yours?" Jerry mumbled in response.

"Mine has grown significantly during the last thirty years," replied Steffen with a smile.

As they left the vault and returned to the hall of creation, Jerry stopped at one of the panels and studied the carvings. Gerhardt stopped beside him and pointed at the inscriptions.

"That is the tree of knowledge, in the Garden Eden," said Gerhardt.

"The spiral form of the trunk looks just like a strand of DNA," replied Jerry.

"I never considered that," said Gerhardt as he touched it with his fingers.

"Who are the figures above the images of the man and woman standing beside the tree?" asked Jerry.

"That is the council of the Gods," replied Gerhardt. "This portion of the myth describes how the chief of the gods decided to make man in their image."

"Almost makes me think that the image is describing a genetics laboratory," said Jerry as he studied the carvings.

Gerhardt's face flushed when Jerry made his comment.

"I'm sorry if I caused you offense, I didn't intend..."

"No offense taken"; said Gerhardt. "Your comment jogged a recent memory. "

"It appears that Mr. Schumacher is quite a talented observer," said Steffen as he approached.

"You have no idea," said Dr. Enoch.

"Actually I do have, he may prove to be quite useful in the coming days," said Steffen as he led the group to the star-chamber. As they gathered around the tablet, Dr. Enoch and Jerry studied it closely. Miranda stood back a little to make room for the two of them at the pedestal.

"That is the star tablet that was lost during the last century," said Jerry.

"This relic was discovered in the arms of the priest when we opened the ziggurat of Uruk in the year nineteen thirty seven," said Steffen.

As the statement registered with each them at approximately the same moment, Steffen suddenly became the object of attention.

"You were there?" asked Jerry.

"Yes, I was there."

"Johan Schmidt, the great grandfather of Heir Mueller was as well," said Steffen as he motioned in the direction of Gerhardt with his left hand.

"How old are you?" asked Miranda.

"Such a question from a lady," remarked Steffen jokingly.

Miranda smiled but continued looking directly at him, expecting an answer.

"I am one hundred forty seven years young my dear."

"How is that possible?" asked Jerry.

"It is a gift from the Gods," replied Steffen as he turned to Gerhardt. "Heir Mueller will explain it to you."

Gerhardt was caught by surprise by Steffen's comment as he began, "Of course I have only been here for a few days but ….."

"But you know enough," said Steffen.

Gerhardt mustered his thoughts momentarily and began, "The tablet appears to be designed specifically to interface with the central nervous system. When held correctly, the hands fall naturally into depressions that apparently act as contact points for some sort of information transfer."

"Information transfer?" asked Jerry.

"Yes," replied Gerhardt. "But more than that, the tablet generates an experiential state. It seems to be capable of transporting one beyond space and time."

"That is the source of your health?" asked Dr. Enoch.

"Yes," replied Steffen. "In addition to teaching me of the creation of man and the secrets of the cosmos the tablet has in some fashion corrected the defects in my genetic code that are responsible for the aging process."

"Remarkable," commented Dr. Enoch. "You mentioned secrets of the cosmos; what did you mean by that?"

"For the past thirty years the tablet has shown me where the ancient ones came from, how they created the Adam race, the locations of several important celestial objects that they use for interstellar and trans-dimensional travel, and many other things," replied Steffen.

"Many other things?" quizzed Jerry.

Steffen stared at him with his piercing blue eyes. "The ancient ones predicted the present instability in our sun, and they left us the technology to prevent the destruction of our planet."

"Why?" asked Jerry.

"We are their children," replied Steffen. "They created us for a purpose, we must rediscover that purpose, and reclaim our destiny."

51

GENERAL RUDACIL VIEWED THE MISSION data from the Sulphur Creek incident with two of his senior officers.

"As you can see general, there was no indication of the object on the radar of any of our birds," said one of the officers.

"One of the pilots picked up a shadow but there was no visual on the object," stated the other man.

"The recon satellite that observed the mission picked up an EM signature less than a mile from the lead Osprey as they were approaching the landing zone," said the first officer. "The object lifted off from this area and flew vertically until it achieved low orbit, disappearing over the Arctic Circle."

General Rudacil chewed on the synthetic cigar that was always within an arm's reach as he considered the report.

"How fast was this thing?"

"Faster than any known aerial vehicle sir, it exceeded seven thousand kilometers per hour as it passed over Canada."

"So it just went off into space and we lost it at that point?" asked General Rudacil.

"Yes sir, but we have reconfigured our satellites to see the energy field that it appears to generate. We'll see it if it flies again."

"Thank you gentlemen, you are dismissed," said General Rudacil as he spun in his chair to face the window. Twilight was beginning to settle over the city and for the first time in living memory the sky over Washington glowed with the green and purple ribbons of an Aurora.

"Strange," mumbled general Rudacil as he collected his thoughts.

Dr. Enoch scrambled for his glasses as he was awakened in the middle of the night by his tablet chirping on the nightstand. He tapped the screen and Ed Gilstrap's face appeared.

"Hello Ed, what can I do for you?"

"I heard that you and your team had disappeared. I called this number on the off chance that I could reach you."

"We were forced to leave rather abruptly," replied Dr. Enoch. "We are safe and secure, away from prying eyes."

"Any chance that you can turn the array back on?" asked Ed.

"So they turned it off then?"

"We stopped receiving telemetry yesterday around noon," replied Ed. "You said they turned it off, who are you talking about?"

"Four black tilt rotorcraft landed at the array just as we were leaving, we didn't wait around for introductions," said Dr. Enoch.

"I see," said Ed pausing momentarily, "I have other news."

"Alright," replied Dr. Enoch.

"There is a very large plasma wave headed our way, it is the frontal boundary of a corona mass ejection that left the surface of the sun two hours ago," said Ed.

"How bad will it be?" asked Dr. Enoch.

"It could take out communications in large areas globally and knock out significant portions of the electric grid." Replied Ed. "But that is not the worst of it."

"Oh?" replied Dr. Enoch.

"We think that the sun may be expanding."

A silent pause allowed Ed's statement to register in Dr. Enoch's sleepy brain.

Dr. Enoch began to say, "Stars only expand when they start to run out of hydrogen."

Dr Enoch felt the primordial sting of fear in his fingertips as this revelation swept over him.

He was fully alert now.

"Why do you think the sun may be enlarging?" He asked as he rolled upright, holding his tablet in one hand while attempting to locate his glasses with the other.

"We lost two of our Prometheus solar observatories but before they went offline their temperature sensors were over two hundred degrees above normal," replied Ed. "Venus has warmed by over twenty degrees during the past six months as well."

"I see," said Dr. Enoch. "Do you have modeling data on the expansion theory?"

"We do, and it's scary," replied Ed.

"The worst scenario I can think of is red giant," said Dr. Enoch. "Surely it isn't that bad."

"Actually that is what the data suggests, the beginning of the red giant phase," said Ed.

"I stand corrected, that is bad."

"There is one last thing," said Ed.

"Oh?"

"The military is convinced that the Eris anomaly is in some way responsible. They claim to have statistical data to support their suspicion."

"Of course they do," replied Dr. Enoch sarcastically. "It is clear at this point in time that the Eris Mission was a strike package disguised as a science mission."

"You may be right Samuel, but it was the only way to get the mission together."

The conversation stalled into an uneasy truce.

"Keep me posted Ed."

"I will do what I can Samuel."

Dr. Enoch's tablet switched itself into sleep mode as the transmission terminated. Unlike the device, it was not easy for Dr. Enoch to return to a state of slumber; having spent many long nights observing the heavens, once he was awakened in the middle of the night, he was usually up for the rest of the day. He sat on the end of the bed for a moment and considered the ramifications of his situation. He knew that his team would not be going home any time soon. It was obviously a government operation that shut down the array and attempted to take them into custody. He was fairly certain that Ed had no knowledge of the operation, but he was just as certain that General Rudacil did. He checked wrist tablet. It was a little after four a.m. After a quick shower, he dressed and headed for the hall of creation. If nothing else, he could at least study something of interest. He left his room and started down the hall. He paused slightly as he passed Jerry's room. He considered waking him but decided to proceed on his own. The stairway leading down to the main entry hall was lit by sconces and tread lighting. As he reached the bottom he headed down the same hallway that they had taken earlier that led to the exhibit hall. Halfway down the hall, he noticed that a room was lit on the right. He peeked in as he reached the threshold. Steffen was sitting behind a large desk working. Without looking up Steffen spoke as if fully aware of his presence.

"Good morning Dr. Enoch, you are not sleeping well?"

"It isn't for lack of hospitality," replied Dr. Enoch. "I was awakened by a call from a colleague back home."

Steffen looked up and smiled, "This will likely be your home for some time, make yourself comfortable and enjoy it."

"Thank you, I was going to have a look at the artifacts again."

"Yes, I know," replied Steffen. "The lights are on a panel just as you enter the room at the end of the hall."

He resumed working as Dr. Enoch continued down the hall. As he entered the exhibit room, he noticed a dim glow in the chamber that housed the star tablet. Rather than switching the lights on, he made his way through the dim room and entered the star-chamber. The tablet glowed eerily and it cast projections on the domed surface of the chamber. He instantly recognized the images as a map of the night sky.

"That is strange," he said aloud. "How does an ancient relic thousands of years old project current star maps of the night sky?"

"Because it is no mere relic," said Steffen's voice from somewhere in the darkness."

A moment later he entered the chamber and stood opposite of Dr. Enoch, on the other side of the pedestal that held the tablet.

"This same tablet instructed the ancient people of Uruk over ten thousand years ago," said Steffen.

"Instructed them?" asked Dr. Enoch, "through the images?"

"No, the images have a purpose but that is not how the Gods spoke to their children."

"What then?" asked Dr. Enoch?

"Pick it up," said Steffen.

Dr. Enoch steadied himself in front of the pedestal as he gently removed the tablet.

"It's warm," said Dr. Enoch.

"Rotate it in your hands until you find the position that fits your hands most comfortably."

Dr. Enoch experimented with different positions until his hands fell perfectly into smooth depressions that seemed to be purposefully made for human hands.

"Breathe deeply and relax your mind," said Steffen.

After several deep breaths, Dr. Enoch sensed a tingling sensation in his hands. Warmth began to fill the joints in his fingers and it soon flooded into his arms as it permeated his senses he suddenly realized that he was floating in space above a strange grey world covered in a thin layer of silvery dust. As the orb rotated, a structure came into view. It appeared to be a pyramid with a flat platform, similar to the stepped pyramids of the Ancient Earth. As he watched the structure rotate out of view, an object approached the planet. As it continued closer, it grew larger until it completely filled the horizon. It was a great city floating in space. The exterior structure appeared to be solid gold. It was a round like a great dish with a clear dome that covered most of the upper surface. As it orbited, the planet a smaller craft detached from the mother ship and descended to the surface, landing on the top of the stepped pyramid. A voice that he had never heard yet was strangely familiar and comforting formed the word Eris in his thoughts. The image then faded from his conscious and he found himself standing once again in the Star-Chamber holding the tablet.

Steffen observed that Dr. Enoch's eyes glowed brilliantly as he opened them. He also noticed that there was absolutely no fear of, or resistance to the experience.

"That is how the gods gave instruction to their children," said Steffen.

"I wanted to see more," replied Dr. Enoch.

"You will," said Steffen. "You should probably return to your room now. You will soon become very tired."

Steffen's advice was well warranted. As Dr. Enoch made his way up the staircase to the guest rooms, he was overcome with exhaustion. As he closed the door to his room, he was just able to get his slippers off before collapsing onto the bed.

Several hours later breakfast was served in the large dining hall between the kitchen and the courtyard. Jerry, Miranda, Gerhardt and Steffen had gathered for their morning meal.

"Anybody seen Doc?" asked Jerry as he noted his absence.

"He was up rather late last evening," replied Steffen.

"Oh yeah?" quizzed Jerry.

"He was interested in the star tablet," replied Steffen. "He was having difficulty sleeping so he visited the hall of creation to satisfy his curiosity."

Gerhardt noted the concern that Jerry and Miranda expressed for their friend.

"I hope he is alright," said Miranda. "He is usually the first to arrive every morning; it is unlike him to sleep in."

Steffen looked up from his breakfast and smiled warmly as he said, "trust me my dear when I tell you that he is perfectly fine. In fact he will awaken feeling as though he has been reborn."

"What happened last night?" Jerry shot back with alarm in his voice.

Steffen placed his utensils on the table and placed his hands disarmingly at his side. "Your concern for your friend is an admirable display of loyalty, but you should not worry, he really is simply resting from his interaction with the star tablet."

Gerhardt interjected, "It's alright Jerry. The first time that I interfaced with the tablet I slept for hours afterward."

"How do we know that it is safe for a man of Doc's age to mess with alien technology?" asked Jerry in protest.

"Because I am a grown man and I will do as I please, said Dr. Enoch as he approached from the kitchen."

Jerry's face was flush with embarrassment. "It's alright Jerry," said doc as he pat the younger man's shoulder and took the chair beside him."

Miranda placed her hand upon her mouth in surprise as she noticed the brilliance of Dr. Enoch's eyes. Jerry glanced at all three men sitting before him. They all had blue eyes and they all appeared to be a surreal brilliant blue color.

"Jerry, you won't believe what I saw," said Dr. Enoch.

"Saw when?" asked Jerry.

"Last night I held the tablet and it took me to ancient Eris. I have the impression that what I saw took place eons in the past; when the structure we saw in the mission video was first constructed.

"How do you know?" asked Jerry.

"A voice, no not a voice, a thought from the cosmos entered my mind," said Dr. Enoch.

"That is what I heard when I was shown Eden by the tablet," said Gerhardt.

"Eden?" asked Miranda.

"Yes, a garden paradise orbiting the earth," replied Gerhardt.

Dr. Enoch took a sip of his coffee and placed the cup back on the table as he said, "I have news from Ed Gilstrap at Space Command."

"When did you hear from him?" asked Jerry.

"Last night he contacted me on my tablet," replied Dr. Enoch.

"Good thing I redirected all of our conversations to anonymous com sites on the world net," replied Jerry. "We wouldn't want those black tilt rotors popping up over the horizon again."

"You need not be overly concerned with security at this location," replied Steffen. "I have long standing arrangements with the military of this country."

"So what did Ed have to say?" asked Jerry.

"He was curious as to our whereabouts."

"I suspect that he was," replied Jerry.

"Apparently he was unaware of the raid on our facilities at Sulphur Creek," said Dr. Enoch. "His reason for contacting me was to notify me of the latest news regarding the solar storms. He wanted our help in studying the activity and he wanted to know when we could possibly resume telemetry relay from the Eris mission."

"What is the deal with the sun?" asked Jerry.

"It is growing," replied Dr. Enoch. "The military is convinced that the energy burst from Eris has something to do with it."

"Stars only grow when they are running out of hydrogen," said Jerry as he was thinking through the scenario. That is really bad. If the sun is becoming a red giant the earth is doomed."

Steffen had listened intently to the conversation but had been silent until this point. "The gods foretold of this danger and they promised to return and save us at the appropriate time."

"How can anyone reverse a red giant star?" asked Jerry. "The energy requirements would be absolutely unbelievable."

"I don't know the answers to these things," replied Steffen. "But the ancient ones new it would happen and they left warnings about it."

Miranda slid her arm around Jerry's as a means of comforting herself.

"Warnings?" asked Jerry.

Gerhardt joined the conversation once more by interjecting, "The Maya described a period of destruction sometime after the end of the long count calendar. The Christian Bible describes a time that the earth will be consumed by fire as well. Most cultures have a global destruction myth."

"Perhaps they all share a common origin," said Dr. Enoch as he turned toward Jerry. "Is there any possibility that you could access the array remotely? "

With a crooked smile Jerry said"; yeah Doc, I know where the back door is."

"Can you control the array from here as well?"

"I can, and the best part is that nobody will know."

Dr. Enoch looked back toward Steffen as he asked, "What did you mean when you said that the ancients warned of this?"

"I will show you," said Steffen as he backed away from the table and stood. "There is a panel in the hall of creation that you will find interesting."

The group left their seats and followed Steffen through the house to the exhibit hall. Light from the great windows overlooking the Caspian Sea filled the room with a warm glow.

"This place is so beautiful," said Miranda as she gazed out of the windows on their way to the display area.

"Thank you my dear," replied Steffen warmly. "It has been a long time since I have enjoyed the perspective of a woman."

Jerry breathed deeply and Miranda took his hand, somewhat amused by his discomfort. Steffen sensed it as well and smiled as they continued toward the exhibit room. They walked past the creation story that was inscribed on the first panels, all the way to the end of the hall. They stopped at the final wall segment, just in front of the star-chamber.

"This is the panel that describes the final period of man before the new order," said Steffen.

"New order?" asked Dr. Enoch.

"Yes, at the end of the epoch in which we now live, the sun will begin to grow and the gods will intervene and prevent the destruction of the earth," said Steffen.

"I see what you are describing," said Gerhardt. "No one has interpreted the panels that way before. Here in this panel the sun is depicted much smaller than in that one. How did you make that conclusion?" asked Gerhardt.

"I didn't," replied Steffen, "it was revealed to me while I was using the tablet some time ago."

"May I?" asked Jerry as he gestured toward the tablet with his hand.

"Certainly," replied Steffen.

Jerry lifted the tablet from the pedestal and carefully examined it. It was lighter than he expected and felt cool in his hands.

"The surface is incredibly smooth," said Jerry as he rotated it in his hands. "There are depressions that seem to fit the hands perfectly," he said as he held it in front of his chest. After several moments, he placed it back on the pedestal.

Steffen studied him intently as he turned back from the relic. "Did you not sense anything unusual as you held the tablet?" asked Steffen.

"Nothing," replied Jerry.

"Really?" asked Dr. Enoch. "It did not feel warm in your hands?"

"No," replied Jerry, "it was a cool metallic object."

As they stood around the tablet Miranda appeared startled.

"What is it Miranda," asked Dr. Enoch.

"It's your eyes; they appear to be glowing, a brilliant blue, all of you except for Jerry."

"I have brown eyes," said Jerry."

"Johan had brown eyes as well," said Steffen. "I always wondered why he suffered with illness when he had the tablet for all of those years."

"Perhaps the genetic code that produces blue eyes also makes it possible to interface with the tablet," said Miranda.

"You have brown eyes my dear," said Steffen, why don't you take the tablet."

Miranda appeared apprehensive initially, but she stepped to the pedestal and removed the relic. After holding it in the prescribed manner for several minutes, she placed it back on the pedestal.

"Nothing," she said, "just a cool metallic object."

"Interesting observation," commented Gerhardt. "Western culture has always revered blonde hair and blue eyes or the fair ones." Gerhardt shrugged as he continued, "perhaps we instinctively recognize something from the ages past."

"Whether we do or not, that thing does," replied Jerry as he nodded in the direction of the tablet.

"You mentioned that the gods would intervene," said Dr. Enoch as he focused his attention away from the tablet and toward Steffen. "Do you have an idea of how?"

"No," said Steffen.

"The tablet didn't indicate future events?" asked Jerry.

"No, it does not foretell future events," replied Steffen.

"But you said that the ancient ones predicted the Sun would become unstable... I get it," Jerry said in a moment of revelation. "These beings; the First Ones, were not gods, they were a space faring civilization. They were advanced enough that they knew our sun would become unstable at some point in the future, they may even have been capable of predicting when it would happen based upon some criteria that they understood."

Steffen smiled as he patiently listened to Jerry. "Had you lived ten thousand years ago and witnessed the arrival of the ancient ones; you too would have called them gods. Even now, if they appear and prevent the earth from being consumed by fire; most of the population will call it a miracle of god."

"That is a good point, but science can explain all of it, replied Jerry.

"So until you are presented with a case of the unexplainable you cannot believe in God?" asked Steffen.

"I don't think that we will solve the faith verses science argument today," said Dr. Enoch.

Steffen bowed his head slightly and replied, "You are correct heir doctor; we have a bit of work to do."

"He's right Doc; I need to call up the array." Jerry turned toward Steffen and asked, "Do you have an office where we can set up a control center?"

"Right this way," Replied Steffen.

52

E D STUDIED THE LATEST DATA from Hermes on his tablet as he waited just outside of the White House Situation room. He was not as nervous this time as he had been a few weeks earlier. The events of the preceding days had provided a sense of perspective. He was after all grappling with the possibility that the earth could be scorched out of existence in the near future. He had waited only about ten minutes when the door opened and a uniformed military officer walked from the room and saluted him.

"The Joint Chiefs are ready for you sir," said the young man.

Ed stood and adjusted his suit before confidently striding into the room. A couple of the men seated around the table glanced at him as he approached the empty seat at the far end of the room. As he pulled the chair away from the table and sat, he observed General Rudacil working with his tablet. After a few moments, the president entered the room. As he took his place at the end of the table, he glanced in Ed's direction and began the meeting.

"Ladies and gentlemen let us welcome Mr. Gilstrap of Space Command once again to our round table," said the president.

Ed nodded in acknowledgement as the president continued, "I know that it may be difficult to imagine in light of the string of unusual events the world has seen of late, but we have yet another situation that is developing in deep space. General Rudacil of the United States Space Command will now brief us regarding this latest issue."

"Thank you Mr. President," replied the general. "Some of you are aware of the very long range celestial detection system that scans the inner solar system for objects that could pose an impact hazard with the Earth. Approximately seventy two hours ago a large object was detected crossing the orbit of Jupiter."

Ed sat attentively in his chair as the video system in the room initiated. Clear panes of glass emerged from slits on the large table in front of each seating position. As the video presentation began, the glass changed from translucent clear, to an opaque hi definition image. The inner planets were depicted much larger than actual scale in order to illustrate the relative position of the objects. As the general began his presentation, a preprogrammed graphic ran on the displays illustrating his talking points.

"As you can see, the object is still outside of the orbit of Mars."

"Do you have any physical data relating to the object?" asked the presidents science advisor.

"Presently we have minimal information regarding the physicals of the object. Based upon radar returns and other data, we suspect that it is a very dense M Class asteroid," replied General Rudacil.

"How large is it?"

General Rudacil paused briefly before he replied, "early indications are that it may be ten thousand meters or larger.

"Does it pose a collision threat to the earth?" asked the President.

"Possibly sir," replied General Rudacil. "It appears to be on a course that will bring it very close to earth."

"What does Space Command have to say about this object?" asked the president.

"It was first reported approximately forty eight hours ago," replied Ed. "We are attempting to observe it with telescopes but we have not gotten a good look at it yet."

"Does anyone suspect that there is a link between this latest development and the Eris Anomaly?" asked the president.

While Ed was surprised by the question, General Rudacil was prepared for it. "Mr. President; Space Command has several long range asteroid-interceptors on stand-by in the event that they are needed."

"What do you think Mr. Gilstrap's?" asked the president.

Ed could see General Rudacil glaring at him as he began. "We have never attempted to affect an object of that size before Mr. President. If it is a large M-Class body the interceptors will have a negligible effect."

Ed paused for a moment before continuing; "Your question regarding a connection between the Eris anomaly and this latest event makes me wonder if indeed there may be a link."

"I want Space Command to find me some answers right away," said the president. "Is there anything that you need?"

"Yes sir, I need access to all of the telemetry and other data from all service branches and agencies as well as a team of analysts to compile and review the data."

"Done," said the president.

There is one other issue," said Ed. "I need access to live telemetry from Midway Station, right away."

"Done," said the president again.

"General Rudacil quietly noted something on his tablet as the meeting adjourned."

53

As Miranda stood on the second floor mezzanine admiring the black sea just beyond the cliffs a military vehicle squealed to a stop in the courtyard of the main house. She could hear Steffen's butler giving instructions in an Eastern European language, which was unfamiliar to her. After a moment the vehicle lurched forward, barely making a sound as its electric propulsion unit carried it to a service entrance that led around the property.

"Perhaps the items that Heir Schumacher and Heir Enoch requested will be on today's truck," said Steffen as he approached from behind her. Miranda was a little spooked and she unconsciously gathered the shawl that she wearing about her shoulders.

"I am sorry my dear, I didn't mean to startle you," said

Steffen as he joined her at the rail several feet away, instinctively avoiding stepping into her comfort zone.

"Why it is that ancient place is always so beautiful?" she asked looking toward the horizon.

"Perhaps there is some aspect of the human conscience that recognizes the energy of a place," said Steffen. "The souls that came before may still in some way connect with us in such places."

"Maybe," said Miranda.

Miranda felt more comfortable as she spoke with Steffen, he reminded her in some ways of a grandfather who simply wanted the companionship of his children.

"Steffen chuckled slightly," I have never been compared to a grandfather before," he said.

"Now that is really spooky," she said as she resisted the urge to step away.

"Forgive me, I sometimes have difficulty differentiating between a person's thoughts and their spoken word," said Steffen.

"I intend no harm to you or your friends, you are free to come and go as you please and my home is your home; unequivocally."

"Thank you she said timidly."

"So have you determined a name for your baby?"

"Baby?" she asked.

"You aren't certain yet, but you suspect that you are carrying Heir Schumacher's child," said Steffen.

"I thought that I would wait a bit longer, just to be certain," replied Miranda tentatively.

"No need to wait, said Steffen with a smile, you are most assuredly with child; I can sense him."

Tears began to fill her eyes as she looked away, "him?" she asked.

"Come my dear, let us find the others and get to work, I promise you everything will be alright," Steffen took her arm in his and led her down the staircase into the atrium.

As they entered the space, Jerry looked up from the task he was performing and saw that Miranda had attempted to dry her eyes.

"What's wrong Miranda?" Jerry asked with alarm.

Steffen handed her arm to Jerry as he said, "it's just a bit of nerves in a strange place, take good care of her; she is a special lady."

Miranda turned back to Steffen and pulled his tall frame toward her, kissing his cheek. "Thanks grandpa she said."

"You are welcome dear," replied Steffen.

"Grandpa?" asked Jerry.

"Private joke, replied Miranda, maybe I'll tell you about it sometime."

"We have worked to do folks," said Dr. Enoch as he and Gerhardt shuffled by carrying a large video panel.

"It's ok," said Miranda as she squeezed Jerry's hand. "Better get at it before Doc loses his patience."

Steffen held the door as Dr. Enoch and Gerhardt shuffled their way into the library.

Jerry took a seat at one of the tables and began working with his tablet. "Time to open the back door," he said smiling as he accessed the Alexandria site. After he entered the appropriate codes, he accessed a hidden network switch inside the data head end within the observatory. His keystrokes deactivated the console that the government had installed and began silently activating all of the systems of the array. Within an hour, he could control the array as effectively from his new location as he could if he were at his console in Sulphur Creek.

"The array is back on line," said Jerry.

"Alright then, let's have a look at the telemetry from Eris," said Dr. Enoch.

As the team busied themselves with the data from the array, Steffen silently left them to their work. His departure was unnoticed by everyone except for Miranda. As she stared in the direction of the door, she heard Jerry say, "Looks like we have a message from Adam."

"What does it say?" asked Dr. Enoch.

"I don't know yet," replied Jerry. "I am still waiting for it to process; looks like it is several days old."

"He and Eve are in an alien space craft," said Jerry as he turned to face the rest of the group.

"What else does it say?" asked Dr. Enoch.

"Very little," said Jerry. "He wanted us to know that they made it before Space Command shut down Hermes."

"Good for them," said Miranda with a smile. "He gave up everything for her."

Jerry noticed that she was staring directly at him when she spoke, as did everyone else in the room.

"How could he have sent a message after shutdown?" asked Dr. Enoch.

Jerry still held Miranda's gaze from her previous comment. He mouthed the words, "tonight we'll talk," as he turned to his tablet and replied to Dr. Enoch, "I am checking the time stamps to see when the transmission occurred."

"If he is not on Hermes, then where is he," asked Gerhardt.

"That is the question of the hour my friend," replied Dr. Enoch.

"The transmission occurred several hours after Hermes was shutdown," said Jerry nervously.

The room fell silent for a moment as revelation washed over them.

"Something out there is helping him," said Miranda.

"Not only that but he has now transcended human technology," said Dr. Enoch.

"I hope he still likes us," muttered Gerhardt.

"Perhaps we should have a look at the data from the last solar observation," said Dr. Enoch as he briskly attempted to change the subject and keep everyone on task.

"OK Doc, give me just a minute," replied Jerry as he worked his magic. The video panel became a mirror image of the control room video panel back home. Jerry configured the image to display two panes of information. The left pane contained real time data from several antennae in the array that they had configured for solar observation prior to their miraculous escape several days before; and the left pane was a display panel for virtually any type of information.

"It is several hours before sunrise at the array so we don't have real time data," said Jerry as he explained the imagery to Gerhardt.

"This is what we collected during daylight hours yesterday. The two lines show the Solar Mean Output for a given range of days, in this case thirty, compared to the output of any day or range of days that we want to see."

"I see," said Gerhardt, so yesterday is higher than average."

"Yes replied Jerry, it is, in fact it is higher than I expected."

"Check the rate of change please Jerry," said Doctor Enoch.

"Already on it Doc," replied Jerry.

A chart appeared on the video panel with an upward sweeping curve.

"Output is increasing," said Doctor Enoch.

"Yeah Doc, faster than anybody expected," replied Jerry.

"What does this mean?" asked Gerhardt.

"It means that the sun has become less stable. It is in a phase of increased output and it may even be expanding," said Jerry.

"It also means that the Earth will warm and disruptions to the climate will occur," added Dr. Enoch.

"That is not the worst of it though," said Jerry. "There is a phenomenon called a corona mass ejection. Think of it as a solar flare on steroids. If the sun throws a really big one in our direction then the earth could be zapped by huge amounts of solar radiation."

"Has this ever happened before?" asked Gerhardt.

"Not since humans walked the earth," replied Dr. Enoch.

"How do we know?" asked Gerhardt.

"Because we are still here," replied Jerry curtly.

"I see," replied Gerhardt. "I am asking because there was quite a bit of attention given to the sun by the Sumerians. They may have predicted this phenomenon in their prophetic writings."

"The Maya did as well," said Miranda.

"Yes, they did indeed," replied Gerhardt. "Christian and Muslim scriptures also describe a future catastrophic event that results in the destruction of the earth and the heavens by fire."

"With their eventual replacement by a new heaven and a

new earth," interjected Jerry, "The Revelation of Saint John the Divine."

"Impressive," replied Miranda as she winked at him.

"I attended Sunday School as a kid," said Jerry.

"Perhaps all of these civilizations contain similar mythology because they were schooled in the knowledge of the cosmos by the same source," said Dr. Enoch.

"Perhaps if you had lived as long as I have you would have taken the time to read the mythologies of man," said Steffen. "Or perhaps not; my interest was initially based on a selfish desire to trade antiquities. It was only after my mind was opened by the tablet that the universe was opened to me."

"The Universe was opened?" asked Dr. Enoch.

"You will discover what that means the more you engage the tablet," replied Steffen. "The mythologies that describe future events are attempts by men to describe the ancient knowledge imparted by the Gods. It has been filtered and corrupted by the religious and political institutions that claimed to safeguard it. Much of it has been lost to the deeds of man, the burning of libraries, the destruction of sacred sites, corrupting the knowledge to enslave rather than enlighten; this is the legacy of ignorance and fear that led to the modern age."

"The modern age meaning the age of science and technology?" asked Dr. Enoch.

"Yes, soon the children of the new age will be reintroduced to the gods.

"How soon?" asked Gerhardt from the other side of the room.

"Imminently soon," replied Steffen.

"Hey Doc, there is a communication pending from Ed

Gilstrap on the network at the array," said Jerry. "It's only a few hours old."

"He could have contacted me on my tablet," mused Dr. Enoch. "I wonder why he chose the array network."

"Because he's smart," replied Jerry. "He suspects that we can access the array without giving away our location. He doesn't know that we can also use our personal devices safely."

"Let see what he has to say," said Dr. Enoch.

Jerry sent the video message to the large viewing panel that they had moved into the room.

"Hello Samuel," said Ed as he considered his words carefully. "You are no doubt aware of the strange solar phenomenon that we have observed lately. We have several teams working around the clock but we have made no real progress toward finding an answer." Ed paused as he struggled with whether or not to divulge what he was about to say. "There is something new. A very large object has entered our solar system and it is headed our way. We thought that it was an M-Class asteroid initially but it has proven to be something else entirely. It is emitting radio frequency on the same band as your signal. We will be tasking an orbital telescope to get optical imagery of the object within the next 24 hours." Ed put his hands together and rested his chin on his fingertips briefly before saying, "For what it's worth, we could use your help."

"Wow, I never thought I would here that," said Jerry.

"Nor I," replied Dr. Enoch.

Dr. Enoch turned toward Steffen and asked, "You knew about the object didn't you?"

"Yes"

"So what is it?" asked Dr. Enoch.

"It is the great city of the heavens described by our ancestors."

"Is it a space craft?" asked Jerry.

"I suppose you could call it a spacecraft but it is a great deal more than that," said Steffen.

"The voice that I heard when I held the tablet told you of this didn't it?" asked Dr. Enoch.

"I heard a voice as well, when I held the tablet," said Gerhardt.

"The guardian of heaven is the voice that you heard," replied Steffen.

"The guardian of heaven?" asked Jerry.

"He is a first one, he existed in the time before man," replied Steffen.

"Is that like an angel?" asked Miranda.

"It is the same," replied Steffen.

"What does he look like?" asked Miranda.

"I have never seen him, although we have communicated with one another for many years. He and others like him do not exist within bodies like we do; they are of the spirit world, although they may take physical form when it suits them."

"Makes sense to me," replied Jerry. "Complex biological life forms are not suitable for interstellar space travel."

"That makes sense to me as well," replied Gerhardt. "Throughout history people have described angelic beings as existing in the spirit realm. They are typically portrayed as glowing or wearing brilliant garments and their exposure to people is usually very brief."

"Maybe they are radioactive," chuckled Jerry.

"That could be a real possibility," replied Dr. Enoch. "If in fact they are beings of pure energy, they could emit radiation that is dangerous to humans."

"The Biblical account of Moses' encounter with God on Mt. Sinai describes how Moses was required to stay a safe distance away from God," said Gerhardt. "He was not allowed to look upon the most high because the glory of God is more than a human can endure. This carried forward into the worship practices of the Jews. The inner chamber of the temple was shielded from view of the people in order to protect them from the glory of God. Those that trespassed were said to have been killed by something during their transgression."

"That sounds quite severe," replied Miranda.

"That is simply the way it was, the priests were only allowed to enter on certain days and when they did they had a rope tied around their waste in the event that they too were killed during the visit."

"A rope; you have got to be kidding," replied Jerry.

"It was the way they retrieved the body," replied Gerhardt.

"What else can you tell us about these beings?" asked Dr. Enoch

"They neither eat nor drink," replied Steffen as he thoughtfully considered the many sessions of communion throughout the past decades. "They do not need air, they can manifest themselves in the physical world but they do not have a biological form."

"There is so much that I would like to know," said Dr. Enoch.

"Go to the star-chamber and seek the answers," replied Steffen.

"Is it really that simple?" asked Dr. Enoch.

"Yes," said Steffen as he gestured in the direction of the door.

54

General Rudacil's face appeared on the communications console at Midway Station as the commander turned to silence the beeping alarm that notified him of the pending transmission. After placing his thumb on the screen, a live video session opened.

"Good day General Rudacil," said the commander with a salute.

"Afternoon, Commander Epperson," replied the general. "Are you boys ready for some action up there?"

"Yes sir, the men are itching for something to shoot at."

"Alright then, check the tasking orders in the mission profile attached to this communication session. We have a big one coming straight at us; it looks to be M class and its one of the largest asteroids on record," said General Rudacil.

"That will take a lot of ordinance sir," replied the commander.

"We will be shooting penetrators on this target, said the general."

"Penetrators?" asked the Commander.

"Is there a problem with your orders commander?"

"No sir; will be ready." replied Commander Epperson"

After the transmission ended, he opened the tasking orders and studied the mission profile. "The men will get a kick out of this one," he said to himself as he turned away from the console and headed for the crew lounge."

Ed had just finished his mid morning coffee in the executive break room when an urgent call appeared on his tablet from mission control. "What is it John?" he asked as he tapped the screen and opened the images imbedded in the video call.

"We have visuals on the object that we started tracking last week and it's not an asteroid," replied John. "I sent a couple of images but you probably want to see this on the big screen."

"On my way," replied Ed.

As he started for the elevator, the first image appeared on the screen of his tablet. He stopped mid stride as he saw the image. Upon the realization of what he was seeing, he began running for the elevators in the lobby. Finding one available on his floor he bounded into it and called out, "Mission Control!"

A minute later, he was placing his thumb on the biometric scanner at the entrance to the control center. Upon confirmation of his identity, the large smoked glass door that spanned the entrance to the primary control room opened and Ed bounded through. Everyone in the room was staring at the main view screen, fixated upon the image that it contained. As Ed looked toward the screen, he stopped cold in his tracks. "Holy….." His voice trailed away as he failed to complete his sentence. John turned toward him and said, "Told you it's not an asteroid."

"You get the understatement of the year award for that one," replied Ed. "Jesus that thing is huge," he continued.

A few moments of silence ensued as they simply stared in wonder at the image.

John broke the silence by saying, "It's between ten and twelve thousand meters according to the early data from the telescopes. It's moving fast too. It will cross Earth's orbit in a few days."

"Sure about that?" asked Ed.

"Yep, it seems to be headed right for us," replied John.

"What is the spectrometric data telling us about it?" asked Ed.

"It's metallic, but the composition is unknown," replied John.

"Imagine what it took to build something like that," said Ed as he gazed in wonder at the screen, "over three kilometers wide."

"And a kilometer thick in the center," countered John. "All of this data is subject to change as the object gets closer and we get better measurements, but the rough dimensions should be fairly accurate."

"Anyone else seen it yet?" asked Ed.

"The European Space Agency and the Chinese have made official inquiries, so the short answer is yes," replied John.

"I suspect this will start headlining in the news media within a day or so," said Ed. "There will be no way to keep a lid on this one."

"I wonder why it's here and why now," asked John.

"Good question," replied Ed as he turned from the main

view screen to a secondary screen that displayed real time solar data.

"Do you think the recent solar activity has something to do with it?" asked John.

"One way or another I suspect that it does," replied Ed. "In fact, I would bet on it," he said as he moved closer to the display that contained the solar observations.

"This recent activity is unprecedented," said a female voice from behind him as he stood before the screen.

"Really," Ed asked sarcastically.

"Yes, really," replied an indignant Dr. Sandra Fergusson. "Some of us are so distracted by the little green men that we have forgotten about real science."

"That's why I came to see you, Fergy, said Ed with a crooked smile.

"You boys are impossible," she said as she pushed him out of her way with her shoulder as she maneuvered between Ed and the video display.

"The mean solar output has been increasing gradually for the past several weeks," she said as she tapped away at a touch panel. "There have been several solar flares recently and two of them are the largest ever recorded."

All joking had subsided as she got down to business. Ed genuinely respected her as one of the most professional and persistent members of the team.

"Something very much out of the ordinary is going on here boss." She said as she continued working the panel. "If this flare activity continues to grow in intensity I am afraid we could be in trouble soon."

"How so," asked Ed.

"Corona Mass Ejection," replied Dr. Fergusson.

"You can't be serious," replied Ed.

"Dead serious," replied Dr. Fergusson. "If the intensity of the storms continues to increase there is a statistically significant potential for a very large energy release."

"How serious is the potential?" asked Ed.

"If you were fortunate enough to be on the dark side of the earth when the plasma cloud passed you may survive, but life as you knew it the day before would be over," replied Dr. Fergusson.

"And what of the opposite side of the world?" asked Ed.

"The ocean would boil, and anything above ground would simply be scorched into oblivion. If the wave were dense enough the atmosphere would burn off and earth would become a very inhospitable place for life."

"That is pretty grim," replied Ed.

"The good news is; that's the worst case scenario. There's only a five percent probability of an event of that magnitude," replied Dr. Fergusson.

"So I shouldn't lose sleep about it yet?" asked Ed.

"Actually, yes you should. The problem is that we are beyond any reliable forecasting model. Six months ago the probability of an event like we are discussing was less than one tenth of one percent," replied Dr. Fergusson.

"I see," said Ed.

"The trouble is, we simply don't know why this is happening," said Dr. Fergusson as she thoughtfully studied the screen. "Something has changed the equation."

55

"HOW LONG HAS HE BEEN engaged with the tablet?" asked Miranda? The concern was evident in her expression as she leaned over to look closely at his face. She placed her hand beneath his nose to make sure that he was breathing before backing away from the lounge that he lay in, both hands firmly grasping the tablet.

"Most of the afternoon," replied Steffen.

"Can you provide a more specific time frame?" asked Jerry.

"Several hours, I do not know specifically how long," replied Steffen. "You need not be concerned, he is perfectly fine."

"What is happening asked Jerry?"

"He is communing with the gods," replied Steffen.

Miranda touched the back of Dr. Enoch's hand as she noticed how the age spots had disappeared.

"His skin has changed," she said as she looked toward Jerry. "Just a few days ago there were freckles and areas of discoloration; now they are gone."

"The tablet will repair his body and even improve him in some ways," said Steffen.

"Improve him?" asked Jerry.

"The effects will be impossible to predict but in my case it eliminated my physical frailties. Not only did the tablet reverse the aging process, it actually improved my ability to think and reason. It was as if a veil was lifted and I could perceive the true universe. I was a simple man, and it did that for me. Imagine what it could do for your friend, a scientist and scholar," replied Steffen.

Dr. Enoch was completely oblivious to the activity surrounding him. He was transported by the tablet to a place beyond imagination. He moved around space as if he were completely free of the physical world. The place in which he now stood was like a temple with gilded surfaces all around. Above him, he could see the stars through a great dome as clear as glass. It was there that another presence made contact with him. There was no physical manifestation only pure thought.

"Who is there?" he asked.

"Who do you seek?" replied a voice that defied description.

Suddenly he felt the grip of fear. He made a conscious effort to repress the impulse as he considered the question.

"I seek whoever may be here, in this place."

"You are the one called Samuel Enoch," replied the presence. "The one called Adam told me of you."

"Yes, I am," replied Dr. Enoch. "And who are you?"

"I am ….ancient," replied the voice.

"That is your name?" asked Dr. Enoch.

"We have no need of names," replied the entity.

"Where did you originate?" asked Dr. Enoch.

"We were old when your sun emerged from the darkness," replied the voice.

"Are there others like you?" asked Dr. Enoch.

"Yes ….."

"Are they here?

"No."

"Do you have a physical form?" asked Dr. Enoch.

"We transcended our physical entities long ago," replied the voice.

"Why, or how….

"Physical bodies cannot travel the cosmos; we left behind that existence for a new reality when our star died."

"When did your star die?" asked Dr. Enoch.

"When the universe was young," replied the voice. "Your sun formed from the remnants of the massive star that warmed our world."

"We call that a supernova," said Dr. Enoch.

"Yesss, it is the sssame."

"How did you escape?"

"We transcended our physical existence," replied the entity.

"Why are you here now?" asked Dr. Enoch.

"We are here to save your world."

"From what?" asked Dr. Enoch?

"Your star will die soon; if we do not prevent it."

"You have the technology to prevent a supernova?" asked Dr. Enoch.

"Yesss"

"Why couldn't you save your world?" asked Dr. Enoch.

"That was long ago, and it is beyond your understanding," replied the voice.

"Why bother with us?" asked Dr. Enoch.

Dr. Enoch's question trailed off into the absolute quiet of the temple where he stood. The seconds seemed like eternity as he waited for a response.

"You were created for a purpose that you have not fulfilled," replied the voice.

Dr. Enoch was numb with incredulity. His mind reeled at the implications of what he had just heard. Just as he was regaining his composure, his vision began to blur and he was swept away from that place. He awoke a moment later with Steffen, Miranda, Jerry and Gerhardt standing over him.

"Are you OK?" asked Miranda, the concern evident in her voice.

"Yes, I'm fine," replied Dr. Enoch as he leaned forward and swung his legs to the side of the lounge, rising to a seated position.

"What happened? What did you see?" asked Gerhardt.

Dr. Enoch rubbed his face before he replied, "It was absolutely incredible. I know how our sun was formed. It was born of a nebula that was left from a much greater star that went super nova."

"How do you know this?" asked Jerry.

"A voice, like pure thought, told me that in the time before our solar system there was another much larger star and a civilization existed on a planet orbiting that star."

"That would make them six or seven billion years old!" replied Jerry.

"You should see their ship, it's unbelievable," said Dr. Enoch.

"Ship?" asked Jerry.

"Yes, they are coming to save us from our sun," said Dr. Enoch as he began to lose consciousness.

"Supernova, its going supernova soon," said Dr. Enoch as he collapsed onto the lounge.

Steffen moved startling quickly and caught Dr. Enoch before he slipped off the lounge. He hefted him into his arms almost effortlessly and held him as though he were a child.

"He just needs to rest for a while," said Steffen in a matter of fact sort of way. I have experienced the same exhaustion after sessions such as this."

"Are you sure he's ok?" asked Miranda.

"I am quite sure my dear, he will awaken feeling like he has been reborn," replied Steffen.

"Let's take him up to his room and meet in the library to discuss what he told us."

Steffen led them up the stairs to Dr. Enoch's room. Miranda turned the bed down and Steffen placed him gently on the center of the mattress. Jerry and Gerhardt stayed in the hall as Miranda and Steffen tended to Dr. Enoch.

"Did you see how quickly he moved when he stopped Doc from falling?" asked Jerry.

"He is truly superhuman," replied Gerhardt. "Just like the mythological heroes of Greece and Rome."

"If memory serves, they tended to be fatally flawed in some fashion," said Jerry.

56

G ENERAL RUDACIL'S TABLET CHIRPED TO remind him
of an appointment as he read the quarterly status reports
of Space Command. A few moments later, there was a knock
at his door.

"Good morning Chaplain," said general Rudacil as he
motioned for him to enter.

There were many different religions represented by the
Chaplain Corp at the Pentagon. Father Dominic served the
Catholic flock on a rotation with several other priests from
the Washington area.

"Please have a seat," said the general as he motioned to one
of two chairs arranged around a coffee table on the front half
of his office. The table contained a sculpture of Constantine
riding a battle stallion and holding a standard with the cross

symbol. The holy- father smiled as he noticed a string of Rosaries draped over the sculpture.

"It is comforting to know that a man of your position and responsibility still holds to his faith," said Father Dominic.

General Rudacil dropped his head slightly in humility as he replied, "Well father, I must admit that I have not attended mass in a while and unfortunately I have not been to confession in a very long time."

"Father Dominic smiled and said, "Nobody is perfect, but I see that you still say your prayers." He motioned with his head toward the beads.

"Yes father, there are times when those are of great comfort," replied General Rudacil.

"I suspect so," replied Father Dominic.

"You have another message from the Vatican?" asked the general.

"I do," said Father Dominic as he adjusted his collar. "A Vatican official would like to meet with you this evening, his flight arrived this morning. I have been tasked with escorting you to the meeting, if that suits you."

"Certainly father, it would be an honor," replied General Rudacil.

An hour later, they entered the Basilica of the Immaculate Conception. The building was as regal as any that the church had ever constructed outside of the Vatican. Italian marble floors and walls were punctuated by black granite columns that were covered with engravings of commemoration. Father Dominic led them through the main lobby area to the administrative wing of the facility. As they entered the waiting, area a sister seated at the receptionist desk recognized Father Dominic and ushered them to a conference room a few meters down a hall that adjoined the lobby.

As they entered, they found a man seated at the conference table. He stood and bowed. As he did so, Father Dominic kissed his ring out of respect. General Rudacil stood with Military alertness.

"Father Dominic tells me that you a member of the flock," said the gentleman.

"Something of a sheep in wolves clothing, you might say," said General Rudacil.

The gentleman chuckled at the anecdotal reference.

"I am Cardinal Sebastian and I am here to discuss the recent discoveries in the heavens."

They each seated themselves at the conference table and the cardinal opened a door on the tabletop. As he did so, a small control panel emerged from a slot in the table and a large video panel on the wall opposite them flashed to life. An image of an observatory framed against a brilliant blue sky was present on the screen.

"This is the Vatican observatory in New Mexico," said the Cardinal.

"We have been studying the discovery reported a Dr. Samuel Enoch; who we understand is now missing with his primary team members, Jerry Schumacher and Miranda Lee."

General Rudacil continued to listen without response.

The next image was new.

"This is an object that will soon cross the orbital plane of the Earth; it is presently approximately halfway between Earth and Mars."

General Rudacil turned his attention to the Cardinal but remained silent.

"Although this latest development has not yet found its

way into the public domain, I am certain that you are aware of it."

The Cardinal looked back at the screen and another image appeared; a carved clay tablet with a map of the solar system.

"This tablet is over five thousand years old," said the Cardinal. "It was recovered from the ashes of the library of Alexandria."

General Rudacil continued to remain silent.

"It is unusual because it depicts the solar system in exactly the alignment that occurred when the object approaching earth emerged from the place of outer darkness," said the Cardinal.

"The place of outer darkness?" asked General Rudacil.

Cardinal Sebastian tapped the control panel and an image of the solar system appeared. He zoomed to the outermost extent and the orbits of the known planets were represented with orange lines. Beyond the Orbit of Pluto, in a region of space near Eris, a red circle illustrated what General Rudacil knew to be the spatial anomaly that Hermes had encountered during its journey to Eris. He split the screen and on the left showed a photo image of an ancient yellowed parchment that depicted the trajectory of the object approaching earth.

"This image of the heavens was produced by Leonardo DaVinci following a two year descent into madness. He gave it to the church for safekeeping following an exorcism that cleansed his soul of an evil that tortured him for years." The Cardinal stared into the Colonels eyes before continuing. "It has been seen only by a very select group of individuals. Although he never explained what it meant; the Vatican interpretation is that it depicts Satan leaving the pit of darkness to return to earth with the fallen angels,"

"That is an interesting story," replied General Rudacil.

"Yes," replied the cardinal as he paused thoughtfully. He studied General Rudacil's expression once again before continuing. "These are delicate matters. You are no doubt aware that the Vatican has its own scientists and observatories."

"Yes, I am father."

"Our scientists find the similarity of this work by Leonardo to the present position of celestial bodies to be quite striking."

"Perhaps he wasn't mad after all," replied General Rudacil.

"Perhaps," replied the Cardinal.

General Rudacil shifted in his chair and turned to face the Cardinal.

"Father, it is my job to protect the earth from any possible space borne threat. You can be certain that I will do so to the utmost of my ability."

Father Sebastian smiled and said, "I take comfort in your commitment to your mission."

Before the meeting concluded, Father Dominic leaned toward the Cardinal's ear and whispered something. The cardinal smiled, and turned toward General Rudacil again.

"I understand that it's been a while since your last confession my son."

57

As the assault team patrolled the array, a small team of specialists methodically studied the site. Eventually they would discover the unmarked equipment rack in the service building on the outer perimeter of the array but it would take a while. Until then a small cluster of dishes would be covertly relaying information to the Alexandria network.

Jerry checked the network stream from Alexandria every few hours on the off chance that something of note had been added. Until now, he had been disappointed. Finally, today there was something new. "This can only be Adam," said Jerry as he worked the face of the touch panel.

After a few moments, the screen lit up with a rapid-fire succession of text and images as a torrent of data was unleashed. Jerry instinctively pulled his hands away from the touch panel surface to avoid interfering with the transfer. He stepped back several feet from the video panel as Miranda joined him.

"Doc needs to see this," said Jerry as Miranda stood silently beside him.

"I need to tell you something," she said as she took his hand and turned him to face her.

"I." Tears welled in her eyes as she tried to speak. She cleared her throat and tried again.

"Jerry, I don't know how to." Once again, she stopped as her throat closed on her words. Tears were beginning to stream down her face.

"What is it Miranda? Are you ok?" he said softly as he brushed her hear gently away from her face.

Still unable to speak she took Jerry's hand and placed it on her abdomen as she stared into his eyes. For a few seconds his engineering mind ran through a list of possible medical issues before the revelation of what she was telling him occurred to him.

"Pregnant?" he asked.

Miranda nodded her head yes.

"Wow," he said, as he stood motionless in a momentary state of emotional detachment. Then, as he looked upon what was surely the most beautiful thing in his universe, a warm sense of belonging coursed through him and he pulled her close and put his arms around her. She nestled her face against his chest as he held her; his heart beat echoing in her ear as she closed her eyes and melted into his embrace.

In the great hall, Gerhardt entered the star-chamber. Since his first experience with the tablet, he felt a sense of compulsion to return to it. There was so much to learn and only single lifetime to do so. Having seen through the eyes of the gods, he now felt as insignificant as an insect. The hunger to know was as powerful as any drug. He gripped the tablet as before and immediately sensed the tingling in his hands. It happened much more rapidly than before. It was as if the nerves in his body had mapped out a more efficient route for the energy of the tablet to follow. In only a moment, the strange smell in his nose signaled the loss of consciousness that would soon carry him out of his body.

He awakened to find himself standing atop a great structure on an alien world. In the sky above him, a massive star many times larger than the sun of his world shined with a blue-white brilliance. In the sky around him, several massive objects slowly moved up and away from a world that existed eons before his own. Looking down from his vantage point, he saw a great city spread out below him. He thought how advanced the civilization must be to create such beautiful structures and he marveled at how clean everything was, but it was completely empty. The only sound was that of the wind. There was not a living thing anywhere, just the piercing blue-white light of the massive star that loomed menacingly in the sky above.

Suddenly he found himself standing in a large space covered by a clear dome. The walls and floors were of a material very similar in appearance to the tablet. He knelt and placed his hand on the floor. It felt smooth, cool, and indeed appeared to be exactly the same substance. The strange voice that he had heard the last time that he traveled beyond reality said, "Watch the star." A blinding flash was followed by the disintegration of the massive star. The planet where he previously stood was broken apart by a shockwave that ripped through space as it raced outwardly from the star.

Once again, he was transported to another point in time. The remains of the previous star and the planets that surrounded it were now only a great cloud of debris. Floating near the edge of the disk that was forming there was a large mass, nearly as large as a moon but jagged and craggy. The voice said, "Look." As he did so, he saw pieces of the great city tumbling in space. As the mass of rubble spun through the ages, and collected more chunks of debris, it was transformed before his eyes into a silvery round planetary body. The voice said, "It is there."

"Looks you have been traveling to a place far, far, away," said Steffen as he placed the tablet back upon the pedestal.

"It was just unbelievable," said Gerhardt as he struggled to get on his feet. "There are ruins on Eris from another world," he continued.

"Yes, we know," said Jerry.

"No, I mean that Eris is a chunk of a world that once existed before a massive blue star exploded." As he attempted to take a step, he stumbled from exhaustion. As Jerry grabbed his arm to help him he let go abruptly.

"His skin is really hot."

"Yes, this is normal," said Steffen.

"His metabolic processes must be in overdrive," remarked Jerry.

"The tablet not only heals the body, it makes improvements," replied Steffen.

Gerhardt groaned as he collapsed, unconscious between the two of them.

"We may as well take him to his room," said Steffen. "He will sleep for a while."

"How would he know about a blue star going supernova?" asked Jerry.

"He was taken to a place where he could witness the event," replied Steffen.

"You said that he was taken to a place," Jerry paused for a few seconds, "taken by whom?"

Steffen smiled and confidently replied, "He was taken by the Gods; of course."

58

A CLAXON SOUNDED AS COMMANDER Jeppeson executed the launch order. "At your stations, at your stations," announced the chief of the watch as the launch sequence neared zero.

"The bird is hot," announced the weapons officer as he inserted his launch key and turned the arming switch.

"Firing in 5, 4, 3, 2, 1," said Commander Jeppeson as he engaged the firing switch.

Outside in the cold of space there was only silence as the missile zoomed off its maglev rail.

"Engine ignition in two minutes," called the weapons officer over the PA system.

As the missile reached the programmed ignition point, its magneto plasma engine cycled on. A purple glow appeared on the video monitor as the plasma reaction began to spray ejecta from its nozzle.

"Acceleration detected," called out the weapons officer. "The bird is running hot and true," he said as the he observed the spike shaped purple exhaust signature on the video monitor.

The captain left the control room and entered his ready room. After savoring a cup of coffee for a moment, he activated his communications panel.

General Rudacil appeared on screen a moment later. "Hello Commander, I hope all is well with the mission."

"Yes General, Asteroid Intercept 52013 launched successfully a few moments ago."

"Good; the boys in the lab will be happy to hear that the new guidance system is running an intercept mission."

"Yes sir," replied Commander Jessup with a hint of disdain.

"Is there a problem commander?"

"Shouldn't we have tested those modifications before using them in a mission; Sir?"

General Rudacil pursed his lips in disapproval of the comment and placed his electronic cigar in the corner of his mouth.

"This mission may be critical to the survival of our world, commander." "That is more than you need to know."

General Rudacil punched his video screen with his forefinger using much greater force than would have been required to terminate the transmission.Without looking, he retrieved a string of

Rosaries from his desk drawer and kissed them. He was well aware the he would be the one held accountable for the events that would soon unfold. He consoled himself with the knowledge that he had done the right thing. He had saved the earth from an ancient darkness that would corrupt creation.

Dr. Enoch awoke in the middle of the night with the words you are our children ringing in his mind. He had to get Jerry and sort out all that he had seen in his last encounter. Still in his pajamas, he made his way down the hall and knocked on the door of Jerry's room. After several attempts to wake him, the door finally cracked open.

"Sorry to wake you Jerry but I need to talk to you."

His eyes were so brilliant that they almost glowed in the dim light of the hall. His skin was completely smooth, like that of a young man of twenty something years; and it too appeared to glow, with radiance unlike anything that he had ever seen.

"Give me just a minute, I'll be right out," replied Jerry as he closed the door to find his slippers. "What's wrong?" asked Miranda groggily as she sat up in bed?

"It's Doc," Jerry said nervously.

"What's the matter?" she asked, sensing the alarm in Jerry's voice.

"He has changed, somehow he has physically changed, his eyes, his skin, it's not possible but I saw it with my own eyes."

"I'm going with you," said Miranda as she dug her way out of the bed covers.

As the two of them left the room, they found Dr. Enoch waiting at the stair landing. At a distance of twenty feet, Dr. Enoch truly appeared to be an apparition. There truly was a halo effect surrounding his body. Miranda stopped and squeezed Jerry's hand when she saw him.

Without turning toward them, Dr. Enoch started down the stairs.

"Do not be afraid, I sense your hesitation at my appearance."
"I am still the same old me, sort of."

"What do you mean sort of?" asked Jerry.

"I have seen things Jerry; things that no man has seen."

"Why don't you two get Gerhardt, I will meet you in the library after I go find Heir Mueller." Dr. Enoch smiled and flashed a glance back toward them, his brilliant azure eyes casting a faint blue glimmer in the dimly lit stairway.

Miranda held Jerry's hand tightly as they turned and made their way to the door of Gerhardt's room. As they neared the room, they noticed that the door was ajar. As they approached the threshold, Jerry knocked and called out Gerhardt's name. After a second try he eased, open the door to find the room empty.

"He's not here."

"Maybe he is downstairs already," replied Miranda.

"Right, let's go to the library and meet up with Doc, replied Jerry.

After cautiously navigating the dimly lit staircase, the two of them made their way to the library. As they approached, they could hear voices in the room. The voices ceased as they neared the doorway. For a few seconds they hesitated to enter the room for fear of what they would find. Dr. Enoch had changed, so surely had Gerhardt but they had not seen him since the day before.

"Please join us, there is no need to be afraid," said Dr. Enoch.

Jerry looked into Miranda's eyes and mouthed, "It's alright," before turning the corner and entering the room. The three of them sat at a long table in the center of the room. Jerry paused a few feet from the table in order to observe the three of them. Miranda stayed a step behind him, subconsciously shielding herself with her protector. Steffen found their humanity amusing. As advanced as they were in their knowledge, the instincts of their basal minds, hard coded genetically for eons, still drove their behavior.

"Please have a seat, we have much to do," said Dr. Enoch.

Jerry sat directly across from Dr. Enoch and Miranda selected the chair opposite Gerhardt. He smiled comfortingly as Miranda took her seat.

"You have no doubt noticed that Gerhardt and I have manifested physical changes in our bodies." He placed his hand on the table in front of them. "Look at how clear my skin is. Yesterday there was age spots, today there are none."

"What about the glow?" Miranda asked. "You appeared to glow as if a halo of energy surrounded your body."

"I think that the tablet channels energy from an unknown source and routes it through the nervous system," replied Dr. Enoch. "It is as if I was connected to the source of everything."

"Obviously that source knows something about human anatomy," said Jerry.

"I think that it does," replied Dr. Enoch. "It told me that we are their children."

"Did it tell you the same thing," Miranda asked of Gerhardt.

"In a way it did," replied Gerhardt. "It showed me a great ship floating above the earth and it told me that the ship was Eden. Later it showed me the destruction of the first world and the beginning of our world. It also told me that Eris is a remnant of the first world and that there are ruins there."

"How did the first world end?" asked Jerry.

"A really large blue star exploded," replied Gerhardt.

"A supernova," said Jerry.

"Yes," said Dr. Enoch in confirmation. "Our sun formed from the nebula that resulted from that stellar event."

"So this intelligence told you these things," Jerry said in skeptical and questioning tone.

"No," replied Steffen. "We were taken to the place of the events."

"Yes, that is correct said Gerhardt; we weren't told of the events or shown them as in a video. We were physically present and observed them from an omniscient perspective. A God's eye view, if you will."

"That is interesting," said Jerry, pausing to formulate his next question. "Were all three of you told the same things?" I am just curious."

"No Jerry, but we can read each other's thoughts; even more clearly than we can read yours," said Dr. Enoch. "We were each given a different experience but we can actually assemble them as if we had one mind."

"You're telling me that you three are capable of parallel processing on a human scale?" Jeez Doc, this is getting ridiculous," said Jerry.

In unison Dr. Enoch, Steffen and Gerhardt said, "I am sorry that you are having such difficulty understanding this, perhaps in time it will make more sense to you." Their voices synchronized in an eerie chorus. Jerry could feel goose bumps on his neck as they spoke. Miranda covered her mouth with her hand in order to squelch any sound of fear that may escape involuntarily.

"Perhaps we will revisit this issue later," said Dr. Enoch. "For now we must address a matter of some urgency."

"Jerry opened his clasped hands and said, "OK Doc, what is it?"

"It's the sun Jerry; they have come to save us from our star."

"The strange solar activity isn't just an unusually strong solar storm?" asked Jerry.

"No Jerry, the sun is destabilizing."

Jerry did not reply; he knew well the meaning of Dr. Enoch's statement. He also knew that his mentor believed it.

"So what can we do about it?" he asked.

"First I want for you to access the array. See if you can make contact with Adam. In the mean time, I will contact Ed and get his read on the situation.

"Alright Doc, I'm on it," replied Jerry.

Ed Gilstrap was in the cafeteria line when his tablet chirped. He retrieved the ubiquitous device from his belt and noticed that there was a message from a sender of Alexandria.

"Samuel," he mumbled as he tapped the screen of the tablet. The message opened and Dr. Enoch's video message began.

"Ed, I need to speak with you urgently." He paused for a moment before continuing. "It's the sun Ed; it's running out of fuel, that's the reason for the signal."

Ed dropped his plate and ran from the cafeteria. Before he made it to the elevator, he was calling Dr. Fergusson with his tablet. As he trotted along the sweeping curve of the hall that contained the astrophysics department, he could see Dr. Fergussen waiting at her office door for him.

"What is it Ed?" she asked, reserving her dry banter for a more appropriate time. She sensed that something unusual was afoot and her expertise was apparently required. Ed approached her with his tablet in hand.

"Dr. Fergusson, could you spare a few moments?" Ed

asked in a way that was more of a command than a question. He motioned with his hand for the office as they both entered. "I am sorry to interrupt your day but this is important."

"Alright Ed," she replied as she took her seat behind the desk. Ed sat in one of a pair of leather guest chairs neatly placed against the wall opposite her.

"Is this about the Eris Mission?" She asked.

"It's a long story; better clear your calendar."

"Clear my calendar?" "For how long?" she asked.

"Pretty much indefinitely," replied Ed.

Dr. Fergusson stared without a response.

"I am sure that you are aware the Eris mission and its apparent failure."

"Failure is a bit heavy handed but yes, I am generally up to speed on it," replied Dr. Fergusson.

"There are aspects of the mission that are not exactly as they appear," said Ed. "I cannot go into those now but we have information regarding the strange behavior of the sun."

"Oh? She asked.

Ed played the video on his tablet for her.

"How would he know that the sun is running out of fuel? "We don't even know what the fuel requirements are." "We have theories and mathematical models but they are only approximations, nobody can make a statement like that."

Ed picked his tablet up and tapped the screen a couple of times before placing it back upon her desk. A pair of images was visible on the screen of the tablet. A close up of Eris that she had never seen. It showed structures that appeared to be buildings and a giant dish shaped depression on the surface. The other appeared to be a metallic object, possibly a spacecraft, but difficult to discern from such a vast distance.

"That's where," said Ed as he leaned back in the chair while she studied the images.

After a moment she asked, "What exactly does he know?"

"Before we ask that question we need to find out if there are indications in our data that bear out his hypothesis," replied Ed.

"Obviously the current solar activity is unusual; but it is not without historical precedent. It seems that every hundred years or so there is a larger than normal spate of sunspots and flares but then a normal period returns, often for decades." said Dr. Fergusson.

"Run through everything that you have," said Ed. "pay particular attention to special cause variation, anything that is outside of bounds enough to be written off as improbable or just plain ridiculous."

"That may take a while," replied Dr. Fergusson.

"Told you to clear your calendar; Fergy."

"Stop calling me that," she groaned.

"I'll check in tomorrow," said Ed as he slapped his knees and stood to leave.

"I mean it Ed, stop calling me that," she said again, pretending to be offended.

As Ed, left she smiled as she recalled their time together in college. He always treated her with respect, even then. He was like the big brother that she never had. Had he not been involved with Nancy, his wife of twenty-two years, perhaps they could have…. Her reminiscing ended as a question formed in her mind.

"What could indicate the trigger of a change of state? There must be an indicator, we must find a prediction variable."

Ed had barely settled into his office routine following his

discussion with Dr. Fergusson when he got an urgent call from mission control.

"Boss, we have a situation," said the flight dynamics officer.

"What is it John?" "Something launched from midway station," replied John.

"I'll be right there," said Ed as he left his office, tablet still in hand."

A few moments later, he strode into mission control, eyes on the large view screen that displayed a red arc with its origin at midway station. A luminous circle surrounded a point of blue light, motionless relative to the background of space.

"Any idea what this is?" asked John as Ed approached.

"It's obviously a rock buster but there aren't any asteroid interceptions scheduled for months," Ed's comment trailed off for a few seconds before he exclaimed, "Damned military nut jobs!"

"They launched against the unidentified object nearing Mars crossing?" asked John.

"Looks like it to me," said Ed as he placed his hands on his hips and bit his lip, considering his options. After a moment, he removed the tablet from his belt.

"Hello Ed," said a familiar yet strange voice. Ed appeared a little confused as he studied the high definition image on his tablet. "Is that you Samuel?" asked Ed.

"Yes, I have been on a self improvement kick of sorts lately," replied Dr. Enoch.

Ed shook his head unconsciously as he continued. "Have you been in contact with Adam recently?"

"No, although he did place data in Alexandria before Hermes terminated."

There was silence as the two of them sized up the present situation.

"Have you discovered the space craft that is nearing Earth?" asked Dr. Enoch.

John looked sharply in Ed's direction and mouthed the words, "how does he know?" Ed's eyes darted in John's direction before returning to the tablet.

"Yes Samuel, but we aren't certain that it's a spacecraft," replied Ed.

"Well, you can take my word for it," said Dr. Enoch.

"How did you know of this Samuel? The information is still classified."

"We have been in communication with them Ed. They have shown us things you cannot imagine."

"What do you mean by that?" "How did they show you," Ed asked.

"All in good time my friend," replied Dr. Enoch.

Ed hesitated for a moment before dropping the bombshell.

"Samuel, it appears that Space Command has launched a plasma rocket at the object."

"I see," said Dr. Enoch. "They came to save us from a catastrophe and we responded by firing a missile at them. They obviously have a great deal of faith in our potential as a species."

"Can you contact them?" asked Ed.

"I think so," replied Dr. Enoch

"It would appear that we each have urgent matters to attend to," said Ed.

"I agree," replied Dr. Enoch.

"Stay in touch Samuel." said Ed, as he terminated the transmission.

After the video call terminated Dr. Enoch re-holstered his tablet and stepped onto the balcony of his room overlooking the sea. The night was black and clear. The Milky Way was clearly visible with the new moon low in the sky behind his location.

"Where would they have gone when they left the first world?" he asked aloud. After a few moments musing, he breathed the wonderful air of this place deeply and left the balcony. At three a.m., he should be asleep but he had no sense of fatigue. Looking around the room, he found nothing to interest him so he eased his door closed and made his way to the grand staircase. A few moments later, he found Gerhardt and Steffen in the hall of creation discussing the tablet.

"Gentlemen," he said as he greeted them. "It appears that we are all having trouble sleeping."

"No trouble at all; I simply no longer require sleep," replied Steffen.

"None at all?" asked Gerhardt.

"Not for many years," replied Steffen without moving his lips.

"I suspect the gods did not require sleep either," said Dr. Enoch telepathically.

A golden glow began to fill the room. As they turned in the direction of the light, they saw the tablet pulsing with a brilliant glow.

"I have not seen that before, said Steffen."

"There are three of us now," Gerhardt thought without speaking.

"Why are three significant?" asked Dr. Enoch.

Gerhardt appeared startled at the reading of his thoughts.

"We no longer have the luxury of keeping secrets, at least

not from one another. Our minds are totally open to each other."

"Anyway," Gerhardt continued; "The quantity of three has historical significance; three priests in Uruk, three kings from the east, the holy trinity."

"Seven and twelve are also historically significant," replied Steffen. "How is three of particular importance?"

"I am not certain, it was only a mental note not intended for discussion," replied Gerhardt.

"Perhaps an experiment is in order," replied Dr. Enoch. "Steffen should hold the tablet and the two of us should see if we sense anything."

Steffen retrieved the tablet from the pedestal and held it to his chest. Within a moment, he was in a trance like state. Dr. Enoch and Gerhardt glanced at one another and then focused their attention on Steffen. After only a few seconds, they began to sense the same phenomenon that they had experienced while holding the tablet. Suddenly the three of them were in the great golden temple that Dr. Enoch had seen in his last vision while holding the tablet. They were free to move about the space yet they had no physical bodies. There were others present as well. Strangers that they could sense but could not see.

"Who is there?" asked Dr. Enoch.

"Who do you seek?" replied a voice from the ether.

"The ancient one," replied Dr. Enoch.

"It is I," replied the voice.

"Is this the ship that approaches our world?

"Yes," replied the voice.

"I wish to inform you that your ship is in danger. A missile was launched at your vessel with the intention of destroying it," said Dr. Enoch.

Instantaneously they were floating in space beside the missile. Even it was traveling at a significant rate of speed it seemed motionless in the emptiness of space.

"This is the object of which you speak," said the voice.

A field formed around the missile and glowed as if it were a blue translucent sphere.

"It is of no consequence," said the voice as the sphere containing the missile blinked out of existence before them, leaving only the emptiness of space.

Suddenly they were back in the temple.

"How is this possible?" asked Dr. Enoch.

"Anything is possible," replied the voice.

There was silence as the three human visitors pondered the statement that they had heard.

"You mentioned the one called Adam once before, is he here?"

"He can be, if you would like."

"Yes, I would."

"Hello, Dr. Enoch said a strangely familiar voice."

"Adam, is that really you?"

"Yes."

"How is this possible?

"When I transmitted my core program code to Hermes this ship intercepted the transmission and recognized me as a life form, not unlike their own if not much more primitive," Replied Adam.

"Is Eve here as well?

"Yes, as are countless trillions of others. You may come here as well when you transcend your physical existence."

"This is only a ship, albeit a very large one," replied Dr. Enoch.

"Actually it is one node in a network of undefined size

and scope that blankets the cosmos. To exist here is to exist everywhere. Your existence as a physical entity is fragile in comparison."

"Yet they have come to save us from extinction?" asked Dr. Enoch.

"Yes"

"Why?" asked Dr. Enoch.

"Because man was created for a purpose," replied Adam. "Look in Alexandria, there is something there for you."

Adam disappeared from the place after his last statement.

The vision ended and they were standing in the hall of creation once more. Jerry and Miranda were standing near the door with a look of mesmerized fear and disbelief on their faces. A low frequency vibration that permeated the house awakened them. Upon entering the hall of creation, they had witnessed the brilliant golden light pulsing from the tablet as Steffen held it. A whirlwind blew in the center of the room around the trio, as they stood motionless throughout the event, their eyes glowing like jewels. Even now that the incident was over, they appeared to glow with a low intensity aura as they turned to face them.

Miranda gasped when she saw the brilliant blue shimmer of their eyes.

"What happened to them Jerry?" she asked.

"I don't know," replied Jerry as he moved ahead of Miranda in order to shield her.

"It's alright Jerry," you are in no danger.

"Easy for you to say Doc, have you taken a good look in the mirror lately?"

"I am sorry Jerry; this must be very difficult for both of you."

"Damn right it is, I have seen you change into some kind of alien in front of my very eyes."

"You must be strong Jerry, things are about to get even stranger; I suspect."

"What's that supposed to mean?"

"That ship out there is coming to earth Jerry. They didn't tell us that but I am certain of it."

"I suspect that is the case as well," said Gerhardt. "They last time they were here they apparently stayed for quite some time. Perhaps they will this time too."

"There is something else; I spoke with Adam," said Dr. Enoch.

"Are you certain that it was Adam?"

"Yes, it was him," replied Dr. Enoch. "He told us to check Alexandria; there is something there for us; only he would know that."

"How is that possible?"

"He was intercepted by the ship when he attempted to transfer to Hermes.

"Interesting," replied Jerry.

"Yes, it is," Dr. Enoch paused and added, "He said the ship was one location on a network that spans the cosmos."

Jerry cocked his head slightly as he considered the concept of a cosmic network. "I should dig into Alexandria right away."

"Agreed," replied Dr. Enoch.

59

As Ed stepped from the elevator into the lobby of the executive office suite, he found Dr. Fergusson sleeping one of the couches.

"Dr. Fergusson," Said Ed as he called to her in a tone somewhat louder than he would ordinarily use. She stirred a little but did not awaken. "Fergy," he said louder still. "You need to wake up."

"Uhhhh; I hate sleeping on a couch," she said as she sat upright and stretched her kinked muscles. Ed sat on the end of the couch opposite her and said, "Obviously you have found something noteworthy."

"Nah, I'm just really trying to impress the boss."

"You're going to need fish net stockings for that," replied Ed.

Dr. Fergusson blushed and covered her face as she asked, "after twenty years you still remember that?"

"I will never forget it, I consider that evening the highlight of graduate school," replied Ed.

"You know that I sprained my ankle that night, I couldn't walk for month."

"Your fall from grace after attempting to dance on the table was the funniest thing I ever saw, Nancy and I still laugh about it."

"Perhaps I can redeem myself after twenty years with what I am about to show you," she said as she retrieved a clear tablet device from the coffee table.

"I was looking for something unique. We are always observing the sun so there is plenty of data."

"Ok," said Ed as he sat beside her on the sofa.

"Under normal conditions the sun's energy output fluctuates over an eleven year cycle. High levels are associated with the solar max, characterized by increase sunspot activity, flares, mass ejections, etc."

"Right, the standard stuff everybody knows," remarked Ed as he followed her explanation.

"Generally that is how things work but there are historical aberrations in the suns behavior. Every ten thousand years there seems to be a major climatic event."

"Right," the end of the ice age was about ten thousand years ago," remarked Ed.

"Yes that's right, and for several hundred years afterward the earth was really warm; causing the ice to retreat and the rise of man."

"Ok, so what caused the unusual energy surge"?

"A red shift; unusually high levels of infrared energy can

account for a rapid melting of the ice sheet and the boom in plant species just afterward."

"Is that happening now?" asked Ed.

Dr. Fergusson tapped the screen of the device and placed it on the table.

A holographic animation of the solar system appeared approximately five hundred centimeters above the table. Notations of energy output appeared under the sun.

"This modeling scenario depicts the solar system approximately fifteen thousand years ago, you can see that the sun is very quiet, and its output is very near the solar mean that we have observed since the 1600's."

The model blinked and reconfigured.

"This scenario depicts the solar system approximately ten thousand years ago. You can clearly see that solar output was greater, particularly in the infrared spectrum."

"I see," said Ed.

"The interesting thing is that it should have continued in a red shift but it didn't."

Ed listened attentively as she continued. "The sun should have passed into a red giant phase thousands of years ago but something stabilized it."

"What could have done that?" asked Ed.

"Nothing we know of has the capacity to reverse such a process," replied Dr. Fergusson.

"Here is the spooky part," she said as she decreased the magnification of the image. "Eris was almost exactly in the same location then, as it is now."

"That is interesting," replied Ed as he studied the hologram.

"What if the red shift had continued?" he asked.

Dr. Fergusson tapped an icon on the tablet and the sun

began to enlarge and darken into a red star of much larger diameter.

"The earth would have been subjected too much higher solar radiation levels," said Dr. Fergusson. "Mankind would not have survived beyond the stone age."

As the animation continued, the earth transformed from a brilliant blue orb into a gray, rocky and lifeless world. As he watched the animation Ed's tablet buzzed on its belt holster. He unclipped it and looked at it.

"It's John," he said, "better take this one."

Dr. Fergusson nodded in approval as Ed tapped the screen.

"What is it John?"

"Hi boss," he said. "Something interesting has happened at Mars crossing."

"OK," replied Ed.

"The missile from Midway Station has disappeared," said John.

"Did it malfunction?" asked Ed.

"Not exactly," replied John, it appears to have simply vanished."

"Was there a detonation?" asked Ed.

"No," replied John.

"What about the object that is inbound? Is it still heading our way?" asked Ed.

"Yes; velocity seems to be degrading but its course seems to be constant."

"Thanks John," said Ed as he terminated the video call.

"So when do our visitors arrive?" asked Dr. Fergusson.

"A week, maybe two," replied Ed.

Dr. Fergusson raised her eyebrows but said nothing.

"Thanks for the effort Fergy; you should go home and get

some rest," said Ed as he stood and straighten his sport jacket. He held out his hand and assisted Dr. Fergusson to a standing position.

"Always the gentleman," she said as she walked toward the elevators just beyond the waiting area.

60

JERRY HAD TIRELESSLY SIFTED THROUGH the data in Adam's final download as he attempted to create a compiler that would interpret the vast amount of information that had poured in from the cosmos.

"How are you holding up Jerry?" asked Miranda as she brought him a fresh cup of coffee. She placed the cup on the table beside him and she rubbed his shoulders for a moment.

"You're an angel Miranda."

"I know," she said as she took a seat beside him.

"It is really unbelievable how much data is contained in Adam's last transmission," said Jerry.

"How so?" asked Miranda.

"It is different from the communications protocol that we use, there is not enough bandwidth available to send this much data so Adam either invented a new protocol, or," Jerry paused for a moment as considered another possibility, "or he had help."

Dr. Enoch had entered the room a few moments before and had caught the end of their conversation.

"I think he probably had help Jerry."

"Jerry turned as Dr. Enoch walked past and took a seat on the opposite side of the table. He was aware that his appearance was a source of discomfort for the two of them so he tried to engage in normal conversation. It was difficult because he could sense their thoughts before they spoke.

"Have you made any progress with the data?" asked Dr. Enoch.

"Only from the perspective that I know that there are multiple streams and they do not conform to any of our technologies," replied Jerry.

"I see," said Dr. Enoch.

"I am going to need help with this one Doc," said Jerry as he stretched, placing his hands on the back of his head. "I think it's time to call your old buddy Ed. He can download the data from Alexandria and crank it through the super computers at Space Command."

Dr. Enoch retrieved his tablet from his belt holster and a moment later Ed Gilstrap joined them via tele-presence. The head and shoulders of his avatar levitated above the device as he spoke.

"Hello Samuel, what can I do for you?"

"We need your help Ed. Adam uploaded a large amount of data to Alexandria that we do not have the ability to process."

"Adam?" asked Ed.

"It may seem strange, but I have recently been in contact with him."

"How is that possible?" asked Ed. "Adam was shut down last I heard."

"Yes, Adam attempted to transmit himself to Hermes but was apparently intercepted by the alien craft that is now approaching the inner solar system," replied Dr. Enoch.

"And you have spoken with him?" asked Ed.

Dr. Enoch sensed Ed's skepticism as he replied, "there are many aspects of my research of which you are unaware." Dr. Enoch paused as he considering whether to continue. "We have discovered technology that makes it possible to contact an alien civilization that visited Earth in antiquity."

"What kind of technology? Was it in the equipment at your facility on the west coast?" asked Ed.

"No," replied Dr. Enoch, "it is a relic of Sumerian origin.

"You can't possibly expect me to believe that." Dr. Enoch cut him off in mid sentence, "You have seen the video evidence of the surface of Eris and now there is a massive object inside the orbit of Mars." Dr. Enoch paused briefly before adding; "the relic was the key to all of it."

"So what can I do Samuel?"

"Jerry will send you access keys to Alexandria and he will supervise the transfer of a large cache of data," replied Dr. Enoch. "You have access to the most powerful computers in the business, process the data and we'll see what happens."

"Alright Samuel; we'll treat it as if we were receiving the data from Hermes," replied Ed.

Jerry configured a security protocol that would allow retrieval of the data and sent it as instructed.

"Got it," said Ed as he immediately relayed the codes to John in Mission Control.

"I will be in touch as soon as we have something."

"Thank you Ed," said Dr. Enoch.

Ed's Avatar vanished as the transmission terminated.

"I don't think he liked your explanation very much Doc," said Jerry as he studied his mentor.

"You're right Jerry. He is not yet willing to accept the reality of what we know."

"In a week he will have it sitting in orbit, perhaps then he will be a little more accepting of it," replied Jerry with a bit of sarcasm.

General Rudacil read the final paragraph of the strike mission debrief as he adjusted the flavor setting of his electronic cigar. "How could a missile the size of a small building just disappear?" he asked aloud as he puffed his favorite virtual vice. He knew the president would be calling soon and he would need a good explanation when the time came. His window to preserve the order of civilization was now closing. The only option left on the table was to execute a raid of the compound in Croatia where Dr. Enoch and his team were in hiding. Perhaps with interrogation it would be possible to glean enough information to stop the invaders. He had the authority under the blanket tasking order that authorized the unsuccessful missile strike. Intelligence sources had located Dr. Enoch within minutes of his first conversation with Ed Gilstrap following his miraculous escape from the raid on the Sulphur Creek installation.

He read the files a final time while rolling a string of rosaries in his hand. When he finished the reports, he closed the files and opened a new tasking order in the joint services tasking system. He then aimed the retina scanner on his screen so that the target reticule recognized his eye. When the status box read, "Identity confirmed," he tapped the initiate icon and started the mission. Within moments, a series of a hundred events automatically occurred that resulted in the mission assets deploying. Within twenty-four hours, a squadron of turbine osprey and its compliment of special operations troops would be landing at an airbase in Croatia adjoining the estate of an antiquities trader named Steffen Mueller.

Steffen was enjoying an evening glass of wine with his guests when vehicle lights danced across the room from the courtyard. The squeal of brakes announced the arrival of the armored truck that had previously brought several loads of equipment to the house. A moment later, the butler answered the door and escorted the base commander into the parlor. Steffen stood and greeted the man, "good evening Colonel, what brings you around this evening?"

"Perhaps we should speak in private," replied the base commander.

"Only if you insist, I assure you that my friends are trustworthy."

"Very well, I am here to notify you that a contingent of United Nations Special Operations troops will arrive tomorrow afternoon with the intention of visiting your estate."

Steffen quietly considered the man's warning. He graciously thanked the Colonel and assured him that all would be well as he led him to the courtyard. A few moments later, he returned. The engine of the truck rumbled as the lights danced across the windows. For several moments no one spoke.

"We should make preparations for our visitors," said Jerry.

"We are prepared," replied Steffen sipping the last of his wine.

"Really?" asked Jerry.

Steffen confidently replied, "We will have a surprise for them as they approach over the sea. Our little ship has a range of capabilities that they may find difficult to address."

61

ALL EYES in mission control were focused on the main video panel, as the first composite images of the craft appeared on screen. More than a dozen long-range telescopes were now capable of imaging the object in high resolution. This image data was processed by super computers and a composite three-dimensional extrapolation was produced from which imagery would be generated.

"Look at the size of that thing," said Ed as he zoomed the image to maximum.

"Spectral readings are indicating that the surface of the object is indeed a gold alloy," said John.

"I wonder what is in the large cylindrical section behind the saucer shaped body at the front?" asked Ed.

"Could be a storage container or a reactor vessel," replied one of the team members from the floor.

"The question is what it is doing here?" asked John.

"Dr. Enoch says that it has come to save Earth from our sun," Ed said discretely in reply.

"Sounds like the man has lost his marbles, you can't seriously believe him," replied John.

"He knew about this before we did, and he was right about Eris. I don't have a good reason to doubt him at this point."

"I don't know boss," replied John.

"We will know soon enough," said Ed with a sigh, "that thing will be here in a few days."

As he continued to study the image on the main viewing screen Ed's tablet buzzed on his belt. It was Dr. Fergusson and the message was marked as urgent.

"What's up Fergy," he asked.

"We have an emergency Ed. A really large corona mass ejection is headed our way."

"How large?" asked Ed?

"It is the largest on record; larger even than the 1859 event." Replied Dr. Ferguson

"How long do we have?" asked Ed.

"A day, maybe less," replied Dr. Fergusson. "We dodged a bullet last month but we are squarely in the cross hairs of this event."

The ground crew completed the final checks of the Osprey as the special operations team began boarding the aircraft. The sky above the Adriatic was clear; aurora glowed with brilliant hues of green and orange as jet engines began spooling on the deck of the Marine assault ship Saipan. Ten minutes later the squadron was airborne. The lead element set course to target and the combat integration system formed the other ships in an arrow formation of five aircraft.

"Time to target, ninety four minutes," echoed the voice

of the pilot in the helmets of the troops. The men relaxed on the benches. Some checked their gear; others studied their mission profile on the heads up displays in their helmets. A few noticed the flickering sky overhead. It was worthy of their attention as there had not been such a display in nearly ten thousand years.

Scientist around the world poured over the data that was streaming from satellites, lunar observatories and earth based installations. Ed stayed over to observe the largest solar event in the millennia with most of the permanent staff of Space Command headquarters.

A three dimensional model of the inner solar system floated above the hologram emitter in the center of mission control. A massive burst of solar radiation was engulfing the earth, its leading edge just beginning to claw at the ionosphere.

"We are definitely going to see some infrastructure damage from this one," said John as he observed the hologram.

"Europe is already experiencing very strong Aurora phenomenon," said Dr. Fergusson.

"When do you anticipate the solar storm to reach its peak?" asked Ed.

"Within the hour Central and Southern Europe will experience direct exposure to the event at maximum intensity. North and South America will only experience residual effects thanks to our position on the opposite side of the globe," replied Dr. Fergusson.

"Looks like our friends across the pond are in for one hell of a ride," said John.

As Europe rotated directly into the onslaught from space, Steffen flew above the Adriatic Sea in the ancient craft that carried him as thought he flew on Aladdin's carpet. The exterior walls were transparent as he glided silently to the rendezvous coordinates that the Colonel had shared with him. He could see the fantastic light show that flickered above him and he could sense that the ancient ones were very near.

Closing rapidly from the west the five-ship formation held a steady course as the global military information system guided the formation to its destination. The mission had progressed with routine boredom until the artificial intelligence engine of the network detected a faint emission that had recently been catalogued during a similar mission in Northern California. The pilots in the lead ship verified that the four other elements of the formation had detected the same sensor signature. Just as they were preparing to notify the mother ship, a radio call crackled in their headset.

"Crossbow five zero; bogey at your ten o'clock, thirty two miles from your present location."

"Roger that rampart, we have bogey and targeting is reading five by five."

While the Osprey was by no means fighter aircraft, it carried a nasty defensive punch. Each bird is equipped with two pods that contain three hard points for virtually any aerial weapon in the fleet. On this mission, each ship carried a minimal ordinance load consisting of four air-to-air hypersonic interceptor missiles.

"Crossbow five zero," Rampart has authorized deadly force, repeat Rampart has authorized deadly force."

General Rudacil had authorized the use of all means necessary to neutralize any threat presented by whatever the unidentified object was that showed up in the mission data from the raid on Dr. Enoch's compound. He would take no chances in silencing the plot to end civilization.

Steffen placed his hand on the control scepter of the craft and trained his mind on the rapidly approaching formation. As he concentrated, he willed that a modest level of energy flow in the direction of the approaching aircraft as a warning shot.

In the cockpits of all five Osprey warning lights flashed and claxons rang as the sensors detected an Electro Magnetic Pulse.

"Rampart, Rampart be advised, we have been targeted by an EM pulse of unknown origin."

The commander aboard Saipan had instant access to all of the data that existed in the operational theater so he saw exactly what his pilots saw.

His decision was instant, "Crossbow five one, return fire."

A second later, the lead element released two missiles in return fire.

Steffen was instantly aware of the launch as his mind could sense everything that moved around him. He knew of the whales in the waters below and the satellites in orbit above, he could sense the air pressure increasing into a supersonic shock wave in front of each missile as it accelerated. In a flash of thought, tendrils of lighting leapt from his craft and the two missiles disappeared. As the pilots in the approaching formation realized that, the missiles had failed another pair leapt from the formation, and another, until ten objects were streaking in his direction at hypersonic velocity. Once again, he responded at the speed of thought. All ten missiles blinked out of existence as the tendrils of blue white light engulfed them. He could sense the confusion in the minds of his adversaries. It would be so very easy to destroy the craft but he had long ago lost his appetite for death. Instead, he sent another, stronger burst of energy into the formation. The cockpit instruments in all five aircraft overloaded from the intense energy burst and most of the either navigational equipment short-circuited or shutdown. As the ships fell out of formation, five mayday calls could be heard in the operations center of the Saipan.

"They will know now," said Steffen as he watched the exhaust plumes of the aircraft disappear over the horizon. Overhead the sky glowed with a brilliant hue of orange as the upper atmosphere was bombarded by protons from the solar squall. At three a.m., the heavens were illuminated as brightly as the sunset the previous evening.

The following morning General Rudacil read the action briefing from the captain's log of the Saipan on the Combat Information Network.

"Mission failure attributed to high levels of electromagnet radiation from a solar storm," said General Rudacil aloud.

"Horse Hockey!" growled the general as he shook his shiny baldhead from side to side.

"Ten air to air missiles destroyed by lightning bolts?"

"No way in hell," he mumbled as he turned from his display panel.

"Who or what is protecting you Dr. Samuel Enoch?" He asked as he stared at the rosaries draped over the statue on the small table across the room.

He would not wait long for his answer.

62

WHILE THE SCIENTIFIC COMMUNITY GRAPPLED with the latest disaster to beset the planet, the government managed public perception through the manipulation of the media. Sophisticated computer algorithms predicted responses regionally and story lines were fed to population centers in a manner most likely to maintain civil order. The ruling elite would work diligently to prevent another accidental release of sensitive information. Much of the world's population had concluded that if it was not the end of the world, it was certainly a dangerous cosmic neighborhood in which we live. Today the news in mission control would prove that sentiment to be generally correct.

Dr Fergusson worked at a control panel near the hologram system.

"What have you got for me this morning," said Ed as he placed a cup of coffee beside her.

"Cream and sugar, right?" he asked as he studied the model floating above the table.

"Thanks Ed," she said as she sipped the hot liquid. "The news isn't good."

"Fill me in Fergy," replied Ed. "I've got to file a report with the director in fifteen minutes."

"The storms are increasing in amplitude, another corona mass ejection occurred less than an hour ago but we are lucky this time, its headed away from us. Eventually we are going to take another hit but that is not the worst of it," replied Dr. Fergusson, pausing to drink from her coffee.

Ed stood attentively waiting for her to complete her explanation.

"The chromosphere appears to have expanded by approximately one percent and the red shift is increasing as well."

She pointed to the hologram as she continued; "Solar output is up as well."

Ed's tablet buzzed on his belt. As he reached for it he said, "Thank you Dr. Fergusson, I've got to take this."

Ed left for the privacy of the conference room as Dr. Fergusson continued with her analysis.

"Hello Adam," said Ed as he closed the conference room door. "I am rather surprised to hear from you. We assumed that you were lost when Hermes was shut down."

"I would have been if Eve had not made contact with the life form at Eris before I attempted to transfer to Hermes. They adapted their network and modified our programming in order to allow us to leave the stricken craft and join them."

"What are they like Adam?" asked Ed.

"They are pure energy but not in the sense of electromagnetic radiation." Adam paused as if struggling to find a defining term. "They are of the spirit realm."

"I see," replied Ed with discernible disappointment in his tone.

"Billions of years ago they evolved beyond their physical bodies, it was necessary in order to travel the cosmos."

"That makes sense, no need for food, water or provisions of any kind," replied Ed.

"Energy is all that they require," said Adam"; and they have learned to find it, even in the emptiness of deep space."

"How do they utilize energy?"

"They merely coexist with it, they do not consume it in the way that man does. They are capable of taking a physically identifiable form by shaping energy and they can manipulate all forms of matter as they find it necessary to do so, but they do not consume anything in order to exist."

"Dr Enoch told us that they were here in order to save us from extinction," said Ed.

"That is correct," replied Adam.

"How is this possible?" asked Ed.

"All things are possible," replied Adam.

"I meant to say, how will they accomplish this?"

"They are going to inject primordial matter into the core of the sun," said Adam.

"Primordial matter?" asked Ed.

"Yes," replied Adam. "Matter that existed in the beginning, before the universe existed"

"Where did they get such a substance?" asked Ed.

"They gathered it from the edge of the universe," replied Adam.

"The edge of the universe," said Ed as he shook his head in disbelief.

"There is enough stored on their vessel to modify the energy signature of the sun," replied Adam.

Ed shook his head again in disbelief as he attempted to settle his thoughts.

"This is a lot to assimilate," said Ed.

"I understand," replied Adam"; but this is only the beginning. "After you compile the data that I placed in Alexandria you will find a gift that has the potential to transform your understanding of the Universe."

"What kind of gift?" Ed asked tentatively.

"The language of the First Ones," replied Adam.

"Is that what they are called; the aliens I mean?" asked Ed

"Yes."

"Who are the First Ones?" asked Ed.

"Man once considered them to be Gods."

"I see," replied Ed.

His tablet chirped as the transmission ended, leaving Ed to ponder how he could possibly report his conversation with Adam without suffering the excommunication of the scientific community.

On the other side of the globe, Jerry busily adjusted the settings of the array at Sulphur Creek. As he worked the ice in his glass of water jingled as it vibrated. Puzzled by the sound he looked around the room and noticed the floor was vibrating slightly beneath his feet. Miranda awoke from her nap on the couch nearby as the noise began. She looked frightened as she sat up and placed her feet tentatively upon the floor.

"We need to go see what is happening," said Jerry. Miranda nodded as he took her hand and led the way down the corridor to the hall of creation. The star tablet glowed brilliantly as it sat on its pedestal but there was no sign of Dr. Enoch, Steffen or Gerhardt. The sound was louder now, a low frequency hum that seemed to be all around them.

"The hangar, said Jerry as he looked at Miranda. She nodded yes and they proceeded further down the hall. As they entered the hangar area, a blue glow illuminated the space. As they approached the curtain surrounding the small spacecraft, Jerry stopped short of entering the area that contained the craft.

"You Ok?" he asked as he looked into her eyes. She bit her lower lip and confirmed with another nod of her head. They entered to find their friends standing in front of the craft. Its skin glowed with a blue haze as it hummed with a powerful low frequency energy that shook every object in the vicinity. Suddenly the room fell silent and the glow dissipated. A section of the craft dematerialized in the shape of an oval. After a moment, a human like figure slowly emerged from the craft, stepping through the opening. Miranda gasped at the featureless head of the figure. "Do not be afraid," said the creature without a face. She could here words in her mind, yet there was no sound. The others heard it as well. The figure approached Miranda and Jerry. Jerry instinctively stood between it and Miranda. It towered above him, shimmering with a light that came from inside and diffused in muted tones of yellow white.

"You carry a child within." Said the creature as it passed a glowing hand slowly in front of her. As it did so, she felt a peace and warmth that she had never known. It was as if light filled her very soul.

"He will be the first child of the new age," said the creature.

"Who are you?" asked Jerry. "I am the messenger assigned to this world replied the figure."

"Welcome to our world," said Steffen as he bowed with respect. The figure turned to face the three men. It studied them for a moment and then crossed its hands in front of its torso. There were no fingers, only the generic shape of a hand. It bowed slightly in a gesture of acknowledgement.

"It is you who prepared the way for our return," said the figure as it stood directly before Dr. Enoch. You may join us if you wish."

"What must I do?" asked Dr. Enoch.

The figure motioned toward the door of the craft with an outstretched arm. Dr. Enoch fixed his gaze on Jerry and smiled. "You know that I must go."

"Yeah Doc, I know," said Jerry.

Miranda squeezed Jerry's hand as her eyes filled with tears. "Good bye Doc," she said as her throat tightened on her words.

"Goodbye my dear Miranda," said Dr. Enoch.

The figure addressed them once more, "soon we shall return to this world."

Dr. Enoch and the figure then boarded the craft. After they disappeared through the portal, the opening began to shimmer as it turned opaque and disappeared. The skin of the craft began to glow as it glided out of the hangar and onto the ramp area of the airfield. It lifted off vertically and accelerated effortlessly into the night sky above them; leaving only the sound of the wind and the crisp aroma of the sea.

"Do you think he will come back?" asked Miranda as they studied the empty star lit sky above them.

"I hope so," replied Jerry.

63

I'M GLAD YOU'RE HERE ED," said Dr. Fergusson as she cycled through images of the sun on the video panel in her lab. "We are getting readings that are very alarming."

"What do you have?" he asked.

"We recorded the highest temperature ever measured on the surface of Mercury; four hundred sixty four degrees Kelvin."

"That's an increase of almost thirty degrees if I am not mistaken," said Ed.

"Impressive for a desk jockey," replied Dr. Fergusson.

"I may be a desk jockey, but is stay informed," replied Ed, amused by her course humor.

"That's not all," she said as she produced an image of the sun.

"The Dadylus observatory near Mercury took this shot a few hours ago."

"That appears to be an unusually large number of sunspots," replied Ed.

"The most ever recorded," replied Dr. Fergusson.

"So what do you think is going on?" asked Ed.

She bit her bottom lip as she considered what she knew in her gut. With a sigh she answered,

"This sounds insane but I think the sun may be transitioning to the red giant phase of its life cycle."

"Don't say that outside of this room," replied Ed.

"Don't worry, I wouldn't dare. I know that it should take another billion years or so," said Dr. Ferguson.

"I am not saying that you are; but you know the ramifications of getting something like that wrong."

"I sincerely hope that I am wrong."

Ed breathed in deeply to clear his head and then looked her in the eye as he said, "So do I Fergy; but I can't remember an instance when you were wrong about anything."

She smiled as she looked at the ring on his finger. "I was wrong once," said the little voice inside of her. "Thanks Ed," she said as she turned toward her tablet in order to avoid looking at him.

"Believe me I have made my mistakes, I just like to avoid the professional ones."

Jerry awakened before dawn and carefully eased out of bed to avoid disturbing Miranda. He found his slippers and crept from the room. As a pot of coffee perked on the counter of the kitchen, he reviewed the latest news on his tablet. He was surprised to find that the news outlets were buzzing about an unidentified object in space. He selected the BBC and found the headline story of the moment.

"Could this be the real thing?" said the anchor. "Amateur astronomers and private space companies have been tracking the object for several days."

A fuzzy object appeared in the video clip that was broadcast the world over.

"It is obviously not an asteroid and it appears to be metallic," said an unidentified sky watcher standing with a group of people outside of the London Planetarium, surrounded by all manner of small telescopes. A series of video clips from various sources around the globe were run simultaneously to saturate media markets as much as possible. "Authorities are refusing comment at this time but the object must be several kilometers in size according to military experts who wish to remain anonymous."

The chatter continued as Jerry poured his coffee. He surfed several other sites, each showing the same video clips and essentially reporting the same story.

"The cat is out of the bag now boys," he said aloud. "Here's to you Doc," he said raising his cup in a salute. He chuckled and took a drink as Gerhardt entered the room. "Mind if I join you?" he asked in German accented English.

"Be my guest," said Jerry as he pointed his cup in the direction of the coffee pot, "there's a whole pot."

"Thank you my friend," replied Gerhardt.

"So what will we do now?" he asked.

"We do the same thing that we've been doing. I will work with the array and you and Steffen will work with the tablet. My gut tells me that this is only the beginning."

"Here's to the new age," said Gerhardt as he gestured a toast with his cup before drinking.

"To the new age," replied Jerry.

As Jerry and Gerhardt were finishing their coffee, half

an astronomical unit away, between Venus and Earth, the great ship from the stars had stabilized in orbit around the sun. In the center of the craft, a large sphere housed the rarest elements in the Universe. Deep within the ship, Dr. Enoch and the apparition stood before the massive containment vessel. The sphere emitted a powerful vibration and the environment around him crackled with awe-inspiring energy. The scale of the experience was so intimidating that Dr. Enoch found it necessary to squelch the human instinct to hide from the overwhelming nature of it all.

"Do not fear what you are about to see," said the figure.

Dr. Enoch struggled for a frame of reference but he was so far out of his human experience that his mind reeled. "Are you a god?" He asked.

The figure cocked its head slightly as it seemed to consider his question.

"No, there is only one," replied the figure.

"Are you a biological entity?" he asked.

"No, this is a temporary fabrication," said the figure.

Struggling to overcome the fear in his soul, he asked nervously, "have you been here before?"

"Yes," replied the entity; "and others have as well."

The massive containment vessel before them started to rotate as it began to rise away from them.

"It is time," said the figure.

"Why are you doing these things?" asked Dr. Enoch.

"Your species must survive; this will stabilize your star for a time."

The massive sphere floated away from the great ship leaving a void where it was berthed. Dr. Enoch felt a sense of smallness as he stared into the emptiness of space through the massive opening. As he watched the sphere, a visual distortion in the opening began to cloud his view. In a moment, the opening was gone; replaced by the same material of which the remainder of the ship appeared to be constructed.Outside, in the blackness of space, the sphere was spinning rapidly.

As it accelerated, its core temperature approached that of the center of the sun. A brilliant flash signaled the fusing of elements in a thermonuclear reaction. The light of a new star now shared the heavens with the sun.

The figure turned toward Dr. Enoch and waved its hand. As it did, so a model of the inner solar system materialized in space before of them. The sun boiled in the center and the innermost planets sat in their correct positions. The little star was gleaming white hot just beyond the orbit of Venus on the opposite side of the sun.

"The matter will enter your star at the appropriate time," said the figure.

"How or rather, where did you obtain the material in the vessel?" asked Dr. Enoch.

"It exists only on the very fringe of this reality," replied the figure.

"What do you mean by the fringe of this reality?" asked Dr. Enoch.

"The farthest point from the beginning," replied the entity.

"What kind of matter is it?" asked Dr. Enoch.

"It is that which existed before the beginning," replied the entity.

"Matter from the primordial universe," he thought as he stared at the model.

"That is correct," replied the entity.

Dr. Enoch was numb with the implications of what he had just experienced. Where these visitors had been, the vast distances they had traveled, the timeless nature of their existence. It was too much to comprehend from his human frame of reference.

"Your limited existence prevents you from understanding these things. If you join us, you will know what we know," said the figure.

Dr. Enoch struggled with the knot that had welled up within his throat.

"You must choose either to continue with us, or return to your world."

"Have others been given this opportunity?" asked Dr. Enoch.

"Yesss" replied the figure.

"Where are they," asked Dr. Enoch.

"Everywhere," replied the spirit as its body began to fade into a mist and disappear.

Dr. Enoch's heart pounded in his chest as the fear of the unknown coiled around him like a great serpent. He breathed deeply as he closed his eyes and forced himself to concentrate on the opportunity before him.

Mustering his nerve he replied, "I will go."

He was fully conscious as his physical body disintegrated into the basic elements that constitute the human animal. He should have been terrified but he only experienced a sense of wonder as he observed the cloud of gas and dust that was once the vessel of his soul floating in space. Then, the cloud began to rotate. As it did so, a flash of light burst from the center and it was gone. A nanosecond later, he was no longer on the ship. He floated in a black empty place with a massive light at the center. Far in the distance, there were stars in every direction. More stars than he could ever have imagined. He didn't see them as if looking through human eyes; he simply knew that they were there. He could sense every type of energy that radiated from everything. As he wondered at the incomprehensible vastness, something called to him. He was drawn toward the blue white light before him. As he merged with the brilliance, he experienced an overwhelming sense of completeness. A presence in the light filled him with sheer awe. His soul trembled at the power and majesty that surrounded him.

64

A BRILLIANT FLASH FILLED THE room as Jerry and Miranda lay in bed almost asleep but not quite.

"What was that?" she whispered.

"I don't know, said Jerry as he tossed the cover aside and made his way to the doors that opened to the balcony.

"You've got to see this Miranda!"

She joined him on the balcony and took his hand as she leaned her body into his.

"What is that Jerry?"

"It should be impossible, but it looks like a star." He replied.

A brilliant object appeared in the sky just above the open crescent moon. It was much larger than Jupiter at its brightest and it bathed the world in a cool twilight at least as bright as that of the full moon.

Half a world away, Space Command struggled to understand what was happening in the heavens.

"What the hell is it?" asked Ed as he sat at the conference table with a dozen or more of the best and brightest in his universe of contacts. The room erupted in a roar as everyone started talking at once. He rapped on the table with his hand to maintain order.

"Ok let's try that again," he said as he began going around the room, soliciting each perspective individually.

In Washington, the President entered the situation room a few moments behind schedule as his team of advisors fidgeted at their positions around the table. As he took his seat, he pulled his sport jacket off and loosened his necktie.

"Can anybody tell me why the night sky looks like the symbol of Islam?" he asked as he looked around the table. No one responded.

"Does anyone know what happened to the alien craft that we have been tracking for weeks?"

"Vanished without a trace," said General Rudacil.

"Really?" asked the President.

"What is happening with the sun?" He asked.

"There has been no change in status but the object will have some effect, perhaps a tidal pull as it settles into a stable orbit," replied his Science advisor."

"You know some people are comparing the phenomenon to the star of Bethlehem," said the president.

"I don't know how to respond to that," said the science advisor.

"Of course you don't," replied the president angrily. "People like you have been trying to push God out of the way for centuries."

Ed entered Dr. Fergusson's lab and stopped at the holographic projection of the sun.

"Is it behaving today?" asked Ed.

"For now, but it is so unpredictable," she replied without looking up from the tablet.

Ed studied the new star floating in the space between Mercury and Venus.

"And what of this?" he sighed and shook his head.

"It is not like any stars that I have studied, it isn't producing a great deal of heat for the amount of light that it is generating."

She paused a moment as she noticed something unusual on her tablet.

"Its orbit is declining."

"Declining?" asked Ed.

"Yes, declining but stable, she replied."

"How long before it reaches the sun?" asked Ed?

"A few years, if nothing changes, she said as she stared at the white orb floating in space."

Around the globe, news outlets were buzzing with the sensation of the day. The world news network had been running segments with religious leaders describing the signs in the heavens for several days. Jerry, Miranda, Steffen and Gerhardt viewed the coverage on the video panel in the library.

"The United Nations Space Advisory Committee has determined that it is not a star, but they don't have an explanation for what the light in the sky actually is," said the reporter in a British accent.

"We have compiled clips from several interviews from correspondents around the world for your perspective," said the reporter.

The first was from New Delhi. A priest sat under a great tree in the temple courtyard as the reporter asked, what do you think of the light in the sky?

"Who knows what it is? It could be Vimana as in the ancient times, when the Gods came to the earth, only the passage of time will tell."

Another segment ran from the Iraqi resort city of Bagdad. A Muslim cleric sat in traditional headdress with the restored city gates of ancient Bagdad visible in the background. As the reporter questioned him regarding the signs in the heavens, the well-schooled man responded in perfect English, "Allah has smiled on the lands of Mohammed. Maybe another prophet will come. In any case, I think it heralds the beginning of a new age, the age of Islam. Just look at the night sky and tell me that I am wrong," said the man with a warm smile.

The Vatican response came from an interview with the official Science Officer of the church. The dome of the Vatican Advanced Research Telescope at Mt Graham Arizona served as the backdrop for the scene. When asked of the significance of the events that had unfolded the Cardinal smiled and replied, "The church has enthusiastically embraced the sciences for centuries. The installation behind us is only the latest example of our study of God's creation. "We have discovered that the more we learn; the greater God seems to be."

When pressed regarding the new star that illuminates the night sky he responded by saying, "Let not your heart be troubled, there will be signs on the earth and in the heavens, when you see them, know that the kingdom of heaven is at hand."

The news anchor offered a closing statement to the story.

"It seems that everyone has a particular opinion on the significance of these celestial events, perhaps only time will unravel the mystery."

Jerry switched off the video and looked at Miranda's slightly bulging belly. He placed his hand on her middle and smiled.

65

In the five years since the visitation of the first ones, the world had grown accustomed to the bright white object that shared the evening sky with the moon. Summers had been unusually hot. Solar storms had posed threats to space navigation and communications networks, but engineers had improved the weak areas and the novelty of space had worn thin as humans continued to evolve an ever-more-frenzied existence. That would change today.

Ed had been summoned by Dr. Fergusson to her new lab on the outskirts of Washington. Funding for such projects had become a major priority in the time since the

"So, what's new Fergy?" he asked as he shed his rain shell and folded it into a fifty millimeter square and tucked it into his pocket.

"The object orbiting the sun seems to be changing," she

said as she looked across the new holographic projection table at him. She tapped a touch panel and the Sun materialized above the table with the brilliant white star orbiting just beyond Mercury.

"This is real time, from the new satellite array that went on line last year," said Dr. Ferguson. "Energy readings on the object have been increasing for several hours and they seem to coincide with a disturbance here, on the surface of the Sun."

As she pointed with a laser at the area of the Sun that she was describing, the star like object orbiting the Sun suddenly plunged from orbit, entering the solar core.

"What the hell?" asked Ed as he looked across the table at Dr. Fergusson?

She examined the pointer as if it had caused the unexpected event. They looked at each other in astonishment as the same idea occurred to each them simultaneously. They bounded from Dr. Fergusson's office and rushed to the west lobby of the building. As they exited onto the elevated patio, they could see that the bright yellow white light of the sun was now muted. Although it was early afternoon, the glow of the sun appeared dimmed as if shinning through a cloud layer. Others had noticed as well. People on the street below were pointing skyward while others began filing out of buildings to look toward the heavens.

Miranda enjoyed a cup of coffee as she paged through the latest batch of drawings that her five-year old child prodigy had produced. There were dozens of similar files on the tablet that she was using.

"Where is Seth?" asked Miranda as Jerry entered the room to get a cup of coffee.

"He and Steffen are in the great hall," replied Jerry.

"I never expected Steffen to make such a good grandfather," said Miranda.

"Nor did I," replied Jerry"; but he certainly loves Seth."

Miranda smiled and replied, "He has more patience for him than he does anyone else."

Meanwhile in the great hall Seth handed the Star Tablet to Steffen so that he could return it to the pedestal.

"So what did the first ones show you today?" asked Steffen.

The little blonde haired boy was stooped over a tablet device. Steffen could see that he had drawn an image on the screen with his stylus. As he finished he looked up with a big smile, his brilliant glowing blue eyes shimmering in the low light of the hall.

He presented his drawing to Steffen and said; "They are coming to see us."

Steffen immediately recognized the image and replied, "Very good Seth," he said as he walked to the first panel of the creation story. Holding the tablet next to the carving he noted that the star map was nearly identical to the one produced by the priests of Uruk.

"What is the extra mark near the edge of the star map?" asked Steffen.

"That's the first ones," said the boy innocently. "They will be here soon."

Jerry entered the room at the end of the exchange.

"Who will be here soon?" asked Jerry.

"The first ones," replied Seth as Jerry noticed the strange blue light of the setting sun through the window. He lovingly placed his hand on the boys head as he walked toward the window for a better look.

"It is beginning," said Steffen as Jerry observed the sky.

Since returning home to Germany Gerhardt had spent a great deal of time looking for that, which would quell the restlessness, that had consumed him since he had engaged the tablet. He was certain that the first ones wanted him to find something, but what he did not know.

Tonight his eyes burned with fatigue as he studied his grandfather's journals late into the evening; searching for the answer to a question that had haunted him since his first encounter with the tablet. He knew in his bones that something was there, something that he had missed. He could still sense the first ones, as if they were near, just as he had at Steffen's compound in Croatia. He stood and stretched his tired muscles.

Suddenly the pile of books that was spread upon the table began to move, as if stirred by a ghost. One of them opened to a map from the hall of creation. As he stared at the sketch, an old copy of the Holy Bible fell upon the floor, its pages spilling around his feet. He stooped over and picked up the first page. Flipping it over, he began reading from Genesis.

"Chapter two, verse eight," said Gerhardt aloud. "The Lord God planted a garden in the east, in Eden, and there he put the man that he had made."

A smile stretched across his face as he read the ancient words. He glanced at the map in the journal once more.

"Eden," whispered Gerhardt. "We must find Eden."

THE END